OZ REIMAGINED

Also Edited by John Joseph Adams

Armored
Brave New Worlds
By Blood We Live
Epic: Legends of Fantasy
Federations
The Improbable Adventures of Sherlock Holmes
Lightspeed Magazine
Lightspeed: Year One
The Living Dead
The Living Dead 2
The Mad Scientist's Guide to World Domination
Nightmare Magazine
Other Worlds Than These
Seeds of Change
Under the Moons of Mars: New Adventures on Barsoom
Wastelands
The Way of the Wizard

Forthcoming Anthologies Edited by John Joseph Adams

Dead Man's Hand
Robot Uprisings (co-edited with Daniel H. Wilson)
Wastelands 2

OZ REIMAGINED

NEW TALES FROM THE EMERALD CITY AND BEYOND

Edited by
John Joseph Adams & Douglas Cohen

47NORTH

Printed in the United States of America.

Published by 47North
P.O. Box 400818
Las Vegas, NV 89140

ISBN-13: 9781611099041
ISBN-10: 1611099048
Library of Congress Control Number: 2012953172

Dedication

For that wonderful wizard,
L. Frank Baum

A NOTE ON THE CONTENT

L. Frank Baum's original Oz books were works of children's fiction—albeit ones that have been known and loved by "children of all ages" throughout their existence. Though many of the stories contained in this anthology are also suitable for the aforementioned children of all ages, *Oz Reimagined* is intended for ages thirteen and up, and as such, some of the stories deal with mature themes, so parental guidance is suggested.

TABLE OF CONTENTS

FOREWORD: OZ AND OURSELVES

BY GREGORY MAGUIRE

When I try to settle upon some approach to the notion of Oz that might suit many different readers, and not just myself, I stumble upon a problem. The unit of measure that works for me might not work for you. Standards and definitions vary from person to person. Oz is nonsense; Oz is musical; Oz is satire; Oz is fantasy; Oz is brilliant; Oz is vaudeville; Oz is obvious. Oz is secret.

Look: imagine waiting at a bus stop with a friend. We're both trying to convey something to each other about childhood. When you say *childhood*, do you mean "childhood as the species lives it"? Do I mean "my childhood upstate in the mid-twentieth century, my house on the north edge of town, my grouchy father, my lost duckie with the red wheels"?

Oz comes to us early in our lives, I think—maybe even in our dreams. It has no name way back then, just "the other place." It's the unspecified site of adventures of the fledgling hero, the battleground for the working out of early dilemmas, and the garden of future delights yet unnamed.

Foreign and familiar at the same time.

Dream space.

Lewis Carroll called it Wonderland, Shakespeare called it the Forest of Arden, the Breton troubadours called it Broceliande, and the Freudians called it Traum. The Greeks called it Theater, except for Plato, who called it Reality. Before we study history, though, before we learn ideas, we *know* childhood through our living of it. And for a century or so, we Americans have called that zone of mystery by the name of Oz.

Your little clutch of postcards from the beyond is a different set than mine, of course. Nobody collects the same souvenirs from any trip, from any life. Yours might be the set derived from those hardcovers in your grandmother's attic, the ones with the John R. Neill line drawings someone colored over in oily Crayola markings. (Crayons were invented at just about the same time as Oz, early in the twentieth century.) Or your souvenir cards might be the popular MGM set starring Margaret Hamilton and Bert Lahr and some child star—I forget her name. Or your souvenirs might be more like mine: memories of being a kid and reenacting (and expanding upon) the adventures of Dorothy using the terrain at hand, which in my case was a filthy alleyway between close-set houses in the early 1960s. Dorothy in her blue-checked gingham and her pigtails is my baby sister in her brother's T-shirt, hair all unbrushed and eyes bright with play.

What, I wonder, did we Americans do to conjure up a universal land of childhood before L. Frank Baum introduced us to Oz? Did the Bavarian forests of Grimm or the English fairylands (sprites and elves beckoning from stands of foxgloves, deep hedgerows) ever quite work for American kids? Or maybe that's a silly question. Perhaps before 1900—when *The Wonderful Wizard of Oz* was first published and the United States was still essentially rural and therefore by definition hardscrabble—there was no time to identify the signposts of childhood. Children's rooms in public libraries hadn't yet been established. Reading for pleasure wasn't for everyone, just for those who could afford their own private books. Few nineteenth-century Americans could relish childhood as a space of play and freedom; instead, childhood was merely the first decade in a life of hard toil on the farm or the factory.

Maybe Oz arose and took hold because urban life began to win out over rural life. Maybe as our horizons became more built up and our childhoods—for some middle-class American kids anyway—a little more free, the Oz that came to us first on the page and later on the screen had a better chance of standing in for childhood. That merry old Land of Oz certainly did, and does, signify childhood for me; I mean this not as the author of *Wicked* and a few other books in that series, but as a man nearing sixty who recognized in Oz, more than half a century ago, a picture of home.

I don't mean to be sentimental. There's a lot to mistrust about home. It's one of the best reasons for growing up: to get away, to make your own bargain with life, and then to look back upon what terms you accepted because you knew no better, and to assess their value. Travel is broadening precisely because it is *away from* as well as *toward.*

As a young man, on my first trip abroad, I went to visit relatives in northern Greece, where my mother's family originates. In the great Balkan upheavals of the last century, the boundaries of political borders had shifted a dozen times, and the family village that had once been part of Greece, in the early twentieth century, lay now in Yugoslavia—still a Communist country in the late 1970s when I first saw it. Stony, poor, oppressed. My ancient, distant relatives, all peasant widows in black coats and neat headscarves, told me how their mother had spent her married life imprisoned in Thessaloniki, Greece, on the top edge of the Aegean; but, of a fine

Sunday afternoon, she would direct her husband to drive her north, to a hillside just this side of the border of Yugoslavia. There she would sit by the side of the road and weep. The village of her childhood was on the other side of the border crossing. From this height she could see it, like Moses examining the Promised Land, but she was not allowed back. She could never go back. She never did, or not in this life, anyway. She never sent us postcards once she finally crossed over.

Oz lives contiguously with us. The Yellow Brick Road, the Emerald City, and the great Witch's castle to the west—these haunts are more than tourist traps and hamburger stands. They are this century's Pilgrim's Progress and Via Dolorosa and Valhalla. Oz is myriad as the Mediterranean with its spotted Homeric islands; Oz is vast as Middle-earth and moral as Camelot. This is to say, of course, that Oz is a mirror. Turn it about and, in the mirror, *OZ* nearly says *ZOE*, the Greek word for life.

Of course we recognize Oz when we see it. Of course we find ourselves there. If we can't find ourselves *there*, well, we don't have much chance of recognizing ourselves *here*. As some farmhand or other might have said to Dorothy, or she to the Wizard.

I will utter a word of caution, though. Perhaps my souvenirs of Oz are darker than yours. I can't help that; life gives what it will. As a young reader, I learned about Oz the way I would later learn about Life on the Mississippi or life sailing to the lighthouse of the Hebrides or life lived on the verges of The Waste Land. And I found the insularity and even parochialism of Oz's separate populations puzzling and, maybe, worrying. Racist even, though I hadn't a word for it yet. Troublingly myopic, exceptionalist. Certainly lacking in intellectual curiosity. When Dorothy first arrived in the land of Munchkins, the kindly Munchkin farmers told her what they'd been told about the Emerald City and about the Wizard. But none of them had had the gumption of Dorothy to pick themselves up and go see for themselves. No firsthand experience. Few of them could predict what kind of population lived over the horizon. None of them cared.

Or maybe I'm being unkind. Maybe those Munchkins all just had to stay on the farm to bring in the crops. But they didn't signal lust for adventure in their remarks about the Emerald City; you'll grant me that.

Well, they had not read any chronicles of Oz to whet their appetites for the adventure, I suppose. Kindly, good, solid working people, they were lacking in vision. They'd never gone far enough away from the villages of their own childhoods to be able to look back down the slope and see childhood for what it is: a paradise from which, if we are to survive, we must escape.

I write this in a small walled garden in what used to be called the Languedoc region of France, where for the past decade I have spent part of every summer. My French is close to execrable; even the birds chirp with a better accent than I do. The plane trees with their coats of mottling bark, and the stiff, brushlike sound of their leaves in the dawn wind—it's all ineffably foreign to me a decade on, and if I can be forgiven an Anglicism, it's ineffably dear to me, too. I like spending time every year in a place I only barely comprehend. It reminds me of childhood, when I was most alive because the world was so new. Being abroad, struggling to understand, reminds me of Oz.

There is more to say, but here comes the bus. It says *OZ* above the front window. Welcome aboard. Welcome home.

Gregory Maguire
Cavillargues
Bastille Day, 2012

INTRODUCTION: THERE'S NO PLACE LIKE OZ

BY JOHN JOSEPH ADAMS & DOUGLAS COHEN

There's no place like home.

The phrase has become one of the most famous in the English language, if not all of Western culture. Although first popularized by John Howard Payne (as a lyric in the song "Home! Sweet Home!" for his opera *Clari, Maid of Milan*), it's safe to say that when most people hear it, they think not of the opera or the song but of L. Frank Baum's most magical creation: Oz. It is to Dorothy Gale that most of us unconsciously attribute these words—perhaps because her innocent longing for her farm while being surrounded by such wondrous magic makes the words all the more poignant. Whatever the reason, there is no denying the resonance of the message. Yet while the words may indeed evoke thoughts of home for some, it is somewhat ironic that those words now transport most of us to that magical Land of Oz.

But if this unassuming phrase should take our thoughts someplace vastly different than Baum intended, it's hardly surprising, because while there's no place like home, it's equally true that there's no place like Oz. It has not only transcended the ranks of fantasy readers; thanks to the beloved MGM film classic *The Wizard of Oz*, it has also transcended the ranks of readers, period. Indeed, Oz has woven itself into the very fabric of our culture.

While the Land of Oz has achieved a level of fame that few fantasies ever manage, and while various political allegorical meanings have been attributed to these works, at its heart Oz remains a series of fairy tales—tales written by a man who continued writing them long after he expected to because he received so many letters from children imploring him to write more Oz adventures. For many of those children—and for many of us even now—Oz became another home.

Of course, sometimes the home you remember can change. You'll find that is the case with these stories. For this project we asked our authors to not only *revisit* Oz—we asked them to *reimagine* it.

And the results were everything we could have hoped for. Some authors chose to fill in the cracks of the existing mythology with their own unique vision. Others revised the original story, making it branch out in wildly unexpected directions. Still others took the bones of Oz and rebuilt it from the ground up, one magical limb at a time.

Characters you know and love might look different. They might *act* different. Their choices might shock you. They may make you laugh. They may make you cry. They may guide you down a gaily colored road to see a great and powerful wizard, but then again you might not even find yourself in Oz. (Though in spirit, all these stories take place in Oz, regardless of their actual location.)

If it seems like we're being vague regarding how our authors have reimagined Oz…guilty as charged. We want you to experience that same delight we did the first time we read these stories, discovering what is familiar versus what is different, seeing how it all fits together. We want you to wander into old, warm dreams only to find they've taken a delightful right turn.

Even so, we do want to mention one important bit of information before you begin your trip to Oz. If you're only familiar with the classic movie, you might notice that certain details in some of the stories are different from what you remember. The reason for this is simple: our authors were tasked with reimagining L. Frank Baum's books rather than the famous film based on them. (Though quite faithful, the movie version does take some liberties with the source material.) As a result, some of the little details you remember may be slightly different here— and not just because the stories have been reimagined. For example, in the movie version, Dorothy famously comes to possess a pair of magical ruby slippers; in the book, the shoes are silver instead. Another difference: thanks to the film, the Wicked Witch's soldiers have come to be known as Flying Monkeys rather than Winged Monkeys, as they were originally. And in the book Glinda is the Witch of the South rather than the North, and so on. So when you encounter these details in the anthology—things that may seem to be changed for no particular reason—rest assured there is a method to our madness. But if the movie is all you know, have no fear: the movie and the book are similar enough that you'll have no trouble following the stories and falling into these new versions of Oz.

Reimagining a creation as enduring and seminal as Oz is no small feat—we all have our memories of it, and for many these memories are dearly cherished. Perhaps this explains why our authors embraced this project with so much enthusiasm. Oz is as special to them as it is to you; it is a land of deep imagination, part of that dreaming landscape they delve into each time they create a new work of fantasy. Most of them discovered Oz in one form or another before they even realized they wanted to write fantasy stories of their own, and so it could be said that L. Frank Baum planted some of the earliest seeds that brought them to where they find themselves today. For those of whom this is true, perhaps this anthology is their chance to say thank you…a chance to celebrate one of the great fantasies of our time…a chance to go back to Oz.

We all change as we pass out of childhood and become adults. Our perceptions of Oz may change as well. So follow the road of yellow brick when you're ready, but prepare for a detour or two along the way. And remember: whatever version of Oz you find yourself in, there's no place like it.

THE GREAT ZEPPELIN HEIST OF OZ

BY RAE CARSON & C.C. FINLAY

Strange in a Stranger Land

Scraps, the Patchwork Girl, witnessed the Wizard's arrival.

She sat beneath a tree watching the most spectacular show ever performed by a summer sky. White clouds swirled above an emerald-colored sky, like whipped marshmallow topping on a glass bowl full of lime jello, spinning round and round and round on a potter's wheel.

She didn't think it could get any more amazing when the clouds cracked open and sunlight burst through, so blinding that she lifted one patchwork arm to shade her button eyes.

That's when she saw the balloon.

It was a big bubble made of brightly colored fabric, with a basket hanging underneath and a man inside the basket, clinging to its rim. And it was coming toward her tree.

She jumped up and shouted. "Turn away!"

"I am rudderless in the maelstrom!" yelled the man in the basket. His small voice was getting louder and closer. "Reinless in my carriage!"

The man was making no sense. Scraps waved her hands to shoo the odd vessel aside. "All right, but steer your picnic basket that way!"

"I can't steer it because—"

The balloon crashed into the branches of the venerable tree, which shook and shook and shook, like a dog shaking off a bath. The balloon deflated, becoming hopelessly entangled, but all the tree's effort did manage one thing, which was to spill the passenger out of the basket.

He hit the ground with a loud thump, and Scraps ran toward him. She reached down to help, but he jumped to his feet like a cat—not all lithe and athletic like a cat making a spectacular leap but rather all arrogant and full of himself like a cat too embarrassed to admit that he'd taken a bad tumble.

"Are you all right?" she asked.

He stared at her uncomprehendingly, so she spoke in a way that he might understand.

"ARE. YOU. ALL. RIGHT?"

"I must have knocked my noggin," he said, feeling his head for lumps. "I've shaken the coin purse, rattled the old dice cup."

"I don't know about that," Scraps said. "But I think you bumped your head—you're not making a lick of sense."

He startled when she spoke again, as if hearing her for the first time. "Merciful blessings," he said. "You're a talking ragdoll! And a filthy one at that."

Scraps, who was very proud of her shiny button eyes, orange yarn hair, and striped knickers, opened her mouth to say something likely to land her in a tussle with the strange man, even though she stood no higher than his knee. But the tree spoke first.

"And you're a blithering idiot," boomed the good-natured old oak.

He was bending over as he said it, and the man from the balloon jumped so high that he hit his head on a branch and accomplished what falling from the sky could not: he knocked himself out cold.

"What a strange man," the tree said, his knotholes frowning. "What do we do with him now?"

"I'll run to the Emerald City and get the Guardian of the Gates," Scraps replied. "He'll know what to do."

Progress!

The Guardian of the Gates had no idea what to do.

The strange man had not stopped talking once since he'd been carried to the guardhouse. He called himself Oz, which was short for Oscar, because he had so many other things to say; there was no time to use a two-syllable name when one syllable was available. His talk was equal parts questions and opinions, although the latter seldom seemed related to the answers he received to the former, until he said, quite out of the blue:

"I'll tell you what's not right about this country."

The statement startled Gigi, which is what the Guardian of the Gates was called by his friends, even though his proper name—George—was only one syllable long. But who in the world used one syllable when two perfectly good syllables were at hand?

"What's wrong with this country?" asked Gigi, who already knew what was wrong with the guardhouse—half his bread and all his butter had been eaten by the stranger.

"Now don't go putting words into my mouth," Oz said. "*Not right* is not the same as *wrong*. There's *right* and *not right*, and there's *right* and *wrong*, and there's *wrong* and *not wrong*. But to insist that *not right* is the same as *wrong* is to infer a transitive property of equivalence that is not supported by the evidence, for we do not yet know the qualities that individually compose *not right* and *wrong*. Am I not right?"

"I think you're wrong," Gigi said, trying desperately to follow.

"You haven't been paying attention at all," Oz snapped. "Have you never studied the mathematical approach to language known as *logic*?"

"I can't say that I have."

"Which is not the same as saying that you haven't," Oz replied. "But I digress. To return to the original—in fact, the essential—point that I was about to make: what's not logical, what's distinctly and preeminently *not right* about this country, as you have described it to me, is that there are four kingdoms."

"No, that's right," Gigi said. "There are definitely four kingdoms."

"There are four kingdoms, *but not one king*. Every kingdom in this land is ruled by a *woman*! Why, in the land I come from, there is a great city called Omaha, not much different than your fine metropolis, in which my father served as a city councilman for two score years, give or take an annum. In all that time, he did not once serve under or even with a woman. And yet here you are ruled by four of them. Glinda, Bastinda, Locasta, and…Canasta?"

He waved his hand in the air, as if it were a matter of no consequence to forget a witch's name.

"Her name is—" Gigi started to say.

"Why, it's poppycock!"

"No, it's…what's poppycock?"

"Poppycock? It's a species of flower. You usually find it planted in gardens along with balderdash and humbug and ample beds of bunkum. Does she have an army?"

"The Witch?" Gigi said. "She has a few soldiers, I suppose. But mostly she has the Winged Monkeys."

"Monkey business, is it?" Oz murmured to himself.

"And she's very capable with magic."

"I can do a bit of magic myself!"

Oz pushed up his sleeves to his elbows and showed Gigi his hands, palms up, then palms down. Then his right hand darted to Gigi's ear, and when he pulled it back, a tiny silver-colored disc was pinched between his thumb and forefinger.

Gigi snatched the disc away and examined it.

On one side was a portrait of a severe-looking man with feathers tucked in the back of his hair. On the other side was a picture of a large, hairy beast with a larger, hairier hump. "What is this?" Gigi asked.

"This is what you call progress," Oz said. "In the land where I come from, which is known as Nebraska, there were once great tribes of Indians and endless herds of buffalo. Then men like me came along, and we achieved progress, which we memorialize by stamping it on a nickel."

"What happened to the Indians and the buffalos?"

"The same thing that is going to happen to your witches now that I'm here," Oz said, snatching the coin away. "Progress!"

"That doesn't make any sense," Gigi said.

"I believe it makes five of them." Oz flipped the coin in the air with his thumb and caught it in his fist, which he held in front of Gigi's nose. Then he opened one finger at a time to reveal an empty hand.

"Hrm," Gigi said skeptically.

But Oz just wiggled his fingers and grinned. "Now *that's* magic."

"Yes," Gigi said. "I'm certain that it is."

He wasn't certain at all, but he would help this Oz fellow anyway, just in case. There was no need to risk getting *progressed.*

The Queen of the Field Mice

"Your Majesty, it is a pleasure of immeasurable proportions, a satisfaction both sublime and profound, an honor far beyond a man of my own humble origins, to make your most regal and diminutive acquaintance," said the whiskered stranger who had come from the Emerald City with the Guardian of the Gates.

"Delighted to meet you, too, I'm sure," the Queen said, glancing up at the Guardian of the Gates, who was deliberately avoiding her gaze. She brushed her whiskers with her paw, in case they held any crumbs. "Who did you say you were again?"

"I am Oscar Diggs, from the wide and narrow land known as Nebraska, which lies across the hills and over the rainbow, where I am a modest purveyor of marvels, an itinerant educator of the masses, and the possessor of great and powerful devices of extraordinary merit. But you may call me Oz."

"Oh my," said the Queen, who thought she could smell a cow patty before she stepped in it. "Well, how can I help you, Mr. Oz?"

"Your Majesty," Oz said. "I'm not here to ask for your help like some beggar far from home. No, indeed! Rather I hope you will allow me to describe the manner in which *I* can help *you.*"

"*You* help *me*?"

"Your Majesty, this field that you occupy is part of a much bigger land—in fact, a kingdom! A kingdom is a structure of government that I trust you, as a fellow monarch, albeit of a more limited domain, approve of and even support. But right now this kingdom has no king, a situation that confounds sense and boggles the cerebrum. Instead you are ruled by a witch, a woman who, instead of a scepter, carries a broom. Do I need to paint a picture for you?"

"Oh, please," said the Queen. "I love paintings."

Oz began to stomp around in a circle. "A broom is the bane of every mouse. It's cold outside, and there is no food, but—look!—over here is a cottage. A simple home. You peer inside the door, and what do you see? A fire on the hearth, providing warmth and safety. You see that there are crumbs upon the floor, so small they've been cast off by the giants who live here—but these tasty, savory crumbs will fill your belly and feed your numerous brood of starving children. Do you follow me so far?"

"I do," said the Queen, but in a tone intended to indicate *not at all.*

But this Oscar person seemed pleased. He thrust his hands dramatically at her. "And then here comes the broom! It slams you against the wall. It pursues you into the corner. No matter where you turn, there waits the broom, relentless and unforgiving, until it has chased you back out into the cold, bruised and battered. Until it has swept up all the crumbs—food that could feed your loyal, hungry subjects—and tossed them into the flames where they can feed no one at all. And is this fair?"

"It's horrifying," said the Queen, her whiskers twitching.

"Exactly," said Oz. "But here you are—you live in a kingdom ruled by a witch with a broom, and what will she do with that broom? She will chase you, and slap you, and destroy the food supplies of your people, and leave you all with nowhere to turn and nowhere to live. Horrifying! But fortunately you have me."

"We do?"

"You do! And Your Majesty," Oz said, bowing low. "If you will just do as I ask, I can put an end to the Witch's broom and guarantee peace and prosperity for the foreseeable future."

The Queen looked at Gigi, who was twirling his toe in the grass and still avoiding eye contact. "I don't know…"

Slam! Oz stomped his boot on the ground, making her jump.

"That's not me," Oz said. "That's what the Witch wants to do to you this very minute."

"What can we do about it?" the Queen said, ready to agree with almost anything the stranger asked if he would just leave her alone.

"I have brought with me, from the land of Nebraska, an element called helium and several things called balloons…"

A Clean Sweep

It was hard for Bobbin, one of the smallest of the field mice, to predict which thing would be more terrifying that day.

Would it be getting tied to a string that was tied to a balloon that was then sent floating aloft to drift over the Witch's castle?

Or maybe while he dangled hundreds of feet in the air, it would be climbing up the string and chewing a tiny hole in the balloon—a hole not so big that the balloon would pop and drop him to his death, but just big enough to allow the balloon to descend slowly into the castle.

Or maybe it would be searching the castle, memorizing everything he saw, never knowing when the Witch's Broom of Doom, as it was now being called among the field mice, would slam down on his tiny body.

As it turned out, the most terrifying thing was none of these.

They started on an observation platform that stood above the trees on a high hill overlooking the valley and the distant Witch's castle. Socks were tied to poles at each corner of the platform. Wind filled them, indicating which direction it was blowing. Only when Oz was satisfied with the wind did he fill the first balloon and set it adrift. They watched it until it floated over the castle and away.

"We'll call that test a success," Oz said as he filled the second balloon from the metal tank. "Now's for the real adventure. Are you ready, my lad?"

"Ready," Bobbin squeaked. He wanted very much to be brave and do a good thing for his fellow mice.

"Your valor and fortitude are deserving of the highest recognition," Oz said. And he tied the string around Bobbin's waist and set him adrift over the forest.

Bobbin kept his eyes mostly closed and drifted over trees that looked at him with puzzled faces. Whispers ran through the leaves, branching out in every direction. Poor Bobbin began to twitch nervously. This was hardly the surreptitious entry that Oz had promised him.

The balloon was barely over the castle wall when other faces appeared in the windows and along the battlements—the Witch's Winged Monkeys, furry little men with leathery wings and sparkling golden vests.

Then there were Monkeys on the roof of the castle.

Then there were Monkeys in the air above the castle.

Bobbin paddled his tiny legs furiously, like a swimmer desperate to make it to shore, even though his intention was only to turn around and climb up the string. The activity made him swing like a pendulum and soon he was all tangled up, which cut off his circulation and made his toes go numb.

The Monkeys flew up in waves, spinning round and round Bobbin's balloon until it was twisting like a leaf in a whirlwind. The more daring Monkeys flew in and poked at the balloon, or—worse!—at Bobbin.

"No no no no no no no no no no no no!" he screamed.

The Monkeys laughed and spun him round and round and batted his balloon until he was screaming at them to—

POP!

The balloon disappeared like a wasted wish, and he plummeted toward the rocks below. At the last second, as the rocks loomed large in his vision, a tiny hairy hand thrust out of nowhere and grabbed him.

The Monkey carried Bobbin high into the air, higher than his balloon had been, and then the Monkeys played a game of keep-away, tossing Bobbin back and forth, dropping and catching him over and over again until he was limp and exhausted with terror.

Eventually the Monkeys grew bored, and they took Bobbin to the castle, where he was presented to the Witch of the East.

"Who sent you to spy on my castle?" the Witch asked.

"Oz," Bobbin said, and then, feeling like that wasn't quite enough, like it might be a good idea to have a powerful protector, he added, "Oz, the great and powerful. He's a wizard! He came from Nebraska, and he…he…has progress, which he keeps in his pocket."

While he spoke, his eyes darted back and forth, looking for the terrible, the awful, the frightening Broom of Doom.

The Witch reached down and, with one long fingernail, scratched between Bobbin's ears. Despite his wariness, Bobbin closed his eyes and sighed.

"Tell me everything you remember," the Witch said.

So that's what Bobbin did, even though when he got to the part about the Broom of Doom, she laughed so hard that tears fell from her eyes.

"That's a good boy," the Witch said when the laughter subsided and her breath returned. "Will you take a message to this wizard for me?"

"Y...y...yes," Bobbin said.

"Tell him, if he's smart, he'll go back to Nebraska."

"I can do that," Bobbin said.

"I know you can," the Witch said, giving him a big yellow-toothed smile. "Now...would you like to walk back to the Wizard's base of operations, or would you like my Monkey friends to fly you there?"

"Walk! Walk! Walk!" Bobbin shouted.

He staggered like a drunk all the way back to the far end of the valley.

When the Wizard saw Bobbin, he snatched him off the ground.

"What did you find out?" he demanded.

"That I don't like flying," Bobbin said.

"How many soldiers does she have? What sort of weapons?"

Oz, in his enthusiasm, gripped Bobbin too tightly, more roughly even than the Monkeys had. So it was a reflex, really, that caused Bobbin to use the only weapons he owned—his teeth—which he sank into Oz's thumb.

Oz yelped and dropped Bobbin, who ran off to a safe distance.

"Go back to Nebraska or you'll smart!" he yelled.

Without waiting for a response, he ran away and didn't stop until he reached the meadow.

Even though Bobbin never saw the Witch's Broom, every time the other field mice gathered to hear about his adventure, when he reached the conversation with the Witch, he told his listeners that the Broom moved tirelessly around the castle of its own accord, cleaning every nook and cranny, every crack and hiding place, so that it was the cleanest castle that had ever been lived in by anyone anywhere.

The baby mice shivered when Bobbin told them that part of the story.

Bobbin shivered too.

Hot Air

Over the years, ever since he ran away from the Peppermint Home for Orphaned and Abandoned Youth, Finagle the Munchkin had been a pickpocket, a highwayman, a mercenary, a Nome wrangler, a goat washer, and once, for two weeks and three Saturdays in the Land of Ev, a wedding cake decorator. Personally, he considered the last two the most dangerous jobs he had ever done.

But then he had never before worked for a wizard.

"So let me get this straight," he said to Oz as they stood on top of his observation platform, where they could see the Witch's castle. "The Witch is a danger, so you want to me to go up in a hot air balloon so I can spy on her."

"I can tell that you are a gentleman of unusual perspicacity and astounding perception, with a mind as sharp as a barber's razor and as quick to snap as a bear trap," Oz said. "And if you do this for me, I promise to pay you all the wealth I previously described, but even that will be as nothing compared to the treasure chests full of glory that shall be heaped upon you."

"I suspect you get paid by the word," the Munchkin muttered.

"What was that, good sir?"

"I said, I expect you are as good as your word," Finagle said. He was puffing on a cheroot and blew a smoke ring in Oz's direction. "But I have three questions I want answered first."

"And I promise you three full and satisfying answers, answers that will erase the stain of any doubt and introduce in your mind a comprehension and understanding of the situation that will engender your whole-hearted commitment to the greater cause."

"No matter how long it takes," the Munchkin muttered.

"I beg your pardon, my dear friend."

"I said, and that's exactly what it takes." He looked at the tiny basket and the large balloon, which was being inflated with hot air as they spoke. "Question, the first. Why is it you want me to climb up in this contraption and float over her castle, when you could clearly do it yourself?"

"An excellent question. A very wise and sage question. A wonderful question."

"And the answer?"

"Why, the answer is obvious, my good friend. You need but consider your size compared with mine. Why, I am twice the man you are—"

"Hold on now!"

"Hear me out, please—simply by way of physical proportions. Why, look at me! I'm bigger than you in every dimension. Taller, wider, and thicker."

"I'm beginning to think you're thick enough."

"See, there you have it. So, with me aboard, this hot air balloon would founder like a boat loaded with rocks, and that would do no good at all, not for anyone. And yet, with you aboard, a man whose size is, I daresay, in inverse proportion to his value, whose courage is worth his weight in gold, why the craft will certainly most positively and absolutely soar like a bird in the wind."

"So, say I soar," Finagle said, looking out over the valley filled with trees to the sharp edges of the Witch's castle perched on a distant crag. "What should I see that a bird can't see—why not just send a bird? I know a crow or two, even a mockingbird, who'll do for you in a pinch."

"That's an excellent question. A very keen and perceptive question—"

"Go on with the answer."

"Why, isn't it obvious? I came to you for your reputation as the most courageous man among your people. Is a bird ever as brave as a man? No! Can a bird hold a weapon in his hands? No! Will a bird count the grains of sand—"

"I get the idea," Finagle said. "So when the Witch's Monkeys come flying up at me, just like they did for that mousy fellow, you want me to fight them off and then count what's inside the castle walls—the soldiers and such."

"Fight them off only long enough to release your ballast and man the hot air pump. Let the balloon rise directly upward until it's beyond the limited flight of these heavy creatures, and then, when you are clear of the castle, release the air from the balloon just as I showed you and float safely back to land, where I will come and meet you. Can you do that?"

"Yeah, I can do that," Finagle said, but it didn't add up with what he'd told that field mouse to do—what was this Oz fellow up to?

"Drop the ballast and pump the hot air," Oz repeated.

"Hot air—I've got it. It seems easier than fighting off a few dozen Monkeys."

"I knew you were the man for the job," Oz said. "Never has a recommendation more recommended itself. Nor commended its recommender, who deserves a commendation..."

He blinked and regarded Finagle with a fixed smile and a blank stare.

"Lost your flow of words there?" Finagle asked.

"Not at all," Oz said. "Not at all. I was simply trying to say that you came highly recommended, and with good and self-evident reason."

"Third and final question then," Finagle said, staring hard at the castle, which protected the valley of the Munchkins from the wild creatures beyond. "What have you got against the Witch?"

Oz paused thoughtfully. He pulled a brass tube from his trouser pocket, held it up to his eye, and stared across the valley to the castle. Finagle was about to repeat his question when the Wizard finally spoke.

"In the land where I come from, we have wonderful institutions of learning, where a man can discover all the secrets of the universe, and that's why these institutions are called universities," Oz said. "And in these universities, there are wise men called philosophers, who ponder the fundamental questions of life. Being in the business of questions, they employ a tool named for their most distinguished predecessor, a philosopher named Socrates, and this tool is called the Socratic Method, and those who use this tool answer questions with more questions in order to reach a more enlightened perspective."

"What?" Finagle said.

"That's precisely how you do it," Oz said. "So permit me to answer your question about the Witch with a question of my own."

"Go ahead," Finagle said.

"Do you know what sort of man the Witch might be interested in?"

Finagle narrowed his eyes. "Where are you going with this?"

"Yes, by Jug! That's how you do it. Socrates would be so proud—OWW!"

Oz hopped on one foot, holding his opposite shin—the one that Finagle had just kicked.

"That's for sending me up in a balloon with a bunch of flying Monkeys chasing me," the Munchkin said. "And I want twice what you offered to pay me."

—

Monkey Business

Wisdom from Omaha: you only have one chance to make a first impression.

Oscar Diggs was not about to waste that chance. He stared at himself in the full-length mirror and admired the work done by the tailors in the Emerald City.

A double-breasted vest in emerald silk with silver buttons. A tailcoat in a complementary green, trimmed in black velvet. Fall front trousers in a lovely shade of fawn. He had never looked so good.

To be fair, the effect was marred somewhat by the straps holding the canister of oxygen to his back, and by the bug-like mask, connected to the tank by a breathing tube, that at the present moment hung loose about his neck where a less inventive and more ill-prepared man would tie an ordinary cravat.

He was, he assured himself, most inventive and well prepared and wholly extraordinary, even without a cravat.

More importantly, he had a plan.

A plan, which, so far, had worked to perfection.

The first part had involved simple helium balloons and an even simpler field mouse. The balloons revealed the direction and speed of the valley's winds while the mouse served up misdirection by relaying his false concerns about soldiers to the Witch.

The second part of the plan employed a hot air balloon, which permitted him to measure the speed and maximum ascent of the Winged Monkeys, who were his real target all along.

Now the third part of his plan—involving a hydrogen balloon, of the type popularly called a zeppelin—was about to be set into motion.

He climbed into the large gondola of the craft, which was moored to the top of the tower that the Emerald Citizens had built for him, and he untied the ropes that held him down.

His heart beat faster as the craft rose majestically into the air.

The Valley of the Witch was long and narrow, split by a gleaming blue ribbon of river, cushioned by thick green orchards on either side, and framed by rugged peaks of bare stone that reached straight up to the sky. At the upper end of the valley, a picturesque castle occupied a bluff overlooking the river.

"The question," Oscar Diggs mused, "is why a witch needs a castle at all. Either she has great wealth, which her army of Winged Monkeys guards for her, or she has great enemies, which her army of Winged Monkeys protects her from. Either way, it's the business with the Monkeys that is key."

His palms grew sweaty as the great airship approached the Witch's castle. He wiped his hands on his trousers and peered through the telescope. The Monkeys were already perched along the battlements and on the rooftops, eyeing his approach.

"The question," Oscar Diggs asked himself, "is, How much is she willing to trade to get the Winged Monkeys back."

Of course the bigger issue was going to be stealing them in the first place. It was too late to double-check his calculations. He had made his plan and—

Here came the Monkeys!

It was much more terrifying to see in person than it was to watch from the safety of his viewing platform. He pulled his mask over his face, turned on the flow of oxygen, and braced for the impact.

The gondola rocked as the first Monkeys landed on the sides and swarmed aboard. They ran all around the rim and rigging, curiously exploring the craft just as he'd seen them do during the previous tests. Then they began creeping down the rigging toward him, eyeing him warily, ready to pounce.

"Not yet, not yet," he muttered to himself, his hands shaking.

More Monkeys jumped on. Then more and more. The moment they were all aboard, he yanked the rope he had prepared, releasing thousands of pounds of ballast.

Straight up the zeppelin went, fast enough to press them all to the floor of the gondola. In four seconds they reached a height where the air was too thin to support the Monkeys' flight. In eight seconds they reached a height where the air was too thin for them to stay awake. The Monkeys in the rigging lost their grip and tumbled into the gondola at his feet.

Oscar shivered in the cold, but the dazed or entirely unconscious Monkeys were now at his mercy. He moved quickly around the gondola, binding them hand and foot and wing with ropes he had brought specifically for that purpose.

When he was certain that all his prisoners were secure, he changed the course of the zeppelin and reduced his altitude, bringing it back toward the Witch's castle. All the way he gave thought to the encomium this daring would win him and the epithets that would cling like laurels to his name forever after.

Oz the Wise!

Oz the Wonderful!

Oz the Triumphant!

He moored to the peak of the Witch's highest tower and descended a rope ladder to the castle's courtyard, where the Witch was waiting for him.

She was older than he expected but certainly not much more so than an old maid or two he had courted briefly back in Omaha. She was taller than he was, but some of that was the tall pointed hat she wore. If he could only convince her to ditch the hat and put her hair up in a more practical bun.

"Very bold, coming here," the Witch said to him when his feet touched ground. "Bold…or foolhardy."

"Merely the logical thing to do…" Oscar started. He swallowed hard. Though he considered himself an accomplished practitioner of the elocutionary arts, this one would require every bit of his skill. He finished, "since I wanted to prove myself worthy of you."

"Worthy?" she said, surprised.

"Worthy!" he said confidently. *Witches love confidence.* "The man who could capture your Winged Monkeys and return them to you is the man who can outsmart your enemies just as easily. Who better to be your ally than the man who could outsmart you...but didn't?"

"What are you getting at?" she said.

He bowed low to her, and when he raised his head again, he smiled. "You have a kingdom without a king. I could be that man. You have a castle without a lord. I could be that man. You have a heart without a helpmeet...I could be that man."

"Are you suggesting that I need you?"

"I'm suggesting that we need each other. Why, we could be like John Smith and Pocahontas, opening up virgin lands for settlement. We could be like Sacajawea and Lewis—or possibly Clark—expanding territories westward. Isn't it manifest? Isn't it destiny?"

She stared at him up and down, and he tried not to pose or preen too much, although he wanted her to notice what a figure he cut. Her glance slipped past his shoulder to the impressive airship moored behind him. A wicked grin played across her lips.

"So is that progress in your pocket," she said, "or are you just happy to see me?"

The conversation went downhill quickly from there.

His New Digs

The two witches shared a cup of tea in the gazebo situated in Locasta's summer garden. Locasta held a cup of tea to her lips and breathed in the minty aroma while her sister from the East retrieved a small hat from her pocket and set it on the table.

"Here's the Golden Cap," she said. "Whoever possesses it can command the Winged Monkeys three times. I've used my three commands, so now I pass it on to you. You may need them next if he chooses to come after you."

"Thank you," Locasta said. "But I don't think I need to fear him much, not after what you've described."

"He'll fool some with his tricks and bluster, like he has the folks in the Emerald City."

"What else did he say to you, then? After he proposed, I mean. That was a proposal of marriage, wasn't it?"

"Oh yes, it most definitely was." She chuckled and tapped her silver shoes in delight. "So then he told me he thought that together, we could unite all four kingdoms into a single country, which, get this, he wanted to name for himself."

"Oz?" asked Locasta.

"No, that's just it," her sister said, pausing to drop in another cube of sugar. "He suggested that we call it *Diggety*."

"And that's when—"

"And that's when I pointed up in the air, to show him the Monkeys had chewed through their ropes and were flying away with my new zeppelin. Smoothest heist ever."

EMERALDS TO EMERALDS, DUST TO DUST

BY SEANAN MCGUIRE

The pillows were cool when I woke up, but they still smelled of Polychrome—fresh ozone and petrichor, sweeter than a thousand flowers. I swore softly as I got out of bed and crossed to the window, opening the curtains to reveal a sky the sunny fuck-you color of a Munchkin swaddling cloth. There was no good reason for the sky to be that violently blue this time of year—no good reason but Ozma, who was clearly getting her pissy bitch on again.

Sometimes I miss the days when all I had to deal with were wicked witches and natural disasters and ravenous beasts who didn't mean anything personal when they devoured you whole. Embittered fairy princesses are a hell of a lot more complicated.

I showed the sky my middle finger, just in case Ozma was watching—and Ozma's always watching—before closing the curtains again. I was up, and my girlfriend was once again banished from the Land of Oz by unseasonably good weather, courtesy of my ex. Time to get ready to face whatever stupidity was going to define my day.

As long as it didn't involve any Ozites, I'd be fine.

The hot water in the shower held out long enough for me to shampoo my hair. That was a rare treat this time of year, and one I could attribute purely to Ozma's maliciousness: lose a girlfriend, get enough sun to fill the batteries on the solar heater. It was a trade I wouldn't have needed to make if I'd had any magic of my own, but magical powers aren't standard issue for little girls from Kansas, and none of the things I've managed to pick up since arriving in Oz are designed for something as basic as boiling water. That would be too easy.

I was toweling off when someone banged on the bathroom door—never the safest of prospects, since the hinges, like everything else in the apartment, were threatening to give up the ghost at any moment. "Dot! You done in there? We've got trouble!"

"What kind of trouble, Jack?" I kept toweling. My roommate can be a little excitable sometimes. It's a natural side effect of having a giant pumpkin for a head.

"I don't know, but Ozma's here! In person!"

My head snapped up, and I met my own startled eyes in the mirror. The silver kiss the Witch of the North left on my forehead the day I arrived in Oz gleamed dully in the sunlight filtering through the bathroom skylight. "I'll be right there. Just keep her happy while I get dressed."

"I'll try," he said glumly. His footsteps moved away down the hall. My surprise faded into annoyance, and I glared at my reflection for a moment before I turned and headed for the door to my room. Ozma—fucking *Ozma*—in *my* apartment. She hadn't been to see me in person since the day she told me we couldn't be together anymore, that I had become a "Political liability" thanks to my unavoidable association with the crossovers.

I would always be a Princess of Oz. Nothing could change that, not even the undying will of Her Fairy Highness. But I was no longer beloved of the Empress, and if I wanted to see her, I had to come to the Palace like everybody else. So what the hell could have brought her to the crossover slums at all, let alone to my door?

I wrenched drawers open and grabbed for clothing, only vaguely aware that I was dressing myself for battle: khaki pants, combat boots, and a white tank top—none of which would have been anything special outside of Oz. Here the tank top was a statement of who and what I was, and why I would be listened to even if I were a crossover and not a natural-born citizen. Only one type of person is allowed to wear white in the Land of Oz; it's the color of witches, and I, Dorothy Gale, Princess of Oz, exile from Kansas, am the Wicked Witch of the West.

Putting in my earrings took a little more care. I would have skipped it if Ozma had sent a representative instead of coming herself, but it was the very fact of her presence that both made me hurry and take my time. Ozma needed to see that I was taking her seriously. So in they went until my ears were a chiming line of dangling silver charms: slippers and umbrellas and field mice and crows. I checked my hair quickly, swiping a finger's-worth of gel through it with one hand. The tips were dyed blue, purple, red, and green—four of the five colors of Oz. I'm a natural blonde. I didn't need dye to display the colors of the Winkie Country.

Clapping the diamond bracelet that represented the favor of the Winkies around my left wrist, I gave myself one last look in the mirror and left the room. I could hear voices drifting through the thin curtain that separated the apartment's narrow back hallway from the main room: Jack, a high tenor, almost genderless and perpetually a little bit confused; a low tenor that had to belong to one of Ozma's guards; and Ozma herself, a sweet, piping soprano that I used to find alluring back when it whispered endearments instead of excuses. I stopped at the curtain, taking a breath to bolster myself, and then swept it aside.

"I'm flattered, Ozma," I said. "I didn't know you remembered where I lived."

The main room served as both our living space and the reception area for my duties as the Crossover Ambassador. It was shabby, as befitted both those roles. Ozma stood out against the mended draperies and twice-repaired furniture like an emerald in gravel.

Her back was to me, facing Jack and a guardsman in royal livery. If we could have conducted the entire meeting that way, I would have been thrilled. Sadly it was not to be. Her shoulders tensed, and then the Undying Empress, Princess Ozma, turned to face me.

She was beautiful. I had to give her that, even if I never wanted to give her anything again. Her hair was as black as the midnight sky, and like the midnight sky, it was spangled with countless shining stars, diamonds woven into every curl. Red poppies were tucked behind her ears, their poisonous pollen sacs carefully clipped by the royal florists. It all served to frame a face that couldn't have been more perfect, from her red cupid's-bow mouth to her pale brown eyes, the same shade as the sands of the Deadly Desert. Her floor-length green silk dress was more simply cut than her court gowns; I recognized it from garden walks and picnics back in the days when I was in favor. She wore it to throw me off balance. I knew that; I rejected it...and it was working all the same.

"I granted you this space," she said sweetly. "Of course I remember. How are you, my dear Dorothy?"

"Peachy," I snapped. "What are you doing here, Ozma?"

"It's such a beautiful day outside, I thought you might need some company." A trickle of poison crept into her words. That was all it ever took with Ozma. Just a trace, to remind you how badly she could hurt you if she wanted to. "Don't you love the sunshine?"

For a moment I just gaped at her, inwardly fumbling for some reply—any reply, as long as it didn't involve hurling something at her head.

Finally I settled for, "Not really. What do you *want,* Ozma? Because I don't want you here."

"Ah. It's to be like that, is it?" The sweetness vanished from her face in an instant as she straightened, looking coldly down her nose at me. "There's been a murder. I expect you to deal with it."

"Uh, maybe you're confused. I'm not a detective, and I'm not a member of your royal guard. I'm the Crossover Ambassador and the Wicked Witch of the West. Neither of those jobs comes with a 'solve murders' requirement."

"No, but both of those jobs come with a 'control your people' requirement, and Dorothy, one of your people is a murderer." Ozma's lips curved in a cruel smile. I balled my hands into fists, pushing them behind my back before I could surrender to the urge to slap that smile right off her smug, pretty little face. "The body was found Downtown, in the old Wizard's Square. My guards are holding it for you. Find the killer, and deliver him to me."

"Or what?" The challenge left my lips before I had a chance to think it through. I winced.

"Or I find a new ambassador to keep the crossovers in line. A proper Ozite, perhaps, one who will have the nation's best interests at heart." Ozma kept smiling. "And you, my dear Dorothy, can look forward to an endless string of cloudless days. Sunshine does keep spirits up in the winter, don't you think? Rinn will stay here to show you to the body. Whenever you're ready—but it had best be soon, for everyone's sake."

She turned, leaving me staring, and swept out of the room. Her guard remained behind, standing uncomfortably beside the door. Jack stepped up beside me, his big orange pumpkin-head tilted downward to show the unhappiness his carved grin wouldn't let him express.

"Well, that wasn't very nice," he said.

"Get my pack," I replied, snapping out of my fugue. "I've got a murder to solve."

—

The Wizard was the first person to cross the shifting sands of the Deadly Desert with body and soul intact. He wasn't the last, not by a long shot. We should have known something was wrong with the spells that protected Oz when I made the crossing over and over again, traveling by every natural disaster in the book, but what did I know? I was just a kid, and Oz was the country of my dreams. I would have done anything to get back there. When Ozma told me I could stay, that we could be best friends and playmates forever, I cried. I would have done anything she asked me, back then. I would have died for her.

The one thing I couldn't do, not even when she asked, was stop the slow trickle of crossovers from appearing in Oz. They each found their own way across the sands, some intentionally, some by mistake…and since each method of crossing back to the "real world" seemed to be a one-shot, once they were in Oz, they were in Oz for keeps. At first Ozma left them to find their own way. It had worked well enough for the early arrivals, but fewer and fewer crossovers were coming from places like Kansas. The farmlands found themselves overrun with people who didn't know which end of the plow was which. They threw the newcomers out, and one by one, the crossovers came to the only destination they had left.

The City of Emeralds. Which was now the Emerald City in nothing but name; only the oldest, richest denizens still wore their green-tinted glasses, updated with a special enchantment that made anyone who wasn't born in Oz disappear completely. This led to a few collisions on the streets, but as far as they were concerned, it was worth it. For them, the Emerald City was still the pristine paradise it had been before the crossovers came. For the rest of us…

Jack and I left the apartment by the back door, with Ozma's guard tagging along awkwardly behind us. He looked as unhappy about the situation as I felt. His look of unhappiness deepened as he realized that we were heading for the stairs. "Are we not taking the skyways?" he asked hesitantly.

My status as Princess-cum-Ambassador-cum-Wicked Witch was confusing for some people—especially the kind of strapping young lad that Ozma liked to employ. "No, we're not," I said curtly and promptly regretted my tone. It wasn't his fault. More kindly I explained, "We're going Downtown, remember? Not every building in this area has connections to both the streets and the skyways. It's better if we go down low as soon as we can. If we take the skyways, we'll come out miles from Wizard's Square."

"I have a piece of the road of yellow brick attuned to my comrades in arms. It would lead us where we needed to go," he said with the pride of a farm boy who'd never had his own magic before.

I remembered being that young, and that naive. I hated him a little in that moment for reminding me. "That's just dandy, but I know where we're going. This door lets out within half a mile of the Square, and I'd rather not walk any farther if I can avoid it. You don't want to walk that far through Downtown either. It's not safe."

"I am in service to the Undying Empress," he said proudly. "I fear nothing in this city."

"Just keep telling yourself that."

Jack snorted. It was an oddly musical sound thanks to the acoustics of his head.

Rinn frowned at us. "I am sorry. Is there something I am unaware of?"

"We're going *Downtown*," I said. "Have you ever been there before? Yes or no?"

"No," he said sullenly.

"I didn't think so. All right. First rule of Downtown: don't act like your position means anything to the people who live there. Most of them were city folks before they crossed, and they're still city folks. They don't appreciate being reminded that things are different now. Second rule of Downtown: don't mention Ozma."

"But why not?" Rinn sounded honestly confused. "Surely they're grateful."

"Grateful? She herds them into slums. She coddles the ones who catch her eye and leaves the rest to fight for scraps. She lets them kill one another, steal from one another, and do whatever they want, as long as she doesn't have to look at them. Downtown isn't grateful. They hate her more than almost anyone or any*thing* in Oz."

Rinn's eyes widened. To him I was speaking blasphemy. "What do they hate more?"

My smile was thin as a poppy's petal. "Me."

We'd been descending as we walked, moving out of the rarefied air of the upper city and down, down, down where the lost things lived. Buildings like mine are rare these days. They're technically considered Uptown since they're connected to the skyways, but they also have doors leading Downtown, making them vulnerable to compromise no matter how many spells are layered on to keep them secure. Good Ozites refuse to live in places like mine.

Good thing I'm not a good Ozite anymore. My building is a liminal space, like me, neither part of Uptown nor Downtown...and like me, it's never going to fit quite right anywhere again.

Jack pushed open the beaten copper door separating our stairwell from the street, and we stepped out into the humid, sour-smelling air of Oz's undercity. The door slammed behind us as soon as we were through, its built-in enchantments forming a seal that couldn't be broken without the appropriate countercharm. A dog barked in the distance. A baby wailed. And even though the sun was shining, so many walkways and structures blocked the light that it was suddenly twilight—a twilight that would never end.

I turned to Rinn, who was still looking staggered by my last word, and gave him my best Princess of Oz curtsey. "Welcome to Downtown."

"Prince—Miss—Sorcer—" Rinn stopped, done in by the perils of nomenclature, and gave me a look so pitiful that I couldn't help thawing a little. "I'm sorry. I don't know what I'm meant to call you."

"Dot is fine," I said and started walking along the cracked brick sidewalk toward the Square. This used to be one of the thoroughfares to the Palace, back when you could get there at ground level; the yellow still showed through in patches, where the grime hadn't managed to turn it as gray as everything else. That's the sick joke of Downtown. I left Kansas for Oz because I was tired of the color gray. Now I'm the Ambassador to the Gray Country of Oz, built in the basement of the City of Emeralds. "If that's too informal, you can call me Dorothy."

"Miss Dorothy, why is the Empress…what I mean to say is…"

"He wants to know why Her Royal Bitchness is threatening you with sunshine," said Jack. Rinn cast him a shocked look. The pumpkin-headed man was walking with more assurance now that we were Downtown. Maybe it was the fact that his shoulders were straight for the first time, showing just how tall he really was. "Weather isn't usually a good incentive."

"You mustn't speak of the Empress like that," said Rinn, sounding stunned. "What would even make you *think* such a thing?"

"My father and I go way, way back," said Jack. The bitterness in his voice was unmistakable. "I'm allowed to say anything about her that I feel like saying."

I patted him on the arm as comfortingly as I could manage. Ozma was a boy named Tip when she created Jack. She'd never liked to talk about that period in her life, and I knew better than to go into it in detail around one of her men. Rinn had probably been trained to regard all mentions of Ozma's boyhood as treason. Instead I said to him, "I'm dating a girl named Polychrome. She's the daughter of the Rainbow. No clouds, no rain. No rain, no rainbows. No rainbows, no girlfriend. She needs clouds if she wants to be here, and that means she'll be gone for as long as the sun stays out. So when Ozma wants me to dance to her song, she threatens me with the weather." I shook my head. "Now get moving. We've got a dead body to see."

Rinn held his official-issue lance at the ready as we progressed through Downtown, waiting for a brigand or a hungry Kalidah to spring out of the shadows. I slouched along next to Jack, eyeing the various speakeasies we passed with an undisguised longing. Jack followed my gaze and sighed.

"No, Dot."

"But—"

"No. Poly doesn't want you drinking, and neither do I."

"I just want a little pick-me-up, that's all."

"Dot, the stuff you can buy here stands a good chance of being a put-you-down one of these days. Poppy juice isn't safe for crossovers."

"Yeah, well." I shook my head, the charms on my ears chiming against one another. "What is?"

"We'll take care of this. Poly will be back by tomorrow night. You'll see."

I sighed. "Stop being optimistic. Or did Ozma remember your name this time?"

Jack didn't answer me.

I wasn't Ozma's first castoff, and I won't be her last. Jack was part of the group responsible for helping her claim her throne, back when she first came out of exile. He was also unpredictable—thanks to the slow decay of the pumpkins he used for heads—and he didn't clean up well for her court. She tolerated him for a long time, first out of love and later out of loyalty, but the day came when Jack was more of a liability than a friend, and he'd found himself banished to the City of Emeralds to sink or swim on his own. I'd chased him down before he could leave the Palace, pressing the key to my then-unused apartment into his hand.

It was an impulsive gesture that I didn't think anything of until years later, when the growing unease over the number of crossovers made it politically unwise for Ozma to keep one as a pet and boon companion. When I'd found myself in Jack's position, I'd staggered to my apartment on instinct, unsure what was going to happen when I got there. I was half-afraid he'd claim squatter's rights and leave me alone in the dark.

Instead he'd proudly shown me the furniture he'd built for my eventual arrival and tucked me safe and warm into my very own bedroom that I didn't have to share and that no one could ever turn me out of. He'd been waiting for me. I guess once you're thrown away you come to recognize the impending signs of someone else being discarded.

Jack was never really my friend when we both lived in the Palace. These days, there's no one I trust more. My first companions in Oz have long since found their place in the political structure. So have I, I suppose. It's just that the place I've found isn't one they can afford to associate with.

This deep into Downtown, things were a curious combination of Ozite tech and crossover ingenuity. Shacks built from every material imaginable squatted on corners and clustered in the bands of watery sunlight that pool between the distant skyways, their solar heaters out and soaking up every drop of energy they could collect. Half the shacks were on wheels, allowing them to move with the sun. The other half belonged to the light-farmers, who jealously guarded their turf against all comers. It would have been enough to make me feel bad about my longing for rain if it wasn't for the fact that rain was actually better for Downtown. It was harder to catch and control, for one thing. It washed everything clean, and it filled the water batteries, which worked just as well as the solar kind. Rain was the most precious commodity Downtown had.

Ozma probably wouldn't have thought to threaten them with a lack of rain if it hadn't been for my relationship with Polychrome. That, if nothing else, I was willing to feel bad about.

People appeared from alleys and shacks, watching us walk by. We made a curious parade, to be sure: a man in Ozma's colors; another with a pumpkin for a head; and me, their hated Ambassador, in my witchy white. Even if they didn't know my face, they knew what the color meant. There were three witches left in Oz, and I was the only one who ever came anywhere near Downtown.

"Miss Dorothy, I'm not sure the people here are very glad to see us," said Rinn, falling back to walk beside us. He was trying to keep his voice low. I appreciated the gesture, useless as it was. "Are we in danger?"

"If we're Downtown we're in danger. Did you miss where I said they hated me here?"

"But you're their Ambassador."

"Yeah, and they're living in hovels while I'm living Uptown. I'm the Empress's former lover, but I can't get them half the things they need, or change the laws so they're starting on an equal playing field, or find a way to send them home. Why would they like me, exactly? I'm failure walking to these people, and they don't understand how much worse it would be without me here. No one does." No one who hadn't been in those council meetings, playing wallflower, while Ozma—not yet broken on the subject of the crossovers, not yet embittered and cruel, although the seeds were already sown—fought with her advisors to keep them from driving the crossovers out into the Deadly Desert to die. I'd seen how bad it could be. How bad it *would* be, if we let certain people take over.

If Ozma wanted this murder solved, I'd solve it. And then I'd get back to the important business of finding a way to send these people home while they still had the option.

I knew we'd reached the Square when we turned a corner and found ourselves facing a crowd. Crowds were rare in Downtown; they left you vulnerable to pickpockets and to surprise raids by the royal guards. If people were gathering, it was because there was something too interesting to be ignored. Dead bodies usually qualified.

Rinn continued marching straight ahead, shouting, "Make way for the Princess!" Guess he'd decided which of my titles he liked best. He might have been surprised to realize that I was already gone, ducking to the side and working my way around the rim of the crowd until I found an opening. I dived in, worming my way between bodies until I broke free into the circle of open space maintained by Ozma's guards. A few people scowled and pointed, but they were sensible enough not to say what they were thinking out loud. They knew that you should never insult a witch to her face.

Jack's round orange head bobbed above the crowd about midway through, marking Rinn's progress. He nodded when he saw me. I nodded back and turned to see what we were dealing with.

The dead man lay in the center of the Square, arms spread as if he had been trying to make snow angels on the pavement before he died. His expression was one of profound confusion, a final perplexity that would never be resolved. I paced a slow circle around him, ignoring the glares from Ozma's guards. Something wasn't right here. I just couldn't quite see what that something was.

He was dressed in Quadling red, six different shades of it: garnet, ruby, crimson, carnelian, scarlet, and macaw. That sort of motley marked him as a member of the upper class, since getting those specific distinctions out of their dyes was difficult and expensive. His boots were wine-red leather, counter-stitched with gold in honor of the road of yellow brick that brought the wastrel sons of rich families marching into the Emerald City. Those boots…

I stopped, crouching down and frowning at the soles of his boots. A brief ruckus behind me marked the arrival of Jack and Rinn. "Jack, look at this," I said, indicating the dead man's feet. "Does this look wrong to you?"

"How did you—" demanded Rinn.

I ignored him. So did Jack, who stooped down next to me, the branches in his back creaking, and said, "They're awfully new boots. Probably expensive, too."

"Not just new. They're pristine. The streets are rough and filthy down here, so how did he wind up in the square without any scuffs or smears on his boots?" I reached out and grabbed his right foot, lifting it away from the pavement. "Look at his heel. Someone dragged him."

"He's still here, Dot. Even if he wasn't killed Downtown, he wound up here."

And that made him my problem. I dropped the dead man's foot, frowning. "Something else isn't right here." Something about the cut of the clothes just wasn't jibing with the man in front of me. I straightened enough to move up to his midsection and began undoing his belt.

Jeers and catcalls rose from the crowd, and from more than a few of the guards. I flipped them off and kept working, first unbuckling his belt and then untying his trousers. The jeers turned disappointed when I left his trousers on and used the slack I'd created to haul his shirt up over his belly. He had the beginnings of a paunch. Not a Quadling trait—Quadlings tend to be tall and skeletally thin—but city living can create anomalies in just about anyone.

The jeers finally turned to disgust and faded into muttering when I stuck my pinkie in the dead man's navel and began rooting around. Behind me Rinn asked in a horrified tone, "What is she doing?"

"Shut up and grow a pair," I snapped, pulling my finger out of the corpse and turning it so I could study what was caught under my nail. Then I smiled thinly. "Jack, get this man's boots off. I think you're going to find that they don't actually fit his feet. He's too short for them."

"What?" demanded one of the other guards.

I looked up and smiled. "Nice of you to say hello. Hello. I'm Dorothy Gale, and this man is a Munchkin." I picked the lint from under my pinkie nail and held it up. "Blue. They changed his clothes, but they didn't give him a shower first."

The guard blinked at me, looking nonplussed. He didn't say anything as I straightened again, this time moving to squat next to the dead man's head. That confused look on his face was bothering me. I just couldn't put my finger on exactly why…

"He died overdosing on the drugs *your* people make," said the guard, recovering his voice. "There's no parlor trick for you to play here."

"I learned humbugging from the best," I said and leaned closer, carefully prying his lips open. The charms in my ears jingled again as I peered into the dry cavern of his mouth. It smelled strange, like the dustbowl fields of Kansas. My eyes widened, and I sat up straight, turning to stare at my companions. "Dust. This isn't a poppy juice overdose. This is *Dust.*"

Everyone—even the parts of the crowd close enough to hear me—went silent. The only sounds were footsteps scuffing against the pavement, and the distant trill of birdsong from the lacy trellises of Uptown far above us.

Poppy juice predated the crossovers. It was a natural intoxicant, refined by the people of Oz when they needed something stronger than absinthe, but still weaker than pure poppy pollen. The crossovers just refined it a little. Dust, on the other hand…that didn't happen until the crossovers were well established and trying to find new ways of supporting themselves.

Because every crossover had to cross the shifting sands, one way or another, many of them arrived in Oz with a few grains of the Deadly Desert stuck to their clothes or hair. I don't know who first got the brilliant idea of grinding the stuff up and snorting it, but if I ever find out, I am going to kick their ass from one end of Oz to the other. Dust was addictive to Ozites and crossovers alike…and if people weren't careful, it could also be deadly, just like the sands it was derived from.

The only thing I didn't understand was where it was all coming from. Crossovers arrived with sand in their shoes and hair, but never more than a pinch. A few new people arrived every week. That should have been enough to provide a small cottage industry, not build an empire. And yet more Dust hit the streets of Downtown daily, and it was starting to appear Uptown as well.

Hatred of Dust was one of the pillars of the anti crossover movement. We'd created Dust. Get rid of us and, clearly, Oz would go back to normal—or what passed for normal, anyway.

What they hadn't considered was that even if the Dust was suddenly gone, the addicts would still remember what they'd craved—and they would still want it. Getting rid of the crossovers wouldn't get rid of the Deadly Desert. Dust would still find a way in.

Ozma's guards bundled up the dead Munchkin and carried him away, presumably bound for the Uptown morgue, where he could be kept preserved by stasis spells until the mystery of his identity could be unsnarled. The crowd dispersed as soon as the show was over. None of them stuck around to talk to us. In a matter of minutes, only Jack, Rinn, and I remained.

"Dust is a scourge," said Rinn in a challenging tone.

"You won't get any argument from me," I said. "The closest I'll come is this: if the crossovers had been treated better after they stopped being cute trinkets to show off at dinner parties, maybe they wouldn't have needed to struggle to survive. Maybe they wouldn't have chosen ways you don't approve of. Dust is horrible. But the crossovers created it because they were starving. This is everyone's fault."

Rinn didn't have an answer for that. He glared in stony silence as we walked back to my apartment, where the charms attached to my diamond bracelet—one spell per stone, thank you, Winkies, thank you—unlocked the door. I led the way up the stairs, past my apartment, and through a second locked door. This one was sealed with even more potent charms and led to the airy spires of Uptown. Here the air was fresh and sweet and tasted like the Oz of my childhood. The sun was neither too hot nor too bright, and the breeze that set my earrings jangling was just cool enough to make the day seem even lovelier.

Ozites strolled on the elevated walkways, many wearing the enchanted green goggles favored by the wealthy. They were all dressed in the latest fashions. I saw several pairs of boots like the ones we'd pulled off our dead Munchkin, done in all five of the citizenry colors. Only the yellow-clad Winkies acknowledged us as they passed, offering small nods or even bows in my direction. I replied with smiles and silence, not drawing attention to them. It was the only reward I could offer for them remembering that I was, after all, officially their Witch.

"Where are we going?" asked Rinn.

"The Munchkin Country embassy," I said. "I'm sure they'll be interested to hear that one of their citizens was found dressed as a Quadling in the middle of Downtown."

"And dead," said Jack. "Mustn't forget dead. That seems to be one of the main selling points of this particular gentleman."

I cast my pumpkin-headed friend a smile. "Oh, believe me, I won't be forgetting that part."

We walked on toward the embassy. It really was an unseasonably beautiful day.

The receptionist was a perfectly coiffed Munchkin woman who would have stood no taller than my chin in her high-heeled boots. She could never have passed for a Quadling. Lucky her. Maybe that would increase her chances of survival.

Although nothing was going to increase her chances of coming away without a bloody nose if she kept looking at me like something she'd just stepped in. "Ambassador Boq isn't seeing visitors today," she said for the third time.

"Well, since I'm an ambassador, too, maybe you could make a little exception."

She smiled thinly. “I’m afraid the Munchkin Country does not recognize Downtown as a territory.”

“Fine, then. Tell Ambassador Boq that Dorothy Gale, Princess of Oz, wants a minute of his time. If that’s not good enough, tell him that Dorothy Gale, Wicked Witch of the West, *will* have a minute of his time. If he’s accommodating now, my minute won’t happen unexpectedly in the middle of the night.” I bared my teeth at her in what might charitably be called a smile.

Her own smile faded. “One moment, please,” she said and slid off her chair, vanishing into the back of the embassy.

“That wasn’t nice, Dot,” said Jack.

“Nope,” I agreed. “It wasn’t.”

Rinn didn’t say anything. I couldn’t tell whether that meant he was getting used to me or had simply been horrified into silence.

The receptionist returned only a few minutes later with the round, blue-clad form of Boq, Ambassador of the Munchkin Country and head of the anti-crossover political faction—not to mention one of my first friends in Oz back before everything changed—following close behind her. “Dorothy!” he bellowed in a tone that implied absolute delight at my presence. “You should have sent a card ahead. I would have met you at the door with cakes and lemonade.”

“I didn’t really have the opportunity, Ambassador Boq,” I said with a polite bow. “We’ve come on business for Ozma. May we retire to your chambers?”

Boq was a consummate politician, but even he couldn’t have faked the look of surprise on his face. It had been a long, long time since I went anywhere on business for Ozma. “Yes, absolutely, my dear. You and your friends, follow me.”

“Thanks.” I offered the receptionist a little wave as we followed Boq down the hall to his private chambers, which were larger than my entire apartment and appointed ten times as well. They still weren't as nice as the quarters I'd shared with Ozma at the Palace.

I waited until Boq was settled in the chair behind his desk, giving him a few moments to feel like I'd been stunned into silence by the opulence of my surroundings. Then, without preamble, I said, "A Munchkin man was found dead in the old Wizard's Square today. He was dressed in Quadling colors. It's pretty clear that we weren't expected to figure out where he was from. Do you have any idea who he might have been? Ozma has tasked me with finding his killers."

Boq's face twisted into a mask of revulsion. "You've come here to talk about Downtown, with *me*? Dorothy. I thought better of you."

"No, Boq, I came here to talk to you about a murder. A Munchkin is dead. Surely that's more important than your hatred of the crossovers."

"Spoken like a girl without a country to defend," he spat. "You deserted your precious Kansas for us. How long before you desert us for something better? It was only a matter of time before the crossovers began killing."

"The fact that they had access to Quadling clothes and knew to re-dress him, that doesn't concern you at all?"

"Crossovers are as cunning as Winged Monkeys and about as trustworthy," Boq countered. "Really, you started killing the day you arrived. No wonder you speak for the rest of them. You're the first murderess of the lot."

"Since it got me a crown and made me a witch, I guess murder is pretty lucrative," I said. "You're the only one who might tell us who the man was, Boq. And you're the one who stands to benefit most from an Ozite dying Downtown. That makes me wonder why you're so defensive. I might just have to tell Ozma about this."

"You can't threaten me with Ozma," said Boq. "She heeds my counsel now, not yours."

"She heeds whatever counsel keeps Oz safest," I corrected gently. "Who was he, Boq? You know every Munchkin in the City of Emeralds. Who's missing?"

Boq hesitated. Then he sighed and said, "Taf. He's a junior clerk here at the embassy. He didn't report for work this morning."

"Why didn't you tell the guards?" asked Rinn. "We would have helped you find him."

"Munchkins police their own." Boq looked at me coolly. "We don't depend on outsiders to fix our problems."

"Funny," I said. "I seem to remember an outsider taking care of your little 'witch' issue a few years back."

Boq reddened, but he didn't look away.

"Thanks for letting us know who he was," I said. "You can probably collect his remains from the morgue later today."

"Dust is a scourge," he said. "I blame you and your kind."

"Yeah, I know," I said and turned to go. Jack and Rinn followed me.

We were almost to the receptionist's desk when I froze, my earrings chiming madly with the sudden motion.

"I'm an idiot," I said.

"What?" said Jack.

"I never told him it was Dust." I turned, running back to Boq's office.

He was in the process of emptying his desk when I burst in—with Jack, Rinn, and the shouting receptionist all close behind me. I didn't hesitate before launching myself across the room, grabbing Boq by the shoulders and pulling him away from what he'd been doing before he could destroy any more evidence. He shouted and threw a sachet of fine gray powder in my face, where it burst and filled the air around me in a choking cloud. I coughed and grabbed for him again. He shied away, stumbling right into Jack's arms. Jack grabbed him and held fast. The pumpkin-head might be made of sticks, but he was stronger than a normal man. Magic can be funny that way.

Boq struggled against Jack's grip for a moment before spitting in my direction and saying, "At least I get to see you die, crossover."

"Uh-huh." I coughed again before wiping the Dust out of my eyes. I was going to need another shower. "Funny thing, Boq. Crossovers can gather this stuff because they're resistant. Crossing the shifting sands makes the Desert a little less potent for them. I've crossed the shifting sands more times than anyone."

His eyes widened. Then he sagged, going limp in Jack's arms. "You bitch."

"It's pronounced *witch*, but that was a good try." I turned to Rinn. He was keeping his distance from me. Smart boy. At this point I probably qualified as a walking intoxicant. "Take him to Ozma. Tell her his clerk overdosed and Boq staged the murder to implicate the crossovers. Also tell her he tried to kill me." I couldn't keep myself from smiling. Ozma and I might not get along, but I was still her property, as far as she was concerned, to coddle or break at her whim and no one else's. She wouldn't take kindly to hearing that Boq had given me a face full of Dust.

Boq knew that too. He whimpered, and kept whimpering as Rinn handcuffed him and pulled him from Jack's arms.

I coughed again. The room was starting to spin. My multiple crossings of the Deadly Desert made me resistant, not immune. Jack's arms caught me before I could hit the carpet, and I let him bear me up and carry me home.

When I woke up, it was raining, and the whole room smelled like petrichor. My head was still spinning, and so I closed my eyes again, waiting for the world to be still.

"Ozma sends her thanks," said a voice from beside me—female, alto, and more welcome than a thousand roads of yellow brick. "She says that Boq will be dealt with appropriately."

"Meaning he'll be out in less than a week."

"He'd have been out in less than a day if he hadn't thrown that Dust in your face." Polychrome's hand touched my forehead. Her skin was cool and faintly damp, like a fine mist. "How are you feeling?"

"Better now." I reached up to catch her wrist without opening my eyes. "How long has it been raining?"

"About eight hours. You've been asleep for ten. We should tell Jack that you're awake—"

"In a minute." Oz was a land divided; the City of Emeralds was only the visual representation of a split that would tear us all apart, if we weren't careful. Boq was my enemy now, if he hadn't been already, and I was deeply afraid that if I started looking for the source of the Dust, all roads would lead me back to the Munchkin Country. Ozma was starting to use me again.

None of that mattered as I opened my eyes and looked up into the face of the woman I loved, wide-eyed and worried and haloed by the rainbow-streaked cloud of her hair. I leaned up as she leaned down, and her kiss was like the end of a yearlong drought. Outside the rain came down, and oh, the sweetness of that storm.

I was so glad to be home again.

Dear Dottie,
This will be a long letter, because I'm going on a trip, and
such a trip
won't believe
me when I
But don't

LOST GIRLS OF OZ

BY THEODORA GOSS

Dear Dottie,

This will be a long letter, because I'm going on a trip—and such a trip! You won't believe me when I tell you! But don't tell Mamsie, because you know how she worries when she thinks either of us girls is doing anything the least bit—well, she would call it *dangerous,* but I'm going to call it *adventurous.*

But I do want to tell you about it, because I want you to know where I am in case anything goes wrong. That makes it sound dangerous, I know—but please don't worry about me. I'm perfectly capable of taking care of myself, and I wouldn't be an intrepid girl reporter if I didn't follow my story wherever it took me. And this is quite a story, my dear. I'm so glad that I came to San Francisco even though it meant leaving you and Mamsie. I would never have gotten a story like this, or the Ogilvie murders either, if I hadn't left sleepy old Sacramento for the big city.

Do you remember how much Mr. Leavis liked my story on the murders? I spent months researching those girls, and when they actually caught and arrested Ogilvie, based on the evidence I had uncovered, it was quite a coup for the *Ledger*, I can tell you!

This morning, Mr. Leavis called me into his office, which always reeks of cigar smoke, and said, "Nell, you know these girls that have been disappearing?" Well, of course I did—they've been in all the papers, and there was a story on them in the *Ledger* last week. You remember the clipping I sent you—girls from respectable neighborhoods, gone missing and no bodies found. Quite the opposite of Ogilvie, who strangled them and left them in alleys. "I want you to look into it," he told me. "You did good work on the Ogilvie case—under my direction, of course." As though he'd had anything to do with it! Honestly, sis, the way he takes credit for everyone's work is just sickening. "The Langs have agreed to be interviewed. We can run a story on the poor grieving family and at the same time launch our own investigation. How about it?" Well, of course I said yes! Imagine if I could find out where those girls have gone—I would be on the front page again, but this time I would insist on my own byline! No more "by Eleanor Dale and Edward Leavis," thank you!

After lunch I went to see the Langs. At first I wasn't sure if I was going to get the interview after all. Mr. Lang was obviously drunk and refused to let me in, but his wife pleaded with him, saying it was "for our Mary." So we sat on the sofa and had a very stiff interview indeed. Luckily Mr. Lang passed out in the middle of it, and then Mrs. Lang really opened up. Poor woman! She was the one who had called the police and then the *Ledger*—her husband hadn't even wanted to file a missing person report. "He said Mary had run off with some boy, but I don't believe it," she told me. "Mary was always a good girl." She talked about how much she missed her daughter and what a help she'd been around the house and with the little ones. And she let me look around Mary's room. She even showed me Mary's diary. There wasn't much in it, just an account of her daily life, but every once in a while, I came across a curious entry: "Father angry today," or "Father especially angry today."

Fathers do get angry, but it was the reoccurrence of the phrase that caught my attention. And there were mentions of a best friend, Sally Russell. I asked Mrs. Lang if she could give me Sally's address. It was only a couple of blocks away. I walked along streets of placid houses surrounded by white picket fences. They seemed to be sleeping in the California sunlight. (Do you like that description? I'm going to use it in the story.)

Sally Russell was a tall, lanky girl with freckles and straw-colored hair. She wasted no time in telling me what was what. "Of course Mary ran away!" she said. "No, she didn't have a boyfriend—Mr. Lang would never have let her. He used to beat her something awful—and her mother, too, but her mother never did anything about it. And he was going to do worse… He wasn't Mary's real father, you know—her father ran off, and then Mrs. Lang married Mr. Lang and had two more children. Mary could never go anywhere, because she had to take care of them. The little imps, she used to call them. I think it was the school nurse that told her—one day when she was afraid Mr. Lang had broken her wrist, it was so swollen, and she just couldn't hide it anymore. The nurse told her that there was this underground—that it could get girls to Oz."

Well, you can imagine how I responded to that! Everyone knows you can't get to Oz anymore, not since the borders were closed. No one even knows where it is now. It could be in the middle of the sea or a great desert. And even if you could find it—what if you ran into Nomes or

Wheelers or Winged Monkeys? I told her, quite sternly, that Mary had probably been tricked and could be in a lot of trouble. She grew frightened at that. There was something she hadn't given the police—it was an address where Mary had said she could send letters. Well, she gave it to me, after I promised that I would investigate and make sure Mary was safe. I promised her I would do it myself and not turn the address over to the police. It was an easy promise to make—I didn't want to be scooped!

I took the address and looked it up on a map. It was in an older, rundown part of the city. The trolley took a while to get there, and it was already dark when I arrived. But that allowed me to sneak around to the back of the house and look in through the windows. Only one room was lit, and in it was a man, rather old and stooped, sitting at a table and writing something in a book.

Well, he didn't seem terribly frightening! And I knew what to do next. Just a few blocks from the house, close to the trolley stop where I had gotten off, was a diner. I asked the waitress if she had any rubber bands and then went into the bathroom and washed all the makeup off my face. I put my hair in two pigtails. When I came out, she looked at me curiously.

"I went to a party with my boyfriend," I told her. "He's in college—he doesn't know I'm just in high school. But someone took my school uniform. I don't know what to do. If I go home like this, my mom is going to kill me."

"I used to do that," she told me sympathetically. "Here, why don't you take my sweater? And I've got some shoes you can borrow. You can tell her that someone accidentally took your uniform at gym, and you had to borrow clothes from another girl."

"I could just kiss you!" I told her. Then I traded my hat and jacket and pumps for her sweater and a pair of rubber-soled shoes. I looked at least five years younger. It's a good thing I carry a leather postman's bag instead of a silly little purse! In the dark I thought it would look enough like a school bag.

When I knocked on the door, the old man answered it and said, "Yes, my dear? What is it?"

"Mary Lang sent me," I said, looking fearfully around as though afraid someone might have followed me. "She said you could help!"

"Oh goodness, come in, come in quickly," he said. "Along that hallway to the back, where we can't be seen."

Well, I was alone in the dark house with him, but I wasn't afraid. He looked so old, and not particularly strong. And you know I've taken jiu-jitsu.

I followed the hallway and found myself in a room at the back of the house. When he turned on the light, I saw that the curtains were drawn. There was a bed along one wall, a dresser, and a table with two chairs. Really, it was a perfectly ordinary room.

"You must be hungry," he said. "What would you like to eat? Ask for anything—anything at all." Laughing at him a little—surely this funny old man couldn't produce anything I asked for—I said I would like a pork chop with mashed potatoes and peas. And then—you won't believe this, Dottie, but it's true—he pulled out a wand from inside his jacket, waved it over the table, and there it all was! With a glass of lemonade to drink. Of course I knew who he was immediately.

"You're Oz, the Great and Terrible," I said.

"Oh, I don't go by that name anymore," he said, smiling modestly. "I just go by Oscar, or Mr. Diggs if you prefer. To make up for the terrible deception I practiced on the Ozites, I spend my life helping Ozma in her great work."

"And what work is that?" I asked.

"Why, helping girls like you and Mary," he said. "By royal decree, any girl who asks for refuge in Oz is granted it. What did you say your name was again, my dear?"

I hadn't said. "Sally Russell," I told him. "Mary gave me your address so I could send her a letter. She didn't know I would need it myself! But my uncle—he lives with us, and he's such a frightening man! He—"

"You don't need to tell me, my dear," said the Wizard. "It's a story I've heard many times, from girls very much like you. But there is a place and a purpose for you in Oz. Finish your dinner, and sleep here tonight—there is a nightgown under your pillow—and tomorrow we shall go to Oz!"

"How will we get there?" I asked him. "Aren't there terrible dangers in the way?"

"Oh, we have our methods," he said. "Don't you worry. Just get some sleep. We have a long journey tomorrow."

Well, Dottie, you can imagine what was going on in my mind! This was undeniably the Wizard: he had made a dinner appear before my eyes, and a very good dinner too! And he was taking girls who had run away from their families to Oz. That's where all the girls were going. What a story this would make! It would be on the front page, to be sure. Imagine if I could go to Oz and interview Mary Lang!

I ate a bit of everything he had given me and then waited half an hour to see if it contained a sedative, but I felt perfectly fine, so I finished my dinner. Now I am sitting at the table, writing this letter to you. As soon as I finish it, I'm going to sneak out through the window and post it in a letter box I saw down the street. Then I'll get some sleep. I don't know what tomorrow will bring, but this is quite the adventure, isn't it?

Don't worry about me, my dear. But I do want you and Mamsie to know where I've gone. Just in case something does happen to me (but it won't). Love you, little sis! I'll write to you again when I can.

Your own,
Nell

Dearest Dottie,

I don't know when or even whether this letter will reach you. Once I finish writing it, I'm going to give it to a woman I met at the Great Market in the Emerald City. She's a traveling merchant who brings rugs to sell in Oz from beyond the Deadly Desert, crossing the sands on one of the ships that sail across it, blown by the wind. There is no way to get to Oz except across that desert, and anyone who touches the sands turns into sand himself! Of course there is no other way to leave Oz either…

Yes, I'm in Oz, in a camp outside the Emerald City. As I sit in my tent, writing you this letter, I can hear the other girls outside, talking and laughing. Girls from all over the country! In this tent there are six of us: two from California, one from Kentucky, one from Oklahoma, and two sisters who ran away together from Massachusetts. The others are outside right now, probably roasting marshmallows, which grow on the marshmallow bushes down by a swampy area close to the city walls. The fields outside the walls are gay with tents and banners: red and yellow and purple and blue, the colors of the four countries of Oz. All of us girls have been assigned to a particular division; the six of us are in the Quadling division, so our tent and uniforms are red, which I think goes quite well with my hair! But I can't explain where I am without telling you the whole story, from the last time I wrote.

After climbing out of the Wizard's window and mailing you my last letter, then climbing back in again undetected, I had a good night's sleep. The next morning, the Wizard woke me and conjured a breakfast of toast with butter and marmalade, and eggs sunny-side up, with a mug of coffee. I have to admit that it was delicious. But his car! It was a Model A that looked as though it had come through the War. Wouldn't you think a wizard could conjure a better car than that? I asked him, but he said he didn't know that kind of magic. We drove down toward San Jose and then east past Fresno. Slowly the verdure faded from the landscape to be replaced by the dun-colored hills of eastern California. (Isn't that a good line? Frances—one of the girls from Massachusetts—used the word *verdure* earlier, when we were talking about the gardens in the Emerald City, and I liked it so much that I wanted to use it myself.) At some point I must have fallen asleep; it was so dull, driving through the desert. The car jounced along, making it hard to talk, and the Wizard was not a particularly good driver—every time I asked him a question, he turned to look at me, and I was afraid he would swerve off the road.

We stopped under a sign that read "Welcome to Nevada" and had a picnic lunch: ham sandwiches, apples, and more lemonade. It's quite useful having a wizard along when you're traveling! Although I wish he could have conjured up an electric fan. At that point I was too awake to sleep. I kept staring at the miles and miles of sand and scrub, wondering how in the world we were supposed to get to Oz. Maybe the Wizard, although undoubtedly a genuine wizard, at least as far as ham sandwiches were concerned, was also a crazy old man who drove girls into the desert and murdered them, leaving their bodies to rot on the desert sands. When I looked over at him, I couldn't bring myself to be scared of him. But maybe that was part of his plan—to seem so harmless? Well, if he was a murderer, he wouldn't find me easy to kill! I went through my jiu-jitsu moves in my head.

Just as the sun was starting to set, we came to a town in the middle of the desert. Well, *town* is too fancy a word for it—it was just a gas station, the first we had seen for hours, and a general store with a "Closed" sign in the window, and some houses that looked as though they might collapse at any moment. Next to the gas station was a motor lodge, and that, at any rate, was still open; there was a "Rooms to Let" sign out front and a car in the parking lot in considerably better shape than ours. We pulled into the parking lot and got out of the car. I was so sore from sitting and jouncing! The rooms were arranged in a semicircle around the parking lot, and one of the doors opened. Out came a girl, about my age, who waved at us.

She was dressed all in green: a green blouse with hearts embroidered on it and green trousers over which she wore thigh-high green leather boots. Around her waist she wore a gun belt with silver pistols in the holsters. She had short green hair that stood up in spikes all over her head.

"Jellia Jamb!" said the Wizard. "It's so good to see you. I've brought a last-minute addition to our party."

"I have two more in the room," said Jellia. "And the Shaggy Man telephoned to say that he will be here tonight with another three. We'll leave in the morning and meet Nick Chopper at the second rendezvous point."

"My friend Nick is a fierce fighter, although no man has a kinder heart," said the Wizard, turning to me. "We'll need his help getting through the Nome Kingdom."

I nodded, not quite knowing what to say. It was like walking into a fairy tale or a film studio—you know how often

Mamsie would tell us about the famous people of Oz, before it was cut off from the world. The Tin Woodman and the Scarecrow and the Cowardly Lion and Scraps, the Patchwork Girl… And here I was going to meet them! Until that moment I had not truly believed that we were going to Oz. But now I knew we were.

In the room at the motor lodge, I met the other two girls. Joan was also from California. She had run away from home to be a film star and had ended up living on the streets of Los Angeles. Ingrid was from a farm in Oklahoma, and she would not talk about why she wanted to run away. She spoke with an accent—I think her family was Swedish or something like that. I told them about being Sally Russell from San Francisco and about my friend Mary Lamb. We sat on the beds and talked a little, but mostly listened as the Wizard and Jellia leaned over a map on the table and made their plans. Jellia said that the Nomes had been especially troublesome lately, which was why Nick Chopper was joining us; once we made it past the Nome Kingdom, we would be fine. "The last time the Growleywogs and Scoodlers bothered us, we had the Hungry Tiger with us, and we showed them what for!" said Jellia. "I don't think they'll be bothering us again soon." Once we reached the third rendezvous point on the border of the Deadly Desert, we would be transported to Oz.

"How will that happen?" I asked.

"Don't you worry," said Jellia. "All that will be taken care of."

Because we were all hungry, the Wizard conjured up some ice cream, the flavors we liked best—I asked for strawberry and chocolate. I was amused to see that Jellia asked for pistachio. Just as we were finishing, we heard a knock on the door. It was the Shaggy Man.

He was exactly the way I had expected: shaggy everywhere, all his clothes in rags, although they weren't really. If you looked carefully, you could see that the cloth had been carefully cut to appear ragged. And his hair and beard were separated into a number of small shags, all tied with ribbons. His clothes were so colorful that he looked like a rainbow. He had brought three more girls: Lula Mae from Kentucky, who immediately started talking to Ingrid about milking cows, and Frances and Enid, two sisters who had run away from a fancy boarding school in Massachusetts. At first I didn't have a lot of sympathy for them, but during our journey, they earned my respect. None of us could build a fire as fast as they could, or put up a tent so it wouldn't blow over during the night.

"Well, Jellia, my dear, and Wizard, my good friend, I'll take the first watch," said the Shaggy Man. As I fell asleep in the bed I was sharing with Joan and Ingrid, I saw him standing in front of the motor lodge, holding what looked like a machine gun out of a gangster film.

The next day we drove across the desert in a caravan, Jellia's car in the rear because it was the most heavily armed. By evening we had reached the second rendezvous point, where Nick Chopper was waiting for us.

I saw him as soon as I stepped out of the Wizard's car: a man made all of metal, gleaming in the light of the setting sun. He was armed with an axe, and although he had a jolly enough smile on his metal face, I would not have liked to make him angry! Next to him stood a boy about my age. He looked as though he had been training for one of the strongman contests at the state fair: his biceps bulged out of his shirtsleeves and blond hair flopped over his eyes. Behind them was a van armored all over with metal plates.

"Will you look at that," said Joan, who was standing next to me. She was staring at the boy with the muscles. I was more impressed with the Tin Woodman.

"This is my friend Nick," said the Wizard. The metal man made us an awkward bow.

"I've brought Button-Bright," he said. "The last caravan we sent through the Nome Kingdom was attacked. They've gotten bolder since Ruggedo III ascended the throne. They don't dare attack Oz itself, not while Ozma has the Magic Belt. But they want to annoy and harass us as much as they can."

"Is that Button-Bright?" I asked, pointing to Mr. Muscles.

"How-dee-do," he said. "They call me Button-Bright because I'm as bright as a button."

"Oh, do they?" I wondered what kind of button they—whoever they were—had in mind. He sounded as thick as his thighs.

"Did you bring ammunition?" asked Jellia, ignoring Button-Bright. I guess she didn't have much use for him either.

Nick Chopper opened the back of the van. It was filled with stacks of cardboard flats—filled with eggs. "As many as we could bring," he said. "And I brought a secret weapon."

Out of the back of the van stepped...a chicken, with yellow feathers and a red comb. "This is Belinda," he said. "She's one of the granddaughters of Billina herself. She generously agreed to accompany us."

"Oh, it's so good to see you again, Belinda," said Jellia. She knelt and embraced the chicken.

"Well, you don't need to squeeze me quite so hard," said Belinda. "I'm not a stuffed chicken, you know!"

"It's a great pleasure to see you again, my dear," said the Wizard. "I haven't seen you since you were quite a young chick and used to hide in my pockets!"

"Well, doesn't that beat all," said Joan, low enough so only I could hear her. "A talking chicken."

"What, they didn't teach you about Oz in school?" I said. "All the animals talk there."

"I dropped out after sixth grade. We never got to talking animals."

We would all be grateful for those eggs and the talking chicken before long. The third rendezvous point was beyond the Nome Kingdom, in the Land of Ev. That night, we slept in the tents for the first time. You wouldn't believe how the Shaggy Man snored! I could hear him all the way across the camp.

The next morning we crossed the border.

The Nome Kingdom was rocky, and the road was in bad repair. It ran between steep cliffs, and several times boulders came crashing down, hitting and sometimes denting one or another of the cars. Now I knew why they all looked so battered!

"They're watching us," said the Wizard grimly. "Waiting to attack."

Ingrid, who was riding in the back next to me, reached over and held my hand.

The attack came on the third day. We had stopped to rest and eat our lunch in a gully. Suddenly, down the rocky faces of the cliffs came the Nomes—so many of them that the cliffs looked as though they were covered with large black spiders. That's what the Nomes look like, with their spindly arms and legs and their round, fat bodies. Ingrid and Lula Mae screamed and held on to each other. Nick took up his axe and the Wizard raised his wand. Button-Bright and the Shaggy Man both aimed their guns. Jellia threw open the back of the van and said, "Girls, to me! Form a circle and throw eggs, as many as you can!"

Well, I would have thought that the farm girls, at least, would have been too scared to fight. But all of us followed Jellia's orders. I don't like to remember what happened next. Do you know what happens to Nomes when they are hit by eggs, Dottie? They *explode.* There we stood in a circle, lobbing egg after egg until our arms were aching, while all around us Nomes were bursting as though they were balloons filled with horrible green goo. Imagine the smell of smashed eggs, of Nome goop, of our own sweat! It was horrible, but we worked together as a team. Meanwhile, the Tin Woodman was chopping their limbs off left and right, the Wizard was turning as many of them as he could into pebbles, and Button-Bright and the Shaggy Man were shooting into the mass coming at us. Bullets don't hurt the Nomes. But the Shaggy Man and Button-Bright did slow them down so we could pelt them with our eggs.

We were so tired, and the Nomes just kept on coming! I could see one standing up on a rock with a hideous crown on his head. He seemed to be directing the others, and didn't he look triumphant to see us girls getting too tired to aim well?

"They've got me!" shouted Nick Chopper. Sure enough, the Nomes had managed to wrench away his axe and were now trying to pull him limb from limb.

"It's time!" shouted Jellia. From the rear of the van flew Belinda, straight at the Nome with the crown on his head. He uttered a high-pitched shriek when he saw her coming and tried to crouch down, but she made straight for his head and beat him with her wings.

"My eyes, my eyes!" he screamed. "Retreat! Retreat, all of you worthless fools!"

Suddenly the Nomes began to scurry back into the rocks, and in another minute, we were the only ones in the gully. We all looked bruised and battered, especially the Tin Woodman, whose left arm was nearly wrenched off.

"Well, at least it's the left one," he said. "I'm a much better fighter with my right."

"I don't think rotten old Ruggedo will be attacking us again soon," said Belinda.

"Why, what did you do?" asked Jellia, smoothing her ruffled feathers and lifting her back into the van.

"Pecked out one of his eyes." She sounded satisfied with herself.

After that attack word must have gotten around, because we were not attacked again. It took several more days to cross the Nome Kingdom, but finally we reached the border of Ev. There the landscape changed: the rocky cliffs gave way to green meadows and pleasant gardens. As we passed each farmhouse, families came out to ask us about our journey through the Nome Kingdom and praise us—especially Belinda—for our bravery.

At the end of that day, we reached the third rendezvous point: a farmhouse on the border of the Deadly Desert, where yet more girls were waiting for us. They had arrived several days ago, some of them with Aunt Em, Ojo the Lucky, and the Scarecrow, who had come through Noland, and some with Polychrome, Johnny Dooit, and the Cowardly Lion. "They had an even more dangerous journey than we did," said the Wizard. "Not even Ruggedo is as dangerous as Queen Zixi. She is a sorceress almost as powerful as Glinda, and although she is hundreds of years old, she has learned to maintain her youth by eating the hearts of young women. You can imagine how much she would like to capture any of our girls!"

After dinner I went out and looked at the place where the green meadow ended and the Deadly Desert began.

"Hello, my dear," said the Wizard. I had not heard him come up behind me.

"What now?" I asked, looking at the endless expanse of sand that would turn you to sand yourself as soon as you stepped on it.

"Don't you worry about that. Now that we're all here, Ozma can wish us over the desert sands with her Magic Belt. She can only make one wish a day, but tomorrow after breakfast, we will gather in the farmyard, and you will see the Emerald City for the first time!"

The next morning, after a breakfast of pancakes with maple syrup, we gathered together in the farmyard. Some of the girls looked scared, and some held each other's hands or put their arms around one another's waists. At nine o'clock exactly, the Wizard made a particular sign—and the next thing I saw was a great palace, all of white stone with turrets and parapets and whatever else palaces have, including great archways flanked by stone lions with emerald eyes. It was the most magnificent thing I had ever seen—even more magnificent than San Francisco! Standing on a balcony above us were five girls. The tallest one, who had long black hair and looked like a film star, said "Welcome to Oz. I am Ozma, and these are Dorothy, Betsy Bobbin, Jinjur, and Trot."

And then she told us.

Have you been wondering, Dottie, while you've been reading this letter, why all these girls are being taken to Oz? Well, I wondered that too—wondered as I lay in my tent, listening to the Shaggy Man snore at night. Wondered as we traveled day after day through the Nome Kingdom. Why all these girls?

Ozma told us.

Standing up on that balcony, she told us about how she had been taken as a baby to the witch Mombi, and how

Mombi had turned her into a boy, and made her work, and beat her. "I never want another girl to be beaten the way I was," she said. "So any girl who wants to come to Oz is welcome. She will find refuge here with me. But we have to save all the other girls, don't you see? That's why I invite any girl to join my army. It will be an army of liberation, sent from Oz to conquer all the lands around and then the rest of the United States of America. But we're not just going to conquer and rule the country, girls. We're going to transform it too, so it becomes like Oz." She held out her arms to us, and I don't think Mary Pickford could have looked more appealing. For a moment even I wanted to sign up right away, to save all those girls—even if it meant conquering the United States. Of course I did sign up—I mean, Sally Russell signed up. We all did.

Are you laughing, Dottie? At the thought of an army of girls—all those runaway girls—fighting our military, with their guns and tanks? Well, you can stop laughing now. After Ozma's speech, which was short (she probably gives it every day, as more and more girls arrive), Dorothy showed us the camp. That's General Dorothy—she, Betsy Bobbin, Jinjur, and Trot are the generals of Ozma's army. Each of them leads a division of the army that is associated with one of the countries of Oz. Joan, Ingrid, Lula Mae, Frances, Enid, and I were put in the Quadling division. We were given our uniforms, and then Dorothy, our General, talked to us about what we would be doing now that we were soldiers.

We stood on a hill, looking down at the camp, which was covered with tents as far as the eye could see—red and yellow and purple and blue.

"Time works differently here than it does in the outer world," said Dorothy. "We've been gathering soldiers for ever so long. If a girl doesn't want to join Ozma's army, she doesn't have to—but almost everyone joins. Who wouldn't want to fight for Ozma and Oz? Anyway, the girls who come here know what it's like out there. I remember what it was like in Kansas—never enough to eat and people passing through who had no place to call home. They were just trying to get to California, where they thought things would be better. Well, here in Oz, if you don't have enough to eat, you find a lunch pail tree!"

"But there are wicked people even in Oz," said Enid.

"Yes, what about old Mombi?" asked Lula Mae.

"Of course," said Dorothy. "But Glinda finds out about them, and they're punished."

"And do you really think a bunch of girls can conquer the American army and air force?" asked Frances dubiously.

"Oh, but we don't just have a bunch of girls," said Dorothy. "We also have the Jack Pumpkinheads, and the Wogglebugs, and the Tik-Tok Men. Come on, I'll show you." And she showed us, all right.

The Jack Pumpkinheads are grown in fields in Gillikin Country, where Ozma created the original Jack when she was a boy. At least, their pumpkin-heads are. Their bodies are made of wood, and when they are put together, they are sprinkled with the Powder of Life. "It's mixed up in large vats in Gillikin Country," said Dorothy. "We can sprinkle it on anything we like, of course. But the Jack Pumpkinheads are good soldiers. They can't be killed, and they just keep on going unless you chop them up into small pieces. If they lose a limb, they can replace it with any old piece of wood."

The Wogglebugs come from hatcheries in Winkie Country. "They reproduce so quickly that we have lots more than we need," said Dorothy. "When they're born, they're just the size of a pea, but if we need them to fight, we highly magnify them. They're pretty scary, aren't they?"

I have to admit, if I had an army of Wogglebugs coming at me, I'd turn around and run! They look sort of like cockroaches, but when they're highly magnified and standing on their hind legs, they're the size of a man.

"The Tik-Tok Men are made in a factory in Munchkin Country," said Dorothy. "They're just about indestructible, and the machine guns are built right in."

You've never seen anything like the Tik-Tok Men, Dottie! When I saw them, I realized that they would plow our soldiers down and keep on marching. For the first time, I was scared. What if I never escaped from Oz? But there's no time to be despondent when you're an intrepid girl reporter, is there? Instead I tried to estimate the size of the Oz forces.

"But the girls are the most important part," said Dorothy. "Girls are a lot fiercer than most people suppose. All these girls—they've come to Oz because of how they were treated out there. I ought to know—I was like them until Uncle Henry and Aunt Em took me in. They can fight—we've been training them. And they can direct the Jack Pumpkinheads and Wogglebugs and Tik-Tok Men, who haven't much brains of their own."

I remembered how we had all fought the Nomes together. Maybe Dorothy was right. Maybe girls don't fight in the world out there because they've never been taught how. As we walked through the camp, between the colorful tents and banners, I saw girls everywhere: some of them were practicing a kind of jiu-jitsu, some of them were loading and unloading their guns, some of them were listening to lectures on how to blow up trains. They looked busy and serious but also festive in their colored uniforms, as though they had gathered for some sort of outing. I began to see that Ozma's army was nothing to laugh at.

"Ozma doesn't want to kill anyone," said Dorothy. "She doesn't even like to swat flies! She says they are as much her subjects as any creature in Oz. She'd be much happier if everyone just surrendered. That's why she's sending the army of Oz first. But things have to change, don't you see? If the army doesn't work, she'll use the Magic Belt. She can wish whole countries dead, if she wants to."

"Will that work outside Oz?" asked Ingrid. She sounded shocked at the thought of such destruction.

"Of course," said Dorothy. "Magic is like electricity. It works the same everywhere."

So you see, Dottie, I've got to get my story out! Don't you tell anyone any of this, because I don't want to be scooped. I'm going to stay here long enough to figure out the size of Ozma's army, and then I'm going to cross the Deadly Desert—I don't know how yet, but if a rug merchant can get across, so can I. And then I'm going to break the largest story that the *Ledger* has ever seen!

Your loving sis,
Nell

My dearest Dotts,

I've asked the Shaggy Man to bring you this letter. When you've read it, I want you to tell Mamsie the whole story—from when I first started investigating Mary Lang's disappearance. Make sure she's sitting down on the parlor sofa, and tell her slowly. It's not good for her to be startled or upset. But she was the one who always told us stories about Oz, so maybe she won't be as startled as you or I would be.

Once you've told her, I want the both of you to pack up whatever you need—but only what you need. The Shaggy Man will bring you back to Oz, and there isn't much room in the Gump. Do you remember the Gump? Ozma made it when she was a boy, out of two sofas lashed together with palm fronds for wings, a broomstick for a tail, and a head that looks as though it once belonged to a peculiar sort of moose. It's the most sarcastic creature, but quite safe to fly in. It will carry you across the Deadly Desert and into the Emerald City. The Shaggy Man will make sure that you arrive safely.

You might be surprised by this letter, after the last one I sent you. But when I sent it, I had just arrived in Oz, and I didn't understand how important this war is—how it must be waged and won. (That's pretty good, isn't it? Waged and won. I think I'm going to use that in my next article.) Ozma has appointed me Royal War Correspondent of Oz, and I'm proud to fulfill that role. Once the war starts, it will be important for you and Mamsie to be safe—and no place will be safer than the Emerald City.

But I'd better tell you what changed my mind about this war. About a week after we had begun our training, General Dorothy came into our tent. She said, "Sally and Jane, you've been chosen to join Glinda's personal guard. Are you willing?" Jane and I looked at each other in amazement. Glinda's personal guard is an elite unit in the army—it contains the bravest, best-trained girls from our division. We both nodded. "You'll be going down to Quadling Country," said Dorothy. "There you will continue your training with Glinda herself. Make me proud, girls!"

That afternoon we packed our kits and set off, about a dozen of us. It took us several days to reach Glinda's palace, but the journey was pleasant—we walked through green fields and sunlit forests, mostly following the road of yellow brick, and had no trouble at all from Hammer-Heads or Fighting Trees. Sometimes we slept in tents, and sometimes we passed farmhouses, where we were given food and beds for the night. When the Quadlings heard we were joining Glinda's personal guard, they bowed and curtseyed with great respect.

Glinda's palace is not as large as Ozma's in the Emerald City, but when I first saw it, with its spires glowing in the light of the setting sun, I was impressed! Instead of tents we were put in barracks made of marble and rare woods, with the most luxurious baths I have ever seen, and were given new uniforms of rose silk.

The next morning we began the most intensive training we had yet received. Do you know, little sis, how to kill someone with a pocket comb, or a mirror, or even a handkerchief—everyday items that a girl might carry in her purse? Do you know how to pick any lock with a hairpin, or make a bomb out of ordinary household ingredients? Well, I do! Glinda's guards aren't just soldiers—they're spies. We were trained by a roly-poly sergeant who could flip any of us on our backs before you could say "Boo!" I can tell you that we gave each other many bruises! At the end of the day, I would lie in one of the baths, in rose-scented water, to ease my aching muscles.

When we had been at Glinda's palace for about a month, we were told that Glinda herself wanted to see us. I thought we would be taken to a throne room of some sort, but instead we were shown into a pleasant parlor. There were sofas and armchairs upholstered in rose chintz, and on the low tables were trays with heart-shaped cookies and chocolate cake. There was also a cut-glass bowl of strawberry punch. As we stood in that room, not quite sure what to do with ourselves, Glinda herself entered. She looked about our age, although I've heard that she's more than a thousand years old. She wore a long rose-colored gown and a gold crown on her head. She was not as beautiful as Ozma—at least, she looked less like a film star and more like a Sunday school teacher, with calm gray eyes. She said, "Girls, please pour yourselves some punch and take some cookies and cake. And then sit down and make yourselves comfortable. I've asked you here because I like to get to know my new recruits."

I piled cake and cookies on my plate—the training had made me hungry! We all sat—some of us on sofas, some in armchairs, some on the floor. When we were all comfortably seated, Glinda said, "Girls, I'd like to hear your stories." So we went around the room and all told where we had come from before we came to Oz.

Oh Dottie! What some of those girls had gone through. I felt ashamed of myself, telling the made-up story of Sally Russell. Some of the girls cried and held each other, and I could see that sometimes tears flowed silently down Glinda's cheeks, although she remained silent.

"Thank you girls for sharing your stories," she said when we had all spoken. "You have gone through pain and loss and grief. I hope that here, at my palace and in Oz, you will find what you have so often missed in the outer world—a sense of sisterhood and of family." Before we left she embraced each one of us.

"I feel so much better now," said Joan when we were back in the barracks, sitting on our bunks. "As though my heart were lighter. Listen to me! Can you believe I just said that?" And you know? It was the first time I had seen her actually smile.

That night I couldn't sleep. I lay awake in the darkness, remembering the stories those girls had told; one had shown us cigarette burns up and down her arms.

The next morning, before the other recruits were awake, I went to the sergeant's quarters. She was already awake, of course, doing her calisthenics. "I need to talk to Glinda," I said.

She looked at me for a moment, keenly, then nodded. "Glinda will be in her study," she said. "If you're not sure of the way, ask one of the porters."

I did have to ask one of the porters, a girl in a rose-colored dress and ruffled apron, who was mopping the marble staircase. She led me to Glinda's study and opened the door. Glinda sat at her desk, doing whatever sorceresses do in the mornings. I walked up to her, boldly enough, and said, "I'm not Sally Russell."

"Who are you, then?" she asked with a kind look on her face.

"My name is Eleanor Dale, and I'm a reporter for the *San Francisco Ledger.* I came here under false pretenses so I could figure out where all the missing girls had gone. Are you going to have me court-martialed?"

Glinda smiled. "My dear, I knew all this long before you arrived at my palace. I was waiting to see if you would tell me."

I stared at her. "How did you know?"

"I have a book that tells me everything that happens, all over the world. It told me you were coming here as soon as you thought of it yourself. The words appeared on the pages of the book as though written by an invisible pen. I do wish it had an index—it can be most unwieldy to use."

"But then why did you let me come into Oz, and come here from the Emerald City?"

"Because you're a brave girl, and I thought that we could use you on our side. Anyway, if your letters had fallen into the wrong hands, Ozma could simply have wished them to disappear. But you're willing to fight for us now, aren't you, Eleanor? To fight for Oz and everything it represents?"

I nodded. "Should I go back and join the others in the barracks, then?"

"No," said Glinda. "I let you train with my guards until you were ready to tell me the truth, but now that you've shown your honesty and loyalty, I have a more important task for you. We need someone to write about the war effort, to create leaflets and pamphlets and articles for the *Emerald City Daily* and all the smaller newspapers in Munchkin Country and the other countries of Oz. You'll be syndicated, my dear."

Well, you can imagine what I thought of that!

So here I am, sitting in my office in Ozma's palace in the Emerald City. Later today I have an interview with Professor H.M. Wogglebug, who developed the Wogglebug strategy, and then I'm reviewing the troops with General Betsy Bobbin and touring a Tik-Tok Man factory. And I'm meeting Scraps the Patchwork Girl for dinner, but that's just because we're friends. Oh, and you won't believe this—I found Mary Lang! She's in the Munchkin division and is becoming a demolitions expert. She says she's happy here in Oz and looking forward to contributing to the war effort. She wanted to let the real Sally Russell know that she was all right, and I said the Shaggy Man could post a letter for her.

I can't wait to see you and Mamsie again! I have a lovely apartment here in the Emerald City, which I'm sure you will both love. And I will be glad to know that you're safe in the coming months as Ozma begins her invasion of California. I'm looking forward to covering the siege of San Francisco! Remember, the Gump is perfectly safe, and the Shaggy Man will be with you the whole time. See you soon, darling!

Your loving sis,

Nell (Royal War Correspondent of Oz)

THE BOY DETECTIVE OF OZ: AN OTHERLAND STORY

BY TAD WILLIAMS

It was hard to imagine anything was actually wrong here. It was the nicest Kansas spring anyone could imagine, the broad prairie sky patched with cottony white clouds. Redbuds cheeky as schoolchildren waved their pink blooms in a momentary breeze, and a huge white oak spread an umbrella of shade over the road and for quite a distance on each side.

As he crossed a little wooden bridge, Orlando Gardiner saw the birches rustling along the edge of the stream, exchanging secrets with the murmuring water. The stream itself was bright and clear, flowing over large, smooth rocks of many colors and festooned with long tendrils of moss that undulated in the current. Fish swam below him and birds flew above him and it seemed like it would be May in this spot forever.

But if everything was as nice as it looked, why was he here?

—

To: HK [Hideki Kunohara]
From: OG [Orlando Gardiner, System Ranger!]
RE: field dispatch, kansas simworld

i'm sub-vocalizing this while i'm actually onsite investigating, so sorry for any confusion. i know you think the kansas world was hopelessly corrupted from the first, and if it really has gone bad you'll utterly have my vote to de-rez it, but first impressions are that everything looks pretty good here, so let me finish checking it out before we make any moves. Like you said, I'm "the one who'll have to deal with the bullshit if it goes wrong," and that's what I'm doing.

He could see the modest roofs and central spire of Emerald in the distance, everything as neat and well kept as a town in a model railroad. The first time he had seen this place, it had looked like something out of a medieval painting of hell: dry, blasted, cratered as if it had been bombed, and populated with creatures so wretched and freakish they might have been the suffering damned. But it was the only Oz simulation in the Otherland network, and Orlando had fought hard to keep it running; it was good to see it thriving. Oz had meant a lot to him when he was a kid confined to a sickbed. When he had been alive.

But that still didn't answer the main question: If everything was good in Kansas, why had he been summoned?

Whatever the reason, someone seemed to be waiting for him. She would have sparkled if the sun had been on her, but since the Glass Cat was sitting in the shade grooming,

Orlando didn't see her until he was almost on top of her. She looked up at Orlando but didn't stop until she had finished licking her glass paw and smoothing down the fur on her glass face. The Glass Cat might be a sim of a cat—and a see-through cat at that—but she was every inch a feline. The only things that kept her from looking like a cheap glass paperweight were her beautiful ruby heart, her emerald eyes, and the pink, pearl-like spheres that were her brains (and also her own favorite attribute).

"I expected you to show up," said the Glass Cat. "But not this quickly."

"I was in the area." Which was both true and nonsensical, since there really was no distance for Orlando to travel. He existed only as information on the massive network and could visit any world he wanted whenever he chose. But as far as the Glass Cat and the others were concerned, there was only one world—this one. The sims didn't even realize they were no longer connected to the Oz part of the simulation, although they remembered it as if they were. "I hear there's a problem," he said. "Do you know what it is?"

She rose, swirling her tail in the air as gracefully as if it had not been solid glass, and sauntered off the path, heading down toward the stream. "Am I supposed to follow you?" he asked.

She tossed him an emerald glance of reproach. "You're so very clever, man from Oz. What do you think?"

Following a snippy, transparent cat, he thought: *Just another day in my new and unfailingly weird life.* Orlando's body had died from a wasting disease as he and others had struggled against the Grail Brotherhood, the network's creators, a cartel of rich monsters and other greedy bastards all looking for eternal life in worlds they made for themselves. But now they were all gone, and this was Orlando's forever instead.

"I hope this is important, Cat," he said as he followed her down the embankment, into the rustle of the birch trees. "I've got plenty of other things to do." And he did. Major glitches had looped Dodge City—the simulated outlaws had been robbing the same simulated train for days—and the gravity had unexpectedly reverted to Earth-normal in one of the flying worlds, leaving bodies all over the ground. He planned to fob at least one of the problems off on Kunohara, who, like most scientists, loved fiddling with that sort of programming problem.

"There," the Cat said, stopping so suddenly he nearly tripped over her. "What do you think of *that*?"

Orlando was so irritated by her tone that for a moment he didn't see what she was talking about, but then he noticed a leg and the long, curled toe of a boot lying half-hidden in the tall wheatgrass. "*Ho Dzang*," he said softly. "Who is it? Do you know?"

"I think it's Omby Amby."

"The Soldier with the Green Whiskers? The Royal Army of Oz?"

"If you mean the Royal Policeman of Kansas, then yes," the Cat said. "You know we don't use those titles and such from the Old Country." She yawned. "I found him this morning."

"What were you doing way out here?" Orlando bent down. The top half of the body was still hidden by grasses, but he could see enough of the man's slender torso and green uniform to be sadly certain the Cat was right.

"I get around." She rose and writhed herself in and out of Orlando's legs. "I travel, you know. I see things. I learn things. I'm curious by nature—isn't that why you chose me to help you?"

"I suppose." As far as he was concerned, she was merely an informant, but of course the Glass Cat would see herself as more important than that. He bent lower to pull back the grasses. "But if you really want to help me, you'd stop bumping m—"

He never finished his sentence. As he exposed the rest of the green-clad figure, Orlando Gardiner was arrested by the sudden realization that while this might indeed be the body of Omby Amby, Royal Policeman of Kansas, that was all it was; his neck ended in a cut as neat and bloodless as if someone had chopped a potato in half with a surgical knife. His head and famous long whiskers were nowhere to be seen.

---

okay, it's a little worse than I first thought, mr. k—there's a body. but it's a minor character, and it might just be an ordinary glitch. My cover story (about being sent by ozma from oz) still holds up though, so give me a little time with this one. i promise I'll get to the other fenfen soon. Maybe you should check out dodge city in the meantime—i think that one has some major programming screwups, because the bridge there fell down and then put itself back up a few months ago, and the native americans are kind of blue-colored. looks hopeless to me, but you might notice something in the numbers I missed.

"Most disturbing!" declared Scarecrow. The Mayor of Emerald shifted in his chair, but his legs wouldn't stay where he left them and kept getting in his way. His friend the Patchwork Girl leaped forward and helped push them into place. "And where is the body of poor Omby Amby now?"

"Being examined by Professor Wogglebug," said Orlando. "Well, all of it that we have, since the head's missing. Amby worked for you, didn't he?"

"Of course!" Scarecrow said. "I'm the mayor, aren't I?" But although he sounded indignant, Scarecrow seemed to lack the spirit to back it up, slumping in his chair like a bag of old washing. His lethargy worried Orlando, reminding him unpleasantly of the bloated, monstrous version of the Scarecrow that had ruled Emerald in the bad old simulation. "And his head's gone, you say?"

"Yes. Professor Wogglebug says he's never seen anything like it."

"He *would* say that," declared the Patchwork Girl, turning cartwheels around the mayoral office. "He's got a terrible memory!" She was not the most focused personality in the simworld, but her heart was good, so Orlando did his best to be patient. That was why he had taken the job instead of leaving it to short-tempered Hideki Kunohara—you had to be very, very patient, because the inhabitants were like weird children frozen in the manners of the early twentieth century.

"Scraps, your foolishness is making my head hurt," Scarecrow complained. "Please stop revolving like a Catherine wheel. This is serious. Omby Amby is dead! Murdered!"

"Hah!" shouted the Patchwork Girl. "Now you're the one who's being foolish, Scarecrow. Nobody dies here in Kansas, just like nobody dies in Oz! Right, Orlando?"

The question caught him by surprise. "I'm not sure, Scraps," he said. "I've certainly never heard of anything like this happening since..." He had almost said *since the simulation was restarted,* which would have only confused his listeners. "Well, since forever, I guess. Was he on some kind of mission for you, Mayor Scarecrow?"

"Mission?" Scarecrow gave him an odd look. "What would make you ask such a thing?"

"Well, he's your police chief. In fact he's your only policeman. He was found on the road that leads to Forest. I thought you might have sent him to Lion about something."

The Scarecrow wrinkled his feed-sack brow and shook his head. "No. Though I did send him to Tinman a few days ago to ask him to stop making such a pounding in his factory at night. The people of Emerald are having trouble sleeping!"

For the second time in a few moments, Orlando felt a tingle of unease. What was Tinman building, working his machines at such hours? The metal man had been one of the worst parts of the corrupted simulation. But this wasn't the same Tinman, he reminded himself; the Kansas world had been restarted and returned to its original specs months ago.

"I suppose I'd better talk to Tinman," Orlando said out loud. "Lion, too."

"I'll come along," the Glass Cat announced. "I like a little excitement, you know."

Orlando wanted to check in at the Wogglebug's Scientific University and Knowledge Emporium, so he and the Cat made their way through the quaint streets of Emerald, a strange hybrid of Oz and an early-twentieth-century Kansas town, full of cheerful people and animals and stolid little houses decorated with all kinds of fantastic trim and paint.

The Wogglebug was bending over the soldier's headless body, which had been laid out on a table in his laboratory, but the man-sized bug (although there was never a real insect who looked anything like him) turned to greet them as they entered. Professor Wogglebug was wearing his usual top hat but also a pair of magnifiers that made his eyes seem huge, as well as a lab apron to protect his fancy waistcoat and tails.

"Goodness!" said the bug. "I can make nothing of it, Orlando! Look, he is completely de-headed. Not *be*-headed, though, which would have been much messier. The head has come off as neat as a whistle."

The Cat leaped onto the table and walked once around the body, sniffing. "Is he really dead?"

"Hard to say." The Wogglebug wiped his magnifiers on his coat. "He does not breathe. He does not move. He certainly cannot speak or think. It seems an awkward way to continue living, if by choice."

---

man, how do we figure out something like this if we can't even figure out whether a sim's really dead or not? i mean simworld-dead, of course—he's not really dead since his patterns are still in the system, and we could just restart him.

by the way, working a possible murder in oz/kansas is like trying to solve an embezzlement at a daycare by questioning the kids. you'll get lots of answers, but none of them will help much.

After leaving the lab, Orlando and the Glass Cat walked back across Emerald, dodging in and out of the Henrys and Emilys now heading home from work to have lunch in their quaint houses. In the corrupted, dystopian version of the world, all the human men and women had been little more than beasts of burden, of which the most obvious proof was that they had all been given the same name: all the men named after Dorothy's Uncle Henry, all the women named after her Aunt Em. But in this new version, they seemed happy and prosperous, dressed in an amalgam of Oz and American fashions from a hundred and fifty years earlier in many shades of green. It was hard to look at their smiling faces and believe something could be truly wrong with this world. But there was that headless policeman.

"Are we going out to visit Lion first?" asked the Cat as they reached Emerald's outer limits. "It would have been quicker to go to the Works. That's right next to town."

"I don't want to wander around in Forest after dark, Glass Cat, so we're going there now." As in the original Oz, the Kansas animals didn't tend to be dangerous, but it was easy to get lost in the deep trees. Orlando might not have a real body anymore, but he still needed to sleep, and he had no urge to spend the night bedded down on the cold, damp ground of the woods.

They passed the spot where the soldier's body had been found, but Orlando didn't bother to examine the crime scene again. The Scarecrow had sent a dozen Henrys to search for the head, but they had come back empty-handed, and any traces of the original crime had doubtless been trampled many times over. Only the stream remained undisturbed, plashing and playing its way between the pale birches.

The current version of the Cowardly Lion was still impressively scary but nowhere near as grotesquely human as the previous corrupted version. If it weren't for a sort of hyperreality, which covered him like a coat of varnish—his magnificent mane all whorls and golden curlicues, his expression just a tiny bit too much like a person's—he would have looked like the biggest, most impressive lion any nature documentary ever showed. As it was, though, he looked a little *too* styled—more like a celebrity lion tamer himself than the creature to be tamed.

Not that he isn't pretty tame already, Orlando thought. *Luckily for everybody.*

The protector of the woods listened to Orlando's news with grave concern, nodding his huge head sadly. "But I just saw Omby Amby last night," he growled. "He was right here in Forest."

"Do you know why, exactly?" Orlando asked.

"He had been to see Tinman and brought a message for me. Scarecrow asked the Works not to make so much noise at night, so Tinman wanted to know if he could expand some of his factories into land on the edge of Forest."

"And what did you say?"

"About that idea? That I'd have to think about it. I wanted to talk to Scarecrow, too. I don't see why my people should give up their territory without getting anything back, and we don't like noisy machines, either."

"And it was Omby Amby who you gave that message to?"

Lion frowned, his furry brow wrinkling like crumpled velvet. "I told him what I thought—that it was a serious issue and nothing to rush into." He raised his head and sniffed the wind. "Why do you ask? Did Omby Amby talk to Tinman? Did he tell him what I said?"

"We have no way of knowing," said Orlando. "I haven't spoken to Tinman yet."

"Ah. Then you came to me first?" Lion seemed to like that. "Well, if he didn't get the message already, tell my tin friend I won't be hurried into a decision. I have my subjects' welfare to think of, you know."

"Of course." Orlando suspected there wasn't going to be much more to be gained here. "Thanks for your help."

"I hope you find out what's going on," said Lion. "I know Ozma will be very upset. She was very fond of the Soldier with Green Whiskers."

Princess Ozma, like Oz itself, was now unused strings of code sleeping in the original specs of the simworld, but Orlando certainly wasn't going to mention that.

He called to the Glass Cat, who had disappeared somewhere. When she finally sauntered back into the clearing, Lion said, "Say, Glass Cat, you get around. Do you know anything about what happened?"

"I found the body," she said. "Nobody else did. Just me. It's because of my superior brains. You've noticed them, of course."

Lion shared a look with Orlando. "We've all admired them, Cat. How did you find him? Were you out searching?"

The Glass Cat looked irritated, her version of embarrassment. "Actually it was sort of an accident. I was on my way back from a trip when I saw him."

The Lion shook his head again. "Someone has done a very bad thing."

—

As he and the Cat made their way out from beneath the pleasant insect-humming shade of Forest, Orlando said, "You couldn't have seen Omby Amby's body from the road."

The Cat was silent for a moment. "Very well, I didn't notice it right away. I heard a noise in the bushes. I thought it might be a mouse. I went to look."

"Was it Omby Amby? Was the noise from him? Or did you see someone else?"

"How should I know who made the noise?" Now the Glass Cat was genuinely annoyed. "Is it important? I didn't see anyone else or I would have told you, and when I found him, he certainly wasn't moving."

The number of things that could have been rustling through the grasses by the side of a Kansas stream, even in this simulated version, was effectively endless. "You said a trip. Where?"

"Just to see some friends. I've been very busy lately, running errands for Scarecrow and the others, and I wanted a little time to myself. I'm very important, you know—they need me for lots of things because Omby Amby was just too slow sometimes."

"Has there been a lot going on here lately?" Orlando asked as innocently as possible. "Lots of activity? Messages going back and forth?"

"Goodness, yes." The Cat stopped to smooth her already smooth glass fur with her tongue. "I've hardly had time to catch my breath, if I had breath in the first place. *Go tell Scarecrow this! Go ask Tinman that!* Sometimes it's quite overwhelming."

"And are any of the messages…strange?"

The Cat gave him an odd look. "As far as I'm concerned, man from Oz, they're *all* strange. But that's just me. Because I have a much better than average set of brains." She leaned her head forward to better display the cluster of pink pearls glistening in her transparent head. "You already know that, of course."

"I'm sure everybody knows that by now," Orlando assured her.

Of all that had changed since Kansas had been rebooted, the Works was the most striking example. The final corruption had been a nightmare of massive gears and steam and dripping oil, with so many wires strung overhead that they blocked out the sky and plunged the place into permanent, sodium-lit twilight. The inhabitants had been either semi-sentient tin toys or mindless human Henrys and Emilys, most with cruel mechanical devices surgically implanted into their bodies. Now the Works looked like something out of one of the real-world Disneylands, all bright, shiny colors and smiling mechanical people marching in and out of cheerful little metal houses. Of course Orlando could not help remembering that those smiles were painted onto their faces.

Not fair, he told himself. *Everybody in Kansas is a sim, even the most human-looking of them. All the faces in this world have been painted on—by programming, if nothing else.*

Still, after experiencing the horrible previous version of the Works, Orlando had never felt quite the same about Nick Chopper again.

---

man, what was with those grail brotherhood people screwing up perfectly good children's stories, mr. k? I mean, you knew some of those people—what was their scan?

Kunohara himself had been an early member of the Grail Brotherhood, but only because he wanted access to the powerful simulation engine to pursue his scientific interests. That was how he told it, anyway. But he had helped Orlando and the others take down the Grail Brotherhood, so Orlando trusted him. Didn't always like him, but trusted him.

—

i mean, dzang! those old scanners turned the first version of kansas into a nightmare, ruined alice's wonderland and pooh corner—remember pigzilla?—and a bunch of other stuff besides. didn't those fenhead bastards ever hear of innocent childlike wonder?

that's a joke, case you didn't know. sort of.

—

"Tell me a bit about Omby Amby," said Orlando as he and the Glass Cat walked down the main street, past clean, bright tin-fringe lawns and polished mailboxes, toward the Shop, the unofficial city hall of the Works. "Did he have family? Friends—or more importantly, enemies? What did he like to do?"

The Cat shook her head. "No family, but I didn't know him very well—to be honest, we do not travel in the same circles. If you'll remember, I am intimate with many of the leading citizens of Kansas and was present to see several of them come to life—like Scraps the Patchwork Girl, for instance. The Policeman with Green Whiskers...well, he was a policeman. A civil servant. You would have to ask around in the workingman's taverns in Emerald."

"Taverns?" That didn't sound very much like the Oz that L. Frank Baum had written about, and it didn't sound like it belonged in this rebooted version of Kansas either. "There are taverns here?"

"Of course," said the Cat. "Where else can that sort of people drink ginger beer, play darts, and generally be loud and not half as amusing as they think they are?"

"Ah," said Orlando. "Ginger beer."

"Although," said the Cat with a little frown of disdain, "I hear that nowadays the younger men are drinking sarsaparilla instead. Straight out of the barrel!"

"Goodness," said Orlando, trying not to smile. "These places sound desperate and dangerous."

"I wouldn't know," the Cat said. "My superior intellect doesn't permit me to visit such low establishments."

Tinman was in the barnlike building known as the Shop, standing beside a large drafting table, surrounded by tin toys of various descriptions—a bear on a ball, a monkey with cymbals, a car with an expressive, smiling face. Tinman stared as Orlando explained why he had come, his brightly polished face devoid of any discernible emotion, although his eyebrows had been welded on in such a way that he always seemed surprised, an effect amplified somewhat by the gaping grill of his mouth, as though he were perpetually hearing news as unusual as Orlando's. Tinman was less human than the drawings in the ancient books, but still a great deal friendlier-looking than the thing that had ruled the Works before the restart, a creature more like a greasy piston with crude arms and legs than anything with thoughts and feelings.

As Orlando finished his recitation of the facts to date, the tin toys standing around the table began to make quiet ratcheting noises and move in place.

"My friends here are upset by your news," Tinman said tonelessly. "As am I. Poor Omby Amby! He was kind to everybody. He lived to help, and although he was a soldier, he would not have hurt a flea." He paused for a moment. "Nor would he flee from hurt, evidently."

The other tin creatures gave little whirring laughs. "Very clever," the rolling bear said. "Your workings are as droll as ever, Tinman."

"But now my heart shames me for making light at such a time," he replied, though Orlando could see no evidence of it on his inscrutable metal face. "What has Scarecrow said? Will he draft another policeman? The whiskered fellow was very useful dealing with small problems and matters of everyday…friction." It was impossible to tell if Tinman was making another joke or talking about something of particular concern to folk whose internal workings were composed of oiled gears. The tin toys began to whisper among themselves, a noise not much louder or different than the sound of their clockwork, until the monkey became excited and clapped his cymbals together with a loud crash, which startled the Glass Cat so badly that she jumped off the table.

"Careful," said Orlando.

"You are right," said the Cat. "Scarecrow was right, too—there are too many hard edges around here for me."

Tinman swiveled his head toward her. "What does that mean, Glass Cat? Has Scarecrow said something unkind about the Works? That would be very disappointing."

"No, no," said the Cat. "Only that he told me I must be careful when I am visiting you here. That all this metal is a threat to my delicate, beautiful glass body."

"Nonsense," said Tinman. "No more so than the brick sidewalks of Emerald or the stone-scattered paths of Forest.

It is too bad to hear my old friend speak about my part of Kansas that way."

Orlando was going to say something conciliatory but instead found himself wondering what was going on behind Tinman's shiny face. Was this exchange really as innocent as it seemed, or had the rivalry, treachery, and ultimately destructive conflict that had ruined the previous version already started again between the leading characters of this simworld?

Orlando asked about Omby Amby's last mission.

"Yes, he took a message to Lion for me," said Tinman.

"And you wanted Lion to let you use some of the Forest land?"

Tinman gave the closest thing he could to a shrug, a brief up-and-down pump of his shoulders. "He has a great deal, and there is much of it going to waste, but here in the Works, we are cramped between Emerald on one side and Lion's domain on the other, with nowhere to grow."

Lebensraum, Orlando thought. *Isn't that what the Nazis called it?* Out loud he said, "Was there anything else to your message? Anything besides the request to use some of his land?"

"I can remember nothing else," said Tinman. "Now if you will excuse me, my associates and I must discuss an addition to one of our factories. We would like to complete it during the dry season. Many of our laborers are Henrys and Emilys, and unlike my own people, they do not enjoy working in bad weather."

"Of course," said Orlando. "We'll find our own way out."

As he led the Glass Cat from the Shop, he considered what Tinman had said. On the surface all was as Orlando would have expected, so why did he feel as though something just as important—perhaps many important things—had gone unsaid?

---

just checked in on tinman. he's still a little weird, but he always was, even in the nicest versions. something about that voice—like a robot with a bucket over its head. can we just redo the way he talks? that's probably most of the problem with the simulation right there—that voice is utterly creepy. if sims can dream, I bet he's giving the others nightmares.

Is this whole world just doomed to go wrong? Orlando wondered. *Maybe the whole network? Something in the original programming that keeps tipping it back toward chaos? Or am I seeing ghosts where there aren't any? Maybe Omby Amby just…tripped or something. And his head fell off. Shit, this is Oz, more or less. Stuff like that happens in Oz all the time.*

But unless he could prove it, it didn't solve the current problem. "I guess we're off to see the Wizard," he told the Cat.

The Wizard, known in the present version of the simworld as Senator Wizard of Kansas, lived in a stately white house on top of a hill between Emerald and Forest, overlooking the city. He was semiretired, leaving the business of governing mostly to Scarecrow and the others.

Orlando had discovered Oz early, first in various vids, then later in the books themselves. For a very sick child who spent most of his short life in bed, the Land of Oz had been the best childhood dream, a place where even someone as prematurely aged as little Orlando would have been just different, not a freak.

Another big part of its appeal: nobody died in Oz.

It was not surprising he had a soft spot for this place, but Orlando had also seen the horror that could be produced here firsthand, and knew that leaving its sims to such a fate would be far more cruel than simply pulling the plug.

A riddle like this was so much more difficult to solve than something like the endless train robbery, which Kunohara and whatever programmers had signed his penalties-worse-than-death nondisclosure agreement could solve just by fixing a few command lines. This Kansas thing was a people problem, at least so far. They might just be code, too, but every single bloodless algorithm had been through the black box of the Otherland network's strange origin, had been effected by its living operating system and its many Grail Brotherhood manipulators, and had evolved and changed even since Kansas had been restarted. They were nearly as complex as real human beings, and although he knew it wasn't that simple, Orlando couldn't stop thinking of them that way. Shutting down the previous version of Oz had been a mercy killing, and it might come to the same thing this time, but it was a lot harder to think about euthanizing a patient who was smiling and happy and enjoying being alive.

"Princess Langwidere of Ev once told me," the Cat said suddenly, "that if everyone had brains like mine, the world would be a less boring place."

Orlando had only the vaguest recollection of Langwidere, a minor royal who lived somewhere on the fringes of Oz, or in this case, obviously, sim-Kansas. "Ah? Did she?"

"She most certainly did. She said that at least it was something to see, interesting enough to make her look away from her mirror every now and then."

"She sounds charming."

"She is. Most regal and discerning. When I visited, she took special trouble to show me her lovely things, her whole collection. She understands my true uniqueness." They had reached the front porch of the Wizard's big white house. The Cat vaulted up and waited for Orlando to open the door. "It is a shame there aren't more people of her...and my...quality."

The Cat was a useful informant, but she wasn't his favorite sim by any means.

The Wizard came down the stairs as they entered the cluttered front parlor.

"Orlando!" he said with obvious pleasure. "Come in, young man, come in! A privilege to see your shining visage—and you, too, Glass Cat! You are even shinier! Hmmm, there was something I wanted to ask you, but I can't think of it just now. Anyway, come in, both of you. May I offer you some lemonade?"

When they were comfortable, Orlando began to explain what had happened, but the Wizard held up his hand. "I have already heard this terrible news. Scarecrow sent me a letter this morning—although I had a devil of a time reading it. I suspect the actual hand was the Patchwork Girl's." He held up a sheet of paper daubed in several different colors, with no hint of sentences or even individual words holding themselves to straight lines. "Her enthusiasm somewhat outstrips her patience." He put on his glasses and squinted at the page. "Scarecrow says that he's keeping up the search for the unfortunate Mr. Amby's head but he thinks he must nominate another policeman."

"Makes sense." Orlando looked around for the Cat, who seemed to have gone missing again, but she had only crossed the room to admire herself in the polished sheen of the Wizard's fireplace fender.

"I suppose, yes," said the Wizard thoughtfully. "In any case, he says he thinks the Shaggy Man would be the best choice, because he is such a great traveler and will be happy to go back and forth wherever he is needed..."

"Piffle," pronounced the Cat in a ringing tone.

"I'm sorry?" The Wizard turned to her with an indulgent smile.

"The Shaggy Man! I'm sorry, Senator Wizard, but I have spent time with the Shaggy Man, and the man is far too irresponsible for such a job. He simply does not care a feather for anything. How could such a man carry out important tasks?"

"Perhaps you're right," said the Wizard. "In any case, you should bring up your objections with Scarecrow, who says he has not made the decision yet. Perhaps you have some preferred candidate...?"

The Cat snorted, a delicate noise like a tiny chime. "Hah. Who needs a policeman anyway, in a place that has no crime?"

"Except for what seems to have happened to Mr. Amby himself," the Wizard pointed out.

The reproof had been a gentle one, but still it was a silent, perhaps even chastened, Glass Cat who accompanied Orlando back across the fading afternoon into the heart of Emerald.

---

note to hk for later: we need to start a serious categorization census, because policing this network is getting a lot more complicated than just me and a bunch of glitchy sims. in the year or so since we took over the system, we've run into simuloids with personalities and memories stolen from real people like my friends that came into the network with me, others that are probably based on real people we don't know, some ghosts created from just a few aspects of real people, and some that are regular sims but seem to be turning into something else all on their own. even if this oz has gone bad, i'm not 100% sure we should get rid of it. i mean, this is evolution in action! okay, it's not the normal kind, but who said it had to be? but these simworlds, these sims, they're definitely changing over time—is that just the complexity of the programs, or is it something else? i know they're supposed to seem real, but sometimes I think it goes a lot deeper than that. yeah, that probably makes you even more certain we should erase kansas and the oz folk, but I don't want to if we can avoid it.

—

Of course Orlando had to admit his feelings might change when he learned what was really going on here.

When they reached City Hall, they were told the Scarecrow was having a private conference with the local balloonmaker's guild. The Cat wandered off on some idleness of her own, so while Orlando waited for Scarecrow's meeting to finish, he went out to wander the gardens and orchard behind City Hall. Every shapely trunk had a great spread of branches, and each branch was heavy with fruit—apples, pears, and sunset-colored oranges—all so lovely and enticing that it reminded Orlando all over again of why he had fallen in love with Oz and its simple but dreamlike pleasures. He wandered a long time, but enchanting as the place was, he could not really enjoy it, too busy picking at the problem of the murdered, or at least dead, soldier from every angle he could conceive.

Perhaps it was simply an isolated glitch. That was the simplest explanation. The old Kansas had been like Pol Pot's Cambodia, but that version was gone; as someone had pointed out, nobody was supposed to die in Oz, and those rules applied in this rebooted version. If it had been an accident, one of the searchers should have stumbled across Omby Amby's head by now. If it was an actual murder—why? The policeman had no enemies, no job that anyone else coveted—hell, the Glass Cat didn't even think they should replace him. And while Orlando might be full of nagging worries about the simworld turning feral, other than the soldier's surprising fate and a little minor squabbling between the three principal rulers, he hadn't seen any evidence of it happening. The people seemed free, happy, and prosperous.

A blare of trumpets in the distance startled him. The loud call didn't quite sound shrill enough to be an alarm—more like the herald of something official, perhaps an announcement. It might be nothing more exciting than a breakthrough in the balloon negotiations, but Orlando thought he should check it out anyway.

He followed the noises out of the gardens and around the front of City Hall, where he found a crowd had gathered: an assortment of Henrys, Emilys, and less human-looking Emerald citizens milling in the lamplit square before the building. As the horns blared again, he saw people standing on tiptoes and heard them *oohing* and *ahhing*. He worked his way to the front just in time to see what looked like a circus parade passing into City Hall—antelope, bears, porcupines, all manner of woodland creature. No, he decided as he saw the beasts' expressions, it was not a circus parade but something more serious, more somber. He was about to follow the last of the animals into the building when he heard people begin to shout behind him. He turned in time to see a solitary figure making its way through the crowd, headed toward the entrance.

"The Wizard!" someone called. "He'll sort things out!"

"Help us!" cried another.

"Ah!" the Wizard said to Orlando, seemingly oblivious of the onlookers. "Do you know where the Glass Cat is? I remembered what I wanted to speak to her about. She carried a message from me to the King and Queen of Ev on her last trip, and I forgot to ask if they had sent back any reply."

"You sent the Cat all the way to Ev?"

"Because it is on the far side of the Deadly Prairie," said the Wizard. "The Cat is nearly the only person who can cross that burning expanse without harm."

"I'm not sure where she is, to be honest," said Orlando, anxious to find out what was going on inside. "She's somewhere on the grounds, though, I'm pretty certain."

The Wizard excused himself and hurried off, apparently completely disinterested in (or, more likely, completely oblivious to) whatever had brought a protest march of forest animals into the center of Emerald. Those of the throng who had not yet made their way into City Hall cheered him as he passed.

Inside, the Forest animals—and many others, Orlando could now see, including a large contingent of tin people from the Works—had gathered in the rotunda at the base of the large ceremonial staircase. Orlando saw a sparkle above him: the Glass Cat was perched on a railing above his head, watching the crowd with grave interest. But before Orlando could ask her if she knew what was going on, the Scarecrow appeared at the top of the stairs with the Shaggy Man and a few of his other advisors. The Scarecrow stopped short, apparently surprised by the size of the waiting crowd and the presence of Lion and Tinman.

"Here, now—hey! What are you all doing here?" Scarecrow's mismatched eyes seemed even wider than usual. "Is it time for a council meeting? Did I forget?"

Scraps came spinning dizzily out onto the landing beside him, whirling like a top. "No!" she shouted as she stumbled to a halt. "It's a revolution! Round and round and round!" She didn't sound too concerned.

The noises from the rotunda floor grew louder; Orlando could hear some of the animals and tin people shouting "Cheat!" and "Liar!" They seemed to be shouting it at Scarecrow.

"I cannot make heads nor tails of any of this," Scarecrow said.

"It doesn't work that way, either!" cried the Patchwork Girl, who was now standing on her head.

"Quiet, please, Scraps," said Scarecrow. "Tinman, Lion, can either of you tell me what is going on here?"

"We know about your plan to seize the Works, brother!" Tinman cried in his harsh, echoing voice. "Is that fair? Is it right?"

"What plan?" said Scarecrow. He seemed honestly confused, although his lumpy face often looked that way because of the slapdash work of the farmer who had painted it.

"Don't listen to his gibble-gabble," rumbled Lion. "Tinman plans to annex part of Forest so he can build more tin people and be the leader of the largest group of citizens!" Lion's animal supporters growled loudly at this. Some of them, like the bears and wolves, were actually quite large and frightening. Orlando was seriously beginning to worry that things might get out of hand.

"That is an untruth!" Tinman's voice grew higher in pitch, like a giant tin whistle. "It is *you*, Lion, who plots with the Scarecrow to absorb my beloved Works and divide it between yourselves. You would make my people your servants, and that is most unfair."

"Never!" cried Tinman's supporters in voices as inhuman as New Year's noisemakers. "Never slaves!" The din made the great room seem even more crowded and dangerous.

Orlando looked up to the landing, where the Wizard had found the Glass Cat and was talking animatedly to her, still seemingly unaware of the angry crowd of animals, toys, and people. Orlando wondered what could be keeping him so busy with the Cat during all this. The slightly absentminded Wizard was certainly capable of overlooking a revolution in the making, but was a message from the royal family in Ev really more important than the growing chaos right below their noses…? Couldn't the two of them do anything to help?

Then somebody threw something at the Scarecrow—an oil can, Orlando thought. It missed the mayor of Emerald by a wide margin and clattered across the landing at the top of the stairs, but it shocked the Scarecrow; even fearless Scraps looked a bit taken aback. As Orlando turned back to the confrontation, an idea, or rather a fragment of memory, drifted up from the back of his mind. *Wait a minute. Ev. The royal family. Princess Langwidere and her collection…*

Krrrunch! One of Scarecrow's anxious supporters, perhaps the Shaggy Man—who was originally from America and not one to ignore an insult—had pushed a large vase off the landing. Orlando didn't believe he meant to hit anyone, only to startle the troublemaker who threw the oil can, but pieces of the vase flew in all directions and bruised more than a few of the animals and people gathered below him. One of Tinman's toy subjects received a large scratch across the shiny paint of his suit coat and let out a ratcheting noise of protest. The entire crowd began to push in closer in an attempt to climb the stairs, which brought the Forest contingent and the Works party together, not always smoothly. Shoving and arguing spread throughout the bottom floor of City Hall, and Scarecrow huddled on the landing with his face between two of the rails, watching it happen. As the first of the Works folk reached the stairs, the mayor tried to stand up again, but his padded head was now caught between the railings. Scraps and the Shaggy Man couldn't get him loose, and Scarecrow began to shout in dismay, which only made the crowd more excited, more certain that somebody was being hurt and that one of them might be next.

Orlando sent out a quick dispatch.

---

okay, worse than I thought—some serious shit is going down here. i'll finish this later, but please stay on call. hate to say it, but maybe you were right about this one all along.

"Who killed Omby Amby?" someone on the rotunda floor shouted. "Who killed the Policeman with Green Whiskers?"

Others picked up the cry, although the different sections of the crowd seemed to have different ideas of who had removed Omby's head, and why. Orlando shoved his way onto the bottom of the stairs, but one of the larger tin toys took exception and tried to obstruct him with a large tin rake. He ducked under the halfhearted swipe, stepped slowly and carefully over a large and very angry porcupine, then turned to the crowd from the steps of the great staircase, raised his arms, and shouted "STOP!"

It took a moment, but the mob quieted and the shoving lessened; at last something like silence fell over the City Hall rotunda. Everyone turned to look at Orlando, and there were suddenly so many painted eyes, shiny button orbs, and outlandish cracked glass eyeballs staring up at him that he felt a moment of real unease, even though he was the only one in the room who was in no actual danger. "Thank you," he said in a loud but more normal tone. "I know you're all upset, but you don't know the entire story. Senator Wizard, can you hear me? Come down, will you? And bring the Glass Cat. These people need explanations."

The Wizard crossed the upper landing, stopping for a moment to help unstick Scarecrow's head from the bars before he descended the stairs. The Cat hesitated before following him.

It was only as he reached Orlando's side that the Wizard finally seemed to notice what was going on around him. His bushy eyebrows rose. "Goodness," he said. "What's happening here?"

"Confusion. But we're about to resolve it. Did you find out what you needed from the Glass Cat?"

"She forgot to give them the message, for some reason." The Wizard shook his head. "I don't know why, after she traveled all the way across the Deadly Prairie to see them."

"Because the message wasn't what interested her." Orlando turned to the Cat, who was watching him with something like alarm. He bent and picked her up. She struggled, but he held her firmly until she stopped fighting. "Let me go!" she demanded. Orlando ignored her.

"I have a few other questions," he said. "Tinman—who told you that Scarecrow and Lion were planning to take your land?"

"It was the Woozy!"

The animal named Woozy was a strange boxlike creature, an old friend of the Patchwork Girl and others. He frequently helped out in the forges of the Works, keeping them roaring hot with his magical fire-eyes. "I heard it from the Glass Cat," Woozy called from the middle of the throng. "She told me it was a secret."

Orlando felt the Cat grow tense in his arms. He tightened his grip. "Ah," he said. "And Lion, perhaps you could let us know who told *you* about Tinman's plans for your forest."

"Easy," the king of the beasts replied. "It was Kik-a-Bray the Donkey."

The donkey stepped forward, embarrassed to be the center of attention. "But I didn't make it up!" the beast protested. "I heard it from Bullfinch!"

The little bird seemed a bit reluctant to speak up in front of an angry crowd, but after some coaxing from Orlando it fluttered up to a railing and announced, "As for me, I heard it directly from the Glass Cat herself."

This time the Cat really tried to get away. Orlando held on as tightly as he could, but it was hard to manage without cutting himself, so he borrowed the Wizard's coat and wrapped it around her until she again stopped struggling. "You're not going anywhere," he said. "You have a lot to answer for."

"I did nothing wrong!" she said. "I was just trying to help!"

"Trying to help start a fight."

"Goodness," said the Wizard. "Goodness! Why would she do such a thing?"

"I'll get to that," said Orlando. "But first I think we should fetch Omby Amby's body and head out to the bridge over the stream on the way into Emerald. I need to show you something." It was a bit of a risk if he hadn't figured everything out correctly, but at least it would get the unhappy mob out of City Hall. "Come on, everybody. Follow me."

Kik-a-Bray the Donkey, perhaps ashamed of his unwitting part in things, allowed himself to be hitched to a cart, and Omby Amby's motionless, headless body was gently loaded onto it. The large party set off, with Orlando walking in front, still holding the angry but temporarily resigned Glass Cat. The Forest animals and Works workers, along with dozens of curious Emerald Citizens, all fell in behind them. Scarecrow, Lion, and Tinman joined the procession too, muttering grumpily among themselves. The Wizard, in his waistcoat and shirtsleeves as though going to a summer picnic, walked with them to forestall any more arguments.

When they reached the bridge, Orlando had them set Omby Amby's body down on the ground before he led the party of onlookers down the bank to the stream. He waded out into the gentle, singing current, the Glass Cat struggling mightily now because although she was made of glass, she still hated water (as most cats do), but Orlando retained his grim grip.

"Put me down!" she spat.

"This is your fault, and I don't want to hear any nonsense from you," he said in his sternest voice. He knew from experience that the best way to talk to Oz folk in times of crisis was in a firm, parental tone. When Orlando stood thigh-deep in the rushing, burbling stream, he began looking carefully into the water while the Kansas sims lined up along the bank to watch him. At last he found what he was looking for—the longest streamer of wiggling, wavering moss at the bottom of the stream. He leaned over and grabbed it, and when he lifted the dripping green mass from the water, the head of Omby Amby hung upside down at the end of it.

"I should have realized that stuff wasn't all moss," said Orlando. "This one was so long! Because it was your beard."

The eyes of the Policeman with Green Whiskers popped open. "Dear me, many thanks!" he said after he had spat out a great deal of water. "It was terribly boring down there on the bottom of the stream. I slept most of the time. If I'd known you were looking for me, I would have tried to make bubbles for you."

"I wasn't looking for you until just now," Orlando said, wading out of the water with the squirming Cat still clutched securely under one arm and the policeman's bearded head cradled in the other. When he reached the spot where Omby Amby's body lay stretched on the ground, Orlando set the head on top of the neck, and the two parts immediately joined together. The Policeman stood up, unharmed except for the water drizzling from his long, green beard. "Goodness, it's nice to be back," he said, rubbing his throat. "I'm not sure what happened. One moment I was kneeling down having a drink; the next I was lying facedown in the stones on the bottom of the stream and unable to move. What happened to me?"

"Curiosity," explained Orlando shortly. "But let's get you back to Emerald and into a warm bed. Your beard should dry by the time we get back."

"But I'm not cold!" Omby Amby protested, but then paused to consider. "Well, my body isn't, but I suppose I do feel a bit of a damp chill on my head..."

Relieved to find it had all been a mistake, or at least that their accusations against each other had been untrue, Tinman and Lion led their charges back to the Works and Forest. Orlando and Scarecrow returned to the Wizard's white house on the hill to talk things over, the Cat still wrapped firmly in the Wizard's coat.

"You wanted things to be exciting, didn't you?" Orlando asked the Cat. "You liked being the center of things."

"What if I did?" She turned her head away. "There's nothing wrong with that."

"There is if you manufacture a quarrel so things will become even *more* exciting," said Orlando.

"I am very disappointed in you, Glass Cat," Scarecrow added as they entered the Wizard's parlor. The mayor of Emerald was doing his best to make his painted smile turn downward, but without much success. "I always thought your good intentions were crystal clear."

"But what about Omby Amby?" asked the Wizard. "What did she do to him?"

After the doors and windows were locked so she couldn't escape, Orlando set the Cat down in a chair and let her wriggle free of the imprisoning coat. She wouldn't even look at him and groomed her long glass tail as if she hadn't a care in the world.

"The Glass Cat had just come back from Ev, where she had forgotten to give your message to the King and Queen. The reason she'd forgotten, I suspect, is because she had been visiting with Princess Langwidere."

"Oh, goodness, of course!" said the Wizard.

"What do you mean? I don't understand." Scarecrow still couldn't make his mouth do anything other than smile, so he was doing his best to squeeze his painted cloth face into an expression of incomprehension. "What does Princess Langwidere have to do with any of this?"

"You might or might not remember, but Langwidere has a collection of heads she likes to wear, one for every day of the month. She simply takes one off and puts another on. She keeps them in glass cabinets—she even once threatened to take Dorothy's, although Dorothy wasn't having it."

"No, I dare say she wasn't," said the Wizard with a chuckle.

"I suspect that the Glass Cat begged Langwidere to teach her the trick, because she thought it would be an entertaining mischief. On her way back to Emerald, she came across Omby Amby having a drink at the stream and decided to play the head-off trick on him that she'd learned from the Princess. But when Omby Amby's head came loose, it rolled into the water. Even though she's made of glass, she wouldn't have wanted to go in after it. Am I right, Cat?"

The Cat looked up long enough to let out a tinkling sniff, then returned to her grooming.

"But that wasn't enough for her, I suspect. She realized that with Omby Amby unable to perform his duties, she'd have a lot more to do. She likes being in the center of things. And if there was going to be a fight, and arguing, and people upset with each other—well, she'd have even *more* to do."

"Is this true, Glass Cat?" asked the Wizard. "If so, it was very wicked of you."

"You people are silly," she said. "You simply don't have the sense of humor to appreciate a clever prank."

"A clever prank that almost started a war." Scarecrow was obviously troubled and stared carefully at the Cat for a long time. Meanwhile Orlando was beginning to worry all over again. At first he had been relieved just to have solved the mystery, but the Glass Cat had proven that things *could* go wrong in the simulation, even if she hadn't meant to cause as much harm as had resulted. How could they deal with her here? What if she decided to cause more trouble as soon as Orlando left? And even if Orlando simply removed the Glass Cat from the Kansas simworld—something he was seriously considering—who was to say someone else wouldn't just start in where she'd left off? The simple-minded, simple-hearted characters could easily be led astray again.

"Ha! My excellent brains, which you gave to me, Senator Wizard, have thought of a possible solution," the Scarecrow said abruptly. "Do you still have that gift that the Shaggy Man brought back to you from the shores of Nonestic Lake?"

The Wizard looked puzzled for a moment. Then he brightened and nodded. "Yes, yes!" he said. "I do indeed. But before we do anything else, I want the Cat to prove she can actually do what she claims, because I am not sure I believe her."

"What are you talking about?" the Cat demanded. "Are you calling me a liar?"

"Well, I've never seen such a thing—making someone's head come off with no harm to them." The Wizard shook his head in wonder. "I find it hard to believe such a thing is even possible."

"I'll show you," the Cat said, jumping abruptly from the chair to his desk. "I'll have your head off in a flash."

"No, no, I am too old for such tricks," said the Wizard. "And everyone knows it is no difficulty to get the Scarecrow's head off, as it is barely sewn on."

"Comes off all the time," agreed Scarecrow cheerfully. "Frightened one of my council members quite badly just the other day."

Orlando was beginning to get the drift. "And it won't work on me," he said. "Because...um...Ozma put a spell on me to protect me against such things."

"Very well," said the Cat, "since you are all such scaredy-people, I'll demonstrate on myself." And without so much as a word of a magical spell or the hint of a magical gesture (although she might have whispered something to herself), the Glass Cat turned her head all the way around once on her neck, and it fell off like the lid of an unscrewed jar. Her body slumped down onto the desk, but her head shot them a look of superior self-satisfaction from where it now lay, bloodless and quite alive, on the Wizard's blotter. "See?" she said. "Easy as pie."

The Wizard lifted her head and examined it. Then he turned it neck-side-down and shook it (the head complaining loudly all the while) until the Glass Cat's pink brains rolled out of it and onto the desk. She immediately stopped speaking, and her emerald eyes closed; even her pretty little ruby heart seemed to stop beating. Then the Wizard opened a drawer in his desk and removed a small jar of what looked like transparent glass marbles.

"Shaggy Man brought back these beautiful crystal pearls from the salty shallows of Nonestic Lake," the Wizard said. "They are made by the very cultured oysters who live there. The oysters are happy in the warm waters, so their pearls are lovely and clear, and I doubt there is an evil or even mischievous thought in them." He cupped the pearls in his hand and poured them into the Cat's head in place of the pink brains. The old brains went into the jar and back in his desk. Then he set the Cat's head back on its neck. "There," said the Wizard. "How do you feel now, Glass Cat?"

She blinked and looked around. "I feel...good. Thank you for asking. It has suddenly occurred to me that I owe a number of apologies, including one to you, Senator Wizard, and one to you, Mayor Scarecrow. But I have upset others, too, and I must get right to work telling them that I'm sorry." She turned to Orlando before jumping down. "Nice to see you again, Orlando. Please give Ozma my love and best wishes."

"What will you do when you've finished apologizing?" the Wizard asked.

"Something useful, I expect," she said. "Something that will make others happy." She jumped down, landed lightly, and walked out the door without a trace of her former swagger.

"But is it real?" Orlando asked. "Has she really changed, just like that?"

"Oh, no need to worry," said the Wizard. "Those pearls will let only the clear light of Truth into her head, which everyone knows makes it impossible to be wicked. I doubt we will have any more trouble from her."

"It is miraculous what brains can do to improve things," said Scarecrow. "Even if they are hand-me-downs."

—

A little while later, as Orlando was preparing to leave not just the Wizard's white house but the entire simulation, his host stopped him. "Just one more question, if you don't mind."

Orlando smiled. "Of course, Senator Wizard."

"We were wondering how you knew that something was wrong here in the first place. Did the Glass Cat call for you?"

"No—in fact, she seemed a bit surprised to see me." But as soon as he said it he wished he hadn't. How could he tell them about all the ways he was monitoring Kansas and the other simworlds? He fell back instead on an old catchall. "Princess Ozma saw it in her magic mirror, of course, and sent me to help straighten things out. She sees everything that happens."

Scarecrow scratched at his head with an understuffed finger. "But if Ozma saw it in her mirror, why didn't she tell you before you left what had really transpired? Why would she keep the Cat's trick a secret from you?" He seemed genuinely puzzled.

Orlando had been formulating another lie, but the deception was beginning to make him feel shabby. "You know, I don't actually know the answer to that. I'll try to find out from Ozma herself. I'll let you know what she says."

"Ah," said the Wizard. "Ah." He exchanged a glance with Scarecrow. "Of course, Orlando. We shall be...interested to hear."

"Is something wrong?" Orlando suddenly felt himself on shaky ground and wasn't sure why.

Scarecrow cleared his throat with a rustling noise. "It's just...well, we are very grateful for your help, Orlando. You've always been a good friend to Emerald and the other counties of Kansas..."

He heard the unspoken. "But?"

"But..." Scarecrow looked embarrassed, or at least as much so as a painted feed sack could. "Well, we...we wondered..."

"We wondered why we never see anyone else from Oz," said the Wizard. His familiar face was kindly, but there was something behind the eyes Orlando hadn't seen before, or perhaps hadn't noticed: a glint of keen intelligence. "Only you. Not that we're unhappy with that, but, well...it does seem strange."

The two best thinkers in Oz had been thinking; that was clear. Orlando wasn't too sure he liked what they'd been thinking about. "I'm sure that will change one day, Senator Wizard. Surely you don't think that Ozma has forgotten about you?"

"No," said the Wizard. "Of course not. Whether in Oz or Kansas, we're all Ozma's subjects, and our lives are good." But something still lurked beneath his words—perhaps doubt, perhaps something more complex. "We miss her, though. We miss our Princess. And all our other friends who don't visit any more, like Jellia Jamb and Sawhorse and Tiktok..."

"And Trot and Button-Bright," finished the Scarecrow sadly. "I cannot remember the last time I saw them. We wonder why they don't come to visit us."

"I'll be sure to mention it to Ozma." Now Orlando wanted only to get out as quickly as he could, before these uppity Turing machines began to ask him to prove his own existence. "I'm sure she'll find a way for your friends to come see you." At the very least, Orlando thought he could reanimate a few more characters from the original simulation without causing any real continuity problems. Which reminded him...

---

false alarm, mr. k—it was something that came completely out of the system itself, not a murder at all. the character wasn't even really dead. no repeat of the kansas war, you'll be glad to hear. (or maybe you won't.) no need to shut it down—it's doing all right. really. nothing to worry about. i'll finish the official report after i get some sleep.
your obedient ranger,

o.

Nothing wrong with a half-truth every now and then, right? For a good cause?

Scarecrow and the Wizard came out onto the veranda of the Wizard's white house to wave good-bye to him, but Orlando couldn't help feeling they would be discussing what he'd said for days, pulling it apart, trying to tease out hidden meanings. Perhaps the Oz folk weren't quite as childlike as he'd assumed.

So was there a moral to this story? Orlando headed down the hill from the Wizard's house and into the outskirts of Forest. Every Eden, he supposed, even the most blissful, was likely to have a snake—in this case the curious, manipulative, and self-absorbed Glass Cat. But Orlando had been so worried that this particular snake would ruin things that he had been willing to consider shutting down the whole garden. Instead the peculiar logic of the place had absorbed the conflict and—with a little assist from Orlando Gardiner, Dead Boy Detective—had resolved the mystery without any drastic remedies. But Orlando had also learned that these sims were not always going to take his word for everything, at least not the cleverest of them. Was that good? Bad? Or just the way things were going to be in this brave new world?

Oh, well, he thought. *Plenty of time for Orlando Gardiner, the only Dead Boy Detective in existence, to think about such things later, after a little well-deserved rest.*

Plenty of time. Maybe even an eternity.

DOROTHY DREAMS

BY SIMON R. GREEN

Dorothy had a bad dream. She dreamed she grew up and grew old, and her children put her in a home. And then she woke up and found it was all real. There's no place like a rest home.

Dorothy sat in her wheelchair, old and frail and very tired, and looked out through the great glass doors at the world beyond—a world that no longer had any place or any use for her. There was a lawn and some trees, all of them carefully pruned and looked after to within an inch of their lives. Dorothy thought she knew how they felt. The doors were always kept closed and locked, because the home's *residents*—never referred to as patients—weren't allowed outside. Far too risky. They might fall or hurt themselves. And there was the insurance to think of, after all. So Dorothy sat in her wheelchair, where she'd been put, and looked out at a world she could no longer reach…a world as far away as Oz.

Sometimes, when she lay in her narrow bed at night, she would wish for a cyclone to come, to carry her away again.

But she wasn't in Kansas anymore. Her children told her they chose this particular home because it was the best. It just happened to be so far away that they couldn't come to visit her very often. Dorothy never missed the weather forecasts on the television; but it seemed there weren't any cyclones in this part of the world.

Dorothy looked down at her hands. Old, wrinkled, covered with liver spots. Knuckles that ached miserably when it rained. She held her hands up before her and turned them back and forth, almost wonderingly. *Whose hands are these?* she thought. *My hands don't look like this.*

A young nurse came and brushed Dorothy's long gray hair with rough, efficient strokes. Suzie, or Shirley, something like that. They all looked the same to Dorothy. Bright young faces, often covered with so much makeup it was a wonder it didn't crack when they smiled. Dorothy remembered her own first experiences with makeup so many years ago. "Been at the flower barrel again?" Uncle Henry would say, trying to sound stern but smiling in spite of himself.

Suzie or Shirley pulled the brush through Dorothy's fine gray hair, jerking her head this way and that, chattering happily all the while about people Dorothy didn't know and things she didn't care about. When the nurse was finished, she showed Dorothy the results of her work in a hand mirror. And Dorothy looked at the sunken, lined face, with its flat gray hair pulled back in a tight bun, and thought *Who's that old person? That's not me. I don't look like that.*

Eventually the nurse went away and left Dorothy in peace, to sit in a chair she couldn't get out of without help. Though that didn't really matter; it wasn't as though there was anything she wanted to do besides sit and think and remember...her memories were all she had left. The only things that still mattered.

"Don't get old, dear," her Aunt Em had said back on the farm. "It's hard work being old."

Dorothy hadn't listened. There was so much she could have learned from wise old Aunt Em and hardworking Uncle Henry. But she was always too busy. Always running around, looking for mischief, dreaming of a better place far away from the grim gray plains of Kansas.

She had dreamed a wonderful dream once, of a magical land called Oz. Sometimes she remembered Oz the way it really was, and sometimes she remembered it the way they showed it in that movie...she'd seen the movie so many times, after all, and only saw the real Oz once. So it wasn't surprising that sometimes she got them muddled up in her mind. The movie people made all kinds of mistakes, got so many of the details wrong. They wouldn't listen to her. *Silver shoes,* she'd insisted, not that garish red. All the colors in the movie Oz had seemed wrong—candy colors, artificial colors. Nothing like the warm and wonderful world of Oz.

Dorothy woke up after dozing off in her wheelchair, and she was back where she belonged: in Oz. A country of almost overwhelming beauty, bright and glorious as the best summer day you ever yearned for. Great stretches of greensward ranged all around her, dotted here and there with groves of tall stately trees bearing every fruit you could think of. Banks of flowers in a hundred delicate, delightful hues. All kinds of birds singing all kinds of songs in the trees and in the bushes. Wonderfully patterned butterflies fluttered in the air like animated scraps of whimsy. A small brook rushed along between the green banks, sparkling in the sunshine, and the open sky was an almost heartbreakingly perfect shade of blue.

Dorothy was just a little disappointed. When she'd imagined returning to Oz in the past, she'd always thought there would be a great crowd of Munchkins waiting for her, with flags and banners and songs, happy to welcome her back. Those marvelous child-sized people in their tall hats with little bells around the brim. But there was no one there to greet her. No one at all.

Dorothy was surprised to find herself a young woman, in a smart blue-and-white dress, with silver shoes, rather than the small child she'd been the last time she visited Oz. Though this was how she'd thought of herself, for many years, long after she stopped seeing that image in the mirror. She patted herself down and was surprised at how solid and real she felt. And not a pain or an ache anywhere.

She jumped up and down and spun around in circles, waving her arms about and laughing out loud, glorying in the simple joy of easy movement. And then she stopped abruptly as a dog came running up to her, wagging his tail furiously. A little black dog with long silky hair and small black eyes that twinkled so very merrily. He danced around her, jumping up at her, almost exploding with joy. Dorothy knelt down to smile at him.

"You look just like the dog I used to have when I was just a little girl," she said. "His name was Toto."

The dog sat back on his haunches and grinned at her. "That's because I *am* Toto," said the dog in a rough breathy voice. "Hello, Dorothy! I've been waiting here for such a long time for you to come and join me."

Dorothy stared at him blankly. "You can talk?"

"Of course!" said Toto, scratching himself briskly. "This is Oz, after all."

"But…you're dead, Toto," Dorothy said slowly. "You died…a long time ago."

"What does that matter where Oz is concerned?" asked the little dog. "Aren't you glad to see me again?"

Dorothy gathered the little dog up in her arms and hugged him tightly, as though to make sure no one could ever take him away from her again. Tears rolled down her cheeks, and Toto lapped them up gently with his little pink tongue.

Finally she had to let him go, if only so she could look at him again. Toto backed away to regard her seriously with his head cocked to one side.

"You have to come with me now, Dorothy."

"Where?"

"Along the road of yellow brick, of course," said Toto. "To where all your old friends are waiting to meet you again."

Dorothy straightened up and looked, and sure enough, there it was: a long straight road stretching off into the distance, paved with yellow bricks. A soft butter-yellow—easy and inviting to the eye. Nothing like the gaudy shade in the movie. Dorothy smiled and set off briskly down the road, with Toto scampering along happily beside her. She had no doubt the road would lead her to answers, just as it always had.

The sun shone brightly, with not a cloud anywhere in that most perfect of skies. Birds sang sweetly, a cool breeze caressed her face, and Dorothy's heart was so full of simple happiness it felt like it might break apart at any moment. It felt good to just be striding along, stretching her legs after so much time in that damned wheelchair. Neat fences painted a delicate duck's-egg blue ran along either side of the road, just as she remembered. Beyond them lay huge open fields full of every kind of crop, so that the whole land was one great checkerboard of primary colors.

Soon enough she came to a small summerhouse of gleaming white wood, standing stiff and upright all on its own at the side of the road. Bright-green jade and rich blue lapis lazuli made delicate patterns over the gleaming white. And there, inside the summerhouse, sitting at a table, were two women she recognized immediately: Glinda the Good Witch and the Wicked Witch. They were taking tea together and chatting quite companionably. They stopped their conversation and put down their teacups to smile brightly at Dorothy.

She stopped a cautious distance away and studied them both carefully. Toto sat down at her feet, apparently entirely undisturbed. The Witches looked pleasant enough—two cheerful young women who didn't seem any older than Dorothy was. Or was *now*. Glinda wore white, and the Wicked Witch wore green, but otherwise there wasn't much to choose between them. They might have been sisters. Dorothy remembered them as being much older the first time she encountered them, but she had been just a small child at the time. All adults seemed old then.

Dorothy crossed her arms tightly and gave both Witches her best hard look. "It seems to me," she said firmly, "that an explanation is in order."

Glinda and the Wicked Witch shared an understanding smile, and then beamed sweetly at Dorothy.

"You were just a child when you came here, my dear," said Glinda. "And you wanted an adventure. So we provided one. In a form you could understand. You can have anything you want here."

"Glinda played the Good Witch, so I played the Bad," said the Witch in green. "Though you were never in any danger, of course."

"So nothing that happened here was real?" asked Dorothy.

"Well," said Toto carelessly, "there's real, and then there's *real.* I always found reality very limiting. I couldn't talk when I was real."

"When you were alive..." said Dorothy slowly.

"Yes," said Toto. He waited a minute, as though for her to grasp something obvious. Then he sighed and got to his feet again. "Look! Here come some more of your old friends!"

Dorothy looked around, and her heart jumped in her chest as she saw the Scarecrow, the Tin Man, and the Lion hurrying down the road of yellow brick to join her, waving and laughing. They all looked just as she remembered them. The Scarecrow was out in front, lurching along, all bulgy and misshapen in his blue suit and pointed blue hat, his head just a sack stuffed with straw with the features painted on. She jumped up and down on the spot, clapping her hands together, until she couldn't wait any longer and ran forward to grab the Scarecrow and hug him fiercely, burying her face in his yielding shoulder. He scrunched comfortably in her arms.

The Tin Man was waiting for her when she finally let go of the Scarecrow. He was all shining metal, with his head and arms and legs jointed on, and not an ounce of give in him anywhere, but she still hugged him as best she could. He patted her back carefully with his heavy hands. And finally there was the Lion. He towered over her, standing tall on his two legs, a great shaggy beast. When Dorothy went to hug him, she couldn't get her arms halfway around him. His breath smelled sweetly of grass.

But when she finally stepped back from her friends, Dorothy was shocked again when they strolled over to the summerhouse and greeted both Witches as warmly as old friends. Dorothy's heart suddenly ran cold. She folded her arms again, and hit them all with her hard stare.

“So,” she said harshly. “If you two just pretended to be Good and Bad Witches, does that mean you three just pretended to be my friends?”

“Of course we were your friends,” said the Scarecrow in his soft husky voice. “That’s what we were there for. To keep you company, so you wouldn’t be alone and scared. So you could enjoy your adventure.”

“Right,” said the Tin Man. “A doll to hug, a metal man to protect you, and a cowardly lion to feel superior to.”

“Wait just a minute,” said the Lion. “There was a lot more to my role than that.”

“I don’t understand,” said Dorothy, suddenly close to tears.

“Then let me explain,” said a familiar voice.

And when Dorothy looked around, there he was, of course. Oz the Great and Terrible. The Wonderful Wizard of Oz. A little old man with a bald head and a wrinkled face, dressed in the kind of clothes no one had worn since… Dorothy was a child. He smiled kindly at her. There was such obvious warmth and compassion in the smile that she couldn’t help but smile back. She felt better, in spite of herself.

“I thought you went back to Omaha,” said Dorothy, “in your balloon.”

“Just another part of your adventure,” said the Wizard. “I never really left. I’m always here, in one form or another.”

“Then…you were just playing a role, like all the others?”

“I am Oz the Great and Terrible, the Kind and Beneficent, and everything else you need me to be. I am the man with all the answers. Come walk with me, Dorothy, and all shall be made clear.”

Reluctantly Dorothy allowed the little old man to lead her to the road of yellow brick, and they walked along together, the Wizard moving easily beside her. It bothered her on some level that all her old friends stayed behind. That even Toto didn't come with her. As though the Wizard had things to tell her that could only be said in private. Or perhaps because they already knew, as though they shared some great and terrible secret that only the Wizard himself could tell her.

"I always was the one with all the answers," said the Wizard. "Even if I wasn't necessarily what I seemed."

"When I first met you, I saw a huge disembodied Head," said Dorothy. "The Scarecrow said he saw a lovely Lady. The Tin Man, he saw an awful Beast with the head of a rhinoceros and five arms and legs growing out of a hairy hide. And the Lion saw a Ball of Fire. But in the end, you turned out to be just an old humbug, a man hiding behind a curtain. Why did you insist we had to kill the Wicked Witch before we could all have what we needed?"

"Because gifts must be earned, and good must triumph over evil if an adventure is to have an end," said the Wizard. "Did you never wonder why the Wicked Witch, so afraid of water, would keep a bucket of water nearby?"

"It was a dream," said Dorothy. "You don't question what happens in a dream."

"Do you remember being old, Dorothy?" the Wizard asked gently.

"Yes," she said slowly. "Though that seems like the dream now."

"You have finally woken up from that nightmare and come home. Where you belong. This is a good place, Dorothy, where good things happen every day, and the day never ends. Unless you want it to, of course. Look…see?"

Dorothy looked where he was pointing, out across the great green plain before them. Off in the distance, two young girls were dancing with a huge and noble Lion. A young girl in sensible Victorian clothes was conversing solemnly with a great White Rabbit. And a boy and his Bear played happily together at the edge of a great Forest.

"I know them," said Dorothy. "Don't I…?"

"Of course," said the little old man. "Everyone knows them and their stories. Just as everyone knows you and your story. All these children dreamed a great dream of a wonderful place where magical things happened. And some author wrote the stories down to share their dreams with others. All of you, in your own ways, caught just a glimpse of this place, this good place yet to come. For a moment, you left your world and came to mine. And because all of you are my children, you all get to come home again in the end."

Dorothy looked steadily at the Wizard. "Who are you, really?"

He smiled at her with eyes full of all the love there is. "Don't you know? Really?"

"And this is…"

"Yes. This is heaven, and you'll never have to leave it again."

"I'm dead, aren't I? Like Toto."

"Of course. Or to put it another way, you have woken up from the dream of living, into a better dream. Everyone you ever loved, everyone you ever lost, is here waiting for you. Look. There are Aunt Em and Uncle Henry."

Dorothy looked down the road to where four young people were waiting. She recognized Em and Henry immediately, though they didn't seem much older than she was.

"Who's that with them?" she asked.

"Your mother and your father," said the old man. "They've been waiting for you for so long, Dorothy. Go and be with them. And then we'll all go on to the Emerald City. Because your adventures are only just beginning."

But Dorothy was already off and running, down the road of yellow brick, in that perfect land, in that most perfect of dreams.

DEAD BLUE

BY DAVID FARLAND

Tin Man's life flashed in memory the way that it always did when rebooting—at least, the part of his life stored within his crystal drive.

He had been traveling with Dorothy, climbing over a razor-backed ridge of gray karst rock, when the Chimeras struck—dropping from the low-hanging fog.

The first inkling of attack came when a huge weight slammed into his back, knocking him over a precipice onto sharp boulders, and suddenly a Baboon was biting at his throat with dirty yellow fangs, hissing "Die, you motherfu—"

Its hands smelled of dung and filth; its breath stank of morning kimchee.

It wrenched Tin Man's head, as if trying to snap his neck with superhuman strength.

Tin Man was so shocked, he barely had time to shout a warning, "Dorothy!"

He activated the vibroblade on his axe and felt it hum to life in his hand.

Something batted the axe to the ground—a fluttering wing, enormous and batlike. Only then did he realize that his attacker was a Chimera, a life form cobbled together by a mechmage.

Dozens of others dropped out of the cloud forest, wings fluttering in a blur. They hurled Scarecrow to the ground, scattered his straw, and snatched up Toto and Dorothy.

Tin Man could not see the Lion and hoped that the coward had made his escape. As the Winged Baboon hit his kill switch, Tin Man marveled at his attackers.

They were perfectly fitted to their humid terrain, where mountain escarpments split the jungle. Such creatures, with DNA from humans, baboons, and giant bats—flying foxes perhaps?—would easily haul ore from the Witch's bauxite and platinum mines.

Tin Man wondered, *Do they even know how beautiful they are?*

Dorothy's eyes were flat blue, the color of television, tuned to a dead channel. Her young face was pale from shock, emotionless, framed by strawberry hair the color of bloodied water.

"Oh, Tin Man, are you all right?" she begged, leaning over him, trying to help him up. He pushed away her hands and tried to rise on his own power.

As he rebooted, memories burst upon him in waves—flashes of his past life as a machine—while sound files all roared at once, louder than the crashing of the sea.

All that came to him now were the mech-memories. Nothing from before, nothing from the days when there had still been a fleshy component to him.

Once, he had been a man. Then he lost a leg and had it replaced with cyberware. As he had aged, more parts came—an artificial lung here, a kidney there, drives and programs to enhance his failing memory—until only a shriveling brain had been left to the cyborg, powered by a dying heart.

He was not sure when he had quit defining himself as a man and accepted that he was a cyborg.

Now, he told himself, *I am not even a cyborg. I am a construct, a golem made from black plasteel and titanium, hardly better than Scarecrow.*

The recognition brought no sense of loss. He recalled that Dorothy had asked a question. His programming required that he offer a reply. "I feel fine, Dorothy."

But can one truly be said to feel *fine* when he feels nothing at all?

He was dead inside. His quest to get a new heart—a simple pump to keep his brain alive, his last connection to the world of emotion—had failed. His olfactory sensors could detect the remains of his own rotting organs.

Tin Man scanned the nearby rocks. The Winged Baboons surrounded them there on the ragged peaks. Dark creatures with gleaming fangs. In infrared, he could see them glowing, as if flames licked their skin. They spread their wings as they sat huffing from a recent flight.

Dorothy and the Lion exhibited no fear of them. Indeed, Toto sat in the arms of one of their leaders as the creature scratched the dog's head.

Several Winged Baboons now leaned over Scarecrow, stuffing the straw back into his clothing, retracing the runes upon his mouth that would let him speak. There is a technology that surpasses mere gears and circuits—a technology so advanced that common men cannot comprehend it.

Tin Man was not versed in technomagic, but when a Winged Baboon brought out a soulgiver—a forked rod fitted with switches and meters that jolted Scarecrow to life—Tin Man knew enough to feel awe.

It seemed that much time had passed since he'd died. Vines had grown over his titanium exoskeleton, with its sleek design and black plasteel joints. Weak electronic stimulation to some circuits in his right arm and leg suggested internal corrosion.

He'd lain here for months.

"What happened?" he asked Dorothy.

"The Wicked Witch caught me," she said. "I killed her."

Killing a technomage wasn't easy. The Witch of the West was an ageless cyborg. Her green skin powered her system by converting sunlight to energy using chlorophyll.

"How?"

"She forced me to wash the floors in her castle," Dorothy said. "She liked to come in and walk on them while they were still wet, leaving muddy tracks. So I waited until she walked in with wet feet, and then I threw down the bare ends of a power strip—and fried her green ass." Dorothy laughed painfully, halfway to a cry. "Now *I'm* the Wicked Witch of the West!"

The Witch's own pettiness had been her end. Tin Man felt the killing was well justified.

Dorothy held out her hand as proof of the deed. She wore the Witch's bracelet, complete with glowing diadems. It looked something like a chronograph, but meters and LEDs tracked the progress of the nanobots that would turn her into a technomage, guided by the bracelet's own AI. Indeed Dorothy's arms had begun turning green, as if they were pieces of rotting fruit.

Deeper within her, other changes would be taking place. Synapses would be growing and expanding, boosting her intelligence to superhuman levels. Already, studs on her brow showed that she had fitted herself with cybernetic implants so that she could access the data stored within the Witch's Cloud.

The leader of the Winged Baboons gave a howling shriek. "All hail Dorothy!" and from every perch on the ragged peak, like loathsome gargoyles upon a castle wall, thousands of its brethren began roaring, tossing grass and leaves into the air in celebration, chanting, "All hail Dorothy!"

But Dorothy did not smile at their obeisance. Her eyes did not glow with pride. On her taut lips there was only pain. She had killed in cold blood. Did she fear what she would become?

"A Witch you may be," Tin Man said, "but you will never be 'wicked.' You've saved my life twice now, and for that I thank you. I think we'll have to find a new name for you. How about the Worthy Witch of the West?"

He did not say it, but he suddenly remembered something: he'd once loved her. He'd loved the little girl that she had been, and he knew that he would love the woman that she would become.

The fleshly component of his body was dead now, along with its capacity to love. But the memory still floated through his RAM, a ghost in the machine.

She was taller now—at least an inch taller than when she'd first made her appearance in Oz. She had grown in more ways than one.

The Winged Baboons finished shocking Scarecrow to life, and he began to speak. "Are we going to Oz?" Scarecrow cried in celebration. "Shall we get our reward?"

Dorothy looked sad at this, as if pitying the fool. "Oh, Scarecrow," she said. She seemed to fight back words that would break his heart, but said carefully, "Of course I want you to have your reward." But there was a distant look in her eyes.

She peered away toward Emerald City, gleaming there beyond the mountains. Its spires rose to heaven, and in the evening, one could see green lights among its towers, winking like stars, guiding in the zeppelin captains who ferried goods from far countries.

There was a wistfulness to Dorothy's gaze, a haunted look, and Tin Man knew that she was accessing memories from the Cloud.

"He can't help us," she said. "He's a charlatan, Scarecrow, no technomage at all. The image we saw of a sagacious wizard was nothing but a disguise, a holograph. Their wizard cannot offer you a brain. The best he might give is a third-rate memory crystal from a broken-down droid."

At that, Scarecrow looked to the ground, hung his head in defeat, and began to bawl.

Dorothy fixed him with a commanding gaze. "I will do better, my friend. I will fit you with a brain unparalleled in the world, and you shall have access to all the data in my Cloud, for you have proven your loyalty over and over again."

Scarecrow's demeanor immediately changed. "Hooray!" he shouted, and he jumped up and began to dance, scattering straw from his stuffed shirt and trousers.

"And me?" the Cowardly Lion roared, stepping forward. He tucked his tail between his legs and cringed, as if afraid that she might whip him.

Dorothy smiled benevolently. "I shall fit your hypothalamus, the back of your brain, with a device that will jolt it. When faced with cruelty and injustice, your rage shall overwhelm your own self-interests, for that is all that *courage* is—outrage over evil."

The Lion frowned, as if he had hoped for more.

"I'm sorry if it seems too little," she said. "But the Wizard of Oz can offer you nothing but patronizing platitudes. He's only an old man whose starship slipped into a wormhole. He can never return home, so he makes his living by foolery. In that industrious city, where all of his people slave beneath a cloud of fear, he produces the least of all, for he creates only lies and illusions and false assurances. He is the ultimate politician. He only takes, while his people give. He sent us on this quest hoping that we would be destroyed."

Tin Man scanned the city where he had once placed his hopes, his electronic eyes registering the scene in infrared, so that certain pillars blazed from heat waste. It looked like a hell of burning green flames. The Wizard was no better than a murderer, he decided. "Then he cannot help you get home?"

"No," Dorothy said. "Even if he were a mechmage, that would be beyond his power. I must make my home in Oz."

"What of me?"

"Your heart died months ago, and your brain with it," she said. "I would bring them back if I could…" She faltered, and a tear slid down her cheek. "I'm sorry. For you, most of all, I'm sorry."

She looked too sad and too wise for her years, but that was the price of knowledge.

"What will you do with the 'Wizard'?" Tin Man asked. "What he does is unjust."

"He should pay for his crimes," Dorothy agreed. "But I won't harm him. In time his people will discover his evil, and then they will bring him to justice."

He wondered why she did not take the Wizard now. He'd nearly sent Dorothy to her death. Tin Man suspected that the Winged Baboons would gladly rip him limb from limb.

He looked into her dead blue eyes, and Tin Man understood. She already grieved over what she had done. Compassion restrained her from bloodshed.

He wondered, *Does she even know how beautiful she is?*

Tin Man no longer suffered from human limitations, not since the Wizard of Oz had masterminded his death.

"No better time to get rid of him than now," Tin Man said.

Activating the vibroblade of his axe, he turned and stalked downhill into the gathering darkness.

ONE FLEW OVER THE RAINBOW

BY ROBIN WASSERMAN

Crow found her first. Never let us forget it either. It was always *my Dorothy* and *before you met Dorothy* and *Dorothy told me,* emphasis on *me.* Crap like that. She staked a claim on her, like it mattered, and I guess it did, because back then we all loved Dorothy, maybe even me. But no one loved her like Crow, who found her first.

Crow's shit at remembering things now, so I have to remember for her. But I usually spare her that one, because what's the point?

I let Crow blame me. I'd let Roar blame me, too, if he could pull it together enough to blame anyone. And I blame me, because I listened to Dorothy, and I knew better, and I got the lighter, and because I can take it.

Because I still have the knife.

Crow was Crow because of her tattoos. Not the ones she did herself with unbent paper clips and ballpoint ink: jagged hearts and lightning bolts and stupid stick figures who all had missing limbs—because when it came to Crow, nothing hurt until it did, and then you had to *STOP*, even if you hadn't gotten to both legs. It was the ink on her back that gave her the name, a murder of crows swooping up her shoulder blades and pecking at the nape of her neck.

A murder of crows. I got that from her. But I found the others on my own:

A bellowing of bullfinches.

A pride of ostriches.

A mutation of thrushes.

A brood of hens.

A charm of finches.

A parliament of owls.

I found them for her. I thought she'd like it, how everything had its own special name, like a secret only we knew, because Crow taught me that names have power, and I figured we needed all we could get. But Crow only cared about the crows.

"A murder of me," she liked to say. She made it into a song to sing when she was bored, and sometimes, when things got dark inside her head, she screamed it, flapping her arms and jumping on tables, screaming and screaming those same four words until the monkeys with the needles came to drag her away.

Monkeys, because "they're all monkeys," Crow said once about the orderlies, watching them fling a softball around the exercise yard. "Look at those monkeys flinging poo," and because she said it, it stuck. Crow was in charge of naming. She could see the *you* inside of you, and she knew its true name.

But Dorothy was only ever Dorothy.

—

My first time in here, Crow and I were roommates. Stuck in south wing together—medical wing—bruised and bandaged because she'd jumped off a roof, and I'd sliced through enough skin to get gangrene or blood poisoning or who even cares what you call it, and we lay in those beds and rolled our eyes at each other when Glind came to ask us in that low, gentle voice why we wanted to die.

He didn't even need a nickname, because: Dr. Glenn Glind, can you imagine? He's got parents who do *that* to him, and he still manages to not shoot himself in the head. No wonder we confused him.

We don't tell him:

I don't want to die.

Crow doesn't want to die.

She wants to *feel* something, that's what she tells me one night after he runs out of questions and leaves us to our reality TV and morphine drips. That's why she jumps.

I feel *too much*, I tell her. That's why the scars crawl up my legs and down my arms, intricate jags and whirls of hardened tissue; that's why I grid myself with the knife, quadrants of lines and angles, my diagram of pain. I was Tina then, but she's already calling me Tiny and Tinny and Tin-Girl, tasting the sound of one name after another until one tastes right. And even though I don't tell her, not then at least, how Tin-Girl sounds good to me—because wouldn't that be a great deal, hard on the outside, hollow on the inside, too hard for the knife, too empty to need it—Crow somehow knows anyway, and I'm Tin from then on.

Her brain doesn't work right, she tells me, because that's what they all told her, and she thinks she's stupid, but she's smarter than any of us, something I figure out pretty fast because I'm not stupid either.

My heart doesn't work right, but I don't tell her that either, because then I'd have to tell her that I'm not supposed to love anymore because it hurts too much, and that even so, I stay awake at night and watch the curve of her body and listen to her breathe, and then she'd laugh, and I'd have more to cut.

Here was Dorothy: electric-blue hair bobbed at her delicate chin. Ironically checkered baby-doll dress, chunky bracelets from her left wrist to her elbow, nails painted black, ruby lips, and big baby-blue "who, me?" eyes, and all that crap that gets people to make asses of themselves and write poems about you.

Before Crow, I never much noticed girls, and I don't notice them after her, because it's not a girl thing, it's a Crow thing, like she's some separate species, some alien who got dropped on this planet by mistake and has to imitate human beings and suffer the consequences when she can't imitate them quite well enough. That was one of Crow's theories, at least. I don't know whether she believed it or not, because with Crow you could never be sure. It was better to play along, not so much that she could laugh at you after if it turned out to be a joke, but enough that she wouldn't have a freak-out and jump on the tables and then get zombified for the rest of the week. But I could believe it: Crow the alien, Crow the stranger in a strange land. Crow, who wasn't like anyone else.

So even though Dorothy was pretty enough, that wasn't the thing about her.

The thing about her was her shoes.

Silver combat boots that sparkled like magic under the fluorescent lights.

The thing was how she howled when they took them away.

We were pressed to the picture window overlooking the ward intake area, not because we were waiting for Dorothy to show, but because we were waiting to give the one-finger salute to the Wicked Bitch of the East. Head nurse of the east ward—excuse me, soon to be *ex*-head nurse, fired for drug smuggling, that's what we heard. She was a yeller, the kind always looking for an excuse to get mad and, we heard, always smiled a creepy little smile when it came time to call in the monkeys to put someone down. Of course, they didn't fire her for that. Even though we were in west, where we still had a Wicked Bitch of our own, we celebrated, because one down seemed pretty good, and at least someone was getting off easy, even if it was the pathetic east wingers. Nutcase solidarity and all that.

So we were watching when they brought Dorothy in, and when they took her shoes and the rest of it, because real clothes meant special privileges and new patients didn't get any of those, she threw a grand mal seizure of a fit, sedated before she even made it onto the ward, maybe some kind of record. It seemed like a good omen, Crow said then, the new girl coming in just as the Bitch was going out, and for a while that's all Dorothy was, the good omen with the shoe fetish. But Crow must have noticed something, something she liked, because the next time I saw Dorothy, she had Crow's arm around her shoulder and Crow was saying to her the same thing she'd said to me, "Now you're one of us."

Here was us: Crow with her scrambled-egg brains. Me with my scars. And Roar, our bodyguard, big enough to scare off anyone who might think to mess with us, big enough to scare even the monkeys into keeping clear, skinhead bald with a bulldog face and barbed wire tattoos, big and mean-looking and too doped up to do much about it. We didn't even know his real name, but he was loyal and useful and kind of sweet when you got to know him, and frightened enough that if anyone but us got too close, he let out a mighty *roooooooar*. And so, his name. And so, Us.

"Those are the monkeys," Crow told Dorothy, and pointed to the poo-flinging orderlies.

"Those are the Munchkins," Crow told Dorothy, and pointed to the pathetic east wingers, anorexic outpatients gnawing on their doughnut holes during group therapy, lording their precious snack over the rest of us even though they could barely choke it down.

"You ever get lost, you follow the road of yellow brick," Crow told Dorothy, and pointed to the ribbon of paint that wound through the tiled corridors, stretching from the mythical doors to the outside all the way to the bolted doors that closed down our wing. Every ward got a different color: south was sky, north was death, east was puke. Ours was sun.

"This is Roar," Crow told Dorothy, and pointed to our giant.

"This is Tin," Crow told Dorothy, and pointed to me.

She gave her all our secret names, and she did it like it was nothing.

"How about me?" Dorothy asked and twirled around. She had one of those song voices, and you wanted her to talk more, even when you wanted her to shut up. "What's my name?"

Crow didn't pause. "Dorothy. You're nothing but Dorothy."

Then Dorothy told me how much she loved my skin art and that she was an artist too, and she showed me the girl on fire she'd markered across her forearm.

I didn't tell her that mine wasn't art. Because when she said it, I thought, *Maybe it is. And she's just the first to notice.*

Dorothy told us that she hated her parents, who'd stuck her in here because they couldn't handle her light, and that her parents, who she called Emily and Henry instead of Mom and Dad, weren't really her parents, that—depending on what kind of mood she was in—her real parents were fugitives, her real parents were deadbeats, her real parents were cult members, her real parents were dead.

"Henry and Emily just want to suffocate me," she told us. "They want me to be as gray and lifeless as they are so I can fit in at their gray and lifeless country club and get good grades at the gray and lifeless school they send me to, then get into a gray and lifeless college, and lead a gray and lifeless life. It's pathetic."

We all nodded, even Roar.

Dorothy had a ragged stuffed goat named Bad Dog that she took with her everywhere because it was her totem animal, whatever that meant. As she talked, she made it do the can-can across her knee. "When that didn't work, they decided I was crazy. Just for not wanting what they want me to want. So I decided if they wanted me to be crazy, I'd be crazy. Is that crazy?"

We shook our heads.

"Oh, it's crazy, all right." Her laugh was even more song than her voice, and when she laughed and shook, her hair flickered around her face like blue flame, and I thought that, crazy or not, she didn't belong here. She was too bright. "But *life* is crazy, right? That's what I figure. And if *life* is crazy, then we're all the sane ones, aren't we? They probably want you to be gray and lifeless too, don't they?" She flung her arms out at the monkeys and the Wicked Bitch and the empty paper cups in the trash, the ones that had held our morning pills. "But I think we should *celebrate* what we are. What we can see. We see life in color, so we know what they don't, am I right? We live life like *artists.*" She pointed at me. Jabbed her finger right into my chest, then traced it across my collarbone to where the scars poked out above my collar. Concentric circles with arrows speared through their centers; I remembered every line. I remembered the cold blade warming in my hand, and I remembered carving myself into a target. You can hurt me, the arrows said to my mother and all her bullshit, to the guy in sixth period who got me up against the wall and rammed his hand up my dress and stuck his fingers inside, to the last person I was stupid enough to love and the one before that. But not as much as I can hurt myself. "Tin understands. Don't you, Tin?"

I saw Crow's eyes follow that finger on my skin, and I saw them narrow, because Crow was jealous for all the wrong reasons, and that made me just jealous enough to smile and say yes.

Sometimes one yes is enough to explain all the rest of them.

Yes, we were special, and *yes,* we shouldn't let them take that away from us.

Yes, we were too doped up, and inside we were just like Roar, tamed and muzzled and all too willing to follow orders.

Yes, we should do something about it.

"I have an idea," Dorothy said. She took our hands, mine and Crow's, and she squeezed. Roar rested his paws on our shoulders, closing the circuit. "Just for fun. Are you in?"

We said yes.

Some days we took each other's pills. Some days we didn't take any at all. Dorothy showed us how to cheek our meds, and after that it was simple: Drop the pill in your mouth, lodge it in a warm, soft place against your tongue, swallow hard, then open wide so the Bitch could see your insides and check you off her list. Later the pills went into our palms, damp and sticky, and they were ours, to do with what we wanted.

It got so every day was a surprise, whether you'd want to dance and fly and scream just to hear the sound of your own voice cutting the air, whether noises were too sharp and colors too bright, whether you felt like hugging or laughing or punching a fist through the webbed glass windows just to have something sharp so you could cut and cut and cut. Roar decided one of the droolers in the rec room was looking at him funny and broke the guy's arm in two places before the monkeys got him down and sent him off for some time in the straps. Crow kissed me, or maybe let me kiss her, or maybe I imagined it, but there wasn't much difference and anyway her lips were harder than I thought they'd be, and when we lay together side by side, with her hand in mine and her head against my cheek, her hair was stiff and rough, like sticks. She rubbed it against my face until I said stop, it hurts, and she laughed and said nothing hurts until it does, and then she took my hand and laid it on her breast and made it squeeze and squeeze. *Like milking a cow,* I thought, because those were the kinds of thoughts I had then, with Dorothy's voice in my head and Crow's meds in my blood and because I knew sometimes you needed that and because I thought maybe it was a dream, I let her make me hurt her until she screamed.

Dorothy got bored.

"Screw the pill thing," she said. "What we need is some booze. How are we supposed to have any fun around here?"

"The Wizard can get us booze," Roar said quietly, because even after two days in the straps, he was still getting ideas, sometimes even good ones. None of us were used to that yet.

Dorothy was still new enough not to understand.

"The Wizard can get anyone anything," Crow said. She always liked to be the one to explain things to Dorothy. "But it'll cost us."

The Wizard lived in green.

Jade. Chartreuse. Citrine. Kelly. Verdigris. Lime. Avocado. Hunter. Rifle. Emerald. He named the colors for us, tapping along the wall where he'd taped pages from magazines, strips of cloth, napkins and leaves and curling locks of hair—a collage covering every inch of plaster in more colors than I ever knew existed, and all of them green.

No one knew what it was the Wizard had about green, like no one knew what he was in for or how long he'd been here or how it was he managed to smuggle in everything that he did—not just booze and the good kinds of drugs but smokes and sharp objects and the kinds of movies we weren't supposed to watch because they might give us the wrong ideas. He had a middle-aged-dad paunch and the big red nose of a drunk or a clown. We'd never been in his room before, because Crow said we had all we needed with just us, and that it wasn't worth it. But now, I guess, because Dorothy said so, it was.

"Vodka," Dorothy told him, one hand on her hip, the other around Bad Dog's neck. "Also cigarettes and a lighter."

"Not cloves," I murmured. I didn't look at Crow, who didn't care about smoke but hated fire. Dorothy said we should do what we wanted, and I wanted cigarettes. Real ones.

"Not cloves," Dorothy said. "And scissors."

The Wizard frowned. "You slice your wrists, it's a mess for all of us."

"No wrist slicing." Dorothy smiled and raised three fingers in salute. "Scout's honor."

Crow gave me a sharp poke in the ribs, which I knew meant when did I ask Dorothy to get me the scissors, and why didn't she know about it. I didn't even have to ask, but I wouldn't tell Crow that, because who was Crow to say Dorothy and I couldn't have secrets together, too?

"And what do I get?" the Wizard said. He was looking at Dorothy, and he was looking at me.

Dorothy gave him a smile that didn't belong here any more than she did, a smile left over from wild late-night bonfires and 3 a.m. beer runs and cutting school to smoke weed in the parking lot and a different life. "What do you want?"

In the Wizard's room, late at night, it's too dark to see the green, but you can smell it, rich and moist and sweet, like a forest after the rain.

In the Wizard's room, late at night, the monkeys down the hall watching hockey and cheering loud enough to cover the noises we make, he tells me to be quiet, even though he doesn't have to. He says he doesn't like the sound of my voice. "It's like metal," he says, and then he laughs.

His breath smells green, and his chest is hairier than I expect.

I do not throw up.

It hurts when he sticks it in, but only a little, and I do not gasp.

It hurts when he is behind me, and his rhythm is a pounding, pounding, pounding, and my head shakes and bumps the wall each time, and it's like I'm his Bad Dog, raggy and boneless and covered in filth.

His hands are on my scars.

"Pretty," he whispers in the dark. "So pretty."

He finds the bare patch on my thigh, the place where skin is only skin, unbroken and waiting. "Mine," he whispers.

I am quiet, like he wants. I breathe beneath him. When it ends, I listen to him snore, and I am still there when he wakes up, so he turns me over and starts again.

"A toast to Tin!" Dorothy crowed, and raised a paper cup of vodka in my direction. "Here's to taking one for the team, and here's hoping it was a *big* one."

She winked, and they all did the shot.

The Wizard supplied us with a bottle of vodka, three packs of cigarettes, a yellow BIC lighter, and most miraculously of all, the key to a supply closet where we could enjoy it all to our hearts' content.

Instead of scissors, he got me a beautiful knife.

He had looked at Dorothy before he looked at me, because who wouldn't, but he wasn't picky. Anyone but the ugly one, he'd said, and we all knew the ugly one was Crow.

He looked at Dorothy, but then Dorothy looked at me, and somehow it was done.

After, we pretended like I volunteered, like I wanted it, like Dorothy was doing me a favor by stepping aside and letting me have all the fun, and maybe we weren't pretending. Maybe that's how it was. Maybe it could be that way if I decided that's how it should be.

So I tipped my vodka back, too, and it burned.

That morning I had taken my secret knife and carved triangles into the bare patch on my thigh—not bare anymore. Interlocking triangles, one corner cutting into the next, so suddenly they weren't triangles at all, just sharp lines doing their own thing. One for the Wizard, one for Crow, one for Dorothy. All of them for me.

Crow scowled when I flicked the lighter, so I flicked it again, right under her nose, yellow flame leaping toward her, and she screeched and punched me in the stomach. The lighter jumped out of my hand and skidded across the linoleum, the flame winking out. Then Roar roared, and Dorothy slapped a hand over his mouth, and Crow laughed and kissed my neck, and I squirmed away and lit up my smoke, and we all got so drunk we puked.

It's good enough that we do it again, and again. When we need more vodka—and more cigarettes along with it, and once some of the graphic novels Crow likes with all the blood, and more than once some pot for Roar, and always something special for Dorothy, brownies or polish or an inferior pair of silver shoes—I do what I have to do.

It gets easier.

The Wicked Bitch never noticed any of it. Neither did the monkeys, neither did the doctors, and if the other patients did, they weren't saying anything, because they all had their own arrangements with the Wizard, or because they couldn't care less. We could have lived like that forever, but instead we did it only until Dorothy pointed out that it wasn't living at all, not as long as we were caged up in the zoo.

"I think you're ready now," she said, proud as if she'd made us herself. "Let's do this thing, for real."

No more sneaking around for the sake of sneaking.

No more pill swapping just to see what would happen.

No more games.

For real.

Crow didn't want to call it anything—Crow didn't even like to talk about it, didn't take part in the planning, just sat there dumb and dull like Roar used to be, while we scribbled maps, timed rounds, scouted exits—and so I had to name it myself. The Great Escape. The Big Breakout. Mission Possible. It wasn't my fault they were stupid; it wasn't supposed to be my job. My job was to get what we needed from the Wizard: The timing. The keycards. The cash. But when I asked Crow, she just shrugged and said whatever Dorothy wants.

Like I didn't exist.

Crow didn't know about the maps I was drawing on my calves, the way the knife tip traced our escape route through the flesh. She didn't come into my room at night anymore, and I didn't want her there, anyway. Once, I peeked through the crack in her door, and I watched her, sitting on her bed in the moonlight, staring at nothing, like she couldn't be bothered to help us escape because she was already gone.

—

Maybe, even though I packed my bag and mouthed goodbye to my roommate and pressed my palm against the Wizard's door like some kind of promise, I knew it would all go to shit. But I didn't think it would go so fast.

We made it out of west, through the intake lobby, and all the way to the last of the locked doors. We made it far enough to start thinking we might actually do it, to whisper to one another, "This is real, this is happening, we're getting out." I told Crow we would run away to the city together, and we would get cool jobs and a cool apartment and live like other people lived, only better, because it was like Dorothy said: We lived in color. We were special. Crow blinked at me and said could we get a goat like Bad Dog and feed it all our dirty laundry, and then she said would the Wizard be at the door every night, collecting the rent, and I just nodded and told her sure, Crow, whatever you want—because Crow was right about her brains being a little scrambled, especially without her blue pills, and sometimes it was good just to say yes and keep going.

Dorothy held her hand, and they skipped along the road of yellow brick, tracing it back and back and back toward where we all started, toward the last of the locked doors, and whatever was on the other side of it. I locked arms with Roar, and he gave me the lopsided grin he'd been trying out lately. He wasn't any good at smiling, and he was worse at skipping, but that was okay, too. On that night in that dark hallway, after it all seemed possible and before we got to the last door, everything was okay. Crow could think whatever she wanted; Roar could stop being afraid; I could watch Crow's curls dance in the darkness and breathe in her smell and see how she looked at Dorothy and still keep the knife in my pocket, because we were close enough to the end that carving my heart out could wait.

The last door.

That was the one that needed the stolen pass, and Dorothy flashed it against the blinking panel, but nothing happened, except a red light. She swiped it again, and there was a noise, a click, a little like a turning lock but more like a warning.

It takes less than five minutes to happen.

It's still happening.

I'm still there, in the dark corridor, choking on panic and the bleat of an alarm. I'm still there, always there, like I'm still in the room with Crow on that first night, like I'm still with the Wizard, will always be in the stink of his breath, in the sweat of his arms, in the bargain no one forced me to make.

When the scars fade, I carve them fresh.

In the dark corridor on the last night, when the alarm blares, and the monkeys spring from all sides, we scatter. We are in a lounge, which means tables to hide beneath and couches to climb over and magazines to throw. Dorothy hides. Roar fights. I draw my knife and think for once I will cut someone else.

There is screaming. Those are the monkeys, as Roar sends them flying through the air and into walls. Roar is the beast we always knew he could be, our fierce giant, the monster we made of him, and it takes six of them and a Taser to pin him down, something I only find out later, because I am focused on my knife.

They come toward me, and I brandish the blade, and I shout warnings, lines from movies that tougher people than me know how to say—"Stand back or else!"—but no one stands back; they come for me, and when I hear a fearsome screech, I know it is Crow coming to rescue me. I want to shout, "No, don't! Save yourself!"—more of the things you say in the movies when there is any saving to go around. But I realize that Crow is not coming for me.

The monkeys have Dorothy and are dragging her out from under the table, dragging her even as she clings to the leg and sobs and begs them to let her go. The monkeys have Dorothy, and Crow somehow has the lighter. And a bottle of hairspray she must have packed in her bag when we all thought we were leaving for a different life.

Crow fires a spray of foul mist.

Crow screams, "Let go of Dorothy!"

Crow flicks the lighter.

And Crow is on fire.

It was the Wicked Bitch of the West, of all people, who put her out. Padded out of her nap room to see what the ruckus was and thought fast—filled a bucket of water, doused Crow's flames. The monkeys found a fire extinguisher somewhere, but by then it was over. We were all quiet and still, except for Roar, who was making strange noises in electrified sleep; except for me, who was slipping a knife back into my pocket unseen; except for Crow, who was screaming.

It doesn't hurt until it does. Crow taught me that.

I could have taught her something, too: that once it starts hurting, it never stops.

They took Roar away to north wing, with its black ribbon of death, and they kept him there for a long time. When they brought him back, he wasn't Roar anymore. He was a body to prop in the corner, on a chair or a stool or a windowsill—a giant body like a piece of furniture that drooled and moaned and didn't notice if you hung towels or bras or signs saying "vegetable" around its neck. Sometimes, if you worked at it, you could get him to rock back and forth, like he was praying.

Roar was back before Crow because of the burns.

When she came back, she was still Crow, but she also wasn't. Because of the scar tissue and the melted skin that turned her face into a cratered moon, because of the nightmares, because of the hair that burned away and wouldn't grow back. Because now she was the one who felt too much, felt everything like it was fire. Or because Dorothy was gone.

"Mommy, I want to go home." That's what Dorothy said into the phone in the hallway, after. She wouldn't talk to me, but she couldn't stop me from watching her, so I did. I played her shadow and followed her to the phone. She called her mommy, and she said the magic words, and then I couldn't follow her anymore because she was gone.

Crow doesn't always remember that Dorothy left. She doesn't remember why she hurts, or why the mirrors have been taken from her room. Sometimes she doesn't even remember Dorothy was ever here, and those are the best times, because we pretend things are like they used to be.

They say it's probably the medicine that makes her like this—foggy and far away. They say it might just be how she wants it, deep down, because why not escape inside if you can't get out.

I think they're wrong. She wants to come back to me. Maybe she's punishing me for what I let happen, and eventually I'll be punished enough. Until then I rub lotion on her ruined skin and kiss the spots on her neck where the crows once flew. I memorized them all, and when she asks, I tell her they're still there. "A murder of crows," I whisper. "A murder of you."

They tell me I won't be here forever. They tell me they will fix me and send me away, and maybe this time I won't come back again, and I let them think I believe them, that I can be fixed, that I am broken, that there is an away where I belong more than I belong here.

They tell me there are people out there who want and need me back, but there is only one person who needs me and only one person I want. I take care of her, because Dorothy's not the only one who wants to run home, and Crow is home. I call to her, and I remind her, and I wait.

I remember for her the things she needs to remember, and I remember for myself the things she needs to forget.

I remember with the knife, which is still and always mine. I do what I need to do to keep it.

THE VEILED SHANGHAI

BY KEN LIU

June 7, 1919, Shanghai

"Don't go into the streets today, Dorothy," Uncle Heng said.

Ever since fourteen-year-old Dorothy Gee started attending the Willard-Pond English School for Chinese Girls, Uncle Heng liked to use her English name instead of her Chinese one—he said it sounded more educated.

"The foreigners in the International Settlement get nervous when the Chinese become unruly. They're scared that the strike and protest are getting out of hand. Soldiers from those British naval ships at the docks came onshore last night. I think something bad is going to happen."

"But the foreigners love freedom," Dorothy said. "That's what Mr. Ward always says in class. This strike is for freedom, too."

Uncle Heng laughed at this, but Dorothy did not see what was so funny.

"The foreigners like freedom sometimes, for some people," Uncle Heng finally said. "Just promise me you'll stay home today." He left to get more groceries from outside the city, as all the merchants had shuttered their stores.

Dorothy nodded reluctantly. This had been the most exciting week in her life. She desperately wanted to go out and join the throngs that filled the streets of Shanghai: workers on strike, students marching and shouting slogans, and merchants closing up their shops and refusing to sell to anyone.

Even the singsong girls and those women standing on street corners in tight cheongsams with long slits were no longer soliciting customers. Instead they linked arms and sang songs like this:

China, China, wake from your slumber,
Strike down those traitors in Peking!

"Other girls from the school are allowed to march," Dorothy said.

"Well, you're not those other girls, are you?" Aunt En said. "If something happens to you, how am I ever going to face your mother in the afterworld?" She handed Dorothy a large bowl. "If you're itching for something to do, you can help me get these carrots peeled."

Dorothy went into the alley so she could dump the peelings directly into the sewer.

Someone was making a speech on Kansu Road, the big street at the end of the alley. As Dorothy worked, snippets from the speech drifted to her, along with the approving shouts from a boisterous crowd.

"...the Western powers have betrayed the people of China and handed Tsingtao to Japan...and now the spineless warlords in Peking are arresting students?...It's not a crime to love one's country!...Free the students!...Down with the warlords!"

The noise from the crowd grew and grew, rising to a crescendo, and then Dorothy heard something new: a scratchy, tinny, almost mechanical voice that was louder than the crowd.

"This is your last warning. The Military Governor and the Shanghai Municipal Council have issued their orders. Disperse immediately, and go back to work!"

The crowd shouted even louder, trying to drown out the loudspeaker. "*The foreigners were in league with the cowardly traitors in Peking!*" Dorothy dropped the bowl and rushed down the alley to Kansu Road.

As she pushed her way into the crowd, she heard angry shouts all around her. Someone picked up a rock and threw it at the loudspeaker; more followed. Then there was the sound of a gun being fired.

The crowd exploded around her like a tornado. Panicked people rushed around in every direction, carrying Dorothy along for the ride. She ran and ran, unable to stop for fear of being trampled, and soon lost track of where she was.

Some people were jumping onto a slow-moving trolleybus in front of her, and a man reached down for her.

"Come on, jump! Before the police get this area cordoned off!"

Dorothy grabbed the man's hand and leaped onto the bus. She was dragged into the safety of the interior, squeezed between tightly packed passengers.

Guess that's the end of my career as a revolutionary, thought Dorothy.

The air was stuffy and warm, and soon Dorothy grew drowsy and fell asleep.

Dorothy awoke with a jolt that made her teeth rattle.

She rubbed her eyes in confusion. It was dark outside, and the bus was empty. There was no one even in the driver's seat. The engine hissed and creaked loudly a few times before falling silent—funny, Dorothy couldn't recall ever hearing a trolleybus make sounds like that.

She got up, almost fell again because the floor of the bus was canted at a sharp angle, and stumbled to the door. She tumbled down the steps and looked around her.

The bus had stopped in a tiny square surrounded by European-style houses, each with a beautiful little garden around it. The residents of those houses, if they were still awake, did not leave their lights on. The cobblestone-paved streets were quiet and deserted. A lone electric streetlamp at the edge of the square cast a sphere of yellow light. This was a part of Shanghai she had never been to.

"*Quelle courage! Merci, merci beaucoup!*"

Dorothy turned around and saw that a few boys and girls were clapping and smiling at her as they approached. The children, European in appearance, ranged in age between five and twelve. They were dressed in rags, and had faces caked in grime.

Apparently she was somewhere in the French Concession.

The children came closer and continued to chatter excitedly at Dorothy.

"*Je m'appelle Sarah. Comment vous appelez-vous?*"

"*Je m'appelle Alissa.*"

"*Je m'appelle Becky.*"

"*Je m'appelle Anton.*"

"I'm sorry," Dorothy said. "But I don't speak French; well, I do know that *merci* means 'thank you,' but I have no idea why you're thanking me."

"They are thanking you for getting rid of the Panopticon that has made this neighborhood extremely unpleasant for street urchins."

Dorothy saw that the speaker was a tall Chinese woman who had followed the French-speaking children and now emerged from the darkness. She wore a brown *kasaya* filled with a pattern of silver threads that glinted in the moonlight. Her head was bald.

"You're a Buddhist nun."

The woman smiled. "Yes. You can call me Beini, for my temple is far in the north. I come here to help the orphaned children who make the streets their home."

Dorothy had seen Buddhist nuns only in pictures in books. She said cautiously, "I'm sorry, Venerable Beini, but I have no idea what a Panopticon is, and I certainly did nothing to it."

The woman pointed to the front of the stopped bus.

Dorothy now saw that the bus had crashed into and toppled what appeared to be a statue. She walked closer and discovered that the statue was actually a tall lamppost of sorts, topped with four telescopes that pointed in four directions like giant eyes. The bus had cracked the structure in half and broken all the lenses.

"A few years ago, the police installed Panopticons in the wealthier neighborhoods of the French Concession," the woman explained. "With these, one policeman can keep watch over an entire neighborhood. The authorities say that the homeless orphans who roam these streets are a gang of thieves—"

"*Nous nous appelons les Munchkins*!" the children sang in unison and laughed.

"—and when the children are caught, they're put into institutions more horrible than prisons, full of cruel headmasters and sadistic teachers. By destroying this Panopticon, you make it easier for the children to hide and move at night. And that is why they're thanking you."

Dorothy was reminded of what Uncle Heng had said about the foreigners: "They like freedom sometimes, for some people."

"Well, I'm glad that the children are happy and free, even if I didn't do anything."

"Your bus did, and that's pretty much the same thing."

Dorothy wasn't sure about this, but she didn't want to argue. "It's very late, and I'm sure my aunt and uncle are worried. Can you tell me how to get back to Kansu Road?"

Beini shook her head. "I don't know where that is."

Dorothy couldn't believe it. Everyone knew where Kansu Road was. "It's in the native city, where there was a large rally today, and the police came to break it up."

"I'm sorry, I don't know what you're talking about."

Dorothy suddenly felt very tired and alone. She tried not to cry.

Beini looked at her more intently. "Ah, you are a child of the Veiled Shanghai. That is why you're afraid."

"What do you mean?"

"There are two Shanghais, one on top of the other. The Shanghai you're from, the Veiled Shanghai, is inhabited by different people, possesses different wonders, and is filled with unfamiliar sorts of machines. It occupies the same space as our city, but a thin veil hides you from us, and us from you. Yet what happens in one Shanghai seems to affect what happens in the other.

"What I do know is that here the night is longer and darker, and the old magic is still strong, the magic that had filled the port with lines of *qi* and crisscrossed the land with currents of power long before the foreigners came and paved it over and covered it with their steam engines and electric automata."

Dorothy was frightened, but she tried not to show it. She looked over at the bus again and saw that in place of the trolley poles, the bus now sprouted a big chimney. This wasn't the vehicle she was familiar with, but a new machine powered by white steam and black coal.

"Oh dear," she said. "How will I ever get home?"

"I don't know," Beini said. She looked thoughtful. "Once in a while we get a visitor from the Veiled Shanghai...but who knows, perhaps you were sent here for a reason, for *yuanfen*...I believe if you want to go home, you must go see Oz."

"Who's Oz?"

"The Great Oz is the most powerful magician in all of Shanghai. He lives in the Emerald House, in the middle of a green park."

"How do I get there?"

"You follow the road of yellow brick."

Dorothy looked down, and she could indeed see yellow bricks embedded here and there in the cobblestones, forming a trail that led out of the square into a dark side street.

Beini bent down and picked something out of the broken Panopticon. "Here, take these." She handed two silver coins to Dorothy, each showing the profile of a bald man.

"The workmen who installed the Panopticon left these coins, the *dayang*, to appease the Chinese ghosts haunting those who disturb their rest. The coins have some charm associated with them, and you might as well keep them in your shoes for luck."

"Thank you," said Dorothy. She took off her shoes, put one coin in each, and stepped into them. "And now I'll be on my way."

"*Merci, merci*!" the children called after her.

"Be safe," Beini said, and she held her hands together and said a benediction for Dorothy.

—

The glow of the lone streetlamp soon faded behind her. After a few minutes of gingerly walking in the dark, Dorothy emerged from the narrow, quiet residential street into a wide avenue, filled with rushing people and cars and loud noise and bright lights and wonders Dorothy had never seen.

In the center of the street were columns of cars sporting large, chrome boilers. Alongside them were rickshaws. But many of the runners before them were not people at all, but man-shaped machines with legs and torsos of iron. Neon signs flashed and blinked everywhere, and vendors in kiosks hawked strange new machines and promised magical results. The strikes in Veiled Shanghai were definitely not taking place here.

"I'm certainly not on Kansu Road anymore," said Dorothy to herself.

Ahead of her, she saw a boy about her own age, tall and gaunt, with a head of messy blond hair and ill-fitting clothes that hung loosely from his frame like a scarecrow's, arguing with a bakery owner in English.

"Get away from here! Go on, shoo!"

"I did everything you asked today. You promised to pay me—"

"You stupid boy! I told you to keep an eye out for those dirty urchins, and you ended up giving them free food!"

"But you told me the buns were going to be thrown out!"

The owner slammed the door in the boy's face.

Dorothy walked up.

"Hello, I'm Dorothy," she said, also in English. After a pause, she added, "That man was mean."

The boy looked away. "You saw that? They used to call me Freddie back home in Iowa, but here, everyone calls me Scarecrow, on account of my looks. My pa always said that I had no sense, got no brains, and whipped me for it. Seems like I'm always doing something wrong, making people mad."

"If you gave food to hungry kids—and I think I know some of those kids—you couldn't have done anything wrong."

Scarecrow smiled. "Thanks. You got anything to eat? I'm starving."

Dorothy realized that her stomach was growling, too. She rummaged about and found that she still had some peeled carrots stuffed into the pockets of her dress. She took two out and handed one to Scarecrow.

He and Dorothy both thought these were the sweetest, juiciest carrots they'd ever had.

"You live near here?" Dorothy asked.

"Sort of." Scarecrow scratched his hair. "I sleep pretty much wherever. I ran away from home because being whipped hurt, and I wanted to see the world, learn some sense. I shipped out of San Francisco as a stowaway on a steamer bound for Shanghai. After I landed, I woke up in the morning and the ship was nowhere to be found. Then I just kind of stuck around. What a strange city."

Sounds like you came from the Veiled Shanghai, too, Dorothy thought. "Think you're learning much?" Dorothy asked.

"I don't know. The things I've learned so far don't seem to make the world any easier to understand."

Dorothy nodded vigorously. "Sometimes the more I find out about the world, the more confusing it becomes—like tonight."

Scarecrow laughed. "Yes, exactly. Where are you going?"

"I'm going to see Oz, a great magician." Just saying it aloud made it seem less ridiculous. A place that could make carrots taste so good must have some strong magic in it. "I'm lost, but Oz, who is very powerful, will get me home. He can make anything happen."

"A great wizard? He must be pretty wise then. Maybe this Oz will make me less foolish. Can I come with you?"

The road of yellow brick turned into a dark alley with no lights at all. The shadows seemed to hide unseen monsters, and the two children slowed down, their hearts pounding.

"Let me walk in front of you," Scarecrow said.

"Aren't you scared?"

"I'm too stupid to be scared." Scarecrow tried to laugh at his own joke, but his voice came out shaky.

"Hold my hand," Dorothy said. "We'll walk together."

After their eyes adjusted, they could see that the yellow bricks cast a faint glow, like a trail of breadcrumbs in a dark forest. They gladly followed it.

A loud creaking came from off to their right. Both stopped.

"What was that?" Dorothy asked.

"It sounded like an old rusty hinge," Scarecrow said.

"Or a man groaning in pain," Dorothy said.

The noise came again. Cautiously, the two moved to the right, tracking the source of the noise.

The side of the alley opened up, and the lights from the sleepless and glamorous heart of the city spilled over and fell against the ground in front of them. They found themselves picking their way across a junk heap, filled with wrecked cars, old, hulking machines with rusting gears, piano wires, and broken wrought-iron fences.

The noise came again, much louder, and the children found themselves staring at a giant iron statue of a man, easily twice as tall as a real man and covered in rust. As they stared at it, the statue's head moved, and it groaned as the old gears lurched and ground against each other.

"It's an automaton," Dorothy said, wonder in her voice. She had read about these in the adventure stories found in the pulpy magazines that the bolder girls sometimes brought to school. But here, in this other Shanghai, they were real.

More grinding and creaking noises filled the air as the automaton continued to turn its head toward Scarecrow and Dorothy and then toward his feet. Following his gaze, Dorothy saw a tool chest filled with steel wool, metal polish, and a can of oil.

"Let's get to work," she said.

Dorothy and Scarecrow began by removing the rust from around the automaton's mouth and oiling the hinges.

"Thank you," the mechanical man said. Now that he could move his mouth, he sounded more like a man than a machine.

"You're welcome," Dorothy said. "What shall we call you?"

"My friends always call me the Tin Woodman, even though I'm made from steel and chrome, not tin."

As more and more shiny skin emerged under the scrubbing hands of the children, the Tin Woodman told the children his story:

"I was once a lumberjack in Manchuria. A Japanese company came and hired me to cut down trees. I was the strongest and the fastest.

"One day, the company brought a new machine into the woods. It belched smoke and steam, and it ran on treads. It looked like a giant crab with two huge axes as its claws.

"*WUMP! WUMP!* It would cut down a one-hundred-year-old tree in five blows.

"'Finally,' the foreman told me, "'here's someone faster, better than you. The Iron Lumberjack is the height of Japanese technology, and it will put you out of a job.'"

"I was about to get married, and my bride-to-be's face turned ashen. I had promised that I'd provide her a good home.

"I went up to the foreman and challenged the machine to a competition. We would see who could cut down ten trees faster.

"I don't think I've ever worked as fast as I did that day. By the time I finished the tenth tree, my arms felt so rubbery it was like they had no bones left in them. That's how rubbery they were. But the machine had been finished long before. Exhausted and disappointed, I let my hand slip, and the axe lopped off my feet and lower legs. I fainted from the pain.

"By the time I woke up, I was a useless wreck of a man. And my bride-to-be had already become engaged to the foreman.

"I left my home on a handcart, pushing the wheels with my hands, and moved a thousand miles to Shanghai, where they say wonders never ceased and anything you desired could be found. I begged for food in the streets during the day and sought out doctors to see if anything could be done.

"Then, one night, I seemed to have entered a part of the city I had never seen before, darker and more dangerous. I met a workshop full of engineers who told me that sure, they could give me what I wanted.

"They attached steel legs to me so that I could walk two hundred miles a day without being tired. I was so happy with the legs that I had my arms cut off and replaced with these mechanical ones so that I could chop down ten trees in a row without being winded. But that was still not enough. I had my face, my lungs, and my stomach replaced so that I could eat coal and breathe steam and give power to all of my limbs. Finally, I replaced my heart with an iron pump so that I could stop feeling the pain of a broken heart.

"I could now do the work of ten men without ever tiring. I thought I finally had what I wanted. I had become the strongest and fastest again, a machine. Like so many others in the city who had gone down this path, I worked and worked and thought about little else. I was happy.

"But one day, while I worked at a shipyard, I saw a pair of lovers kissing. They were so sweet and so happy, and I realized that I could feel nothing at all. All the power in the world meant nothing without a heart.

"I stood still and stopped working, and before long my joints started to rust and fuse together, and soon I couldn't move at all. The shipyard owners left me here for scrap, and if you hadn't come along, I don't know how much longer I'd have waited."

—

"Come along with us then," Dorothy said. "We're going to see the Great Oz, who can make any wish come true. He'll get me home."

"He'll give me some sense," said Scarecrow.

"You think he'll give me a heart?" asked the Tin Woodman.

"It's worth a try," said Dorothy.

—

The road of yellow brick now passed through a neighborhood full of the sort of places Dorothy had been told to avoid: dark houses with red lanterns hanging outside their walls, halls full of loud men shouting as they played cards and argued about money, pavilions with no signs except hanging banners painted with poppy flowers.

As the three turned a corner, they saw a door open up, and some people inside pushed a large man out. He fell facedown into a puddle in the street without moving, and the men inside the house closed and locked the door behind him.

Dorothy hurried over and tried to drag the fallen man out so he would not drown. But she could not move his frame.

"Help me!" she cried to her companions.

Scarecrow wasn't much stronger than Dorothy, but the Tin Woodman easily lifted the large man out of the puddle and sat him down gently so that he leaned against the wall of the house he had been thrown out of.

"This is an opium den," said the Tin Woodman. "He's an addict, and there's nothing we can do. They probably threw him out because he could no longer pay."

"There must be something we can do for him," said Dorothy.

The Tin Woodman considered. "Perhaps I'm too quick to dismiss him." He hung his head. "If I had a real heart, I would be more compassionate."

"Why don't we get the opium out of him so that he's clean?" said Scarecrow.

"I don't think that's a very good idea," said the Tin Woodman. "If it were that easy, opium wouldn't have claimed so many lives."

"I don't have much sense," admitted Scarecrow. "That is why I come up with ideas like that."

But Dorothy didn't think it was such a foolish idea. She remembered Aunt En, who believed in the traditional ways, once telling her that ants belonged to the element of fire and were a good cure for any poison, which belonged to the element of wood. Uncle Heng had told her that this was an old wives' tale, but in this Shanghai, where magic was alive, maybe it would work.

She took some sweet carrots out of her pocket and began to chew them into a paste. Then she spread the paste all over the bare arms and face of the unconscious man.

Soon, ants, enticed by the sweet smell of the carrots, crawled out of the cracks in the walls and began to bite the sleeping figure.

"I hope the poison from the opium will leave with the bites," Dorothy said, her hands squeezed into tight fists.

The large man began to thrash and curse, and Dorothy and Scarecrow jumped back, frightened. But the Tin Woodman held the man down as he continued to scream and fight and the ants went on biting him. The Tin Man kept his eyes averted because he thought the expressions of pain on the man's face would make him queasy, and he tried to keep his touch gentle so that the man did not suffer needlessly.

Eventually the ants had removed every bit of sweet carrot from the man's body and left, and the large man sat up by himself, looking amazed at the three strangers around him.

"Thank you," he said. "For the first time in a long while, I feel awake."

"I was once a fighter, a member of the Boxer Rebellion. I was so fearless that they called me the Lion.

"We invoked the old magic of China, the power of the craggy mountains and misty air, the deep marshes and the clear streams. We called on the old temples, built before the coming of Christian missionaries and their contempt for all that we revered. We painted ourselves with words of power so that bullets could not harm us.

"We rose, a thousand voices shouting as one, to drive the foreigners out of China, so that our children could walk with their backs straight, so that their children would know that they belong to a free people, not a people addicted to opium and subservient to the will of others.

"And for a while, we believed we could win.

"Then came that battle outside the bounds of Shanghai. The foreigners shot at us with their guns and cannons while we rushed at them with our spears and swords.

"My friend fell to the left of me. My brother fell to the right of me. Why was the old magic not working? Was it too weak to stop steel and gunpowder, much as the junks were too weak to stop British gunboats?

"And my courage, the faith that had sustained me for so long, suddenly fled. And the next thing I knew, I fell too, even though I hadn't been shot. I hid myself among the bodies of my fallen comrades and watched as the rest of the Boxers were killed.

"I survived as a coward, and since that day, I have sought refuge in the oblivion brought by opium."

The Lion sat quietly, his wild mane of unkempt hair obscuring his downcast eyes.

"You have saved me from drowning to death in an opium dream, but I'd rather be dead. I have no courage."

"Come with us to see the Great Oz," Dorothy said. "He is a powerful magician, and he will give you courage."

The Lion did not believe this, for he had seen how the old magic failed when he had been most in need. But Dorothy looked so earnest that he could not bear to disappoint her, and so he nodded and agreed to come.

The four companions walked on, as the golden bricks glistened in the moonlight in front of their feet.

For a while they walked along the Bund, next to the Huangpu River. Like its twin in the Veiled Shanghai that Dorothy came from, even at night, the placid, wide river of commerce was filled with cargo ships from around the world, their steam engines puffing and their copper bells clanging.

Dorothy was a little worried that the four of them would make an odd sight. But as they passed through the crowd promenading along the Bund—Portuguese dancing girls flouncing about in puffy skirts and heavy makeup; bare-armed and tattooed Malay sailors flashing black-stained teeth; American "flappers" puffing on cigarettes; well-dressed Russian noblemen and noblewomen taking a night stroll; European businessmen surrounded by Chinese mistresses and servants; a troupe of acrobats with a lion, a tiger, and a dancing bear surrounded by a cheering crowd—she realized that the four of them were far too drab to stand out.

A large, well-dressed man in a crisp new suit barreled down the Bund, and Dorothy couldn't dodge out of the way quickly enough. His shoulder collided with her and almost knocked her off her feet. He stopped to glare at her as she stumbled, his blue eyes icy cold.

"Watch where you're going!" said Scarecrow.

The man looked from him to Dorothy, frowning as if he had seen something deeply distasteful.

"Oh, I'm terribly sorry," Dorothy said. She didn't think it was her fault at all, but she had always been taught to be polite.

The man looked at her contemptuously. "You think because you've learned a bit of English, you belong here? Think you're free to corrupt our youth? Think you're better than the other Chinese whores?"

Dorothy didn't know how to answer this. Her heart pounded and her face felt hot. She backed up a few steps. The other pedestrians on the Bund kept their distance, though a few stopped to look at the confrontation.

"You need to learn some manners," the man said. He raised his cane to strike Dorothy.

But a strong arm shot out from the side and grabbed the cane mid-swing. The Lion stepped in front of Dorothy, still holding the tip of the cane.

"You dare to strike at a European?" said the incredulous owner of the cane. He pulled at the cane, but the Lion's hold was so solid that it might as well have been embedded in stone. "Let go now or else by the time the police are through with you, you won't even be able to crawl back to your muddy village!"

The Lion flinched. But he continued to hold the cane, even though his arm trembled.

Dorothy looked around and saw a few more of the Panopticons rising high above the crowd. If Beini was right, the police would have already seen this and were probably on their way.

"It's okay," she whispered to the Lion. "Let go. We don't want to be caught by the police before we get to see Oz."

The Lion stared at the man with the cane as though his eyes were on fire. He began to twist his wrist, and the man yelped as the cane was finally pulled out of his hand. The Lion snapped it in half and tossed the pieces into the Huangpu River. The man stared in disbelief at the pieces of his cane arcing over the water.

The bobbing hats of the Shanghai Municipal Police could be seen in the distance.

"Run!" Scarecrow yelled.

The Tin Woodman hung by his hands from the levee, dangling his feet over the Huangpu River while the others clung to him so they could not be seen from the Bund. After they were sure the police were gone, they climbed back up.

"I wish I were brave," the Lion said. "I should have punched him in the face. But I'm just a coward in hiding."

"If you had done that," Dorothy said, "then all of us would have been arrested. Sometimes just because you don't fight doesn't mean you aren't brave."

But the Lion wasn't convinced.

They looked around at the splendid, gaudy, European-style buildings that lined the Bund and housed the foreign banks and trading houses whose names Dorothy knew well.

"That's where the real power and magic of Shanghai lies," the Lion said, his voice filled with equal measures of awe and contempt. "The wealth of China somehow flows always to those who do not care about the Chinese."

Dorothy gazed up at the brightly lit windows in the pulsing heart of the city and imagined the power that flowed through the offices.

"I thought Oz was the most powerful magician in all of Shanghai," said Scarecrow.

The Lion snorted and said nothing. But the Tin Woodman answered, "There are different kinds of power, and maybe Oz can give us what we want, even if he doesn't own any steamships or have much money."

They picked up the road of golden bricks again. It took a turn away from the river, and the four followed.

They came to a green park filled with freshly mown grass and trimmed hedgerows. In the middle of the park was a little two-story house with a green-tiled roof, green walls, and green shutters. The road of yellow bricks ended at the green door of the house.

Dorothy pressed the doorbell, and a Chinese woman came to the door. She wore a green dress and scowled at the strange party.

"We're here to see Oz," Dorothy said.

The woman scrutinized them. "You're not with a newspaper, are you?"

"No," Dorothy said.

"Are you here for money?"

"No. We're here to ask for his help but not for money. We admire him because we heard how powerful he is."

The woman seemed doubtful, but at least her scowl relaxed. "Well, it might do him good to see some visitors who admire him. But you mustn't tell him any news about what's going on in the world outside these walls."

"What do you mean?"

"Well, for instance, don't mention the Wicked Warlord of the West, or the Mechanical Cavalry of the Rising Sun.

Don't talk about the Treaty of Broken China Figurines or the Prison of a Hundred Young Flowers either. It would upset him."

Since Dorothy had no idea what any of these things were, she assured the woman that she had no plans to mention them.

"You're probably annoyed that we seem to be hiding everything from Oz, as though we are showing him the world through colored glasses and musical filters. But it's not his fault that his magic didn't work out the way he wanted it to."

Dorothy grew even more confused, but she nodded, just to move things along.

"All right, come with me."

The room they were in was small and lit by a faint lamp. The walls were filled with framed photographs and newspaper articles.

The woman left them and closed the door behind her.

"Hey, I know this man," said Scarecrow. He walked up to a few of the English articles on the wall. "This is Sun Yat-sen, the George Washington of China. He loves freedom almost as much as an American."

"It's Nakayama Sho," said the Tin Woodman. He looked at some of the Japanese articles framed on the wall. "I'd heard some of the officers at the Japanese company back in Manchuria speak of him. They think of him as almost an honorary Japanese."

"It's Sun Rixin," said the Lion. "He's a Christian who did not believe in the old magic that the Boxers fought for. He's almost a foreigner himself."

"This is President Sun," said Dorothy. "I've seen his pictures in the textbooks. He's the most famous revolutionary in China. He brought down the Last Manchu Emperor and was going to free China, but then he disappeared."

The four of them began to argue, each asserting that he or she was right about who the man in the pictures was.

"I am all of these things and none of these things," a thin and weak voice spoke from the dark.

Gingerly, Dorothy walked over and pulled back a curtain. They saw an old man lying in bed, only his wizened face visible above the blanket.

"How did you end up here?" asked Dorothy. "How did you become the Great Oz?"

The Great Oz was sitting up, propped up by pillows. The four companions stood around the bed.

"If I'm not mistaken," said the Great Oz, "all of you came from the Veiled Shanghai, because you spoke of things I had done there."

Dorothy and her friends nodded.

"In the world that you all came from, I was once known for my skill with words. I suppose some might say I was a magician, able to conjure up armies out of peasants, create revolutions with a few well-placed tracts.

"For years, the Qing Court hounded me, and I was a man of many names and many disguises, and everyone had a different idea of who I was. Some saw me as the man to bring China into the modern world as a colonial base for Japan. Others saw me as an advocate of complete Westernization, abandoning China's traditions. Yet others thought I was a nationalist, blinded by zeal to the problems of the common people. Still others thought I might be a Communist.

"Yet through it all, I had only one wish: for China to be respected as an equal of the other nations of the world and not subjugated as the Sick Man of East Asia. I believed I could strengthen this anemic land with an injection of ideas I learned from the West and Japan.

"When the Revolution succeeded in 1912, I thought my dreams would come true. Yet all that followed was more suffering for the people of China. The Great Powers did not live up to their ideals for the respect of the rights of all mankind, and they preferred China to be weak and divided, a carcass to feast upon. The Chinese warlords placed their own interests above those of the people and fought for spoils. I was too naive, and those I thought were my comrades betrayed the revolution until the man I once trusted the most drove me from China. In exile, I became a nobody.

"And one morning, I woke up in this new Shanghai, this Shanghai through a dark mirror. Everyone told me that I was a great magician—that I could make things happen just by thinking and speaking. But I am not a magician at all, only a bad revolutionary. The man who betrayed me, the Wicked Warlord of the West, defeated me with his magic and made sure that my powerlessness was plain for all to see.

"And so the few who still have faith in me allow me to hide in this house, and they hide the truth of the world from me, thinking that it would break my heart. I call myself the Great Oz as a joke, like Ozymandias, whose accomplishments were once thought so great and turned out to be so many mirages."

"So you're not a magician at all?" Dorothy asked.

"No," the Great Oz shook his head sadly. "I am just an old man living with dreams and memories."

"How will you get us home?" asked Dorothy. "Beini said that you could."

"How will you give me brains?" asked Scarecrow.

"How will you give me a heart?" asked the Tin Woodman.

"How will you give me courage?" asked the Lion. And he stood up menacingly over the frail figure of the Great Oz.

"I cannot," said the old man. "I'm sorry."

"You must," said Dorothy. "I believe in you. You might not believe that you have any power, but back in the Veiled Shanghai, young students are marching in the streets shouting your words; workers and merchants are on strike for a future you promised; even the lowliest and meanest Chinese have faith that there is hope to your vision, and they do not care if you don't believe in yourself."

A hint of the red blow of health came into the Great Oz's sallow cheeks. "Is everything you said true? The people of Veiled Shanghai are united?"

Dorothy nodded. "They're risking everything to bring down the traitors in Peking."

"Then you must defeat the Wicked Warlord of the West," the Great Oz said.

"He's behind the warlords imprisoning the students in Peking," Dorothy realized. "He's the greatest of the traitors they're protesting against in the Veiled Shanghai. But how can I defeat him? I'm just a girl."

"Yet defeat him you must, or else none of us can wake from this dream."

And so the four companions began their trek toward Peking, the distant citadel of the Wicked Warlord of the

West. It would be a journey of many days and many nights, but Dorothy, being young and determined, did not think that was a problem.

The Wicked Warlord's name was Yuan Shikai, and he was once the most trusted friend of the Great Oz.

"A revolution!" he had said. "A revolution is exactly what China needs!"

And then, when the revolution had finally toppled the Manchu Emperor, he had forced the Great Oz into exile and declared himself a new emperor. Promptly he made all the Chinese his slaves again.

Now the Wicked Warlord always kept on eye on the Emerald House. He looked through his Panopticon and saw Dorothy and her companions leave the Emerald House for his citadel.

He's sending them to come after me, he thought. *The Great Oz has some fight left in him after all.*

He picked up the phone and called his friends in the International Settlement, for the Wicked Warlord was a good friend of the Great Powers—they gave him the Panopticon, and then enjoyed all the concessions he was willing to give them as ruler of the docile Chinese.

A team of Shanghai Municipal Police officers had blocked off the road ahead of Dorothy and her companions. The officers wore hats with brims in the front, and in the night they looked like the beaks of crows.

"Oh no," said Dorothy. "I think they're looking for vagrants who are out after curfew."

Any other path they could take would probably have checkpoints, too. The companions huddled in a corner and debated what to do.

"I have an idea," said Scarecrow. And then he explained himself.

"That's a very risky idea," said the Lion. "And not well thought out at all."

"Exactly," said Scarecrow, "I haven't got any sense." And he smiled.

The police captain watched as the strange party approached. In the lead was a young American man, who was clearly inebriated and wearing a jacket several sizes too large.

"Hold it there!" the captain said. "Why are you out so late? Don't you know that's against curfew?"

"S-sorry," the young man said, slurring his speech. "Guess I had too-too much fun tonight."

The young man was supported on his left side by a young Chinese girl—likely his maid, judging by her prim dress and the timid way she behaved—and on his right side by a middle-aged Chinese man—likely his driver or manservant, who looked terrified at the sight of the uniforms of the Municipal Police.

The police captain was very proud of his sharp observation and deduction skills. He straightened up and puffed out his chest. He liked feeling powerful in front of others.

But behind the boy: What was this? An automaton bodyguard! Its surface was polished to shine brightly, and it looked to be as strong as ten men. Someone who could afford such a machine was bound to be important.

The police captain had been told to watch for a ragtag band of Chinese vagrants up to no good, but surely headquarters didn't mean these people.

"It's all right, sir," said the police captain. "Just be careful. A lot of hooligans out at night. Do you live far from here?"

"No, not at all. Just a few—a few more steps, er, locks, er, blocks."

The officers stepped aside respectfully as the Lion, the Tin Woodman, and Dorothy half-carried Scarecrow across the checkpoint and disappeared around the next turn.

"I put on a pretty good show, don't I?" said Scarecrow, and everyone laughed.

The Wicked Warlord saw how the companions evaded capture, and he grew angrier.

"Useless," he cursed under his breath. "I have to do everything myself."

Now that Dorothy and her companions were outside Shanghai, they rode on the back of the Tin Woodman as he marched with giant steps through the fields and country roads, heading toward Peking. Dorothy felt as though she were riding a train.

On the second day of their journey, the Wicked Warlord sent a team of soldiers with steam-powered bicycles to come after them. These were among his best-trained men, known as the Wolf Brigade.

As the rumbling wheels surrounded the companions, Dorothy became very frightened. The riders wore thick armor and helmets painted with sharp teeth dripping with blood. They really did seem like a pack of wolves.

"Don't worry," said the Tin Woodman. "I'll take care of this."

He asked Dorothy and the others to hide behind a bale of hay while he took his axe off his belt and strode toward the soldiers on bicycles.

"Stop!" the captain of the Wolf Brigade shouted, but the Tin Woodman did not stop.

They began to shoot at him, but the bullets bounced off the metal carapace harmlessly like bees trying to sting an oak tree. The Tin Woodman strode purposefully around, and with each swing of his mighty axe, split apart a bicycle. He was careful not to harm any of the men, for he did not want to hurt anyone, just the way he imagined someone with a real heart would not.

The soldiers, having seen how their iron mounts were so easily destroyed by the Tin Woodman, shouted and scattered, terrified of this mechanical menace. Some dropped their armor and helmets as they ran.

The Tin Woodman tied the axe back on his belt and squatted down. "Get on," he said to his friends. "We still have a long way to go."

There was nothing to do now but for the Wicked Warlord to send out his army against the companions. They caught Dorothy and the others on the third day of their journey. These were not bad men, just boys forced to fight for the Wicked Warlord because they had no other way to feed themselves.

"Let me deal with them," said the Lion. And Dorothy and the others stepped back.

"I know you're afraid," said the Lion. His voice was somber and resonant; it carried very far in the empty fields. "I am afraid too.

"But this young woman taught me that just because you're afraid doesn't mean that you can't do the right thing. We're here to fight for you! You should be taking up arms against those who have invaded this country, as we Boxers once did, not against your own brothers and sisters. For that is the true old magic of this country: four hundred million hearts beating as one."

And the soldiers looked at the Lion and at each other, and none made a move against him or his friends.

The companions passed the soldiers and went on toward Peking.

Finally, the Wicked Warlord summoned his Secret Police, the elite fighting men known as the Winged Monkeys. These were men who could walk on walls and leap onto roofs in a single bound. They were as practiced in the art of fighting as they were in the art of blending into shadows.

Wordlessly they snuck up behind the Tin Woodman and disabled him by shocking him with an electric prod. They threw a net over the Lion, who fought but could not break the silken threads. They held Scarecrow down and cuffed his thin arms. Finally, they arrested Dorothy and took her to see the Wicked Warlord.

Dorothy faced the Wicked Warlord, a bald and rotund man with a face full of glee and cruelty. He wore a military uniform decorated with so many medals and ribbons that he looked a bit like a gaudy Christmas tree.

Dorothy recognized him from his portrait on all the *dayang*. She was afraid at first, but then she remembered that she was standing on two coins in her shoes, and so she was, in a way, standing on *him*. She calmed down.

“You young people,” the Wicked Warlord said, *tsk-tsk*ing, “always think you know everything. You do not know how the world works.”

“I know that you should free the students you’ve imprisoned,” said Dorothy. “You should give the Republic back to the people.”

“And why is that? The people would not know what to do with themselves without someone like me in charge. I think I’m happy just the way things are.”

Dorothy thought back to the girls standing on street corners singing patriotic songs, to the students fearlessly marching through the streets, to the workers standing and listening to speeches while they lost their wages. She thought about the Tin Woodman’s bravery, Scarecrow’s compassion, the Lion’s wisdom.

“You can’t win,” said Dorothy. “There are many of us, and only one of you.”

And she turned around and picked up the pot of tea on the table and threw it at the Wicked Warlord.

She had meant only to humiliate him, but to her surprise, as the hot water drenched the Wicked Warlord, the Wicked Warlord screamed.

“What have you done?”

And color began to drain from him—literally. The green of his uniform, the gold in his medals, the flushed red cheeks—the colors ran down his body in streaks, leaving behind blurry lines.

The Wicked Warlord was made of paper, and he was falling apart like an ink-brush painting in the rain.

And as the water pooled around his feet, the Palace began to melt, too.

The Wicked Warlord’s power had always been but a mirage and only as strong as the paper tigers and dragons that children played with at the Lantern Festival.

Soon the Wicked Warlord and the Palace were gone, leaving Dorothy in the middle of a square with a lot of other dazed-looking people, prisoners who were now free.

The celebration in Tiananmen Square was like nothing Dorothy had ever seen. So many firecrackers! So much dancing and singing!

Now that the Wicked Warlord was no more, the Winged Monkeys were quick to shift their stance. They brought back the Lion, the Tin Woodman, and Scarecrow, and their reunion with Dorothy added even more joy.

And who should arrive in the middle of the celebration? It was the Great Oz, carried here on the shoulders of the Wolf Brigade—whose legs pumped hard at their bicycles—and the soldiers who had deserted the Wicked Warlord of the West.

"Thank you," said the Great Oz. "You have proven to me that faith does matter, that as long as the young people are willing to go to prison for what they believe is right, this country will always have hope."

"And now, can I go home?" asked Dorothy.

"And now, can I have some brains?" asked Scarecrow.

"And now, can I have a heart?" asked the Tin Woodman.

"And now, can I have courage?" asked the Lion.

The Great Oz smiled and spoke to each of them.

Dorothy was very sleepy and tired by the time the train pulled into Shanghai North Railway Station.

She yawned as she got off the train.

She wondered if the Tin Woodman liked his new job.

"You'll be the new Head of the Peking Police," said the Great Oz. "You have the gentlest heart of all, and the people should no longer be afraid of those entrusted to keep them safe."

She looked around at her. Something felt different about the air, familiar and fresh at the same time. Did the sun seem brighter? The sound of the crowd happier?

She thought about the Lion and whether he was now content.

"You'll be my General of the Army," said the Great Oz. "There is none braver, for you have always been afraid, and yet you always knew that the right thing must be done."

"Going somewhere, Miss?" asked a rickshaw runner, who pulled up to the curb outside the station.

"Yes," Dorothy said. "But isn't there a strike going on?"

"You haven't heard? The government in Peking caved! They had to let the students go and fired the ministers responsible for the unequal treaties. Who'd ever thought that the government would be afraid of the people! We won! They're celebrating all over Shanghai."

Dorothy smiled, thinking about Scarecrow—no, Freddie.

"You have a lot of ideas that others think of as foolish," said the Great Oz. "But sometimes those are the only ideas that will work."

"I am an American, after all," said Freddie, and grinned.

"You'll be my Advisor. The Revolution is still a long way from success, and all of us comrades must continue to strive. Just as only America did not approve of the unequal treaty, you're the only one who stood with us in our struggle. You have more sense than all the Western powers put together—they who only want to keep things as they are."

"Kansu Road, please," Dorothy said as she got into the rickshaw.

She took off her shoes and found the two *dayang* coins, engraved with Yuan Shikai's head. Beini had been right. There was indeed some charm associated with these: they were enough for the fare home.

—

Author's Note: By the time of the May Fourth Movement, Yuan Shikai had already died. But his successors in the Beiyang Government in Peking were not very different from the Wicked Warlord himself. For more on the historical events fictionalized here, Joseph T. Chen's *The May Fourth Movement in Shanghai* is a good introduction in English.

BEYOND THE NAKED EYE

BY RACHEL SWIRSKY

WISH.

The letters are chipped from emerald. Serifs sparkle. They hover in midair like insects with faceted carapaces. Their shadows fall, rich and dark, over a haze of yellow, which as the view widens becomes distinguishable as part of a brick and then as part of a road, which itself becomes a winding yellow ribbon that crosses verdant farmland.

Ten contestants. One boon from the Wizard.

Whose wish will come true?

We all watch in our crystal globes. Blue-tinted ones sit on rough tables in Munchkin Country. Red-tinted ones float beside Quadlings. Green-tinted ones are held aloft in the lacquered fingernails of Emerald Citizens.

Convex glass distorts our view. We see wide, but we do not see deep.

After revealing the rich lands of Oz, the view soars upward until it shows nothing but sky. A silver swing drops down. It's shaped like a crescent moon. Glinda, the Good Witch of the South, perches on it. She wears a drop-waisted, sleeveless gown. Sparkling white fabric falls in loose folds to just above her ankles.

Her voice is as sweet as honeydew.

"We're down to our four finalists. They've worked together to make it down the road of yellow brick. They've almost made it to the Emerald City. What will happen next? Only one can win. Will it be Lion, Tin Man, Scarecrow, or Dorothy?"

She raises her finger to her lips, telling a secret to everyone watching.

"Remember, in Oz, wishes really do come true."

Those of us who fancy ourselves members of the City's intellectual elite gather in fashionable bathhouses to watch the show. This season, it is unthinkable not to wear hats during social gatherings, even when otherwise nude. This makes for awkward bathhouse situations. We hold ourselves stiffly, craning our necks to keep silk and felt dry.

Despite our collective ridiculousness, we still feel entitled to laugh at Glinda's dramatic pronouncements, and at the overblown challenges she puts to the contestants.

"Bread and circuses," we call it.

Some are of the opinion that it's all propaganda. "The Wizard wants to rub everyone's noses in how powerful he is," they remark.

"Not possible," others argue. "He's not that stupid. He could grant all of those people's wishes if he wanted to. He's losing public sympathy by the day." Smugly they tap the sides of their noses. "Someone's making this to show him up."

The two camps argue back and forth. Periodically, wild passion overcomes someone's good sense, and they gesticulate wildly, splashing everyone with emerald-hued water.

In the end we all agree on one thing: bread and circuses.

Effective bread and circuses, though. Everyone watches. Even us.

I keep quiet during the evenings at the bathhouse. I prefer to watch and listen. Few people know the name Kristol Kristoff, and I prefer it that way.

I'm a jeweler.

I have a loupe that I inherited from my great-grandfather. It magnifies everything by ten times.

Sometimes I find it frustrating to look at the mundane, unmagnified world. There are so many blemishes that one can't see with the naked eye. It's impractical to evaluate everything by what's superficially visible. If I had my preference, the ubiquitous Emerald City glasses would come with jeweler's loupes attached.

Working in the Emerald City, I perform most of my work on emeralds, which are actually a form of beryl green due to the intrusion of other minerals, usually chromium. Most emeralds are included—which means that they contain a relatively high proportion of other minerals—and also fragile. This makes them both motley and transitory.

The Emerald City is the same. Like any city, it's composed of a variety of minerals. It contains inclusions of Munchkins, Gillikins, Winkies, and Quadlings. An emerald would not be green without inclusions; a city would not be a city without immigrants.

An emerald will crack under high pressure. The Emerald City will do the same. Introduce a famine, ignite a fire, depose a leader. Stones or cities will shatter.

It's happened before.

The show began with the image of a farmhouse whirling through a tornado. It crashed to the ground in an explosion of dirt and debris. Slowly the wind blew the detritus away, revealing what lay below.

Two skinny, old legs poked out from beneath the farmhouse. Two wrinkled, old feet wore two shiny silver slippers.

"Congratulations, Dorothy!" Glinda beamed. "You've killed the Wicked Witch of the East and won the first challenge!"

She removed the shoes from the corpse and presented them to the little girl.

"These silver slippers will give you an advantage in later elimination rounds," Glinda said.

Smiling, Dorothy put on the shoes. She didn't seem to care that they'd just been taken from a dead woman.

In the Emerald City, we wear green, which is regrettable for my complexion.

Still, I am fortunate enough to own a very fine silk cloak, clasped with a very fine emerald cloak pin, both of which I inherited from my grandfather. While the former is threadbare, few people notice such things, as few people are used to looking at the world with a jeweler's eye for detail. It makes me seem much richer than I am, which is useful from time to time, such as when I visit the Palace.

A maid in a short frilly uniform, all white thighs and rouged knees, greeted me when I arrived. She threw her arms around my neck with overwhelming familiarity.

"Mr. Kristoff!" she exclaimed.

When I paused to take a second look, I noticed with embarrassment that she was not actually a maid at all, but Lady Flashgleam Sparkle in costume.

"Why in the name of Lurline are you dressed like that?" I asked.

Flashgleam scanned for witnesses. "Not here. Come on."

She took my hand—so forward!—and pulled me across the threshold into one of the Palace's many emerald-accented parlors. As she led me briskly through corridors lined with gems and mirrors, I expected someone to stop us and ask Flashgleam why she was in costume, but apparently no one pays heed to maids who are escorting visitors.

We reached her rooms. She closed the door behind us and then went to her windows—which overlooked a courtyard where gardeners grew green orchids, green roses, and green hydrangeas—and swept the velvet curtains closed.

Flashgleam Sparkle is the only remaining scion of the house Sparkle, which had once sent its noble sons and daughters to attend the courts of Ozma III through Ozma XVI. Now that the line of the Ozmas has been broken, and the Wizard sits in their stead, most of the old noble families have departed the Emerald City for country estates.

Flashgleam, as the sole Sparkle heir, remained in the City of Emeralds, surrounded by the remnants of her family's glory. Last year, after she had the family's town house closed, declaring it too large for a single person, the Wizard offered her accommodations in his Palace as suited a person with her venerable lineage.

This was all according to plan.

While two people of our relative stations would not normally have interacted, Flashgleam had been my client for a number of years. Whenever she received gifts of jewelry—for instance, from suitors—she had the habit of commissioning me to craft facsimiles with which she could replace the original ornaments. Subsequently, she sold the genuine jewels through black market connections. It is always important—she says—for a woman to have unexpected reservoirs of cash.

My discretion in helping her create such forgeries had encouraged her to invite me into her secret cabal.

It has, I must say, made my life considerably more interesting than it was before.

Flashgleam arrayed herself on a divan. She crossed her legs, exposing white thigh with the casual disregard of dignity that only women of high station can afford. She said, "When I'm wearing this uniform, I can poke around anywhere."

I asked, "What did you find?"

"The pot of treasure," she said with a broadening smile. "We were right about everything. He's a charlatan."

—

When the show began, there were ten individual contestants. First thing, Glinda split them into teams. Team Dorothy (so named because she'd won the first challenge) approached the City from Munchkin Country. A group of three approached from Quadling Country and another three-entity group approached from Gillikin.

None started in Winkie Country due to the embargo against the Wicked Witch of the West.

The Quadling Team was the first to be eliminated. Their team leader, a lanky Quadling boy, lost a wrestling match with a Fighting Tree. After that, Dairy Belle, the animated butter pat, couldn't figure out how to do a glamour shoot reflecting her unique Quadling heritage, not least because she melted under the spotlights.

At first it seemed as though Pulp, who was one of the famous living paper dolls fashioned by Mrs. Cuttenclip, might make it on her own. She folded herself into a paper airplane and caught a passing wind. It would have carried her to the Emerald City much faster than the other teams could manage, but alas, the wind blew her into a river, where she turned into mulch and was swept downstream.

Initially, the viewers—the cynical bathhouse crowd among them—were in it to watch blood and teeth. The Kalidah challenge mustered a great deal of excitement. The bathhouses echoed with ladies' screams as the monsters' ursine bodies lumbered into view. Even I admit having felt a tremor when the light flashed across their bared tiger-teeth.

If it hadn't been for the first interview with Dorothy, perhaps the show would never have been anything more than a blood sport.

Glinda began the interview during a quiet moment. Dorothy sat under a peach tree in the evening light, her dog, Toto, running circles around her feet. Glinda knelt so that she was eye-to-eye with the child. She asked, "What do you wish for?"

Dorothy looked up. Breeze stirred her wheat-blond curls.

"I just want to go home," she said.

"Don't you like Oz?" asked Glinda.

Dorothy's hand flew to her mouth. Her cheeks flushed with embarrassment. "Oh! I should mind my manners! Of course I like Oz. It's a beautiful place!"

"So why not stay?"

Dorothy's cornflower eyes cut shyly away. She smoothed her pinafore. "Kansas is...well, it may be boring, but it's home. You have to go back home. It's where you belong."

A drop glittered in her eye.

She murmured, "And Aunt Em must miss me terribly."

In the bathhouse, the intellectuals snorted derisively. "Sentimental manipulation," they called it.

Even so, Dorothy's words had taken what had been a silly amusement—no more significant than any game of cards—and transformed it into something that could tug at any of us.

We all remembered being children. We all remembered wanting to go home.

I am reasonably certain that Flashgleam Sparkle is the mastermind behind WISH.

I have not asked, and she has not volunteered the information. Still, the Good Witch of the South is reputed to be sympathetic to her cause, although the affiliations of witches are ever fickle.

More to the point, while Flashgleam and I avoided the subject of the show's derivation, we *had* discussed how well it suits her agenda.

If the Wizard was indeed a fraud—as we had long suspected—then the show would present him a terrible dilemma.

Once WISH became popular—an instantaneous phenomenon—he couldn't shut it down without revealing not only that he wasn't the architect behind it, but also that he had so little control of what was going on in his own territory that he hadn't been able to identify and halt such a large, rebellious magical undertaking before it began.

If he let the show run, he found himself tangled in yet another dilemma—he couldn't refuse to grant an audience to the winner unless he was willing to show himself as both incompetent *and* heartless. Yet, if he was a fraud, he couldn't admit the winner without being exposed as unable to grant their wish.

So far the Wizard had appeared to be biding his time, plotting his strategy as he allowed the competition to unfold. Flashgleam believed that he would eventually find a way to cut himself free of the dilemma; fraud or not, the Wizard was not stupid.

However, she also believed that the show would cause turmoil behind the throne. Frantic and furious, the Wizard would interrogate his staff, searching for his betrayer, disturbing the loyalties he'd so carefully built. During his reign, he'd quelled nascent rebellions with the mere threat of magic. Flashgleam hoped that disorder in his administration would give her the fingerholds she needed to pry the Wizard loose from his throne.

All this hinged, of course, on the thesis that he was actually a fraud.

"It's all done with gears," Flashgleam said. She smoothed the ruffled maid's collar over her bosom. "And pulleys and levers and…I don't know, I'm not a machinist. But it's all machines."

"The Wizard?" I asked.

"His audience chamber," she corrected. "There's a curtain drawn in front of it. But behind, it's all machines. There's something like a projector focused on the emerald throne. I think he's using photographic stills to create illusions."

"That's why everyone reports seeing different things in the throne room," I said.

"Right!" She raised her hands in excitement. Her fingers shone with the convincing forgeries of rings her lovers had gifted her. "Flames, and bats, and women carved from wood. They're photographs. Manipulations."

"So this is proof."

"Proof," she agreed. "Finally."

I was no watchmaker, but as a jeweler, I had more experience than most with the intricacies of machinery. "If you can give me fifteen minutes or so with the machines, I can figure out how to disrupt them."

Flashgleam looked up, a slight frown on her face. "Hmm?"

"He'll be able to repair them eventually, of course."

"Oh." Flashgleam laughed indulgently. "Always thinking like a craftsman, aren't you? You'd solve everything with a chisel if you could." She leaned forward. "Chaos is well and good, but assassinations are simpler."

I shouldn't have been taken aback, but I was. I had allowed myself to be lulled by the fact that Flashgleam Sparkle had, so far, limited herself to subterfuge. I'd hoped that we might expose the Wizard as a hapless marionette and let the Emerald

Citizens themselves demand regime change without any need for cloaks and daggers.

"You're going to kill the Wizard?" I asked.

"We needed to know if he was a fraud. He is. He has no magic. He won't see us coming." She shook her head. "But no, I'm not going to kill the Wizard."

I knew what she was going to say next. I knew, but I still was unhappy when the words came from her lips.

"You are."

When Glinda caught him alone, the Lion giggled nervously.

"I think I want to win. I mean, I wouldn't be here if I didn't, right?" His amber eyes darted back and forth. "But then, thinking about it, if I had courage then I'd want to fight, right? And fighting…anything could happen. There could be, like, a bear. And he'd run at me, and I'd, like, snarl back, because I'd be brave, and he'd probably chew my ears off."

His tail twitched.

"Is that what I'm competing for? A chance to, you know, have a bear chew my ears off?"

He rested his head on his paws. His downturned muzzle looked mournful despite his massive teeth.

"But I want to win. Of course I do. Uh. Courage. Give it to me. Yeah."

Hesitantly, he swiped his paw through the air.

"Rawr."

Despite a strong early showing, Team Gillikin fizzled midway.

Another child was heading that team, a twelve-year-old from Uptown with purple skin and telescoping limbs. She traveled with a nymph from the Gillikin fog banks and a melancholy man from the Flathead Mountains who carried his brain in a jug.

In the Forest of the Winged Monkeys, they were kidnapped by the location's simian namesakes. One hundred feet into the air, the Flathead panicked and dropped his jug. At two hundred feet, a rising wind dispersed the mist maiden into the clouds.

Only the little girl survived; when the Monkeys lifted her into the air, she telescoped her legs so that no matter how high they took her, she was always touching the ground.

Though saddened by the loss of her companions, she was able to travel much more quickly without worrying about how they'd keep up. She telescoped her legs out as far as they would go and bounded by leagues.

Not far from the border, she glimpsed a pair of telescoping green legs doing the same. Upon investigation, they turned out to belong to a young green boy, who was off to seek his fortune in Quadling Country. Their conversation further revealed that they were both odd-colored, telescoping children born to tan, fixed-length parents, and—more importantly—that they enjoyed each other's company.

The girl revealed that her wish had been to find someone else like her. As it had been fulfilled, she left the competition and telescoped into the clouds with her new green friend.

———

The first time that Lady Sparkle broached the subject of revolution with me, she was wearing a woolen traveling cloak, as if she planned to leave the City. A petite fascinator fashioned from feathers and silk left her head almost shockingly bare.

She handed me a pair of jade hair sticks and watched my hands as I examined the carvings I'd need to replicate in order to make convincing facsimiles.

She ordinarily made pleasant small talk, which was unusual for someone of her status. For weeks I'd been noticing that her superficially inane conversation was in fact driving at something. She'd been feeling out my politics, I was sure, though I didn't know to what end.

That day, however, she made a direct assay. "I've heard stories about your grandfather, you know."

I made a noncommittal noise and squinted at the hair sticks. The kinds of stories that aristocrats told about my grandfather were not my favorite subject of conversation.

She pressed me on it. "He was the royal jeweler, wasn't he?"

Matter-of-factly I said, "He was."

She gestured at my little shop with its dusty shelves and poor lighting. "So how did you end up here?"

I shrugged. Though I refused to meet her eye, I could feel her glance on me.

"You're not untalented," she continued. "In fact, you're very talented indeed."

With a sigh I looked up, still holding the jeweler's loupe to my eye. Flashgleam Sparkle is a pretty woman, but under magnification, she looked all powder and artifice: a woman made of paint.

"You've heard stories about my grandfather," I said. "So why don't you tell me?"

Her dimples deepened, as if she was merely trying out a piece of juicy gossip, but her tone remained serious. "He was caught in a plot to overthrow Ozma the Sixteenth."

"That's right."

Her smile broadened. She lifted her glasses away from her face. I barely contained my gasp—I was a man of the world, but still, a woman like her baring her eyes while alone with a man?

"He imbued her diadem with a sleeping spell," Flashgleam continued.

I allowed myself a raised brow. "That part isn't common knowledge."

"I'm not a common woman."

She leaned toward me, placing her hands on my desk. Her eye loomed giant in my jeweler's loupe, an aristocratic shade of deep river-green.

"I think you're more like him than you let on," Flashgleam said. "Am I right?"

When I said nothing, she reached into the purse hung on her sash and pulled out a handful of sparkling green chips.

"I can offer incentive," she said.

As I looked into her palm, I struggled to maintain my equanimity.

"They're genuine," she said, answering my unspoken question. "Lurline emeralds."

Lurline emeralds were the most valuable gem in all of Oz. They'd been created when Lurline made fairyland, and they were imbued with her magic. My grandfather had worked with them when he was a jeweler for the court. None were supposed to exist outside of the Ozmas' treasury.

Exercising my steeliest will, I waved my hand in refusal. "If I help you, I will do it out of conviction. Not avarice."

The rest of our conversation is easy to imagine, but I'll add one corroborating detail:

When Flashgleam Sparkle left my shop that afternoon wearing her woolen traveling cloak, neither I nor anyone else in the City saw her for several days. It wasn't long after she returned that all the globes in the City lit up with those sparkling emerald serifs.

WISH.

There are many people in the Emerald City who are discontented with the Wizard.

Some are Ozma purists, waiting for the return of Ozma XVII. Others note his fascistic tendencies: public punishments, harsh curfews, a large and well-armored imperial guard.

Where the Ozmas had always delegated policy-making to the Witches of the Realms, the Wizard insisted on deciding all matters without regard for local hierarchies. Against his advisors' warnings, he'd implemented the embargo against the Wicked Witch of the West, ostensibly motivated by concern for the Winkie people, but it was well-known that the actual dispute was about the Wizard's attempts to control the provinces.

Flashgleam Sparkle dislikes the Wizard because, unlike the Ozmas, he declines to be controlled by the nobility. She finds herself cut loose from the power she'd always assumed would be hers by right of inheritance.

I myself dislike the Wizard for much the same reason that I expect my grandfather disliked Ozma XVI. My family has served monarchs as their jewelers for generations. We've always paid attention to their flaws. The Wizard doesn't really care about the people. Ozma XVI didn't either.

Maybe Flashgleam Sparkle will.

—

"I'm a bit different from the others," the Tin Man told Glinda when it was his turn with her. "The Scarecrow never had a brain. The Lion never had any courage. I used to have a heart."

He rapped his knuckles against the side of his head. The sound echoed in his empty skull. "I don't have a brain anymore either, but what I miss is my heart."

The illusion of emotion clouded his eyes, something complicated and delicate like wistfulness or regret.

"I don't have blood anymore, so I won't need my heart to pump," he said. "All I need to do is feel. More deeply and more complexly than I ever did. Every minute. Every hour. I want to understand what it feels like to hate and love and laugh at something at the same time. I want to feel the poignant pain of looking at something beautiful and knowing it's going to die. I want to feel everything. Everything."

His fingers grasped the air, trying to hold on to something that wasn't there, a gesture that could easily have been mistaken for passion.

His hand drifted back to his side.

"If I win, of course," he added softly.

—

Last night's poppy challenge was a bit silly. Make the best bouquet you can in ten minutes. But oops, there's a twist. The bouquet was only a decoy. The real challenge was to get out of the poppy field before falling asleep.

The Tin Man and the Scarecrow, having no circulatory systems, were immune to poppy pollen, which everyone agreed was unfair. They carried Dorothy out of the poppy field when she fell asleep, but the Lion was too heavy for them to bring along.

It looked as though the Lion was out until the Tin Man accidentally rescued the Queen of the Field Mice, earning a challenge advantage. The Queen of the Field Mice promised him a favor, which he immediately spent by asking her tiny, squeaking subjects to drag the Lion out of the poppy field.

A lady sitting near me gestured angrily at her emerald globe. "That doesn't even make sense!"

Her hat was wide-brimmed with dense feathers, and her anger had caused her to gesture with such passion that she was in danger of losing her headgear to the water.

"It does seem a bit silly," agreed a friend of hers who was wearing a rather more sensible cloche.

"*Deus ex mus*!" shouted a mustachioed gentleman.

"Stupid strategy," someone else muttered. "They should have ditched Dorothy and the Lion and taken a ticket to the top two."

"But they made a pact!" cried the lady again. "You wouldn't leave behind a sweet girl like that, would you?"

"Bread and circuses, my dear fellows, bread and circuses," said a man near the middle of the pool. He wore a homburg and a stern expression, reminding us that, as intellectuals, we were there to analyze, not involve ourselves in drama.

In our globes we saw the field mice returning. Squeaking, they emerged from the field of flowers, each harnessed with fine thread to a wagon.

Atop the wagon, the Cowardly Lion lay, drowsing, an upturned scarlet poppy capping his nose. He woke with a sneeze that sent the poppy tumbling.

"Oh!" he exclaimed. "What happened? Is there a monster? Don't let it eat me!"

His eyes were so round with fear that even the man in the homburg laughed.

After watching my fellow Emerald intellectuals discuss the poppy challenge, I learned two things. First, that I am strangely reassured to find that even the most jaded of my fellow Citizens can still feel tenderly for a lost child. Second, that the contestants had finally made their way to the emerald gates, and whatever was going to happen was going to happen soon.

I learned to cut gems while sitting—as the saying goes—at my grandfather's knee. Literally on his knee, in my case; I needed the boost so I could see his worktable. I watched his face as often as I watched his hands. He squinted while he worked. His nostrils flared with concentration.

He was an unmade man by then, cast down from courtly heights to the small corner where my shop still resides. His days of working with Lurline emeralds were long past, but his unmatched work brought many aristocrats to him anyway, toting their unset sapphires and their rubies of unknown provenance.

Ozma herself had spared his life. With a yawn and a tinkling laugh, she'd said, "Oz must preserve beautiful things!"

Still, she let her witches weave chains around my grandfather's ankles so that he could not leave his allotted rooms.

When customers came in, he'd sweep me off his knee and hand me a spare loupe. He'd push the loupe against my eye and then lean down, speaking quietly, so that no one could hear him. "Watch for the imperfections. There are imperfections everywhere. Never trust anyone who pretends to be flawless."

Glinda finds the Scarecrow in the chamber on the outskirts of the royal sector that he's been given for the night. He trips over the loose straw in his feet as he escorts her in and lands with a thump on the floor.

A concerned expression flashes across Glinda's face. The Scarecrow waves it away.

"If I had a fit every time I did something stupid, I'd spend all day stomping around."

He's a good-natured fellow, the Scarecrow, quick to mock himself, which I'd guess he'd have to be with those guilelessly painted eyes and that swaying, straw-stuffed gait.

Glinda asks him why he wishes he had a brain. "That's a good question!" he exclaims. "I don't know why I think I want to think since I don't have a brain to think I want to think with. But I'd like to think anyway. At least I think so. You think?"

He sits on the bed and leans against the emerald headboard. At his feet, there's a pair of complimentary emerald-encrusted slippers, which must be awful to wear.

"I was only born the day before yesterday," the Scarecrow says, "so maybe my opinion doesn't count. But it's awfully pretty, isn't it?"

Glinda turns to see what he's looking at. It's sunset blazing through the window, reds and golds and violets refracting through the City's crystalline towers.

The Scarecrow's voice is lower when he continues. "I want a brain, but I think if I get one, I'll be sad that my friends couldn't get what they want, too. Is that what thinking gets you? Understanding that a sweet thing can be bitter, too?"

He looks sadly at Glinda.

"Maybe that's not right. You'd know better than I do. You have a brain."

—

Tonight. Whatever is going to happen will happen tonight.

Everyone in Flashgleam's rebellion wears a watch that I have calibrated. When the tick tells me to, I depart the bathhouse—where everyone is still watching Glinda and the Scarecrow—and head into the corridor.

The City is a labyrinthine place, built as a single creation. It's not like the towns out in Gillikin Country, where one house is distinct from the next. In the City, towers share walls and are connected by archways. Central towers look down on courtyards; those on the outskirts look out over Oz. The royal spire rises above all others, gazing imperially downward.

I work my way along jeweled corridors. Few people are out; most of the population is congregated in bathhouses and parlors. Those that aren't walk swiftly, hunched over handheld globes.

I wear my grandfather's cloak anyway. For disguise. For confidence.

The corridors grow increasingly ornate as I near the royal sector. Gold embellishes the archways. Statues of the Ozmas (their nameplates removed by the new regime) pose gracefully in niches. The hundred passages that wind through the City's outskirts converge into a few main arteries.

From behind me I hear a page trumpeting. Footsteps echo. Bad luck for me. The royal pages have chosen to escort the contestants down this corridor.

I shrink against the wall. It's best they don't see me. I don't want to be delayed.

Still, I admit, I'm fascinated to watch the finalists pass. The Tin Man walks first, each movement clanking. The Scarecrow follows, his straw fingers wrapped around those of the little girl. The Tin Man and Scarecrow look more wary than hopeful. Perhaps they are concerned that there will be another challenge waiting, or perhaps they are wondering whether everything that's happened is a trick. The Tin Man tightens his fingers around his axe, and the Scarecrow clutches the little girl's hand, both of them protecting her as best they know how.

Dorothy dances delightedly down the hall, exclaiming over the jewels and statues, without a hint of fright in her eyes.

The Cowardly Lion slinks after them, belly low to the ground.

How cruel it seems that none of them will get their wish.

What would I wish for?

What would I tell Glinda if she were sitting beside me, the fabric of her gown pooling around her knees?

I'd tell her, I think, that I wish everyone had a jeweler's loupe.

I wish that everyone would try to see things as they really are.

I wish that everyone would understand that glamour is often deceit.

I wish that everyone would realize that when you know a flaw is there, you can figure out how to work with it, how to cut around it, how to make the gem glow despite the cracks. Everyone should know how to make the most beautiful objects they can out of things that aren't perfect.

Because nothing is perfect.

Eight anterooms branch off of the Wizard's audience chamber. We meet in the one Flashgleam described. Today she's more suitably attired, wearing a high-waisted gown with a narrow skirt draped in tiers. Her head is bare except for a single peacock feather pinned over one ear.

She's deep in conversation with the other conspirators. There are perhaps half a dozen; it's difficult for me to distinguish one from the next, as they are all cloaked and in the shadows.

I stand quietly aside until Flashgleam notices my presence. She claps me familiarly on the shoulder. She means to compliment, I think, but her touch is uncomfortable.

From within her cloak, she withdraws an enormous emerald that's been carved into a spike. The wickedly sharp tip glints even in this dark room. She offers it, blunt end first.

"Symbols," she says, "It's all about symbols. The City itself is purging him. The emeralds themselves are rising up."

The spike is cool in my palm. A real emerald would be too fragile to wield as a weapon—this one must be enchanted. It must be a Lurline emerald, purloined from Ozma's treasury. To think that anyone could steal such an enormous jewel is startling, but if anyone can, it's Lady Sparkle.

"You're the perfect one to do this." Her voice is soft and charismatic and urgent. "The avatar of emerald."

Perhaps it's the magic of the emerald in my palm that blunts my tongue. "And this way no one noble has to dirty their hands."

"No, of course that's not why," she assures me rapidly. Despite her shocked tone, we both know she's lying.

I wish I had my jeweler's loupe today, but all I have are my eyes. Lady Sparkle's skin is smooth. Her lips are beautifully rounded. There's not a blemish on her cheek, not a discoloration on her costume, not a barbule out of place in the peacock feather behind her ear.

At normal magnification she's flawless.

Jewelers are trained to cut gems, not break them, but in training for the first, one must inevitably learn the second.

A chisel, misplaced, will transform a jewel that was once worth Ozma's ransom into something worthless and fractured.

You can crack a gem in two. You can shatter it. You can do many things that a jeweler ought not to.

A jeweler understands the vulnerability of stone.

The other conspirators rush around at whatever business Flashgleam has assigned them. They pay me no attention.

I recognize one of them now that she's thrown off her cloak. It's Glinda, wearing a white robe with a starched collar. She stands at the entrance to the audience chamber, holding back the velvet curtain that separates us from where the Wizard is receiving Dorothy and her fellows. She only holds it open a fraction, but it still seems a silly risk to me.

Not, apparently, to Flashgleam, who moves to join her. She peers over Glinda's shoulder and gestures to me.

A risk it may be, but I might as well. If the Wizard finds us now, it will make little difference whether I'm at the forefront or standing back.

"There it is," Flashgleam whispers to me, pointing. "The throne with the screen on it. Do you see?"

"He's a clever old bastard," Glinda says. Surprisingly, despite her harsh words, her voice is as honeydew as ever.

"Shh," says Flashgleam.

She points again, this time indicating the contestants who are entering the chamber. The Tin Man stands at the forefront, axe in hand, protecting the other three.

Lights flash through the audience chamber. Flashgleam points to the spots on the ceiling where concealed bulbs are shining down magenta and cerulean.

Suddenly the throne seems to ignite. A Ball of Fire rages without consuming anything. In a shower of sparks, it disappears and becomes a lovely Lady and then a snarling Beast. Finally it settles in the form of an enormous Head with blood-hued skin and faceted eyes.

"What do you want of the Wizard?" it booms.

Timorously each contestant states his or her wish.

The Head answers, "I will grant your favors."

The contestants rejoice. The Head interrupts.

His roar cuts into their celebration. "If you meet my condition!"

They fall silent.

"You must kill the Wicked Witch of the West!"

Dorothy stammers. Glinda shakes her head. "Clever old bastard," she repeats, "Taking advantage of the show. He's given them his own challenge."

"Doesn't matter now," Flashgleam answers.

Glinda drops the curtain. It sways back into place. She departs the anteroom on her own mission.

The conspirators' voices rise as they enter the final throes of their plans.

Flashgleam's fingertips brush mine. "We're almost ready. Don't worry about anything. He'll be incapacitated. He won't be able to hurt you."

I look toward the curtain.

"What are you going to do about Dorothy?" I ask.

Flashgleam blinks. Her brow draws down. "What do you mean?"

"Dorothy. How are you going to get her home?"

"That's not what we should be worried about now."

I push past her and tear the curtain aside. The contestants in the audience chamber don't notice the noise. The Tin Man looks poised to attack the throne. The Lion's low growl fills the room.

Dorothy sniffles into her apron. The Scarecrow wraps his arms around her shoulders, and she turns into the embrace. Tears leave glistening marks on her cheeks. I lose my breath.

Even the most jaded Citizen of Oz feels tenderly toward a child who has lost her home.

I round on Flashgleam. Angrily I repeat, "What are you going to do for Dorothy?"

She's still staring at me as if my words make no sense. She gives some calculated, reassuring answer, but I don't even hear her. The spike is cold in my hand. Lurline emerald.

All my life I've been the one who held the loupe to my eye, who strove to see beyond the superficial. All my life I've been the one who looked for imperfections.

All my life I've been a fool. All my life I've looked for the flaws in what stands before me, not for the flaws in my own thoughts.

It's foolish to hope for a ruler who will be benevolent and just. Ozma XVI, the Wizard, Lady Flashgleam Sparkle—they're all the same. No monarch is ever going to care more about the people than they do about themselves.

I rush forward. Lady Sparkle exclaims, "They're not ready yet!"

I push past her. Everyone looks up as I enter the audience chamber. Even the Wizard's giant avatar regards me with surprise clouding his faceted eyes.

Lurline emerald can break through a man's sternum. It can break through anything.

The Emerald City is named for the emerald from which it was carved. It's held together by magic that keeps it from shattering, but the magic in a Lurline emerald is stronger than any other enchantment.

I pass the Wizard's hidden niche without a glance. Nearby, a place in the wall shines with a translucence I've learned indicates a weak point in the rock.

I'm a jeweler. I know the vulnerability of stone.

There's a horrible noise as I drive the spike into the wall. A crack appears. Slowly it branches toward the floor, casting its roots into the ground. The tower shudders.

Lady Flashgleam rushes toward me, but she stops when she sees the fracture. She staggers backward. For once, even her seemingly perfect lips are stunned into silence.

The magic will die slowly. There will be plenty of time for everyone to get out.

But the Palace will splinter. The Palace will fall.

Its collapse will resonate throughout the Emerald City, of course. The City is all built from one piece. One can't extricate the Palace from the City without consequence, just as one can't depose a ruler without pain.

But I know this City. The highest spire is the weakest. The rest may tremble, but it won't collapse.

We won't collapse.

I push between the Tin Man and the Scarecrow. They've intuited that I'm on their side. They let me pass.

I take Dorothy's hand and lead her and her friends out of the audience chamber and down into the City. I don't know if I can grant her wish. I don't know if I can grant any of them their wishes. It's a flawed world we live in, and not everyone can get what he or she wants. But at least I won't forget her. At least I won't cast her aside while I search for power.

Even the most jaded Emerald Citizen can feel for a child who's lost her home.

A TORNADO OF DOROTHYS

BY KAT HOWARD

When a path has been set, it is very hard not to take it. That difficulty increases when the path is one that has been made just for your feet.

Or at least made for the shoes your feet are wearing.

Everything changes after a storm.

Kansas was gray. The fields were gray and the dirt was gray. The sun, which was not gray but was merciless, faded everything that might once have had color into one flat tone. Even the people of Kansas were gray: Aunt Em, the harsh, unbending gray of steel, and Uncle Henry, the thin pale gray of the shadow that stood behind her. The only thing that was not gray was Dorothy's small dog, Toto, whose comforting fur was a dark, unfaded black.

The tornado was gray, too, at least until Dorothy was inside it. Then the clouds were striated purple and the light was an acid green. Dorothy looked out the window as the house spun in the center of the tornado, her hands toying with the ends of Toto's shiny black fur.

Dorothy did not notice when the spinning stopped, nor did she feel the bump when the tornado set the small house on the ground. What she did notice was the color. Even through the worn gray calico of the curtains, she had to narrow her eyes against the strength of the blue. Dorothy blinked, then looked again. She nudged the half-awake Toto from her lap, then walked to the window.

Dorothy stared at the blue of the sky, the green of the grass, the clearness of the air, until her eyes burned and tears wet her cheeks. Something inside of her fell, caught, flew. Her hands made fists in her dress. "We're home, Toto. We're home."

The door of the house flung open behind her. "So you're the new one, then? Well, I'm sorry for you. Put on the shoes, and off you go."

Dorothy turned around. There was a girl, about her age, holding a pair of silver shoes.

"Those are beautiful," Dorothy said. And they were, the shoes, as bright and beautiful as everything else here, wherever this was. "But the new what?"

"The new Dorothy," said the girl. "Soon to be the new Witch of the East. If you're lucky." The girl extended her arm with such force that one of the silver shoes slid from her grasp and clattered to the floor.

"I'm Glinda. The Witch of the South. South is always the Glinda. That's the way it has to be.

"Once you get to be East, you can be the Eva. But until you get there, you have to be the Dorothy."

Dorothy looked at Glinda. "I *am* Dorothy."

Glinda rolled her eyes and tossed the second silver shoe on the floor with the first. "That's what I just said. Until you're East, you're the Dorothy. Now put on the shoes.

They'll take you where you have to go. But hurry up. Oz doesn't like to wait."

The shoes gleamed at Dorothy, brilliant as the sky outside. Outside. Glinda was rude, and Dorothy had no idea who Oz was, but the shoes were beautiful, and she wanted to go outside. She sat and began to put them on.

"It's my name, I mean. Dorothy. The name I was born with. Dorothy Gale."

"Well, maybe that will help you, maybe it won't. But you've got to *be* the Dorothy now, until you've become East. Oz needs to have a Dorothy."

Dorothy had finished buckling the silver shoes while Glinda was talking. She stood up and took a couple of steps. The shoes were comfortable, more flexible and less heavy then she had expected. She clicked her heels together, and they rang like the tolling of a bell.

Glinda looked at Dorothy and sneered. "This isn't the story where doing that takes you home, even if you had said the words."

"I don't know what story you're talking about, and I don't want to go home." Dorothy pushed past her, out the door of her transplanted house, and into the fantasy of color beyond.

Behind her she heard Glinda say, "You will."

When a path has been set, it is very hard not to take it. That difficulty increases when the path is one that has been made just for your feet.

Or at least for the shoes your feet are wearing.

There was a path outside the door to the house that had carried Dorothy and Toto from Kansas. It was laid with bricks, bricks a rich, welcoming color, the golden yellow of buttercups. Dorothy stepped onto it, because that is what you do when there is a path right outside your door.

You do not think that it is strange that your house that has been picked up and flown elsewhere in a storm, has also been set down so perfectly in its new location that the door frame lines up exactly with the boundaries of the path. Nor do you—if your eyes are dazzled by the glint of silver on your feet, the gold of the path, the emerald of the surrounding grass—look back on the one gray splotch in the midst of this rainbow: that very house.

And because you do not look back, you do not see that your house has begun to fade. Not further into gray but into invisibility, as if it has become less present now that you are out of it. As if it no longer matters.

Nor do you see the bare feet, small enough to fit into the silver shoes that you are now wearing, attached to the legs that are crushed beneath that house.

Everything changes after a storm.

—

When twilight fell, even Technicolor Oz became gray. A textured gray, a gray with nuance and depth, but gray all the same. Perhaps because she was used to seeing in such a palette, when the colors of Oz faded with the light, Dorothy saw what the rainbow brilliance of the day had been hiding.

Oz was full of the shades of girls.

They were there, in the fields just beyond the yellow-gold path she walked on, in the fields of corn and the fields of poppies, in the forest beneath the twisted limbs of the trees. So many girls. Watching.

They looked to be about Dorothy's age. They watched her as she walked, and Toto's ears and tail drooped under the weight of their eyes. He whined, and Dorothy wanted to droop and whine as well.

She looked deeper into the gray, at the girls hanging in the air. None of the girls were wearing shoes.

When she stopped for the night, Dorothy tried to take her shoes off.

The straps had seemed to glue themselves together, and she could not unfasten them. She tried to slide the shoes from her feet, but they wouldn't move.

Dorothy hit the shoes with a stick and then with a rock. She bruised her ankle—a blossom of blue and purple—but the shoes didn't even scuff.

Oz needed a Dorothy, Glinda had said.

Dorothy needed to walk until she was East, Glinda had said. Dorothy hadn't asked, not then, who—or what—Oz was. She had just wanted to put on the shoes, to go outside, to walk into the bright and into the color, and questions would have gotten in the way of that. But she wondered now, in the watching dark, and she wished that she had asked those questions.

Dorothy did not think the other girl's name was really Glinda, not anymore. She didn't think it was Dorothy either, though she thought that maybe the other girl had been called that once, as she walked south in a pair of shoes that wouldn't come off her feet.

She thought that maybe all the girls she had seen, hanging shoeless in the shadows, had been called Dorothy, once. She wondered who—or what—had watched them, in the gray twilight, in the dark.

Dorothy patted her lap so that Toto would come and rest his head in it. She did not fall asleep until it had gotten so dark she could no longer tell his fur from the night.

—

The sunrise was brilliant, shades of lavender and orange. The air smelled like flowers, and the clean scent of hay. The path of yellow brick unrolled beneath Dorothy's feet, secure in her silver shoes.

The path had moved in the night.

Dorothy had stepped into the grass when she sat down to rest the night before. Not far—she was a sensible girl, and she didn't want to get lost, but she had wanted to sleep somewhere comfortable. She had curled up near enough to still see the curving line of yellow, and she had not moved during the night.

But with the rising of the sun, the yellow bricks were there, beneath her shoes as she stood.

Dorothy stepped off the path. Nothing happened.

She walked farther away from it, her feet getting heavier, and her steps getting smaller, until it was impossible for her to take another step. The air shimmered with purple, hung green at the edges, and in a small whirl—a tornado in miniature—the yellow bricks were in front of her again.

Oz needed a Dorothy, and seemed to have specific ideas about what it was that Dorothy needed to be doing. There was only one path for her to take, and it was the path that Oz put in front of her.

East.

Dorothy took a deep breath, stepped onto the inescapable road, and kept walking.

—

"Have you asked yet?"

Dorothy turned around to see Glinda just behind her, walking along the yellow bricks. "Asked what?"

"To go home." As if this was the obvious question, as if everyone who came here would want to leave again.

"Why are you so sure I'll ask that?"

"All the Dorothys ask to go home. It's part of the story." Glinda bent down and scratched Toto behind the ears as she walked. "Home is never here. It's always the place you want to go back to."

"Well, I don't want to leave. I like it better here." Dorothy began the words as reflex, but they were truth by the time she finished speaking them.

"You don't miss anything? Or anyone?"

"No. I hated Kansas. And Toto's here. He's the only one I would have missed."

"Not even your parents, your family?"

"My parents are dead. Aunt Em didn't like me, and Uncle Henry didn't care. I don't miss anything about that place. It's not my home. And I don't want to go back."

There were shadow shapes in the colors when the sun came up. Image after image of lions, scarecrows, and tin woodmen lined the sides of the yellow bricks that Dorothy never once tried to step too far from.

Except, when she saw them, just out of the corner of her eye, they looked like people. Like people wearing the shapes of lions and tin woodmen and scarecrows.

Most of them watched her, but one watched Toto. "You can pet him, if you want," Dorothy said.

The lion, who was sometimes a boy, put his hand out for Toto to sniff. Toto sat, and the lion scratched the dog's neck and rubbed his belly when Toto rolled over.

"How come you don't have anyone?" the lion asked.

"I have Toto."

"But Oz should have brought others with you, to be the Scarecrow, or Tin Woodman, or the Lion. I was the Lion for my sister, when she was the Dorothy."

"Then what happened?" Dorothy asked.

"Witches don't have lions. It's not part of the story. She became a witch, and I became a ghost." The lion looked very much like a boy then. He scratched Toto behind the ears. "What's your name?"

"Dorothy."

"I mean your real name."

"Dorothy."

"Maybe that will help," the lion said. He gave Toto one more scratch, then bent down and hugged the dog. "Thank you."

—

Oz needed a Dorothy, Glinda kept telling her. Dorothy was happy to be that. She just didn't understand why she needed to change. She already knew who she was.

On and on Dorothy walked, past iterations of the things Oz had needed in the past. Through a field of red flowers that shimmered before her, and then parted like the sea. Through all who had been hurled in a whirlwind to a stranger place and translated into shapes not their own. Dorothy walked through all the props in Oz's story, and still she did not ask to go home.

—

"Have you made plans to see the Wizard yet?" Glinda asked.

"Have you ever thought it might be easier to tell people the rules at the beginning?" Dorothy asked. "Or do you just like it when people get in trouble for breaking them?"

Glinda didn't answer but turned around slowly, shoes the pale pink of candy floss spun into glass, tinkling against the yellow bricks as she revolved. Her eyes narrowed. "You're still alone."

"I'm not alone. I have Toto."

"The others should be with you by now. A Scarecrow, a Tin Woodman, a Lion. Don't you understand how this works?" There was fear crouched behind the words of the question.

"No," said Dorothy, feeling as old and gray as Kansas. "No, I don't."

"You're going to get a house dropped on you before you even become a Witch," Glinda said.

"My house got dropped on someone?"

"How do you think you got those shoes you're wearing? They don't come off until you're dead.

"That's the way this works." Glinda was talking faster now. "The story has to be told the same way every time. That's what Oz wants. If something goes wrong in the story, then one of us gets replaced. Another house. Another tornado. Another Dorothy." The words came out of Glinda in a whirlwind. "Another Dorothy, and no one knows which of us it will be until the house falls."

"So I'm stuck like this until someone drops a house on me. Then I'm dead. And it's the same for everyone else here?" Dorothy said.

Glinda nodded. "For all the Dorothys. It's different for the others. It's not their story." Her face went hard then, for the space of a memory. "Houses don't get dropped on them, but they're gone anyway."

"How do I fix it?"

"You don't fix it. Oz needed a Dorothy, and it sent a tornado that picked you up and brought you here. You put the shoes on. You became the Dorothy. The story gets told whether you like it or not."

Dorothy stared at the other girl. "You're the one who gave me the shoes. You told me to put them on."

"I'm in this story, too. And I don't want a house dropped on me either."

Later Dorothy asked, "What happened to you? When you tried to go home?"

Glinda didn't say anything.

"You told me I would. You told me everyone does. So what happened when you did?"

"I left the path. I became a witch."

"You became a witch because you tried to go home?"

"No, I became a witch because I couldn't go home. And neither could anyone else. Becoming a witch was the only thing left, the only thing that meant having power. I didn't want anything I loved to get taken away from me again."

Dorothy picked up Toto, rested her chin on his head, and rubbed her cheek against his wiry fur. Witches didn't need lions, the lion whose sister had once been a Dorothy had said.

"If being a witch is the thing that gives you power, how come you haven't gone home if that's what you want? Why are you still afraid that a house is going to fall on you?"

"Because the power comes from Oz, not from us."

"Oz is the Wizard?"

Glinda shook her head. "There is no Wizard. Looking for him is just a thing you're supposed to do, to tell the story. Oz is the place. That's what brings us here."

"With the storm."

"Yes," said Glinda. "A tornado of Dorothys."

"Do you still want to go home?" asked Dorothy.

"No," said Glinda. "I just want to live."

That was what they looked like, hanging there in the gray of twilight. A tornado of Dorothys gathered like a storm about to break. All the girls who had been whirled to Oz from elsewhere, stolen to make pieces of a story, set walking on a path they had not chosen. They had been promised power, even held it for a bit. Girls who had become witches, and now were ghosts.

None of them wearing shoes.

Dorothy looked down at the silver shoes on her feet, a brilliant sparkle against the darkening sky.

Glinda said they didn't come off unless you were dead. But maybe she didn't need to take off her shoes to share them with the ghosts.

Dorothy looked at the waiting girls. "I think," she said, "these belong to you."

Their feet in her shoes were cold, and they tore through her like the wind, like a storm, this tornado of Dorothys that had once worn the silver shoes of Oz.

"Go home," she told them. "Wherever your home is, go there. The shoes will take you."

They paused in her body, ghost-feet sharing the shoes that she wore, shoes that would carry them where they needed to go. As they disappeared, Oz's other ghosts followed: scarecrows, tin woodmen, lions that were only called cowardly. One, or two, or sometimes all three. The tornado traveled though Oz this time, and the ghosts were the winds that drove it.

This, Dorothy Gale thought, this is what it was to become a witch. This is what power was, to stand still in the center of a tornado. To be the storm that brought the change.

Somewhere she had left behind, or at the back of her thoughts, a house lifted itself from the ground and flew to a home that was no longer hers—a whirlwind in reverse.

As she stood in the eye of the storm of ghosts, Dorothy heard Toto whimper beside her. She reached down and clutched him to her chest. The winds of Oz plucked and pulled at him, but she held fast, his heart beating against hers. This was not a trade or a sacrifice. This was knowing what was wanted and walking toward it on her own path.

The tornado ended.

The silver shoes were loose, and Dorothy stepped free of them.

Some of the ghost Dorothys remained. Dorothy had expected they would.

Home is always a choice.

—

The colors of Oz were still there, but they were more solid now, less perfect and more true. There was no more path of yellow brick stretched out in front of her. Still, Dorothy walked.

She walked across Oz, south, south, south, beyond where the path of yellow brick had been. Now that she no longer wore the silver shoes, Dorothy could choose her own path, could walk anywhere she needed to.

Now that she no longer wore the silver shoes, she was no longer bound inside the story Oz wanted told. Oz had needed a Dorothy—not to keep telling the story but to end it.

Poppies an impossibly bright blood-red bloomed in her footsteps.

"What did you do?" Glinda asked.

"I became a witch," said Dorothy. "I took off the shoes."

"But Oz—"

"Is just a place. Look."

Glinda looked down at the path of perfect yellow bricks that had led precisely to her door. It was broken, crumbling. She stepped out of her shoes then flung them down. They shattered—shards of pink candy floss, sparkling in the sun. She kicked the shards, stomped through them until blood poppies blossomed on her feet.

"My brother," she said, "is still gone. Oz doesn't let witches have lions."

"What Oz wants," Dorothy said, "doesn't matter anymore. This is our place now. We're home."

EMERALD
CIRCUS

BLOWN AWAY

BY JANE YOLEN

1.

That little Dorothy Gale was the sorriest child I ever saw. She wore her hair in two braids that—however tight in the morning her aunt had made them—they seemed to crawl out of their tidy fittings by noon. She had the goshdarnedest big gap between her upper front teeth and a snub nose that seemed too small for her face. And she was always squinting as if she had trouble seeing things clearly, or as if she was trying hard not to cry.

Well, I suppose she had a lot to cry about, though didn't we all in those days. Both her parents had got themselves killed in a train crash coming home from a weekend in Kansas City. Not unexpected. They'd tried balloon ascension the year before and it went down into the Kansas River, which—luckily—wasn't flooding.

They weren't exactly *on* the train; it was their car got stuck—one of the first in our part of Kansas—and it had run out of gas, because Martin Gale had been too tightfisted to buy a full tank in Manhattan. And of course his luck being what it was, they ran out just as they were at a crossing where the streamliner, the *Southern Belle,* usually passed around noon.

They were the only ones who died, because it wasn't the *Belle* at all, thank the Lord, just a freight hauler. But the two of them were dead before an ambulance could even get to them.

That meant little Dorothy, not quite eight, was sent to her aunt and uncle's farm to live out here in Middle of Nowhere, Kansas. It was a small holding with some pigs, horses, a few cows. And the chickens. Always the chickens, who were in Em's special care.

The house itself was quite small, just one room really, there having always been just the two of them—Henry and Em—so in Henry's mind there'd never been a need to build bigger. No kids, though Em had wanted them of course, but by that time she was long past bearing and worn down to a crabbed, stooped, gray, middle-aged woman.

Henry was Dorothy's blood uncle, being her father's only brother, though ten years his senior. He might as well have been fifty years older, if you judged by his looks. He was just as tightfisted, and not particularly welcoming to the little girl either, since now the one room seemed crowded, what with Henry and Em's bed at one end and little Dorothy's at the other, over by the stove.

At least Em, long-suffering as she was, tried to give the child a bit of her heart, which—after all those years of living with Henry on that old gray farm in the middle of the gray prairie—was as dried up as an old pea. She tried, but she wasn't much good at it. It was a bit like trying to water a budding flower in the middle of a dry Kansas summer with a watering can poked through with holes.

'Course the Gale brothers weren't the only misers in those years. I could name a whole bunch more right in our little town and need six extra hands to count them on, especially my mother-in-law, that old witch, who didn't even have the decency to die till she was well into her eighties, having burned through a good portion of the money that should have come to my wife and me. That money would have changed our story, I'll tell you that.

I'd trained as a carpenter once, loved working with wood, but things being so difficult those days, I never got to make much, and I sold less. Instead I spent my best years hiring out to one tightfisted farmer after another. About the time Dorothy Gale came to stay with Henry and Em, I was working there, bad luck to me.

Henry had enough money saved at that time to hire three farmhands. Though he paid a pittance, it was better than nothing. And a pitiful lot we were: me, Stan, who was a big joking presence even when there was nothing to joke about, and Rand, Stan's younger brother, who was as scared of life as he was of death, having been in a near-drowning as a boy and never gotten over it. Imagine finding somewhere in dry Kansas to drown that wasn't the Kansas River!

None of us had kids, and we felt so awful for little Dorothy, we did what we could to cheer her up.

Rand found her a puppy, the runt of an unwanted litter that Old Man Baum, who owns the farm down the road, was about to drown. Rand had an immediate fellow-feeling for that dog, as you would guess. Old Man Baum had already sold the other pups in the litter, but no one wanted this stunted rat of a dog—black, with long hair, berry-black eyes, a real yapper. Even so, young Dorothy took to it the moment she laid eyes on it.

"You done a goodly deed this day," Stan said, after Rand handed her the dog. "Even a Godly one." Stan had recently been saved in a tent meeting and couldn't stop talking about it. Joking about it, too. Called it his *Tent*ative change of life.

And that he had a *Tent*dency toward God. We just learned to ignore him.

Stan gave Dorothy a cracked bowl he'd found thrown out on the road, only about good enough to use for a dog's dinner. Just as well, as she couldn't actually feed the ratty thing from one of Em's best china now, could she? Not that Em fed anybody with that china. It was saved for some special event that never came.

I gave Dorothy a leather rope I'd braided myself, plus a collar cut down from a bridle I'd found in my mother-in-law's barn. And no, I didn't ask permission. She'd have said no anyway.

Dorothy's eyes got big. "For me? Really? For me?" It was about the longest speech I'd heard from her up to that time. We were afraid she was going to try and kiss us or something right then and there, and so we shuffled out the door to get back to our chores. But when I turned around to see how she was making out, she had her little pug nose on the dog's nose, as if they'd been stuck together by glue.

After that there wasn't a moment those two weren't in one another's pockets. She named the dog Toto, though where she came up with that, we were never to know. I thought for sure it would be something like Silky or Blackie or Fido. But Dorothy, she was always a queer kind of kid, as you will see.

2.

There were two twisters, not one as has been reported. Old Man Baum liked to tidy things up, you know. Dogs, tornadoes, you name it. He tidied. Made for a clean house, but his stories…well, take it from me, they weren't to be believed.

Of course we always get twisters around here. It's kind of an alley for them where we get mugged on a regular basis. But mostly we just hunker down in our dark little underground rooms that are dug into the unforgiving soil. Some folks like to call that kind of hole a cellar. More like a tomb for the hopeful living.

Usually the wind goes zigzagging past a farmhouse, picking up cows and plows, flinging them a county or two away, which does neither cow nor plow any good at all. But sometimes it flattens a whole house and everything in it, which is why we hide ourselves away.

That first twister young Dorothy was part of was one that had the Gale farm in its sights from the very first.

I was the only hand about that day; Stan and Rand were off at a cousin's funeral. Sorry man shot himself on account of losing his farm and land to the bank. He was never meant to be a farmer and was bad at it—and worse at keeping accounts—so no one was surprised.

There I was out in the back acres, hoeing along—*furrowing* I sometimes called it—and suddenly I felt the air pressure change. I heard a low wail of wind, and when I looked north, I could see the long prairie grass bowing in waves all the way to the horizon where the shape of a gray funnel cloud could be seen heading our way.

I dropped the hoe and ran for the house, yelling for Henry and Em and Dorothy to hightail it to the tornado cellar. It was going to be a tight squeeze, even without Stan and Rand, but the one good thing about twisters is that they don't hang around very long. Just a minute or two, though the damage may last a lifetime.

Inside the Gale farmhouse, like many of the houses hereabouts, was a trapdoor with a ladder leading down into the cellar hole. By the time I got inside, Em was already lifting the trapdoor up and climbing in. Henry was looking frantically out the window.

"Where's Dorothy?" he cried, his long beard waggling as he spoke.

Em called up, “Probably chasing that dang dog.”

Henry grunted and said something like, “You never should have let her keep that blasted animal. It’ll be the death of us all.” He not only looked like a prophet out of the Good Book, he often sounded like one.

“Well,” Em called back, “what was I to do, that poor child so broken-hearted and all?”

While Henry searched for an answer, I turned and ran out the door and around the side of the house, where I saw Dorothy laying on her belly and trying to coax the frightened Toto out from under the porch.

“He’ll be safe enough there,” I said, and because I never lie, she believed me. I held out my hand. “But unless you can crawl down there with him, and me after you, we’d better get into the cellar.”

She was reluctant to leave the dog, but she trusted me, took my hand, and we raced back inside and climbed down into the hole with hardly a moment or an inch to spare.

Well, you never can tell with a twister. They are as mean, as ornery, and as unpredictable as an unhappy woman. This one only nudged the house off its cinderblocks. We could feel the hump and bump as the house slid onto the ground. But then the wind scooped in under the porch and dragged the poor dog out of there. We could hear it yelping, a sound that got farther and farther away the longer we listened till it was overpowered by the runaway-train sounds a twister makes.

The Lord only knows how long the storm played with the little yapper, tossing him up and down, spinning him around, before finally flinging him into a coal bin some five counties away.

Henry posted a twenty-dollar reward for anyone who found the dog, which was nineteen dollars more than the animal was worth and five dollars more than Em said he should post. The woman who owned the coal bin sent a note, but she declined the reward, which was both Christian and silly of her, one and the same.

The twister had watered Toto well, and the coal bin woman had combed out his long silky hair. He was a good deal prettier than he'd been in some time. But he was also dead as could be, and no amount of weeping and snuffling and flinging guilt around that little farmhouse for days, like a baseball going around the bases in a game of pepper, was going to bring him back.

Rand had taken a course in taxidermy when he was still in high school, so he volunteered to skin, stuff, and mount little Toto for Dorothy. I was the only one who thought that a bad idea.

"More than likely scare the bejeebies out of her," I said. But to show I was a good sort, I made a little cart out of an old piece of oak I had lying about, too small for a table or anything other than a serving tray, which the wife didn't need. I sanded it down, shaped it a bit, and put on some wheels from a soapbox car I'd scavenged a while back. Then Rand mounted the dog on that.

Now, Rand hadn't done any taxidermy in years, so the dog didn't look very alive. The glass eyes were ones he took from a moth-eaten goose he'd mounted on his first try at taxidermy in high school. But Dorothy took to that stuffed dog like she'd taken to the live one and pulled it after her everywhere she went, using the plaited leash I'd made for Toto when he first came to the farm.

You squinted your eyes some, it looked like the dog was following her around. And now it didn't need much maintaining. That pleased Dorothy as much as it pleased Henry and Em.

So maybe she wasn't the only queer one in the family. After that, I kept my opinions to myself.

3.

We went on like that for three years, and the only thing to change was that Dorothy began to grow up. Grew a little prettier, too, the gap in her teeth closing so it looked more like a path than a main highway.

And then when she was thirteen, after years of near misses with twisters, the farmhouse was hit big. Other houses in the county had gotten flattened in those years, and one little town was just plain wiped off the map. People got parceled out to relatives, or they moved to the East Coast or the West, and we never saw them again after that. But for some reason, Henry and Em's place had been spared year after year.

The big hit began just like the last one, except I was cleaning out the pigpen. Rand was working on Henry's plow, which had developed a kind of hiccup between rows, as had his old plow horse, Frank. Henry and Stan were out checking on fencing, and they came roaring back, Henry shouting, "In the cellar! Everyone! It's the biggest twister I've ever seen, and it's heading right this way. I'm going to let the horses and cows out into the field."

We piled in, one on top of another, Henry coming in last.

About a minute later, Stan noticed that Dorothy wasn't with us. We found out much, much later that she'd gone under her bed to pull out that little dog on wheels. She hadn't played with it for a couple of years. Too grown up, I'd guess. But she wasn't about to have Toto taken from her again.

Well, we kept the trapdoor open for her till the wind hit, howling like a freight train running right through the center of the house. And then Henry reached up and slammed the door down.

That left Dorothy under her bed, the dog on wheels clutched in her arms. Which, under the usual circumstances, might have been just fine.

But there was nothing usual about *this* wind. It was a killer. Should have had its name on a reward poster. It was that bad.

It just lifted up the little house and carried it away. Henry had never gotten it back on the cinderblocks, but that didn't seem to matter. Off that house flew, with Dorothy in it. And we never saw the house again.

We sat cowering in the hole, in the dark. Me, I wondered about my wife and her mother and our chickens, but there was nothing we could do except sit while that wind fretted and banged and gnawed around the house.

When the noise was finally gone and Henry lifted the trapdoor, the light nearly blinded us. We were expecting to find ourselves in the house, of course.

"Lord's sake," Em whispered, as if the wind had taken her voice away, too. "There's nothing left." She was too shocked to weep.

But surprising us all, including himself, Henry began to sob, though the only word he got out, over and over and over again, was *Dorothy*. "Dorothy, Dorothy, Dorothy." Who would have guessed he loved that little child so.

They posted notices all the way to Kansas City, that being the direction the wind had been tracked. And Henry even hired a private detective to search for her. But she was as gone as if she'd never been.

In less than a week, there was a four-room house-raising that all the neighbors attended. One room was set aside for Dorothy. The neighbors brought pies and hot pots and cider. We men got that new house up and tight in a day, and I did a lot of the inside woodwork, including the bed frames. It felt good to be doing what I loved best for once, being a woodman again.

The newspaper covered the house as it went up, taking some close photographs of the hearth I made, with carvings of the little dog on wheels. I got calls from all around the state for work after that, and my wife and I set a bit of money aside. Not in the banks. We didn't trust the banks any more than Henry did, so we bought land instead. I did really well for almost a year, and then some newspaper reporter wrote that I didn't have a lot of polish, meaning—I think—I couldn't make small talk with the customers. But other people thought it was a judgment on my furniture-making, so the work dried up after that, and I was glad to get my old job back with Henry.

The five of us often sat in front of the hearth after the day's chores were done. Fire lit, cider in hand, we'd talk about where Dorothy might be now.

Em thought maybe she'd married, because she'd have been sixteen, close to seventeen. "Maybe to a lawyer," she said, "her memory all blowed away by that wind, or she would have sent us an invite. Maybe even to a doctor."

Henry shook his head. "That girl was bound to be a teacher. She read books."

Stan and Rand said, "Bank teller." Stan added, "Bank manager soon enough."

Once in a while, I would wax a bit fanciful. "Balloonist," I said once, "flying through the clouds."

Henry always laughed at my fancies, a slow laugh with little happiness in it. "I think she'd have had enough of flying through the air."

None of us said she was dead. But we all knew that was the most likely.

Em put it this way, "I hope wherever she is, she's treated well. She never did a hurtful thing to anyone."

It was as close to an epitaph as any of us wanted to go, but it was a good one.

4.

I have to say this about the predictable life: it's easier on the body, easier on the soul. We worked the seasons on the Gale farm, we drank cider and talked a bit at the end of the day. Months turned into years.

My mother-in-law went from difficult and cranky to forgetful and cranky. When she became bedridden, my wife took care of her as if she was a colicky infant, the only one we ever had.

I hoed, cleaned pigsties, walked the plow on occasion, anything Henry asked me to do I set my hand to. I rarely thought about working wood unless it was to mend fences. I mean, what was the point?

Then one afternoon in late autumn, after the chores were all done, we five were sitting watching the fire. We'd grown silent with the years and with the predictability of our lives. None of us seemed to miss the old conversations. If Dorothy was still alive, she wasn't interesting enough to talk about anymore. Or we'd run out of *what-ifs*, which is the way stories get started. In the living room, the only thing contributing to the conversation was the fire, spitting out snappy one-liners none of us tried to top.

There was a knock on the door. I wondered briefly if someone had come to tell me my mother-in-law had died, so I stood up to see. No use letting Em have to come face-to-face with that particular announcement. She'd been worn down by enough bad news in her life. I wasn't going to let her be bothered by mine.

As I walked out of the room, for the first time in months the others all began to speculate. Their ideas followed me into the hallway. *Police? Twister? Telegram? Doctor's assistant?*

When I opened the door, standing there was a tall, pretty young woman, her hair in a short bob. Unlike the local farm girls, she wore careful makeup on her face. It enhanced her odd beauty. The women in Kansas City, the two or three times I'd been there, used makeup as a weapon or as a disguise.

She smiled at me with strong, evenly spaced teeth. If she hadn't been carrying the little dog on wheels, along with a satchel, I wouldn't have known her.

"Dorothy!" I cried out, my voice carrying back into the living room, where suddenly everything went silent—even the fire.

"Come on in," I said, as if this was an everyday visit, as if it was my house to invite her into.

She entered, looking around in wonder. "Golly!" is all she said.

It took me a minute to remember that this wasn't the old farmhouse she recalled. "The neighbors all helped to build it after…after…" I hesitated.

"After I was blown away." So she *had* remembered. I wondered why it'd taken her so long to get in touch. I mean it had been seven years after all.

Before I could ask, the hallway was as crowded as the cellar hole had once been. Everyone was touching Dorothy—her hair, her shoulders, her hands—saying her name in soft wonder.

I pulled back, not trusting this part of the story. Could such a glamorous creature really be our Dorothy? And why had she returned, why now?

They drew her into the living room, where the fire had resumed its one-sided conversation, only this time everyone ignored its snap.

"Where have you been, Dorothy?" Rand was the only one innocent enough to just come right out and say it. "All this time?"

Her next words surprised us. "Why, in the Emerald Circus. The performers heard a huge crash near their Missouri campsite and found me under a tree, pieces of wood scattered all around. My memory was as shattered as the farmhouse. All my clothes blown away but my shoes. The little people got to me first."

I refused to dignify her story with questions, but no one else had the same reaction.

"Little people?" asked Em.

"Dwarfs, used to be miners in Munich. Though they don't like to be called so," Dorothy said. "Just Little People."

"Oh," said Em, "the clowns who run around through the audience. I've seen them. You did, too, Dorothy," she said. "We went to the circus once. Together."

Dorothy got an odd look on her face. "I don't remember." It turned out to be something she was to say many times over the next weeks.

If Dorothy was to be believed, her life in the circus over seven years had been like a dream. Little people. A freak show full of oddities. Wire walkers. A lion that jumped through hoops. Dancing dogs. Bareback riders. Even an elephant.

"And yet," she added quickly, "all just people. Like you, like me." Then she laughed softly. "The dogs, the horse, the lions, the elephant—not them of course."

Well, of course circus folk are just people, I thought, *only* not *like us at all.* Though I didn't say it out loud.

Dorothy had become part of the show, dressing in tights, a fitted bodice, and silver shoes.

"Tights! Land sakes!" Em said, her hand on her heart as if she was going to faint.

Dorothy even got to wear a blond wig.

"Think of that!" Henry put in.

Her toenails were painted gold.

"Real gold?" asked Rand.

"Don't be stupid," Stan said, pounding a fist into his brother's shoulder.

At first Dorothy had just walked around the ring, smiling at the folks in the audience, turning and turning like a whirligig. But all the while, when it wasn't show time, she practiced wire-walking with the Italian acrobats, the Antonioni Family, until she was good enough to become part of their act. They even wanted her to marry their son, Little Tony, and carry on the family tradition.

"But I told them I was too young, and besides, I wasn't the marrying kind." She smiled at Uncle Henry. "I knew that one day I would remember where I came from and want to go back there." She opened her arms and turned around and around, like she was still performing. "And here I am."

"Here you are," Henry said, grinning.

But I wondered if it was true.

All of it.

Any of it.

Dorothy stayed, taking her turn at the house chores, gathering eggs, making lunches, cooking soups, plucking chickens. The usual. She seemed content.

But then, about a month later, she convinced Stan to get a bunch of strands of strong wire, which she braided together. Then he stretched the wire from one part of the pigsty fence all the way across to the other, nailing it down hard on each end.

We watched as she climbed onto the fence, wearing overalls and a silver shirt. Those little silver dancing slippers on her feet.

The piglets looked up at her and squealed, but the sow seemed unconcerned.

I was probably the only who thought we were going to be picking her out of the pigpen, covered with mud.

She started off cautiously, one small slippered foot after another, testing the tightness of the wire. But after about three steps, she walked as if going along a wide asphalt road. Even stopped in the middle to turn like a whirligig, arms wide open, before lifting one leg high in the air behind her.

"Arabesque," she said, as if that was an explanation.

When she reached the other side of the pen, we all broke into applause.

So the wire-walking at least was true. I told my wife Amelia about it and she insisted on coming over to watch the next time Dorothy did it, which was every Saturday after that. Amelia watched Dorothy on the wire with an intensity she'd never shown for anything else. Then she turned to me and said it was a homey piece of magic and she wanted to learn it. I put my foot down. Something I rarely ever do. I didn't fancy her falling in the mud. It would have been me having to clean her up. Somehow, at our ages, I didn't like the sound of that.

5.

About three months after that, I was coming back for lunch where I'd been fixing fences—the prairie wind just devils the wires. I was heading to the cabbage field to give the cabbages a good soaking. Suddenly I noticed a figure standing at the farmhouse door just fixing to knock. I could only see her from the back, but she looked to be a blond-haired, shapely woman. In fact her hair wasn't just blond but an ashy white-blond, a color you don't see on a grown woman unless she spends a lot of time at the hair-dresser's.

"Pardon me, miss," I called, wondering who it might be, guessing she was there to visit Dorothy.

She turned and I got the shock of my life, because she was sporting a beard. Not just a few face hairs like some women get in later life—my mother-in-law has them sprouting from her chin and from a mole on her cheek. But a full beard, kind of reddish color, the bottom half of which was tied off with a pink bow.

A bearded lady, by golly, I thought. *Freak show standard.* I'd always figured they were just regular women in makeup. Or a womanish man dressed in female clothes. This one had the bluest eyes I'd ever seen—an eerie color really.

"Are you looking for Dorothy?" I asked, to cover my embarrassment.

"Dottie, yes, is she here? It's where I dropped her off some months ago," the bearded lady said. "She hasn't written since."

"She does that," I said nodding. "We didn't hear from her for seven years."

"Well, it took her all that time to remember," she told me.

I thought that made for a convenient memory but said nothing.

She held out her hand. "Ozmandia," she said.

"Circus name? Last name?"

She smiled, her teeth pearly above the beard. "Actually, Shirley Osmond, so you're kind of right either way."

The door opened and Em looked out. It took her a moment to put it all together. Then her hand went to her heart. "My word."

"I'm a friend of Dottie's," Ozmandia said, but even as she said it, Dorothy pushed past Em and threw herself into the bearded lady's arms.

"Ozzy!" she cried. "I've missed you so."

"Little bird," the bearded lady said and kissed Dorothy full on the lips, the way a man might do. Then she drew back and looked at Dorothy critically. "You've gained some weight. It might make you too heavy for the wire, but it suits you."

"I've been practicing."

"She has," said Em. "And performing."

"Then no potatoes," Ozmandia said. "No bread. No starch."

"What's starch?" Em asked. The only starch she knew was what she ironed with.

"I'll make a list," Ozmandia told her.

She turned to Dorothy. "We're starting again next month. Barnum and Bailey have bought the old man out."

"No more Mr. Wizard?" Dorothy said. "But it's *his* circus."

"He's retiring to Florida," said Ozmandia. "For what they paid him, he can afford it. Him and that elephant."

"Will you stay awhile?" Dorothy said, speaking to her circus friend as if the rest of us hardly mattered. And indeed, probably we didn't.

"Just tonight, Baby Bird," Ozmandia said. "I'm getting around to everyone."

"But I'm special," Dorothy said.

"You always were, falling out of the sky that way." She turned to Em. "I assume, madam, that it is all right for me to stay the one night? I can sleep in Dottie's bed with her. It's an old circus custom."

I bet it is, I thought, but didn't say it aloud.

She stayed two nights, and no one spoke about it until long after. That first evening, being a Saturday, Dorothy did her wire walk over the pigsty. Ozmandia played a flute as Dorothy performed, and though you probably won't believe it, the sow and piglets got up on their hind trotters and danced.

Amelia was there as usual, of course, and she and Ozmandia became instant pals, both of them enthusing over Dorothy's talents.

When we walked home, I tried to hold Amelia's hand, feeling a sudden tenderness toward her I hadn't felt in years, but she pulled her hand away.

"I can't," she said. "I just can't any more."

Amelia's mother died that very night, with such a peaceful smile on her face she hardly looked like the same woman. Only Henry and Em, Stan and Rand, and Dorothy came to the funeral.

Ozmandia sent a message the next month, and Dorothy packed up her carpetbag, ready to leave the next morning. Stan was driving her by cart into the city—she was taking a steam engine train from there.

Em watched her go dry-eyed, but Henry was sobbing enough for the two of them. Stan and Rand were open-mouthed, breathing hard.

I was there as well, watching Amelia go with her.

"Tom," she'd told me last night, "I have never done anything for myself before. First there was Mother, and then there was you. I've taken the housekeeping money. I've been saving some for months. Sell Mother's house for me, and you keep half. Start that woodworking business for real this time. It's the only thing you've ever really loved. I'll write and tell you where to send my portion when I know."

"Are you going to be a wire walker?" I asked.

"I'll take tickets, sell popcorn, clean out the lion's cage. I'll do anything they need, wear many hats, many heads. After all," she said, "I'm well practiced in that sort of thing."

And maybe she was, after all.

"Perhaps eventually they'll let me try the wire." She smiled. "Even though I'm probably too old."

"Never too old," I said, remembering her on our wedding day.

"Tom, you never could tell a lie," she said. "Don't start now."

The cart pulled away and rolled down the dusty road, making it look for a minute like little imps were running behind. If you start thinking that way about the world once, it seems to go on and on.

I watched till the cart with my wife in it was out of sight. When I turned back, Henry was still standing there, the little dog on wheels cradled in his arms. I guess Dorothy didn't need it anymore.

I guess Henry did.

CITY SO BRIGHT

BY DALE BAILEY

So Joe fell the other day.

One minute he's hanging on the wall, maybe twenty feet away from me, and we're shouting back and forth, razzing each other the way you do—polish polish polish, till your arms feel so numb they could fall off and you wouldn't even notice and just razzing each other: *your wife is so heinous you get a mouthful of fur when you give her a hickey,* and *your mom is so fat she gets mistaken for a dirigible.* The kind of thing you do, and nobody's feelings get hurt. My wife says guys do this because they're so emotionally stunted that they can't express their real feelings. But I know this to be bullshit of the most preposterous variety, because when Joe fell I cried like a baby, and that's not emotionally stunted if you know what I mean.

But I've always been a little bit on the sensitive side, even for a Munchkin.

So here's what happens. We're on the wall, maybe seventy feet up, razzing each other, when two of Joe's lines snap. Not one but two, is what I'm saying. His bucket goes clattering down the side of the wall, spraying polish everywhere—it smells like an ammonia bomb has exploded—and his platform swings down on one side, hanging vertically. His safety harness engages, and he's suddenly dangling below the platform, still holding on to his rag. He's just kind of swinging there, this panicky expression on his face, and I say in this very calming voice, the kind of voice you use with your kids when they scrape a knee or something, I say, "Everything's cool, hang tight," you know what I mean, only not thinking till later that *hang tight* is not the best thing I could have said under these particular circumstances. But still, the safety harness is engaged, and the guys up top are going to winch him up—that's the way it always happens—and we'll all go out for a cold one somewhere after our shift. We'll clap Joe on the back and say things like *You looked pretty scared up there, pal* and *Did you shit your britches or what? I can fucking smell you, man,* and we'll have a few laughs, and then we'll go home to do it all over again, another day on the wall, polish polish polish. That's the way it always goes down, no pun intended. I wouldn't disrespect Joe's memory that way, not for all the world with a cherry on top.

Not even for the Wizard's head on a spike, which is something I shouldn't have written, but hell, sometimes you have to tell the truth or you can't look at yourself in the mirror the next morning.

Then this next thing happens, which is Joe's safety harness snaps, and down he goes like the bucket, bouncing off the wall, which has this gentle slope to it. *Thump thump thumpity-thump crunch kersplat*—this meaty sound like a squadron of monkeys has just dropped a side of beef from a hundred feet up just to see what will happen. Fucking monkeys. Anyway, that's what I remember most is that sound, *crunch kersplat,* blood and bones, you know, blood and fucking bones. Looking down, it's like a kid has dropped a jar of strawberry jelly. Joe's just exploded like a meat bag full of blood, and what I'm thinking is, some poor son of a bitch is going to have to scrape him off the pavement, and some other poor son of a bitch is going to have to wipe down the wall and polish polish polish till it's like it never happened. I'm hoping it's not me, too, which makes me feel kind of guilty, because even though he's a Winkie, Joe's my best friend, you know.

That's what got us thinking—me, Dizzy, and Hops. We go out for a cold one, this little hole-in-the-wall in the tunnels, Frankie's, where we go sometimes after a shift. There are two overlapping shifts, fourteen hours each, six and a half days a week with half a day Sunday, which you're supposed to spend with your wife and kids tossing the old Frisbee around and grilling burgers, but you can't ever do that because you're just so fucking tired—you know what I mean. You're just so *tired.* Calixta always complains about it, prodding me with her foot and saying *Get up lazy bones. Don't you wanna see your kids?* And I do, but I'm just so tired. My arms feel like they're not connected to the rest of me, my hands are clenched into these hooks or claws. It takes me all afternoon and evening to work them back into hands again, and I'm supposed to throw a Frisbee? Besides, where we gonna throw it? You can't do it in the tunnels, with all these sad little holes-in-the-walls that we rent as "apartments," if you know what I'm saying, these one-room little dens with a couple of stinking straw pallets, all infested with lice and bedbugs, one for Calixta and me and one for the kids. We usually end up screwing Sunday night once my hands uncramp, but there's no real pleasure in it. All the time I'm worried about my snot-nosed little apes—are they awake or are they asleep, and what kind of psychological damage is it doing to them to watch their parents humping away on that stinking mess of straw.

But I appreciate it, because Calixta is bone-tired, too. She works in the Wizard's kitchens, buried deep underground like these fucking sewer tunnels where we live, and her hands are always blistered and burned from taking bread out of the ovens or stirring the stew, with the chef riding her ass all day long like she's his own personal horse and he's in a hurry. But there she goes riding me or hunkering over on all fours so I can take her from behind, because she knows a man's got needs, and she's a good wife. I couldn't have done better, even if she's running to fat these days, and her hair is always limp and draggled and kind of greasy from the hairnet she wears all day at the office. Get that? That's a joke. Office, like a sweltering kitchen where you raise blisters on your hands four or five times a day is a fucking office. The only advantage to the office is that she can pinch the leftovers now and then, so we eat better than your average Munchkin.

But I guess I've got sidetracked. Calixta does that to me. What I was trying to say is that me, Dizzy, and Hops stop in at Frankie's the day Joe goes tumbling down the wall, and we get to talking. And here's the thing: people *do not* fall off the wall. Oh, they injure their backs, and the work makes you old so quick that nobody lasts, and you have to go find easier work, which there is none, so you take to begging—but never on the streets, not unless you want to be arrested by the City guard, in their red-breasted uniforms, and beaten or pummeled with fire hoses for your trouble. A lot of guys, they get arrested, and you never see them again. And their wives take to the streets, if you get what I'm saying—but never up top—and their children take to stealing so bad that you practically have to nail down the little bit of stuff you've managed to pull together or it's like to just up and disappear. What I'm saying is there are two cities, one right on top of the other: the Emerald City above, all shining and clean and green with its immaculate polished walls and not a speck of litter on the grass, where everything is fresh and aromatic, and the city below, which I've pretty much described to you, where the smell of sewage hangs in the air so thick that it's almost a pleasure to go to work, and the flies swarm so bad sometimes you can't even see.

But there I go getting distracted again. Writing is not my thing, if you understand, and the only reason I can do it at all is that my mother was a schoolteacher in the days before the Wizard came, and she worked hard to learn me my letters even after he did. I remember working late hours into the night on my letters—this after my mom put in fourteen-hour shifts as a seamstress in the Wizard's sweatshops, sewing up this rich apparel for state dinners and whatever. Anyway, what I was saying is that me and Dizzy and Hops went to Frankie's after work that day. Dizzy is called Dizzy because he used to be a Winged Monkey until they chopped his wings off and sent him below for shitting on the sidewalk upstairs, which he couldn't help because he had dysentery, or that's what he says. But when they cut off his wings they threw off his balance, and he's been dizzy ever since. Most folks won't serve his kind, but Frankie's liberal on the issue, unless the joint is hopping. Which brings me to Hops. Hops is called Hops because that's what his mother named him—he's a Munchkin like me—but he lives up to it because he can put down prodigious quantities of the cold stuff without ever acting drunk or getting hungover in the morning.

And Dizzy—you can see these awful red stumps where his wings used to be, but otherwise he just looks like a Monkey—Dizzy leans close and whispers about two rounds in, "Funny thing about old Joe today."

So we all toast the memory of Joe, and we talk about how his widow is doing, and his three kids, but that's all just make-talk, I've already told you what's going to happen to them.

Then Hops—who's so dim we ought to call him Dim—says right out loud, "What's so funny about Joe?" Because he don't see anything funny about it at all.

"Not funny, ha-ha," Dizzy says. "Funny strange."

And it *was* funny strange. The supervisors don't give a shit, I'll grant you that, but the winch men are working stiffs like us—Winkies and Munchkins mainly, but mainly Winkies—and they *do* care because we're all in this together. So every morning before you go over the wall, the winch men, they check over your equipment real good, and then, because it's your life on the line, you double-check it twice as good. Are the boards of your platform level and solid? Are they secured tightly to your ropes, and are your ropes unfrayed? Are your pulleys secure, solid, and untangled? Is your safety harness tight, safe, and in good condition? And let me be clear: your safety harness is always in good condition or you don't go over the wall to polish the emerald. Period. So your equipment is checked and double-checked before you ever go over the wall.

"What do you mean?" Hops says, again too loud, and right now I'm wishing I'd gone straight home to Calixta. But what's a man to do when he loses his best friend, right? You want a drink and you want to commiserate with men—or Munchkins and Monkeys, more accurately—who know the job the way you do, with all its attendant dangers. What you don't want to do is get into some unsavory details that might send *you* plunging over the wall, and sooner rather than later.

But Hops is too dim ever to unpack all that luggage. So he says it again, even louder this time, "What's funny about old Joe? It was just an accident, wasn't it?"

Dizzy shushes him, and once again, whispering even lower, "Funny strange, is all I'm saying."

And Hops, in a stage whisper you can hear all over the bar, "Funny strange, how?"

And me, I'm wishing the old Witches were still alive. Don't believe any of that shit about them being wicked, that's just propaganda—only Glinda had any drawbacks, and even she was all right before she became the Wizard's main squeeze. But I was saying: right then I'm wishing the old Witches were still alive and one of them would conjure me right out of Frankie's and into my pile of straw with Calixta warm beside me.

I drop some change on the table and stand. "Well, that's all for me, boys. Have a good night."

But Dizzy's hand closes around my forearm and yanks me back into my seat. "Sit down," he says, and I do, slowly, trying not to make a scene. Monkeys—even crippled monkeys—are strong as shit.

"Look here," he whispers. "Joe didn't die in no accident, and you know it."

"Accident," Hops says. "'Course it was an accident."

And this time, Dizzy hauls off and lays him one right across the smacker.

Hops collapses back into his seat, his eyes stinging with tears. You can already see the bruise coming up on his cheek. "What was that for?"

"For not shutting the fuck up and listening. Okay?" And then, leveling one hairy finger at me, he says, "It wasn't no accident, and you know it."

"Me?"

"You. For instance, you got four lines on a platform, right?"

"Yeah," I said all innocent, but I knew where he was going all right.

"So you ever see two lines fail at once?"

"Well..."

"Hey, what are you saying?" Hops says. He was slow on the uptake, but he wasn't that slow.

"What I'm saying is that Joe's accident wasn't no accident," the Monkey says. "You follow?"

"And then the safety harness failed, too." I'd already worked all this out in my head, of course, but Dizzy had drawn me in. And looking back on it, I think he *was* dizzy, dizzy-stupid for bringing it up, double dizzy-stupid for bringing it up in front of Hops, who had reached the conclusion in his dim, fumbling way that maybe he ought to be a little quieter, too. And the whole thing would have consequences for all of us, but I don't want to get ahead of myself.

"But why?" Hops whispered.

"He was talking about organizing," Dizzy said. "He talked to you, didn't he?"

I sat there unmoving, like one of those statues of the Wizard he's put up of himself all over the City. I could have been made of marble. I wish I had been. Maybe things would have turned out different then. But probably not. Probably they'd had their eye on Joe from the start. He was too smart for his own good, and I'd bet they already had a pretty good idea of who he'd been talking too, as well: the monkey, and me, and Hops among them, Hops being an example of Joe being too smart for his own good, if you take my meaning. Who in the hell would confide something like that to Hops in the first place, even if he is muscled like a Monkey and might be useful come crunch time? And I was a little surprised that Dizzy—who was smarter even than Joe, even if he was just a Monkey—had brought it up in front of him, too. But Dizzy wasn't done yet, and it turns out I hadn't sussed out where he was going after all. But now he got there. "Well?" he says.

"He might have mentioned something," I allowed. "But that was just Joe. He was always a bullshitter, old Joe."

And just saying the words, just saying his name like that, I got all teary-eyed, and I had to swipe at them with the back of one hand. "Stinks in here," I said, and it did—it reeked of cheap beer and cheaper gin and the even cheaper tapers Frankie used to light the place. I swear the things smoked more than the coal mines up north, where most of the Munchkins had been shipped. We're little folk, you know, and I'd been luckier than some—Hops and I both—in getting assigned to polish the walls instead. Something had to fuel what the Wizard had taken to calling the Industrial Revolution, after all, and somebody had to mine the coal. So I'm swiping at my eyes like I'm about to burst into tears, and nobody's fooled.

Even Hops looks away, embarrassed.

"He say something to you?" Dizzy asked Hops. He's still clutching my forearm so hard that I'll have the bruises for days. I'm not going anywhere.

And Hops gets this sly look in his stupid little eyes, and I wonder why I ever made friends with him in the first place. Probably just glad to see another Munchkin among all the Winkies, but still, a man has to draw the line somewhere, and I could see now that I'd drawn it in the wrong place.

"Organizing is sedition," Hops says, and I find myself wondering if he even knows what the words mean. But one thing is sure, he's heard the phrase a thousand times—there are dozens of them, and we've *all* heard them a thousand times, these memorable little nuggets that are designed to keep all the people in Oz—who had once been free—thoroughly in line. Though I guess we're still free, technically. There's nothing to keep us from walking away from our jobs. It's just there's nowhere else to go. But I'm getting sidetracked again.

What happens is that sly look comes into Hops' squinchy little eyes, and he says, "Organization is sedition."

"Exactly," Dizzy says, and now he releases me. "So we gotta keep quiet about this unless we want to have an accident, too."

I'm rubbing my forearm as he says this last bit, and I'm thinking he's right and how wrong that is—how wrong it is that we should be trapped like this, scattered from our native lands, "employed," and worked down to the bone. I'll even say the real truth here between you and me—enslaved. How wrong it is that we should be enslaved like this, while the real people—that's the words the Wizard uses for the humans, "real people"—walk around free in the City above the City and farm our lands and scare off all the talking animals into the Haunted Forest (a place you *do not* want to go)—the ones they didn't beat into submission and silence, that is. You see them sometimes, the intelligent animals, beaten like brutes, the knowing and the bitterness shining in their bright eyes.

That girl from another place you hear about, the one who dropped a house on the Good Witch of the East, supposedly exposed the Great and Powerful Oz as a fraud. But he's no fraud. He *is* great and powerful, and he's used guns and bombs—he turned some of the Winged Monkeys to his cause early on, even if they aren't all bad, like old Dizzy here—to conquer Oz, to claim its name as his own, and bit by bit drive out all the magic in the land. But they say something else about her as well: that she really believes he *is* a powerless old man, that she's just a child, a perfect innocent, a rube. And that's important here. But I'm getting ahead of myself again.

For now, back in the bar, me rubbing my forearm like the damn Monkey had about half torn it off, Dizzy goes, "We gotta forget it ever happened. You understand me. You understand me, Hops? Not a word, okay. Not a word to anyone."

And Hops nodded his stupid nod, like he was down with that. But that sly look was still shining in his eyes, and I thought that Dizzy, too, was too smart for his own good, and that he might come to regret that smack across the face he'd given the Munchkin. Hops's cheek was turning a deep purplish blue, and I remember thinking, *These damn Monkeys don't know their own strength and sometimes it comes back to bite them.*

I was still thinking that when I headed home, and that night when Calixta and I blew out the last of the tapers and the kids had fallen asleep, I told her the whole thing: about Joe's fall and Dizzy's sermon in the bar and the way he smacked Hops, turning his face all blue and purple as a storm hoving up on the far horizon. She cried a little, and I held her close until the tears stopped, and then we had slow sex in the darkness, and when I cried out and broke inside her, it was a sweet and sensuous thing.

After that, nothing much happened for a while, except they moved Dizzy next to me in the polishing line, and we hung down the wall side by side. We didn't razz each other or even talk much. It was like that day in Frankie's had marked the end of our friendship, or at least its outward expression. Like it was too dangerous to be seen being chummy. The few times we did talk it was in hurried asides, just to wonder aloud—and barely aloud—why we'd been put on the wall side by side like that, and was someone watching us or listening.

We didn't see much of Hops. They'd moved him way down the line, and when I did run into him, he didn't have much to say either. He still had that bruise—it took a month to fade, from black to blue to a yellowish sallow color—and he still had that sly secret look in his eyes, like he knew something I didn't, and more than ever I regretted going to the bar with him that day, or even being friends with him in the first place, but a man—a Munchkin—has to have someone to confide in and like calls out to like, as they say. I'd never really hit it off with any Winkies besides Joe. My remaining friends were misfits, living oxymorons (and in Hops' case, just a moron), a Winged Monkey without his wings and a brute of a Munchkin.

And then I had no friends at all, except that I continued to nurse a place in my heart for Dizzy, even if he was too smart for his own good, because what's a Winged Monkey without his wings? Calixta always said I had a soft spot for losers and ne'er-do-wells and that someday it would do me in, but you know how it is with wives, they talk and talk and talk and you don't listen and you don't listen and you don't listen, and by the time you figure out they were right all along it's too late. After all, I was consorting with a known criminal—a Monkey who'd lost his wings—and an idiot, what did I expect? But like I said, like calls out to like, so maybe I'm a misfit myself, or even a criminal. But that's getting ahead of the story again.

What happened next is they made an example of Dizzy. Like cutting off his wings hadn't been enough. They hung a sign around his neck—ORGANIZATION IS SEDITION, it read—and hung old Dizzy himself from the top of the wall, where we could see him while we worked. They didn't hang him the good way either, where they break your neck with the drop. No, they let him strangle slowly, his hands grasping and pulling at the rope for a single extra breath, and when his strength finally ran out, they let him hang some more, till the birds pecked out his eyes and stripped the flesh from his bones.

Meanwhile, Hops' bruise slowly faded, but I had a sneaking suspicion that the humiliation of it had never faded from his heart, for that sly knowing look hadn't faded from his eyes, and now that Dizzy was gone, I felt it turn ever more certainly on me. And this time Calixta talked and talked and talked, and this time, because every day I got to see old Dizzy hanging there from the wall, I listened.

It was time to get out.

I'm smart too, you see, but I'm not too smart for my own good. That's what I like to think anyway. So I made a plan, and part of the plan is what I've written here. Tonight me and Calixta and the kids, we're vacating this shithole forever. We're going to cross the fields of poppy and take our chances in the Haunted Forest. We don't care that the talking animals are angry and capable of just about anything, and we don't care what they say about the trees. We're going to make a home there, close by the road of yellow brick. They say this girl, this Dorothy, comes back to Oz upon occasion and takes the road of yellow brick up to the Emerald City. And what I'm going to do is, I'm going to give her this letter—and hope, because if the rumors and legends are right, she managed to kill the Good Witch of the East and the Good Witch of the West all on her own. She must be a sorceress of great power to have done the deeds that are attributed to her. And I'm hoping something else as well: that she really *was* an innocent, a rube, and that when she realizes what she's done, she'll set things to right.

"Dorothy," I will say, "the Emerald City is built upon the backs of millions."

"Dorothy," I will say, "the Munchkins no longer have a song in their hearts."

"Dorothy," I will say, "help us."

Help us.

OFF TO SEE THE EMPEROR

BY ORSON SCOTT CARD

A four-room school in Aberdeen, Dakota Territory, September 1889

The teacher introduced six-year-old Frank Joslyn Baum as one of the new first-graders. "Young Frank's father is Mr. L. Frank Baum, editor of our town's newspaper. Does anyone know the name of the newspaper?"

One hand went up—that of a nine-year-old girl. Frank noticed that the bands of fabric around the bottom of her dress were darker, the colors deeper. The dress must always have been too big for the girl, but over the years during which she wore it, the hem had been let down three times, exposing fabric less faded by the sun. Frank liked to notice things like that and figure out what they meant.

The teacher seemed reluctant to call on the girl. "Why don't you tell us the name of your father's paper?" the teacher asked him.

"*She* knows," said Frank, pointing at the girl, who was now sitting with both hands tucked under her bottom.

"Do you think she does?" asked the teacher with an air of condescension. "Dotty, what were you raising your hand to say?"

Dotty looked straight at Frank. "Your father's store went bust," she said. "He owned Baum's Bazaar."

Frank blushed. It was shameful that the store went out of business; no one spoke of it.

"I fail to see what that has to do with the name of the newspaper," said the teacher. Then, in a voice loud enough for all to hear, she said to Frank, "Now you know why I rarely choose to call on Dotty."

"It was a *wonderful* store," said Dotty. "Your father gave Auntie Bess credit, and it got us through the winter."

"That is enough, Dotty," said the teacher.

Auntie Bess. Frank knew Bess Krassner was one of the customers whose failure to pay had led to the bankruptcy. Frank didn't miss much. Mrs. Krassner was a stern woman who frightened most children with her cold glare, but Frank was not afraid of her. He could look right at her even when she glared.

"The newspaper is the *Aberdeen Saturday Pioneer*," said Dotty, "and Mr. Baum writes the column 'Our Landlady.'"

Then Dotty sat down.

Frank read his father's column every week, every word. He should not be in first grade, but the teacher would not hear of advancing him. "Children learn raggedly unless they have guidance," she had said. "Whatever he thinks he has learned on his own will almost certainly have to be taught to him again, but now in its proper order."

When Mother told this to Father, he laughed. "I'm sure our poor boy has his letters all inside out. She'll set him straight."

At first Frank wanted to tell his father that he did not have *any* letters inside out, but then he realized that Father was joking. Father always made everything either funny or very dramatic. Father was an actor at heart. He used to own a theater but it burned down. Father had written plays. Mother often said that a man like that had no business running a store. Frank heard everything. He remembered everything.

After school, instead of walking straight home, he went up to the older girl, Dotty. "Why do you care about my father?"

"I don't," said Dotty. "And I don't care about you."

"Why did you say that about him giving credit? Your aunt never paid him back."

"She will," said Dotty. "She is a woman of integrity." She turned her back on him and started walking along the dusty road, the opposite direction from Frank's way home. He followed behind her.

"It's too late to pay him now," said Frank. "The store's already out of business."

"It is never too late to pay a debt," said Dotty.

"It's too late for it to do any good," said Frank.

She turned to face him. "Do you want me to poke you in the nose?"

"Why did you tell about your family needing credit to get through the winter?"

"One must never be ashamed of poverty, my Auntie Bess says. One must only be ashamed of wealth that one does not share with those in need. Your father shared. Auntie Bess says that makes him a good man, even if he does hate Indians."

"Everybody hates Indians," said Frank. "They scalp people and they're savages."

"It's also good for children to have minds of their own, and not to echo the opinions of adults."

"Your aunt says."

"I am wise enough to pay close attention to my aunt."

"So you echo her opinions," said Frank.

Dotty glared at him, but it was not as icy a glare as Bess Krassner's. "I have independently reached the conclusion that my aunt is right."

"About everything?" asked Frank.

"So far," said Dotty.

"Why are you bothering to talk to a six-year-old?" asked Frank. "The other fourth-graders don't talk to us younger children."

"One must be especially kind to the little and stupid," said Dotty, "or they will not get wiser along with bigger."

"Auntie Bess again?" asked Frank.

"No," said Dotty. "It was one of my own. Here's why I'm talking to you. First, your father is a good man, so I owe courtesy to his son. Second, you can already read and write as well as a fourth-grader, but you don't make a show of it. Third, you followed me and won't shut up."

She stepped out of the lane and into the brown scruffy grass beside it.

"Where are you going?" asked Frank.

"I'm following the road," said Dotty. She continued walking farther into the grass, heading for a cornfield.

"No you're not," said Frank. "It goes that way."

"*That* road goes that way," said Dotty. "Feel free to follow *that* road, if you want."

"What road are you following, then?"

"I always follow the yellow road," said Dotty. She walked on resolutely.

Frank followed her. "Where is it?"

"I admit that even I can hardly see it here," said Dotty. "There's only a brick or two visible, and then only when the light is right. But by now I know this part of the road by heart."

"What bricks?"

"The light isn't right," said Dotty. "But there's one right there, in the morning, on a clear day."

Frank looked where she was pointing. "I don't see anything."

"Because you are not sufficiently observant."

"I'm *very* observant," said Frank hotly. "Father says so."

"And yet you are not observant enough." Dotty broke into a run.

"Dotty!" Frank called. "I can't run as fast as you."

"I'm counting on that," she called back.

He ran as fast as he could and caught up with her by the scarecrow in the middle of the field, its pants and a shirt and a hat stuck on a pole, with straw stuffed in the clothes. Crows sat on its shoulders. It was clearly not very effective. Dotty was conversing with it.

"If he can follow me, then he can come," Dotty said.

The scarecrow said nothing, but Dotty answered him as if he had spoken. "See? Here he is. Nobody else has been able to follow me this far."

Again, silence from the scarecrow.

"Of course he can't hear you," said Dotty. "He hasn't yet been noticed by the Emperor."

Silence.

"I have so, or I could never have found you and talked to you in the first place. So I'm going on, and as long as he can follow me, I'm taking him with me."

Again she seemed to listen, until she grew quite impatient and held out a hand toward Frank. "Hold my hand," she said. "I'm taking you with me no matter what he says."

"Taking me where?"

"To see the Emperor of the Air," she said.

"Where does he live?"

"In. The. Air," she said.

"We're on the ground," Frank pointed out. But he made his legs trot along fast enough to keep up with her, despite her long-legged strides farther through the corn. "Are there more yellow bricks now?"

"Yes, there are," said Dotty, "and I don't mind that you can't see them. Everybody knows I'm crazy, which is why they call me 'dotty' even though my name is Theodora."

"I'll call you Theodora if you want," said Frank.

"Just keep up," she said. "You're doing very well so far, but we have a long way to go before dark. I brought an oil-can, you see." She reached into her lunch bag and held it up.

This made no sense to Frank, but it was an adventure, and she was a big kid who admired Father, and he was sure that eventually the small oilcan she brandished would make some kind of sense.

"Be careful now," she said. "We're coming into the trees. And don't let go of my hand. I don't want to lose you half-way between."

There were no trees at all. Not any.

"Stop looking with the fronts of your eyes," said Dotty—no, Theodora. "Stop looking at what everybody sees. This is a magical land if you're willing to see it."

"Says Auntie Bess?"

"She can't see anything," said Theodora. "Or I should say, she refuses to come and refuses to hear me talk about the Empire of the Air, so there's no chance that she'll ever see it. But here you are."

"It's a cornfield," said Frank.

"But you're still with me," said Theodora. "You can still see me. And I'm well inside the Empire." She stamped her foot. "Yellow bricks all over now."

Frank looked at the ground, trying to see anything but dry dirt between the rows of corn.

"Don't try so hard," said Theodora. "Squinting doesn't work. When your eyes are pointing *here*, then the bricks start being visible *there*. And when you look there, you can see them here. At least that's how it is at first."

Frank tried to do as she said, but it seemed to require looking at two things at once.

"Look at my hand," she said.

He looked at the hand that was holding his.

"Now keep staring at my hand, but notice the fact that my other hand is moving over here. No, don't look at my left hand, keep looking at my right, but then *notice* my left."

Oh, was that all she meant? That was easy enough, to think about something he wasn't looking at.

There was a glint of yellow on the ground. He looked at it, and there was nothing there.

"You saw it for a moment, didn't you?" said Theodora.

"I don't know," said Frank.

"That's good," said Theodora. "You didn't deny what you saw, you just admitted that you weren't sure. That's important, not to deny it just because you know it *shouldn't* be there. The more you deny it, the less it's there—to you. Because people can't see what they refuse to see."

Frank was looking at the hand that was holding his. And now it was definite. That glint of yellow. Not gold-yellow. *Yellow* yellow. "Like a goldfinch," he said aloud.

"I told the old scarecrow you'd be able to see it."

"This is very strange."

"No," said Theodora. "It's the Empire of the Air. It's just as much a part of the natural universe as anything else. It's not strange, it's *wondrous.*"

"It's wondrous strange," murmured Frank.

But now he could see shadowy tree trunks on either side. Not if he looked at them; but as long as he kept his eyes forward, he could see that they were moving through a stand of woods—though he could still see the corn on either side, as well.

"How can I be in two places at once?" asked Frank.

"You're in only one place," said Theodora. "It's the two *places* that are in the same place. Because they *are* the same place. Welcome to the Empire of the Air."

Frank blinked. And each time he blinked, the trees were a little more solid, the corn a little more shadowy. So by the time they came to the abandoned carnival, he felt as if he were emerging from a dense stand of trees, and the cornfields were now nothing but a vague shadowy movement in the breeze.

Theodora led him among the tattered tents, which now held out neither rain nor light. There was not a soul in sight, though here and there a crow landed or rose from the ground as if patrolling the area.

"I never knew this was here," said Frank.

"It's in the Empire of the Air, not in Aberdeen," said Theodora.

"But it's old and faded and tattered and…gone," said Frank.

"Things get old here, too. People stop coming, the carnival goes out of business, and it gets like this."

"I bet it was wonderful when it was new," said Frank.

"It was a carnival," said Theodora. "Only the acrobats didn't need wires or nets or swings, and the lions had no cages, and all the tricks the magicians did were real."

"Why would people stop coming?"

"How do you know they've stopped?" asked Theodora. "We're here."

"But you said..."

He didn't finish, because they came to the mechanical man—or rather, half-man. From the waist up, he was a man of metal, but the bottom half of him either was, or was inside, a flamboyantly-painted box that was now faded, more gray than anything else.

"I know he has something to say to me," said Theodora. "But he just whimpers. His mouth is all rusted up."

"Is he real all the way down?" asked Frank.

She looked at him like he was crazy but then understood. "Oh, I have no idea whether he goes on inside the box, or whether the top half is all there is. But if I can get his jaw working, maybe he can tell us."

She waved the oilcan in front of his face. Frank heard nothing and saw no change, but Theodora smiled. "Hear that? He's *so* excited."

"I don't hear anything," murmured Frank.

"But you can *see* him," said Theodora. "So reach out and touch him. Hold on tight, because I have to use both hands to work the can and lubricate the joints, and I don't want you disappearing on me."

Frank gripped the arm of the metal man.

Theodora applied a drop of oil in several places along the jaw, and then worked the jaw up and down, side to side.

Meanwhile, Frank tried to do with his ears what he had done with his eyes, to notice sounds that he was not actually listening to, the sounds behind the sounds.

"Stop that," said a very, very faint voice.

"I'll stop when I'm sure I've got you working again."

"Make the boy let go of my arm," said the voice.

"Don't let go!" Theodora said to Frank, her hand flying out to grab him. "People here are always trying to trick you into going away, back to Aberdeen. *Never* obey people here until you're sure it's not a trick."

"I'm not tricking him, I want to get my arm back," said the faint voice; but it was louder now, and Frank could see that the jaw was moving along with the words.

"You won't have your arm back until I oil it, which I *won't* do if you make him disappear," said Theodora.

"I love him," said the voice. "He's very lively."

"Are you *in* the box," asked Frank, "or *on* the box?"

"I *am* the box," said mechanical man. "With a lovely metal decoration on top."

"He's a sarcastic twit," said Theodora. "They all feel so superior to groundlings, which is what they call people who don't naturally dwell in the Empire of the Air."

"Are you a groundling?" asked Frank.

"Not if I can help it," said Theodora. "They can't kick me out anymore, and once I know where things are I can always go back. I'm still a visitor, though. Not a citizen. Yet."

"You are a lovely person, and I love you," said the mechanical man.

"You love everybody," said Theodora. "And yet somebody must have been very angry to box you up and metallize you like this."

"Some people don't want to be loved," said the mechanical man.

"I do," said Theodora. "I want you to tell me how to find out where the crow took my mother's ring, and where I can go to get it back."

"Though my heart is filled with love for you, I must respectfully ask how in hades you expect me to know?"

"Because the scarecrow said that you see everything that passes near you, and the crow carrying the ring passed near you, so spit it out, please."

"If only I had any spit to spit with," said the mechanical man. "How did you find your way here? Just wondering."

"I've oiled you," said Theodora. "Can't you be grateful enough to answer my questions?"

"Did you oil me so I can walk away from here?" asked the mechanical man.

"I've oiled all the parts I can see. Should I break open the box?"

"I don't know," said the mechanical man. "I have no idea whether there's any *me* in there or not."

"I can do it," said Frank.

"You're only six," said Theodora, "and I'm nine, and twice as strong, and besides, you can't let go of me and him at the same time, which means you can't have both hands free, so you're not going to open the box."

In answer, Frank kicked the lower-right corner of the box, about four inches in from the bottom and the side. The fabric tore free. Frank reached down with his free hand and pulled the fabric up, ripping it away from the frame. "It's just stretched canvas," he said. "Like stage scenery."

"Clever wretched boy, exposing my nakedness," said the mechanical man. "How I would love him, if either he or I were real."

Theodora was already on her knees. "He does go on down inside the box, but he has wheels instead of legs. If we tear away this box, maybe we can get him moving."

"Wheels?" asked the mechanical man. "No wonder I couldn't wiggle my toes. I used to have toes, you know. Before I was mechanized."

"Did you mean that I'm not real?" asked Frank, thinking back on what the mechanical man had said.

"Tear away this frame and I'll believe you're real, if you want me to," said the mechanical man.

Theodora pried apart the wood frame of the box. Frank helped as much as he could without letting go of her wrist. Finally the box lay in slats and tatters on the ground, and the mechanical man on wheels was fully oiled in all his parts. His motor whirred and the wheels spun one way to send him backward and the other way to go forward, and both ways at once to send him spinning in a circle.

"I'm ecstatic," said the mechanical man. "I'm filled with joy." His inflection, however, was unchanged from normal.

"We've done what you asked," said Theodora. "Where did the crow take my mother's ring?"

"That way!" cried the mechanical man. Then he whirled and began speeding off in a different direction entirely.

"That's all you can tell me?" called Theodora to his back.

"It's all I know!" he called back. "I love you so very much! I love you both!"

"Well, that was barely helpful," said Theodora.

"Maybe it was completely helpful," said Frank. "If you start walking in the direction he pointed."

"His pointing was very vague."

"I know it wasn't precise," said Frank, "but we know it wasn't that way or that way or that way." He pointed in various other directions. "So it narrows down our choice of routes quite a bit."

Theodora nodded. "That makes more sense than standing here being angry at that ungrateful mechanical toad."

"Very much untoadlike," muttered Frank.

"He sounded like a toad and he was less helpful," said Theodora. She had been looking beyond the carnival, in the general direction the mechanical man had specified, and now, gripping Frank's wrist, she took off at a bold stride.

"You hold too tight," said Frank. "Let *me* hold *you*."

"You're more useful than you look," said Theodora. "But you're not very strong. If I hold you there's less chance of my losing you."

"And more chance of your bruising me," said Frank.

"What a clever little poet you are," said Theodora.

They reached the far side of the abandoned carnival, and now Frank could see the yellow road, bright as could be, stretching off in just the direction the mechanical man had indicated. Frank couldn't even see the shimmering of the waving fields of corn; the woods and the yellow bricks were completely solid to his visions, especially when he stared right at them. He said so.

"Don't be fooled," said Theodora. "If I let go of you, you could pop right back to Aberdeen."

"How do you know that?" asked Frank.

"Because I tried to bring my dog a dozen times. A leash doesn't work. Eventually I had to set him down, and every time, poof, he was gone."

"How about a basket?" asked Frank.

"He'd only jump out."

"Picnic basket with a lid?"

"We aren't rich," said Theodora. "We don't have baskets for picnics, and we don't have baskets with lids."

"I'll bring one next time."

"There won't be a next time," said Theodora. "Either I'll find my mother's ring today or not at all."

"Why?" asked Frank.

"Because we just let the mechanical man go, so I'll never be able to ask him again."

"But you have his answer."

"I have *today's* answer," said Theodora. "Do you think I haven't asked him before?"

"Have you ever let him out of his box before?" asked Frank.

"If I had, do you think he would still have been here?"

"So maybe this time he told you the truth," said Frank.

"I hope so," said Theodora, "because I've been coming here for years. Twice I was captured by winged monkeys. Once a wicked witch screamed at me. Once I was attacked by angry trees. This is not a reliable world."

"What did the wicked witch scream?"

"She screamed. There weren't any words."

"Then how do you know she's wicked?"

"Because she was even uglier and meaner-looking than Auntie Bess," said Theodora. "That's my standard. One inch uglier, plus the screaming, and I know you're wicked."

"How much ugly is there in an inch of it?" asked Frank. "I never knew it could be measured."

"Is your mother ugly?" asked Theodora.

"Not at all. She's mostly pretty."

"But not entirely."

"Very close."

"Let's say she's three inches away from totally pretty. Auntie Bess is one inch away from purity of ugliness. You do the arithmetic."

Frank wasn't very sure of his arithmetic—he had learned his numbers, plus adding and subtracting very small numbers, without borrowing or carrying, though he'd heard of such operations. It was all very mysterious, so he decided to take her word for it.

They walked into very deep woods. The road stayed yellow, but under the shade the yellow wasn't half so bright, and as they climbed higher and higher, it became more and more autumnal, and more fallen leaves were strewn and blown across the road. Also Frank was quite sure he heard a distant roaring sound from time to time. Each time it sounded less distant.

"Do you hear that?" he finally asked.

"It's only a lion."

"A lion from the carnival?" asked Frank.

"Do I look like Queen of the Lion Tribe?" asked Theodora.

"You know more than I do," said Frank.

"And don't you forget it," said Theodora.

The roaring got very close, until at last it was right in front of them, in the form of a very large lion. Frank could easily imagine his whole head fitting inside its mouth, with room left over for two mice and a toothpick.

"So you finally got here," said Theodora.

The lion roared very fiercely and moved closer. Slobber dribbled from its mouth.

Theodora reached out with the hem of her dress and wiped the lip. Frank expected her hand to disappear, but the lion did not bite.

"What was that about?" asked Frank.

"I think it's so untidy for him to be letting spittle drip all over the road," said Theodora. "Somebody might slip on that and hurt himself."

The lion gave the fiercest roar of all, and then snapped its jaws down on their held hands.

Theodora at once kicked the lion in the throat. Its mouth flew open, and the animal made gagging noises as it backed away.

"Is kicking a lion really a good idea?" asked Frank.

"I don't know," said Theodora. "But I do know that biting off our hands would be a very *bad* idea."

"I wasn't going to bite off your stupid nasty hands," said the lion. Its voice rasped as if it were trying to cough up a hairball. "I was just tasting."

"Well, you got your nasty spit all over our hands, and because we can't let go of each other we can't even wash it off," said Theodora.

Frank was beginning to get the idea that either Theodora was always rude to everyone, or she was rude to everyone in the Empire of the Air.

"Since you're the first talking creature we met since we left the mechanical man at the carnival," said Theodora, "I expect you to be able to tell me: Where did the crow take my mother's ring?"

"Funny you should ask," said the lion. "I ate the crow and pooped out the ring three days ago."

"The crow took my mother's ring three *years* ago."

"And you think I can remember?"

"I think you'd better tell me instead of playing dumb," said Theodora.

"Maybe he's not playing," said Frank.

"Do you want me to bite off your head?" asked the lion. "I could, you know."

Frank did not doubt it.

Theodora kicked the lion in the throat again. This time the coughing and choking and gagging went on even longer. "What was that for?"

"For threatening my friend and for not answering my question."

"I did answer it," said the lion.

"With a lie, so that doesn't count."

"How do you know I was lying?" asked the lion.

"Because you couldn't eat it and poop it out. It's filled with my mother's love. It would have burned a hole right through you and you'd be pooping out of everywhere, like all the holes in a sponge."

"That is such an unpleasant image," said the lion.

"My mother said that ring had all her love in it, and it was supposed to come to the person who needed it most, and that was me. But a crow from the air stole it right off the table beside her bed, and in that very moment she died," said Theodora. "So you *know* that ring could not have passed by you and you not see it."

"I was asleep."

"I'll put you to sleep, you bag of hair."

"I'll ask around and see if one of the other woodland beasts has seen it," said the lion. "I'm king here, you know. They all obey me."

"Nobody obeys you," said Theodora. "Because you're a liar and clearly you're afraid of the crows and don't want to get caught telling their secrets." She gestured with a shoulder toward a nearby tree, where there was indeed a crow perched on a low branch.

"I'm not afraid of crows," said the lion. But Frank had seen him jump a little when he saw the crow. What with Theodora kicking him in the throat and him being scared of crows, Frank was reaching some unfortunate preliminary conclusions about the amount of the lion's courage, and whether it existed at all.

"How many inches from a coward is this lion?" asked Frank softly.

"No inches," said Theodora. "He's obviously a carnival lion. Look at the scars on his behind. He was trained to the whip. He's a beaten lion."

The lion burst into tears. "He waved a chair at me," he wailed.

"I'll wave more than a chair at you," said Theodora. "Where is my mother's ring?"

"The crow would have taken it to the Emperor of the Air," said the lion. "Where else?"

"How would I know?" asked Theodora. "I've never been a crow, and I'm not from around here."

"That's where everything shiny and beautiful and strong gets taken, so where did you think?"

"I thought maybe the witch. Or the crow's nest."

"First, it's not really a crow, it's a raven. And the ravens are his agents. He sends them out into the world to watch. You are a very young and ignorant child, if you don't know that."

Theodora turned to Frank. "I bet the scarecrow and the mechanical man both knew that."

"I bet you didn't ask them where the crow would take the ring, did you," said the lion.

"They knew what I wanted," said Theodora.

"They knew what you asked," said the lion. "I bet you asked which way the crow went."

"All right, take us there," said Theodora.

"Where?"

"To the Emperor of the Air," said Theodora.

"He's the Emperor *of the Air*," said the lion. "How would I know where he is?"

"The raven knew," she said.

"He can fly. Do you see any wings here?"

Theodora kicked the lion in the throat for the third time. This time his legs collapsed under him and he splayed out on the road, coughing feebly. Finally he whispered, "I'm going to get angry very soon now."

"You're going to take us to the Emperor of the Air."

"I told you that I—"

"You asked me how would you know where he is," said Theodora. "But you didn't say that you don't know. If you didn't know, you would have said so." She turned to Frank. "I believe that in the Empire of the Air, nobody can actually lie straight out. But they're very good at dodging."

"Not good enough," coughed the lion.

"Take us there," said Theodora.

"He doesn't want to see you," said the lion.

"Did he tell you that this very morning?" asked Theodora.

"It's a general principle," said the lion.

"He'll see me because he has something that belongs to me and I want it back and he's a good emperor!"

"Who told you *that*?" asked the lion.

"You see?" said Theodora to Frank. "A question, not an answer. If he really wasn't a good emperor, the lion would have said so."

"I hate you even more than the mechanical man loves you," said the lion.

"By the power of my mother's ring, I command you to take me."

"When you grow up," said the lion to Frank, "do not marry this girl. I can promise you, she's a future witch."

"I'm not going to marry her!" said Frank. "She's nine and I'm six."

"I'm not a future witch," said Theodora. "I'm a witch *now*."

"The question is, are you a good witch or a bad witch?" asked the lion.

"I'm the witch who asked you where I can find the Emperor of the Air," said Theodora. "It's up to you whether I'm good or bad."

"You're already bad," said the lion.

"But I can get worse," said Theodora. "Or better. You pick."

"Follow me," said the lion.

And so they did. They walked a long time. The yellow road forked three times, but the lion seemed to know which way to go. Theodora stayed with him, holding on to his tail, and Frank held on to her.

"You do realize that my parents will be upset if I'm not home for supper," said Frank.

"You will be," said Theodora.

"We've walked a long way, and we still have to get back."

"We're in the Empire of the Air," said Theodora. "The rules are different here."

"My parents are back in Aberdeen, and in our house *they* make the rules."

"The Emperor of the Air rules over everybody in both worlds," said Theodora.

"I know who the president is, and I know who's queen of England, but I've never heard of the Emperor of the Air."

"Who's president?" asked Theodora.

"Benjamin Harrison," said Frank.

"Not here he isn't," said Theodora. "But the Emperor of the Air is emperor everywhere."

"Even under water?"

"There's air under water," said Theodora. "That's how fish breathe."

"They don't breathe, they have gills, Father said."

"They have gills, but their gills still need air. There has to be air mixed in with the water, so the Emperor of the Air rules there, too."

"You are so ridiculous," said the lion. "Thinking that your thinking is worth thinking about."

At last they came to a place where the forest opened up and there in the distance were the spires and turrets and towers of a great city. The towers were every color and texture, some bright-colored and shiny in the late afternoon sunlight, and some rich in color but not shiny, and some black as a cloudless night. Only one was gleaming pure white. It glowed as if its light came from within; it did not seem to reflect the reddening sunlight at all.

"Is the white tower where he lives?" asked Frank.

"He is alive wherever he goes," said the lion. "How ridiculous to think he lives in only one place, when he can go anywhere he wants."

"I wonder if London looks like this," said Theodora.

"I've seen Chicago, and it does not," said Frank.

"You've never."

"Have so," said Frank. "I was only four, but I remember. I've also been to New York City, but I don't really remember that."

"This is the City of the Emperor of the Air," said the lion. "There are no other cities worthy of the name."

Frank did not argue with him. He was not one of those foolish boys who has to quarrel and claim that whatever he likes or knows is better than whatever he doesn't like or doesn't know. Several such boys had tried to pick a fight with him that very day, at noon recess. But there could be no quarrel when Frank cheerfully agreed that their fathers could lick his father, their brothers his brothers, their mothers his mother, and they him. He only disagreed about sisters, and then only because he hadn't any. "But if I had a sister, I'm sure your sisters could lick her." Frank's willingness to admit complete inferiority kept him from getting a black eye, and as his father had long since explained to him, "Let fools believe their foolishness; there's no point in arguing with imbeciles." This coincided nicely with Frank's native disposition, which was to quarrel with no one and keep his innate superiority a secret from all. If it became general knowledge, it would only cause resentment.

Besides, what if Theodora really was smarter than Frank and not just older and more experienced? Wouldn't *that* be a shocker?

As for the Emperor of the Air, Frank still held on to a bit of skepticism about whether he existed at all. After meeting the mechanical man and the talking lion, Frank was beginning to think that the world was a very different place than his experience had led him to believe. Wasn't it possible, given what he'd already seen, that Theodora really was a witch? Anyone who could kick a lion three times in the throat and not get her head bitten off must have some kind of magical power. Or incredible luck.

It seemed almost as long a time as they had already traveled, to get from the forest edge across the endless meadowland, close-cropped by goats and sheep, to finally arrive at the city, though they could see the city all the way. The yellow road changed color as soon as they entered the city, with strands of many colors arising among the bricks, coalescing, and then leading off in many directions. But always there was at least one street that was mostly yellow, or had a yellow band through it, and that was the road the lion followed.

They passed many people dressed in many odd costumes. None of them seemed to care that a wild lion was walking among them—though some of them did stare at Theodora as if they sensed something important about her. They spared nary a glance at Frank, and he wondered if he might still be a bit invisible here in this place.

The yellow street at last led them to a broad gate of intertwining iron rods. They could see through the gate into a garden, lush with greenery of many hues and alive with birds that lighted and took flight, usually alone but sometimes in great flocks. He knew many of the kinds of birds, because he was an observant child with a fine memory for names and classifications. But there were far more birds that he had never heard of, or seen, or even seen pictures of.

"Is this the Garden of the Air?" he asked.

"It's the garden of the Emperor," said the lion, "but I think he would like your name for it. It's the birds, yes? So many birds, it makes it seem as if the whole garden were about to rise up and fly away. As if the birds were the lacework of the land, and someone were tossing the lace up and down like a blanket being aired out in the yard."

"You're talking in very fine language now," said Theodora.

"I'm so much wiser inside the boundaries of this city," said the lion. "Especially when I'm not being kicked in the throat."

The lion led them to the center of the garden, where a little stool sat in the middle of a green patch of low vegetation—not a lawn, but rather a broad cushion of small leaves undulating over the ground, with tiny blossoms scattered like stars in the sky.

The lion circled the stool three times and then sat upon it. In that instant he became a man in a robe of tawny silk, with a circlet of woven lion's mane hairs around his head.

"How long have you been the Emperor of the Air?" asked Theodora.

"As long as there has been need of one," said the Emperor. "But you're asking at what point I took the lion's place and sent him back to rule over the woods and refrain from roaring until his throat healed, is that not so?"

"Why did we have to come all the way here," asked Frank, "if you were already with us?"

"I could have come to you as a shabby man on the road, or in the guise of a clever scarecrow or as a love-besotted mechanical man or as a cowardly lion, but would you have known me then, or believed me if I named myself?"

"I knew you before I saw you," said Theodora, and she knelt before him and held out her hand. "You know why I'm here. You have something of mine."

"I think not," said the Emperor of the Air. "You are quick to claim what you never owned."

“She’s dead, and I’m her only daughter, so it’s mine.”

“Her daughter, yes,” said the Emperor, and he reached into his mouth and took from it a golden ring. “Was this tasty thing what you came here for?” He dropped it into Theodora’s open hand.

At once Theodora’s fingers closed over it. Then she tried to push it onto each finger of the other hand in turn.

It was too small for any of them.

Theodora handed it back. “This is not the ring.”

“You know it is,” said the Emperor. “You knew your mother’s love; you felt it every day of your life. You recognize it here.”

Theodora’s eyes filled with tears, which quickly spilled out onto her cheeks in two thin shiny trails. “But it doesn’t fit my hand.”

“No, because it wasn’t meant for you,” said the Emperor kindly. Then he reached out a hand and touched Theodora’s forehead. “You are already filled with your mother’s love. You had no need of this ring. She gave it all to you when she was alive, all that she had. She gave it to you, and it lives inside you, child. It never left you when she died.”

“Then what’s the ring?” asked Frank.

“It’s also Theodora’s mother’s love, every bit of it,” said the Emperor of the Air. “Love is infinitely divisible, and the more it’s divided, the greater the whole of it becomes. Sadly enough, hate and rage work much the same way, as do loss and suffering. You have them all, don’t you, Theodora? I felt them when you kicked me.”

“It wasn’t *you* when I kicked the lion!” she protested.

“That doesn’t mean I didn’t feel it,” said the Emperor of the Air.

“I’m sorry,” said Theodora. “I never would have hurt you. But the lion wouldn’t take me to you.”

"The lion didn't know where I was," said the Emperor of the Air, "but he would have taken you here, to wait for me. His pain called to me, though he had no idea of how to summon me. And who were you, anyway, to command him?"

"I am the…I was the master of…it was my ring that was taken…it was my mother's ring."

"All this searching, only to find an outward token of a thing you already had in its entirety," said the Emperor of the Air.

"You think I'm a foolish child."

"I think everyone is a foolish child," said the Emperor of the Air. "I know I'm one."

"I'll go now," said Theodora. "Frank needs to get back before suppertime."

Theodora rose to her feet and gripped Frank's hand again. That was the first he realized that she had let go of him, and he hadn't disappeared. Reluctantly, he let her lead him away from the stool in the middle of the greensward, though he could not help but look back again and again at the Emperor of the Air.

The Emperor reached out his hand and spoke—softly, yet the words were clear and bright in the air. "Theodora," he said. "My little Dotty. Aren't you forgetting what you came for?"

He held her mother's ring in his hand.

"But it's not for me," said Theodora. "You said."

"That doesn't mean it's for no one," said the Emperor. "It's a great inheritance, and it must be passed along."

"Then who is supposed to inherit it?"

"The one who doesn't know she needs it. The one who never wanted it when it was offered to her so many times when your mother was alive. The one who inherited your mother's burdens and yet hasn't the strength to bear them all without breaking."

And in that moment, Frank could see understanding come to Theodora and burst inside her, and now she wept in earnest, great sobs. "Oh, give it to me, give it to me quickly!" she cried through her crying. "I must hurry home with it!"

The ring dropped from his hand into hers. Theodora clutched it in her fist and started running toward the gate.

"Don't forget the boy," said the Emperor of the Air. "I'm sure he's delightful company, but he'll quickly tire of the life here without you."

Theodora ran back, grabbed Frank by the hand, and led him toward the gate. She didn't run now—he couldn't have kept up. And so she walked, still crying. "Help me get back," she whispered to him. "See the edges, where the cornfields are."

"We must have walked a hundred miles," said Frank. "We'll never make it home by dark."

"At the edges of your vision, where the cornfields are," she said.

Only then did he see that in fact the cornfields were still there. And with every step they became clearer, and the palace of the Emperor of the Air grew dimmer, and the road beneath their feet turned from yellow brick to the dust of Aberdeen, and they were in front of a certain house.

A tiny house, barely two rooms wide and two rooms deep, and a woman sat asleep in a rocking chair on the little sagging porch. She looked exhausted and sad, and her face was etched with the harsh lines of a farmwife, though it occurred to Frank that he had never heard she was a wife of any kind, only the aunt to this girl. Auntie Bess. Bess Krassner, who had helped contribute to his father's bankruptcy. Whose niece was grateful to her father for the credit he extended, which had saved her while it ruined him.

Theodora let go of Frank's wrist. His wrist was immediately cold where she had held him, for she and he had sweated profusely in their haste. He watched silently as she tiptoed up the steps and walked along the porch. It creaked under her foot, and Auntie Bess stirred and frowned but did not wake.

Theodora took the woman's suntanned left hand in hers, and with the other hand slipped the golden ring onto the finger where it belonged. It slid on easily, though the fingers were much thicker than Theodora's, and for her the ring had been too small.

In her sleep the woman's face changed a little, just the tiniest bit, but now she seemed at peace, and the frown became one of concern and weariness instead of anger and loneliness. So much to see in such a tiny change, but Frank had learned that there were things to be seen at the edges of vision.

Theodora moved behind the chair and touched the woman's hair with her fingers, and then placed her hand across the woman's brow and smoothed the lines there. The woman woke and her hand flew up and found her niece's fingers there, and the hands held each other, and the woman smiled.

"Theodora," she said. "You lingered late at school? You weren't in trouble, were you?"

"I had a job to do," said Theodora. "And I made a friend."

Only then did Bess notice the boy standing off the porch a little way. "Why, you're Frank Baum's boy, aren't you?" she said.

"I better get home now," said Frank.

"Your father is a good man," said Bess Krassner. "Grow up like him."

Frank saw at once the impossibility of such a thing. "I can only grow up like me," he said. And then, because he couldn't hold it in another moment, he shouted, "I saw the Emperor of the Air!"

Bess Krassner looked in puzzlement to her niece, and Theodora laughed and kissed her aunt on the cheek. "It's just a game we played," she said. "And today I won, but Frank here didn't mind, because he's a good friend already."

Frank waved good-bye, and Bess and Theodora both waved back, and then he was gone, running the dirt roads of Aberdeen until he reached the house where Father and Mother and his three younger brothers lived. Where he lived too, though it seemed so small and colorless, for he had seen the City of the Emperor, and he had stood on the green where the Emperor of the Air sat upon his simple stone and granted, not the wishes wished for, but the sweet relief owed to the dutiful who never hoped, who never thought to ask, but whose unwitting messenger had come to bring her the inheritance that she had earned so well.

Frank burst into the house and could hardly form sentences of all he had to tell his father, his mother, his brothers. The boys listened in wonderment and Mother laughed in delight and Father nodded. "That's how it's done, boy," he said. "That's how you tell a story. And much better than the ones about ordinary life!"

Then Frank understood that they did not believe that any of it really happened. But they loved the story anyway, and remembered it in bits and pieces, and over the next few days his brothers asked for it again and again, and even acted out the parts of lion, scarecrow, mechanical man, and Emperor.

Ten years later, his father would write it down, after embellishing it greatly, and having another man draw pictures of it, and he got so much of it wrong, but Frank loved it anyway, and was proud of his father for writing it, especially because it made them very rich, and Frank was old enough by then to appreciate just how much that meant, not to be poor.

By then they lived in Chicago, the Aberdeen paper having long since failed. Frank didn't really miss Aberdeen, with its bitter winters and hot and dusty summers. Bess Krassner and her niece Theodora had already moved away—had moved that very fall, because they knew they'd never last another South Dakota winter. With her, Theodora took Frank's last hope of ever returning to the Empire of the Air, though he walked the route many times, looking through the edges of his eyes but never catching a glimpse of yellow, not even once.

She was a witch, he thought. A good one, a magical person. And I'm not. I could only get there by holding her hand.

But maybe the Emperor of the Air remembers me.

He held on to that thought, even after he became a man and understood that there was no Emperor, that it had all been a dream. A vivid dream, unforgettable, not a detail ever lost, more vivid than life itself.

Even if he doesn't exist, the Emperor of the Air remembers me, as he remembered dotty Theodora and her hard-edged Auntie Bess, and gave a treasure to them all those years ago.

A MEETING IN OZ

BY JEFFREY FORD

The last time Dorothy returned to Oz, the silver slippers barely fit, the gingham dress was a dust rag in her broom closet back home, and Toto had been in the ground for fifteen years. She carried a briefcase instead of a basket. Her long overcoat covered a rumpled business suit—midlength skirt, a mint-green dress shirt, and a blazer. Her hair was cut short, dyed the pale color of Winkie Country, and already in need of another cut. A puffy face, wrinkles where the freckles had been. Shadows beneath her eyes. She landed in the field of poppies, along the road of yellow brick on the way to the Emerald City. The flight from Kansas had made her dizzy. She breathed deeply, sighed, and walked toward the spires in the distance, cutting a trail through jade blossoms, their scent like a cloud of vanilla.

When she was younger the perfume of the flowers always drew her down into sleep, but over the years their hold on her had weakened, now bestowing only the desire to sleep, but also a fierce alertness in the dark hollows of the mind. She trudged across the field to the edge of the road, where she stopped and set down her briefcase. She removed her overcoat and threw it back into the field. She kicked off the silver shoes and threw them after the coat. From the open case, she took a pair of sea green pumps and slipped them on her stockinged feet. Also from the case, she drew a Colt .22 pistol and pocketed it inside her blazer.

Weeds poked up between the yellow bricks of the road, and its famous color was subdued beneath scuff marks and mold. Here and there, though, a brick was freshly shattered, revealing within the vibrant golden glow of her youth. Although she carried her years in Kansas City with a weary posture, one glimpse of that shining hue lifted the shadows and set her mind to memory. As she strode along, the faces of her old friends returned. The Scarecrow, the Tin Woodman, the Lion, and dear Toto walked with her again. She thought about them till she smiled, and then she shook her head and breathed deeply, knowing her vision was a result of the poppies. Their scent stayed with you nearly a mile after leaving the field.

She was surprised to see no Munchkins on the road, no horse carts carrying corn and pumpkins from the fields. No children gleaning for grains of wheat left behind by the threshers. No scarecrow conversing with a fox. No soldiers on maneuvers outside the city walls. It was as if the land were sleeping. She scanned the skies out over the barren trees in the distance, but there was no sign of crows, no Winged Monkeys. A cold wind blew up the road from behind her. When she'd last left, the Emerald City had exactly 57,318 Munchkins. She thought it odd that no one would have come to greet her. What was forty years to the ageless? She wondered if they'd forgotten her so as not to wonder if she was alone in Oz.

At the main gate to the City, which was open and unguarded, she stopped and took a pair of glasses out of her shirt pocket. Their lenses were a deep emerald green. She slipped them on and continued forward amid the sparkling glass architecture and the warren of twisting streets that wound through it. She knew the way to the Palace and didn't pass a soul. The stalls in the marketplace were empty.

No laughter came from the open windows, no chatter from the cafe. At the village square, which had lost its grass and was now a plot of hardened dirt, she watched the wind whip up a dust devil and send it off toward Quadling Country.

She turned down Gollyawp Way, a narrow lane where the buildings on either side cast the street in perpetual shadow. When last she lived in the Land of Oz, it was on this street. In a second-story apartment, by herself, at the age of eleven. Dorothy came to her old building and stopped to look up at the second-floor window. She pictured the view from it, sitting at a small table in her parlor. She'd been content there for the first two years of her four-year stay. She'd intended to never go back to Kansas. Shopping at the stalls, mingling in Munchkin society, trips to Gillikin Country with Ozma, or tea at the Palace with the Wizard. It was during the time when all who lived in the Land of Oz ceased to age. Dorothy turned away from the old house and began walking again. Her knees hurt, and the street was colder than the others for lack of sun.

At the entrance to the Palace, she found the great wooden doors, as ornate as those of a cathedral, flung open. The guard with the long mustache sat there, leaning back in his chair, wide mouth gaping. His tall fuzzy hat and long coat were tattered. His rifle lay across his lap. She drew near and nearly gasped when she saw his desiccated face, empty eye sockets and leather flesh made green like everything else. She stared at him for a moment, recalling his self-important way, and thought about how much he would have suffered in Kansas.

On her journey up the grand hallway, her shoes echoed against the glass floor, the reverberations bouncing off curving whale-rib columns and the vaulted ceiling. Ahead, a fiery ball the circumference of a hot air balloon spun slowly over a low altar, bright threads of electricity scribbling the air around it. When Dorothy drew within twenty yards of it, the image of a face coalesced out of the green gas within. Eyelids sprang open. It glared at her, transforming rapidly from face to face—a wicked witch, a Winged Monkey, her dead husband, even a skull (the only one laughing).

"Halt!" said the thing in the floating globe. "Who dares to disturb the great Oz?" Its voice boomed down the hall, and she felt its power in the vibration of the floor.

"Dorothy Gale of Kansas," she said.

"The Wizard is busy. Go away!" it shouted.

Dorothy walked past the globe and around behind the altar, where there was a curtained entrance to a room. As she swept the silken fabric back and stepped in, the Wizard turned from the mechanical controls that gave life and light to the remarkable Head. He looked over at her and laughed. She removed the glasses and took him in. His hair was white as a cloud and hung mid-length down his back. Bushy white eyebrows, a trimmed mustache, a sharp goatee. He was dressed in a purple smoking jacket and striped trousers. He wore no shirt, only a vest, with the white hair of his chest showing atop the plunging collar. A thin golden chair clung snugly to the folds of his neck. His cheeks were prodigious and his belly redefined the term.

He came toward her still laughing, and she took a step back.

"You remember me, don't you?" she asked.

"My dear, I knew you'd come back before you did." She cowered, and he lightly embraced her. She heard a whisper of a kiss in the air. As he backed away, he clapped his hands and smiled. "You look wonderful."

"No, I don't," she said.

"You're tired from the trip. Come sit at the table and I'll brew us a cup of Tamornas tea." She followed him across the room, noting the fireplace, the shelves of books, the vanitas paintings by the Quadling master artist, Heshrow. She'd seen it all before but not in a long while, and seeing it again drew a sigh from her.

"That doesn't sound good," said the Wizard. He pulled a padded chair out for her at the table and then turned to fix the tea. She sat back in the chair and folded her arms across her chest.

"So," said the Wizard, "I heard you were working in a shoe store in Kansas City."

Dorothy laughed.

"Were you surprised?" he asked.

"When I was in the stockroom, going through the boxes, searching for something I knew wasn't there but the customer insisted I look, I found them."

The Wizard put the water on to boil and clapped his hands again. He twirled around slowly like a mechanism in need of oil and took the chair across from her. "Ozma told me she'd dreamed they'd fallen off your feet when you left last time."

"Yes, out over the Deadly Desert. It's a miracle I landed in Kansas."

"You should have seen what I went through to get them back."

"I'm flattered," whispered Dorothy.

"Twenty Munchkins on four magic carpets, so they might never touch the life-sapping sands for more than an hour or so at a time. Nick Chopper led the expedition for me, since he's the ruler of Winkie Country now. Their journey took a year, flying each day from the realm of the Squirrel King out over the wastes. The Munchkin members of the expedition all returned as old men, wizened and hobbled, their life drawn away by treading the interminable dunes. The Tin Woodman, of course, didn't age, but the fierce winds blew sand against him, scratching their will into his metal form. Finally, one day, they spotted something glittering in the distance."

"But the sands were deadly? When I was here last, an enchantment had been cast to make all in Oz ageless," said Dorothy.

"Yes, well, my dear, in a land of magic, all things accomplished by enchantment can be just as easily undone."

"And what undid that spell?"

"It's a long story," said the Wizard. "But an interesting discovery of the expedition, other than the shoes, was that the Deadly Desert, at its farthest reaches, is littered with fossilized corpses, frozen in the act of trying to reach the Land of Oz. They brought me one of these unfortunate Desert statues, a man who had turned to leathery rock, and I saw that this person was a gentleman from Kansas, or Nebraska, or Oklahoma, etcetera, etcetera. Hundreds of souls, burnished by the sand and the bright Desert sun, seized in the pursuit of their desire to reach this place. The poor fools didn't know that you can only find Oz without a map."

Dorothy closed her eyes and pictured the stony forms, covered to the elbows in sand, leaning forward in their desperation. As she shook her head, the tea whistle blew, and the Wizard got up to fetch the cups.

"Well, the world is not what it used to be," she said.

"Here or there?" he asked, pouring the hot water.

She looked around at the rug, the tablecloth, his smoking jacket—all threadbare. There was a crack in the glass fixture of the gas lamp. The books and knickknacks on the shelves hadn't been dusted in an age. "I guess both," she said. "More there than here, though."

"I had my spies," said the Wizard, dipping the tea ball as if he was fishing for snappers. A delicious fruit smell pervaded his parlor.

She reached for the gun but caught herself at the last second and directed her hand to her face, where she scratched a nonexistent itch. "How much do you know?" she asked.

He set her tea down in front of her and then his at his place. He took a seat and smoothed the front of the smoking jacket over his gut. "From your earliest days after you last left Oz. The year you were twelve and began working in the leather trimming factory, your hunger, your poverty, your innocence. No parents to guide you or look after you." He scowled, and she almost believed he meant it.

Dorothy nodded. "I suffered for my decision to go back. Fourteen-hour shifts, a bowl of gruel, the heat, the constant grinding noise and darkness, the groping hands of filthy men. All that while carrying in my head a knowledge of the gleaming Land of Oz. Every fall was made harsher, every disgrace more obvious for having traveled the road of yellow brick."

"Why did you leave?" he asked. "You could have stayed here and never even grown old. Been eleven forever."

"I thought you said it didn't work that way anymore."

"Yes, because you left. Ozma was hitching the reins of that enchantment to the magic of your youth and energy. You were powering, like a generator, the immortality of Oz. You can't understand what a profound effect it had on the merry old Land."

"I had no idea," said Dorothy.

"For everything that happened to you in Kansas City, something happened here in Oz." He paused and took a sip of tea. "Not all of it good."

"Such as?"

"Back when you were working at the shoe store, a job you loathed if my spies were correct, you met a young man who also worked in the store. On your lunch hours you would go down to the store's basement, into a small alcove behind the oil burner, and in total darkness you would kiss. Every time you kissed, one of the Citizens of China Plate Land here in Oz shattered, and when first his hand found a way into your undergarments, scores of children abruptly died in Quadling Country."

She tried to stand, but as she rose, he reached out and gently touched her shoulder. She sat back into the chair.

"When your wealthy husband cheated on you, that, my dear, was calamitous. Your shame inspired that fiery ball of a Head out there, that roiling cloud of snarling electricity, to break from its moorings and fly out over the Land, Citizens and cattle disintegrating in its maw. It took all the humbug in Oz to get it back under my control. But even that time held no candle to your quiet later years. Secretary at a shoe factory. Fifteen long years of monotony, and oh how that dimmed the colors of Oz and made its magic stupid."

She pulled the gun.

The Wizard took a sip of tea and laughed.

"Where are the Munchkins?" she said.

"Those ungrateful troglodytes deserted me."

"Did they flee to Gillikin Country?"

"I'll tell you where they are. They're out in the Deadly Desert, no doubt turned to leather stone, seized as if crawling, hands outstretched, fingers frozen only inches from those of the fossils from Kansas and Nebraska. Why did you leave?"

Her gun hand trembled. "I didn't want to be eleven forever. I spent four years here as an eleven-year-old living on my own. The last I was truly happy was when Aunt Em and Uncle Henry came to stay for a while. Do you remember how I showed them around? Before they left to return to Kansas, Aunt Em drew me aside one day and whispered in my ear, 'You've got to get out.' That was all she said. It made me wonder what twelve would be like."

"What's the gun for, if I might ask?"

"I'm going to shoot you."

"I see," he said. He winced and turned away from the barrel. "Now that you've used me up, before you do what you will, I beg you to tell me what happened in the last years. My spies deserted me along with the others some time ago."

"That secretary job went on and on, and then one day, Mr. Steers, my boss, called me into his office. Sitting there in front of his desk was a young blond woman, very pretty. I hated her instantly. Her smile was like the Nome King's. Mr. Steers motioned for me to take the chair next to this woman, and he introduced us. Her name was Edna. She would be his second secretary. I would be in competition with her for two months, and whichever one of us did better would get the job I'd already had for years.

"I worked so diligently—late nights, early mornings. She came late every day, and then he would call her into his office for, as he always said loud enough for the rest of the office staff to hear, 'dictation.' Once I put my ear to the door when they were in there and heard her grunting and him calling out to the Lord. I could already see the outcome of the competition. Of course I was laid off. The day I left, Steers called me into his office. Edna was sitting close to him, preparing to take dictation. He reached into his pocket and threw two crumpled twenty-dollar bills on his desk. 'Nice knowing you,' he said. I scooped up the money and left. With it, I bought this gun.

"Two nights later, I followed them to the local theater and sat three rows back from them in the dark, watching *The Lost Weekend*, starring Ray Milland and Jane Wyman. When the movie was over, I let them leave first. I kept my face in my box of popcorn, and they never noticed me. I eventually followed. As they strolled down the street to where Steers had parked, I picked up my step and passed them, walking fast. I had my hair up under a hat, and I was dressed in clothes I'd never have worn to the office. Once I got a few feet in front of them, I turned, lifted the pistol, and pulled the trigger. The bullet went right into his left eye. He screamed, and I put one in his throat. Blood burbled out and he dropped.

"Edna took off running in her high heels. I caught her by her long blond hair and jerked her head back. She made a sound like the pigs did under the slaughter knife on Aunt Em and Uncle Henry's farm. I shot her twice in the ass to take the fight out of her, and then I gave her two in the back of the head. She was on the ground but still twitching when I took to the alleys. I made it back to my place just in time. As I slipped the silver shoes on and stored the pistol in my briefcase, the police cars pulled up in front of my building. The cops were running up the stairs when I called out for Oz, and I was gone by the time they burst through the door."

"Harrowing," he said.

"Believe me, I enjoyed it."

"Tsk-tsk," said the Wizard. "Did you never know happiness back in the world? Not even for a few minutes? You were married for a full decade. What about love?"

"My husband was wealthy from wheat futures. We had everything, but everything in Kansas was like a box of broken toys compared to Oz, where one of my best friends was a fellow with a pumpkin for a head, and all our adventures ended brilliantly."

"Did you love your husband?"

Dorothy cocked the trigger and brought her other hand up to steady her aim. "How could we be in love? I was daydreaming about Oz, and he was daydreaming about money. When the bottom fell out of the wheat market, when the country was turned to dust by his greed and his dreams rotted in a matter of days, he grew so angry. He took his rage out on me. When Toto came to my defense, barking and maneuvering to get between us, he beat the poor dog to death with his cane. Not long after, he leaped to his death from the widow's walk atop the mansion."

"Leaped?" said the Wizard and cocked an eyebrow.

"He was a runtish man with a bad leg," said Dorothy. "A good shove was all it took. His lawyers threatened to implicate me, and for their silence I forfeited whatever was left after the market crashed."

"And how is this all my fault?"

"Because you're the secret humbug behind it."

"Preposterous," he said and stood up.

Dorothy pulled the trigger twice, but there were no blasts from the gun. No bullets emerged, just two small black moths, which fluttered from the barrel and lazily wove their way toward the ceiling. She dropped the pistol on the table and stared as if in shock. "Oz is hell, isn't it?" she screamed.

The Wizard laughed so hard his stomach shook and his cheeks grew red. As his glee subsided, he clapped his hands and whistled.

Dorothy, trembling, turned in her chair to see a half dozen Winged Monkeys gallop into the room through the curtained entrance. They snarled and spit and barely stood at bay, awaiting the Wizard's command.

"Fly her out to the middle of the Deadly Desert and drop her," he commanded.

She leaped from the chair, but they were already on her, their hairy knuckled fingers clamping her arms and legs. Their brutal faces in hers. The stink of them swirled with the action of their wings and made her weak.

"Here's one adventure that won't end brilliantly," he said to her. "Fly!" he commanded.

The pack of growling creatures swept her toward the exit. Dorothy whimpered, and as she fainted, she heard the Wizard say, "There's no place like home."

THE COBBLER OF OZ

BY JONATHAN MABERRY

-1-

"I need a pair of traveling shoes."

When the cobbler heard the voice, he peered up over the tops of his half-glasses, but there was no one there. The counter that separated him from the rest of the town square was littered with all the tools of his trade—hammers and scissors, awls and stout needles, glue and grommets. However, beyond the edge of the counter there was nothing.

Well, that was not precisely the case, because beyond the empty space that was beyond the counter were a thousand chattering, noisy, moving, bustling, shopping, buying, selling, yelling, laughing people. They were there in all the colors of the rainbow; green was the most common color here in the Emerald City, but the other colors were well represented, too. There were Winkies in a dozen shades of yellow; Munchkins in two dozen shades of blue; Quadlings in scarlets and crimsons and tomato reds; and Gillikins in twilight purples and plum purples and the purple of ripe eggplants.

But there was no one who seemed to own the tiny voice that had spoken.

The cobbler set down the boot he was repairing for a Palace guard.

"Hello?" he asked.

"Sir," said the voice of the invisible person, "I need a pair of traveling shoes, if you please."

"I do indeed please," said the cobbler, "or I would if I could see your feet or indeed any part of you. Though, admittedly, your feet are necessary to any further discussion on the matter of shoes, traveling or otherwise."

"But I'm right here," said the voice. "Can't you see me at all?"

The cobbler stood up and leaned over, first looking right and then looking left and finally looking down, and there stood a figure.

It was a figure even in the cobbler's mind, because he could not call the figure a man or a woman because that would never be correct. Nor could he call it a boy or a girl, because neither of those labels would hang correctly on the person who stood there wringing its tiny hands.

"I thought you were an invisible little girl," said the cobbler.

"No, sir," said the figure. "Neither invisible nor a girl. Though I am little, and to my own people I am a girl, for I am not yet fully grown."

"I see that you are quite little, my dear. But why stand down there, where no one but a giraffe can look over and see you? Why not fly up here onto the counter? There's plenty of space," he said, pushing some of his tools aside.

The little figure looked sad—or at least the cobbler *supposed* that she looked sad, because he had very little experience reading the expressions of persons of her kind. She turned around so that he could see her back. Then she raised her arms to her sides, and with a soft grunt of effort, expanded the pair of miniature wings.

The wings were lovely to see. Gold and tan in color, with nicely formed primary feathers, as well as all the requisite secondary and tertiary feathers, and quite attractive emarginations.

However, upon seeing the feathers, the cobbler felt his mouth turn into a small round *O*, and he even spoke that aloud. "Oh," he said, faintly and with an equal mix of surprise, and consternation and pity.

The wings slumped, and the little figure turned.

"I know," she said sadly. "They look perfect, but they're so small that they wouldn't lift a pigeon, let alone a Monkey."

"Ah," said the cobbler. It was not a great change in his response, but it conveyed a different emotion—sympathy. A Winged Monkey whose wings were so small she could never ever fly.

The little Monkey fluttered her wings so they beat with the blurred speed of a hummingbird, but there was no corresponding change in the elevation of the owner. All that the cobbler could see was a bit of a flutter in the brocade vest the Monkey-child wore, stirred by a faint breeze from those stunted wings.

Once more the wings sagged back in defeat, and the little figure seemed to deflate with them. She hung her head for a moment, shaking it sadly.

"My sisters and my brothers all have normal wings, even my littlest brother, who is only two. Momma has to tie a tether to him to keep him from flying out of the nursery window. And Dadda has great wings. Big ones, with a pattern like a hunting falcon. He can fly way above the tops of the tallest trees in the forest and then soar down among the trunks, swooping past our windows. Sometimes he flies past and without even a flutter or a pause, he'll toss walnuts and coconuts in through the window, and they land on our beds as if placed there by a slow and careful hand." She sighed and shook her head. "My wings are almost the same size now as they were after I was born. They grew a little and then stopped, but I never stopped growing, and I'm still growing. Soon I'll be full-grown, and I'll still have wings that can barely lift a small bird."

Then she drew in a breath and looked up at the cobbler, who still leaned forward over the counter.

"And now you see why I need a pair of traveling shoes."

-2-

The cobbler stepped out from behind his market stall and addressed the little Winged Monkey. He extended a large and callused hand.

"My name is Bucklebelt," he said.

The Winged Monkey curtseyed. "I'm Nyla of the Green Forest Clan. It's a pleasure to make your acquaintance, Mr. Bucklebelt."

"And a pleasure to make yours, Miss Nyla." He tilted his head toward his counter. "As it is rather difficult to hold a conversation with you with my counter in the way, and entirely impossible to measure you for shoes, traveling or otherwise, may I assist you by lifting you onto the counter?"

Nyla sighed again and cast a sad glance around the bustling square. "I suppose everyone who is likely to laugh at a nearly wingless Winged Monkey has already had their fill of snortles and chuckles, I don't see how being lifted onto a counter can cause me any greater embarrassment."

He winked at her. "If anyone so much as sniggers, I will tonk them all a good one on their noggins in the hopes that it helps them remember their manners. This is the Emerald City after all, and the Wizard requires that everyone has manners." Now he sighed. "But of course we both know that for some folks, manners come and go like the phases of the moon."

She nodded, knowing full well that this was true. Some of the other Winged Monkeys her age laughed and made jokes about what they called her "butterfly" wings, but they never did that when the adults were around.

With her permission Bucklebelt lifted Miss Nyla onto the counter. He did it gently and made sure not to set her down on anything sharp. Then he went back around to his side of the counter and climbed onto a stool, for in truth even though he was a grown man, the cobbler was not a large man. Only parts of him were large—his nose was a red bulb, his eyes were as big as the largest blueberries in the southern groves, and his eyebrows stood up like giant caterpillars.

For her part Nyla was graceful and small, with dark brown fur, a soft gray muzzle, and big brown eyes that were the exact color of polished oak. She wore a vest stitched with every color from the Land of Oz, along with a leather satchel that was hung slantwise across her body. The leather was dyed red and green and delicately stitched with a pattern of ripe bananas under lustrous green leaves.

The cobbler noticed the bag and nodded his approval. "That's good work," he said. "And if it's not the work of Salander the Leathermaker then I'm a Munchkin."

"It is!" she cried, delighted at his recognition. The bag was Nyla's prized possession. "My grandmomma bought this for me when I started school. You wouldn't believe how many things I can keep in here."

"Oh yes I would," he said with a knowing smile. "Salander is the genius of our age when it comes to leather goods. There's a saying that if it's a Salander bag, then you can put six things in a bag made for five."

"Or even seven or eight," she said.

He nodded. "Your grandmomma must be shrewd and wise. That bag will never wear out, and you'll never lose anything you put in it. There's no better place to keep your hopes and dreams."

That put a smile on Nyla's face.

"Now," said Mr. Bucklebelt, "let's talk about traveling shoes. Exactly what *kind* of traveling shoes are you looking for? Because there are traveling shoes, and then there are *traveling shoes.* Some will get you home, and some will get you far, far from home. Some will take you places that you want to go, and others will take you to places that you *need* to go—even if you don't know that that's where you need to be."

Nyla settled herself on a soft roll of yarn, pulling her bag around so that it rested on her lap. She took a moment to compose her thoughts, and then said, "I want traveling shoes that will take me to places I don't even know about."

"Ah," he said, adjusting his glasses. "You want *magic* shoes."

"But…aren't *all* traveling shoes magical?"

"Oh no," he said. "Not at all. Most traveling shoes are very civilized and proper, and as you know, when you're too civilized then there's no magic at all."

"How can those kinds of shoes take you to wonderful places?" she asked, confused.

He took a moment before he answered that. "Well, it's because there are different kinds of magic. In the most civilized places—in gray places where everything is normal—then shoes will protect your feet from ordinary things like stones in the road or nettles in the grass. They'll keep your feet from burning on the hot sand or from freezing in the snow. And when you're walking in mud, they won't let squishy worms wriggle between your toes."

"I don't mind worms," said Nyla, but she said it to herself.

Mr. Bucklebelt said, "That kind of traveling shoes will help you run indoors when there's lightning or help you run fast to catch a boat that's about to sail. They won't squeak when you sneak, and they won't flop when you hop. A good pair of traveling shoes—even the non magical kind that people wear here in Oz and everywhere where people have feet—will be a comfort on a long journey. And—maybe there's just the tiniest spark of magic in them, because when you put on any pair of traveling shoes, your feet just want to go find somewhere new to walk."

"Then what about shoes with *real* magic?"

"Ah," he said sagely, touching his finger to the side of his nose, "that's another thing entirely. There are very few genuinely magical traveling shoes. In my whole career as a cobbler, I've seen only three pairs."

"Three?"

"One was a pair of stalking boots worn by the Huntsman of Hungry Hall. When he put those boots on, he never needed horse nor even hounds to find a stag or a wild boar for the village roast. Those boots always found the trail and kept him on it until his prey was within easy bowshot. No one in all the district ever went hungry because of the Huntsman's stalking boots."

"Wow!"

"Then there are the dancing slippers of the Ash Princess. The shoes looked like ordinary slippers on anyone else's feet, but on her feet, they transformed into the second most elegant shoes in all the world, and even though they were as soft as calfskin leather, they were as clear as polished crystal." He leaned in close and whispered. "Made from the leather of dragon's wings. With those shoes, the Ash Princess and her Prince danced on moonbeams and starlight, high above the heads of everyone else at their wedding."

"Wait...you said they were the *second* most elegant shoes in the world. What are the first?"

Mr. Bucklebelt sighed very softly, and when he spoke, his voice was hushed. "Ah, now...that brings us to the third pair of traveling shoes. The dragon-scale walking shoes. Now there is a pair of shoes, my girl. The finest craftsmanship in all the world. I'm only a humble cobbler—I *repair* shoes—but those were made by the finest cordwainer, the finest shoemaker in all the land. Do you know the story? No? Shall I tell you?"

Nyla nodded, her eyes alight with excitement.

"Then tell you I shall, for it is a tale anyone looking for traveling shoes really *should* know." He settled himself more comfortably on his stool. "This is a very old story because it happened a very long time ago. Back in an age when there were griffins and dragons and herds of unicorns. Back when fish with scales of true gold swam in rivers that flowed to a great sea called Shallasa. Ah, but that was so long ago that most people don't believe it's anything but an old story. I know, though, that Shallasa is neither a made-up story nor myth, nor even a dream. And yet all we have left of that sea are its bones."

"The bones of a sea?" asked Nyla. "How can a sea have bones?"

"They don't look like bones as you and I know them, but everything has a part of itself that remains even when all of this is gone." He gave her arm a gentle pinch. "When a sea dies, it leaves behind a great waste of salt and sand."

"The Deadly Desert!" cried Nyla in horror.

"Yes indeed. That cruel waste that no one can cross," he said, nodding gravely. "It stretches beyond our knowing and surrounds all of Oz. No one can cross it and live, and we know this because many have tried. So many. Even heroes and fast horses, even scorpions in their armor and birds on their wings. Nothing that lives can traverse the Deadly Desert. And what a sadness that is, because even though the dragon-scale walking shoes were made in what is now Munchkin Country, the materials—the *key* materials, mind you—came from a land far beyond the Sea of Shallasa. A land not even remembered in fairytales and old songs, more's the pity. It was a land of tall castles and deep valleys, a place where jewel-birds flitted among the trees and the mountains sang old songs every night at the setting of the sun. It was there, in a place in whose very soil the soul of magic thrived. That is the only place where the silver sequins that were used to cover the shoes can be found."

"But...can't someone *make* silver sequins? There is plenty of silver around and—"

"Ah," said Bucklebelt, shaking his head, "like traveling shoes, there is silver and then there is *silver.* The silver I'm talking about isn't a cold metal chopped from a mine. No, this is living silver, and there is only one source for it. Just one in all the world."

"What is it?" asked Nyla in a wondering little voice.

He bent down closer, and his whisper was hushed and secret. "Dragon's tears," he said.

Her eyes went as wide as eyes could go. "*D-dragon's* tears?"

"Oh yes. When Shallasa was still a shining sea, there were dragons in those far-off lands. Only a few, mind you, because even way back then, dragons were becoming scarce. But they were there. And there were different kinds of dragons. There were puffer dragons whose exhalations could chase the clouds through the sky and blow rainstorms away into other lands. There were soot dragons that ate fire and slept in the mouths of volcanoes. And, of course, there were silver dragons. Great, gleaming beasts made of living metal."

"Oh my," said Nyla. "Were they friendly dragons?"

Bucklebelt laughed. "Friendly? Whoever heard of a friendly dragon?"

"I read about talking dragons in stories," said Nyla. "Sometimes they're nice."

"Those are stories, little one," said the cobbler. "Stories are made up except when they're not."

Nyla blinked. "But...but..." Her face wrinkled with confusion as she tried to understand what Mr. Bucklebelt just said.

He chuckled. "I suppose *some* dragons have been civil, but I don't know if any of them have ever been *nice.* At least not to edible, crunchable folks like you and me. Long, long ago, though, there were people who found a way to talk to those dragons. Not all of them...but the less grouchy ones. There are old songs—songs so old that half the words aren't even words to us anymore—about people talking to dragons. High on a cliff or under a mountain or deep in the darkest woods."

"What did they talk about?"

"About sad things," said Mr. Bucklebelt, and he felt sad to say it. "The dragons were the last of their kind. Each of them, be it shadow dragon or red-clay dragon or corn dragon, they were the last of their kind."

"What happened to all the others? To their mommas and daddas and all their sisters and brothers and aunts and uncles and cousins?"

"Dead," said the cobbler. "All dead. Just as most of those dragons are probably dead now. Bones and dust, like Shallasa the sea is salt and sand. Nothing lives forever. Not even dragons."

Nyla looked sad. "That's terrible. Dragons are immortal; they're forever."

"Even mountains don't last forever and ever." The cobbler took a breath and shook his head as if shaking off sad thoughts. He got up and tottered over to a big chest that had been placed on painted sawhorses. Mr. Bucklebelt fished inside his shirt and produced a golden key that hung from a silver chain. He looked forlornly at the key, then inserted it in the chest and opened the lock. The cobbler raised the lid and removed several items that he carefully set aside. Then he removed a parcel that was wrapped in the very finest silk. He brought this over to the counter and placed it with great reverence in front of Nyla. The cobbler licked his lips nervously and then peeled back the corners of the silk wrapping to reveal the ugliest pair of shoes the little Monkey had ever seen.

They were tiny and battered, with holes in each sole and many signs of damage and wear. And though there were sequins sewn onto them, each sequin was as pale as ash and devoid of luster.

Nyla gave Bucklebelt a puzzled expression. "What shoes are these?"

"Why," he cried, "these are the dragon-scale traveling shoes!"

"But...they aren't magical shoes at all. These are just a pair of dirty old shoes." Tears sprang into the Monkey's eyes. "You're trying to fool me. You're making fun of me like everyone else does. I thought you might be different, but you're just as cruel."

The cobbler leaned back and laughed. And yet it was not a mocking laugh, or a cruel laugh, or even an embarrassed laugh of someone whose prank has been found out. No, this was a hearty laugh filled with jolly merriment.

"But my girl, these *are* the dragon-scale shoes, make no mistake."

"How can they be? They're so old and ugly and small."

Bucklebelt shook his head. "Don't be so quick to judge. These shoes have walked more miles than there are stars in the summer sky. They were made for a little princess who wanted to see the whole world before she ascended to her throne to become a queen. She wanted to walk on every street, dance at every ball, and play with every child. She wanted to walk behind the ploughman and stroll the streets with the flower sellers and climb the watchtower steps with the sentinels. This little princess wanted to know everything about her kingdom so that she could rule with knowledge and understanding."

"That must have taken a long, long time."

"The observing took time but not the traveling," he said. "For with these shoes, she could run from Gillikin Country to Quadling Country and back twice in an afternoon. To anyone else that's a journey of weeks upon weeks. And run she did, because it was important to her to know everything she needed to know before she wore the crown."

"She must have been a very great princess."

"A great princess she was…but a great queen she did not become."

"Why not? If the shoes could take her everywhere…"

The cobbler looked left and right to make sure no one stood near his market stall. Then he leaned in close again. "Because the Wizard of Oz came and destroyed all her dreams."

"I don't understand…the Wizard is the savior of Oz."

"Is he? Is that what they teach in schools these days? Oh, sad times. Oz, the Great and Terrible, came from far away and with his magic, he overthrew the kingdom and set himself up as the Wizard King of the Emerald City." He sighed.

"It is treason to say this much, but I must because it is part of the story of the dragon-scale traveling shoes."

"Oh dear, what happened?" cried Nyla, clutching her leather bag to her chest.

"What happened indeed," Bucklebelt mused, and he had to fight to keep the bitterness out of his voice. "When the princess returned here after all her journeys, she was prepared to be empress of all the land, and a fair and just empress she would have been. All the lands, all the people would have been one under her rule, and with the dragon-scale shoes she could have walked abroad over her entire reign to see that justice was done and that everyone lived according to her laws. We would have had a golden age."

"Surely she could not have worn these shoes when she was a queen. They are so—"

"Dirty and damaged?" He shook his head. "With the magic broken, they simply show the wear of all those miles she walked."

"No, I mean that they are so small. If she wore them as a little girl, she could not have worn them as an adult."

"Ah, now," he said, grinning, "that's part of their magic. When they were working properly, they grew with her and changed with her. They would have become the shoes of a young woman and then a full-grown woman. And if she left them to a daughter or heir, those shoes would change to perfectly fit the feet of whoever had the right to wear them. But that is all broken, as the shoes are broken. The magic in them sleeps."

Nyla looked confused and sad, and she hung her head.

"Can nothing be done? You're a cobbler; you repair shoes. Can't you fix them? Can't you awaken the magic?"

"Well," he said, "I have done much to repair these shoes. I've tightened every sequin, and I've done what else could be done. However, there is only one way to fix these shoes, to make the magic within come alive again."

"How? Oh, tell me please."

"If I tell you, will you promise to help me fix them?"

"I will!" she said, clasping her tiny hands together. "I will…I *will.*"

He nodded, satisfied. "Even if it means going on an adventure?"

Nyla's eyes went wide. "Would it be a dangerous adventure?"

"Now, what kind of question is that from a girl who came here looking for traveling shoes? There are dangers in your own garden. There are dangers climbing to the tree house where you live…after all, if you fell, your wings could not save you."

She thought about it and nodded.

The cobbler smiled. "The only way to repair these shoes—the most wonderful traveling shoes ever made—is to replace the missing scales."

"How?"

"The only way to replace the missing sales is by finding *new* scales."

"But there are no more dragons."

"Are there not? How can you be so sure?"

"How can there be? No one ever sees a dragon. People would talk about it if they did. Everyone would say if they saw a dragon. They'd tell us that in school."

"School tells you about everything that happens in Oz—that much I know. Schools are great that way," said the cobbler. "But…they don't tell you about anything that happens *outside* of Oz."

"Outside?"

"The dragons never lived in Oz," he said. "Never ever. Dragons only ever lived in one place."

"But...but...that's all the way over the sea. I mean...where the sea used to be. On the far, far side of the Deadly Desert."

He gave the tip of her nose a tiny little touch. "You are so very correct, my girl. Across the bones of the Sea of Shallasa in the land where dragons once lived there is a single dragon living still." He raised his eyebrows. "And can you guess what kind of dragon still lives there?"

"A...a...*silver* dragon?"

"Yes, indeed. A great and vastly old silver dragon. The very dragon, in fact, whose scales were used to make this pair of shoes."

-3-

"Oh my!" gasped Nyla. "But the dragon is on the other side of the Deadly Desert. No one can cross it and live."

"That is very nearly true," agreed the cobbler, "but it is not absolutely unreservedly true."

"What do you mean?"

He pointed to the shoes. "These are magical shoes as we both know. Magic *traveling* shoes covered in the scales of a dragon. Such shoes can take the wearer anywhere. Across the whole Land of Oz, up and down the tallest mountain, and even across the burning sand of the deadliest of Deadly Deserts."

"But...how?"

"That's the right question. The dragon-scale shoes let the wearer travel so fast that nothing can catch up—not heat or cold or anything that troubles the foot or troubles the wearer. Remember, the princess for whom these were made traveled the whole length and breadth of Oz. She went everywhere and anywhere, and she did it quick as a wink."

"But the shoes are broken. The magic is asleep."

"The magic sleeps," he said. "However, when the right person puts on the shoes, it will wake the magic from its slumber. Not all the magic—oh, no. Unfortunately much of the magic of the shoes was lost when the scales fell off. But even a little magic is still magic, and to cross the sand in shoes like these, you only need a little magic."

"Why hasn't anyone else used the shoes to find the dragon scales?"

"They won't fit anyone else," said the cobbler sadly. "Until they've been restored to their full glory, these shoes will remain as small and as ugly as they have been since the Wizard of Oz stole the Land from the princess."

She shook her head, unable to understand that.

"It doesn't matter," said the cobbler. "What matters is that the *right* person could wear the shoes and awaken enough magic to cross the Desert. Do you know why?"

She shook her head.

"Because in these shoes, the journey—even across the Deadly Desert—will take only a few seconds. Your feet will move so fast that the Desert won't even know you're there."

"My feet?" Nyla raised one leg to show him her foot. "The shoes were made for girl feet and I have Monkey feet. Will they fit?"

Bucklebelt shrugged. He touched the bunched silk and pushed the shoes toward Nyla.

"Why don't you try them and we'll both find out?"

Nyla stared at him for a moment and then looked at the shoes. They really did look bad. There were at least a dozen scales missing from each shoe, and the soles looked very thin. It was hard to imagine that those shoes had once adorned the feet of a great princess.

"Go on," urged the cobbler. "Try them on."

Nyla chewed her lower lip for a moment. Then she reached out to take one of the shoes from where it nestled in the silk. She gave a soft cry at what happened when her fingers touched the shoe. It was like touching something warm and alive. The shoe seemed to shudder under her fingers, and Nyla almost dropped the shoe. But the feeling was not unpleasant. Not at all. In fact it was as comforting as picking up her pet hamster. The shoe seemed to *want* her to pick it up.

Is that was magic was like? Was it that way for everyone?

Nyla held the shoe, turning it this way and that. At close range the shoe did not seem to be that badly damaged. The holes in the sole no longer seemed to go all the way through. The heel wasn't ground down quite as much as she thought. And not as many of the stitches were frayed as had initially seemed apparent. How strange.

"Try it on," coaxed Bucklebelt.

Nyla did so, and to her surprise and delight, the shoe fit perfectly. Even though it had been crafted for a human princess, it seemed perfectly suited to her Monkey foot. She eagerly reached for the other one and put it on as well. Like the first, it was less weathered and battered than she thought, and it fit like a dream.

"Let me help you down," said the cobbler, and he lifted Nyla to the floor. "Now, try walking in them. But be careful...the magic may wake up at any time."

Nyla took a single step, and suddenly the cobbler and his stall and the whole market was gone. She yipped in fear and surprise as she turned and looked around to see that she stood by the east gate of the Emerald City.

"But I…" She backed away from the grim-faced guards who stood at the gate. But as she took that backward step, suddenly she was in a meadow of wildflowers that grew inside the west gate. It was impossible. A single backward step had taken her all the way across the Emerald City.

She turned her head but was very careful to keep her feet where they were.

She was close to the yellow road that curved and snaked its way back into the heart of the City. That road ended at the market square. Nyla knew that she had to go back to Mr. Bucklebelt's stall, but how to get there if every step took her too far?

In her consternation she took a half-step, and suddenly she stood in front of the cobbler's stall. He still sat on his stool, and he wore a great grin, which stretched from ear to ear.

"Ah-ha," he said with a chuckle, "and is that a great princess I see before me wearing dragon-scale traveling shoes?"

"I—I—I…"

"That's exactly what I *thought* you would say."

"These are *amazing*!"

"Now," he said with bright eyes glowing in his face, "do you see how a person wearing these shoes could go anywhere? Even all the way across the Deadly Desert?"

"Yes," said Nyla, almost hopping with delight and wonder. "Oh, yes!"

Then she stopped, and her smile faded.

"But…even if I could cross the Desert, how would I ever find the last silver dragon?"

The cobbler chuckled again and went once more to the chest. He rummaged around until he found a scroll tied with silver cord. He undid the knot and carefully opened the scroll to show that it was a map of such great age that it crackled and seemed on the verge of falling apart. It showed a map of the Land of Oz, with the Emerald City in the center.

"This map was made by the great-great-great-great-great-ten-more-times-great-grandson of the cordwainer who made the dragon-scale shoes. See here? That dot is the town square right here in the Emerald City with the four major countries around it. All around Oz was the broad gray waste. To the Gillikins of the north, it was the Impassable Desert; in Munchkin Country to the west, it was the Shifting Sands; the Quadlings of the south called it the Great Sandy Waste; and to the Winkies of the east, it was the Deadly Desert, which is also what it is generally called here in the Emerald City."

Beyond that desolation were other places, though, and Nyla had never before seen a map that gave names to those nameless and forgotten places. The Kingdom of Ix, the Land of Ev, the Vegetable Kingdom, Mifkits and Merryland, and others. Most fearsome of all was the Dominion of the Nome King, and even Nyla and her people had heard dark things of that terrible place. But the spot that was marked with an *X* was to the far southeast.

The Country of the Gargoyles.

"Oh dear!" whispered Nyla. "Must I go there?"

"If you want me to fix the dragon-scale shoes, then go you must, and go *now.*"

"Now?"

"The shoes are awake," said the cobbler. "But they are not strong, and if you don't hurry, they will soon fall asleep once more."

Twenty-six different reasons why she was sure that she should not do this occurred to her, but Mr. Bucklebelt pressed the map into her hand and gave her the gentlest of pushes toward the southwest.

Before Nyla could utter a single one of her twenty-six very good reasons, she was no longer in the market square. Nor in the Emerald City nor even in the Land of Oz.

She stood under a sun so hot that it made her gasp, and on sands that were hotter than a bread oven. All around her the flat and lifeless sands stretched away.

She was in the middle of the Deadly Desert.

-4-

Nyla took in a huge breath, intending to scream her head off—because finding yourself alone in the middle of the Deadly Desert is really an appropriate reason to scream one's head off—but the air was so hot that it scorched her mouth and throat. She did scream, but it was so tiny and high-pitched that even she didn't hear it.

There were bones in the sands. Human skulls and the rib cages of animals and some bones that she couldn't tell what they were from. There were even gigantic bones and Nyla wondered if these were the bones of dragons, or of great fishes that once swam in the Sea of Shallasa.

Nyla felt herself suddenly growing very drowsy and weak and she realized with horror that the terrible heat of the desert was already sapping her strength and her life. She tried to flap her tiny wings, but all they did was tremble and flutter uselessly.

She managed to murmur a single word as she stumbled forward.

"Southeast."

The Desert wind blew past the spot like a hot scream, but there was no one there to hear it.

-5-

When Nyla opened her eyes she expected to see that unrelenting Desert stretched out all around her, but a cool breeze blew across her face and the ground beneath her feet was covered in green grass. Flowers grew upward on long stems that towered over her like young trees, and butterflies as big as kites danced from blossom to blossom.

"Oh dear," said Nyla. "I must be dreaming..."

"We are all dreaming," a voice behind her said. "Everything is a dream."

Nyla yelped and whirled and then stood quite aghast.

For a moment she was quite sure that a house had just spoken to her. It was huge—many times as high as Mr. Bucklebelt's market stall—and covered all over in plates of polished metal. A chimney smoked at an odd angle.

However, it was not a house at all, and the smoking chimney was not a chimney.

It was a dragon.

A dragon that was as big as a house, with a tail that lay threaded through the grass like a giant snake. A long, long neck rose higher than a chimney and smoke puffed from nostrils that were bigger than feast-day dinner plates. The whole thing, from the tip of the tail to the crest of horns on its massive head, was coated in silver metal. In plates and ringlets, in shingles and in sequins. But as the beast breathed, the metal expanded and contracted the way an animal's hide would, for this metal was clearly alive.

And yet...

Nyla could see that the metal around the dragon's face was tarnished with great age, and many of the scales and plates were cracked and uneven. The eyes of the dragon were large and red, but although they may once have been fierce, now those eyes were rheumy with age and sickness.

It broke her heart to know it, but Nyla could tell that this great silver dragon was dying. Even though it was a dragon and not at all a monkey, it looked like her grandpoppa had looked before he climbed into the great tree that leads all the way up to the stars.

"You...you...you..." she said, but that was the only word her mind could think of.

"I...I...I...what?" asked the dragon.

"You're a dragon."

The red eyes blinked once and the big head turned to look at its tail and its bulk. "Why, yes. It appears I am. Now how about that? It took a monkey from who knows where to tell me that I am a dragon, when all this time I thought I was a teapot."

"That's not what I meant!" insisted Nyla. "It's just that I've never seen a dragon before."

"Clearly. But, to be fair," said the dragon, "I have never seen a talking monkey before who didn't have wings."

"I...I do have wings," said Nyla, and she felt the sting of shameful tears in her eyes.

"Let me see them."

Nyla turned and showed him the tiny wings that sprouted from the brown fur of her back. She fluttered them and then her wings and her shoulders slumped.

"Oh my my my," said the dragon, and Nyla thought she heard real sympathy in the beast's booming voice. He sat there in the green field, his silvery body shining with reflected sunlight as fleets of white cloud sailed above his head.

"Do you have wings?" she asked, craning to see over his bulk.

"Alas, my wings are gone," he said heavily.

"Gone? What happened to them?"

"They broke off," said the dragon and Nyla thought that he looked a little embarrassed. "You see...when I was a much younger dragon I had wings so huge, so great that the shadow of them would darken this entire field. I needed them, you see, because I am made of metal and metal is very heavy. Other dragons had smaller wings, like the corn dragon, who weighed very little, or the fire dragon whose body was filled with hot gases. I was always the heaviest of the dragons, but in my prime I could fly. Oh…how I could fly! I would climb up the side of a mountain and hurl myself into the wind, and my wings would spread out all the way to the horizon on either side and when I beat my wings the world shook and trembled. I would fly high and high on my wings until the world was nothing but a pretty blue marble below me. Ah…ah, those were the days. Those were lovely days," he said sadly, "but they were long ago. Over the years I kept growing and growing until I was so big that my wings could not even lift me. One day, as I stood atop a mountain preparing to fly, I wondered if I had become too big, too old, and too fat for my wings. But I leaped into the air anyway. My wings beat once, twice, and then I heard a crack and a clang like the breaking of a thousand swords. Down, down I went, tumbling over and over—me, the big, old, fat dragon and the broken pieces of my wings." He sighed.

"That must have been terrible. Did it hurt much?"

"Hurt? No, I'm made of metal and I don't feel pain. Not in the way flesh-and-blood creatures feel pain. But I suppose it did hurt here." He touched one claw to his chest. "To know that I would never fly again was a terrible thing. I wept for days and filled pools with tears of liquid silver."

"I'm so very sorry," said little Nyla. "But at least you did fly and you can remember flying."

The dragon nodded. "And here I am lamenting the loss of my wings when here you are, a little child who should have a lifetime of flying ahead of you, and not even a moment of that joy is open to you. It is I who feel sorry for you, my dear."

Nyla sniffed back the tears that formed in her eyes. "It's okay," she said bravely. "I've known for a long time now that I'll never fly."

"A 'long time,'" echoed the dragon. "You are not two handfuls of years old and I can't even count the millennia of my life. When I was full-grown the mountains were not yet born and the Desert was a new sea in which the first fish swam. I pity myself like an old fool."

"No! You're a dragon," said Nyla. "The very last of dragons. I came all this way just to see you and I will remember this moment forever. It is the greatest honor of my life."

The dragon smiled. "You are very kind to say so. Tell me, though, why did you come on such a long journey? And where did your journey begin?"

So Nyla told the dragon everything, from her own decision to go out in search of traveling shoes, to her meeting with Mr. Bucklebelt, to the astonishing speed with which her new shoes carried her across the burning Desert sands. The dragon listened with the patience of a dragon and it studied her with the shrewd intelligence of a dragon. Then it bent low to study her shoes.

"Ah," he said. "Those are truly my scales. I recognize them."

"You do?"

"A dragon cannot forget its own scales, my dear. We know each and every one of them just as you know every hair on your body."

"But I don't! There are too many and besides they fall out and new ones grow."

"Alas, not for dragons. Our scales may grow larger as we grow, but they do not fall out and if one is somehow lost, it is never replaced. See here." He coiled his tail around where they stood and she could see that there were several patches where scales had been lost. The skin beneath was also silver, but it looked much more like the skin of a crocodile than that of a dragon. "Once when I was sleeping a long winter's sleep a thief snuck in and scraped off enough scales to... well, to make a pair of magic traveling shoes."

"Oh no!" Nyla immediately took off her shoes and held them out to the dragon. "I had no idea that these scales were *stolen* from you. How horrible! How unfair! Here, please take them back."

The dragon peered at her. "Are you serious? You have come here to find more scales and yet you'd give all of them back?"

"Of course I would," said Nyla. "If they were stolen from you then they belong to you."

Smoke curled up from the silvery nostrils as the dragon studied her. "Do you understand what you offer? If I take back my scales then your traveling shoes will be only ordinary shoes. And in the condition they're in they won't want to take you traveling anywhere."

She nodded slowly. "I...I know."

"You'd be trapped here. On this side of the Desert. Far away from your family and the trees where they live."

"Yes...but I could never keep something that was stolen...especially something stolen from your poor tail! Besides...my dadda always told me that the Winged Monkeys are good people. We give our word and never break it, and we never act unjustly."

"Ah," said the dragon, "if only all races upon the earth held to such values then the sun would shine on a happier world."

Nyla stood, still holding out the shoes.

The dragon extended one claw and delicately touched one of the sequin scales. "You offer a great gift to an old dragon to whom you owe no obligation. You are willing to make a sacrifice that was unasked of you. Noble indeed are the Winged Monkeys of Oz. Even those with little, little wings."

With his claw, the dragon gently pushed the shoes back. "Take them, my girl."

"But..."

"And here..." The dragon used the same claw to scrape a line of scales from his tail. They fell like silver rain. "Take these as well. Take them to your cobbler and let him remake those shoes. It is a pity to see something so perfectly intended look so incomplete."

Tears sprang into Nyla's eyes and she could barely speak as she gathered up the scales. Then the dragon handed her a piece of silvery leather.

"Wrap them in this and put them in your bag," he said gently.

Nyla did as she was told and then she rushed forward and hugged the foreleg of the big creature—for the foreleg was all she could reach.

"Thank you, thank you!" she said excitedly. "Now Mr. Bucklebelt will be able to repair the shoes and I'll be able to travel everywhere and see everything. I'll go to places I could never go even if I had full-sized wings."

There was sadness in the dragon's eyes, though, when she stepped back from him. "Now listen to me, little Nyla, for there are two things that you must know, and one may break your innocent heart."

"What is it?" she asked, aghast.

"The cobbler will be able to repair those shoes, but magical shoes are unpredictable. These were made for a special purpose and for a certain person. Once they are repaired the shoes may no longer fit your tiny feet. The shoes may also want to find the feet for whom they were made. Magic is a wondrous thing, but it isn't always a nice thing."

Fresh tears burned in the corners of Nyla's eyes but she fought them back.

"And what is the other thing?" she asked in a tiny, fearful voice.

"There is a different kind of magic in the world, and it's older and more powerful than sorcery or witchcraft. It's a magic that comes from the world itself. I will whisper one secret about it to you." He bent down so that his metal lips were an inch away. "Goodness," he said, "is always rewarded. Not always in ways you can see, not always in ways you know or expect, but this world loves goodness. It is a thing that many people think is as rare as dragon scales, but believe me, little girl of the trees, goodness shows everywhere."

Nyla tried to think of how to respond to that. A hundred questions crowded her tongue at once, but the dragon straightened and shook his head.

"The shoes are not yet repaired and the magic that's in them is starting to fall asleep. I can feel it in my scales. Put them on, little Nyla, and run, run, run for home before there is no magic left to carry you over the burning sands."

Nyla did as she was told, and even though she could feel the power of the shoes, it was indeed drowsy.

"Thank you, Mr. Dragon!" she cried. She clutched her leather bag to her chest. "I hope your kindness is rewarded a thousand times."

He winked at her.

"Run away, little Monkey," he said. "Run for your life."

And so she ran.

-6-

She ran the wrong way first and found herself on the slopes of a mountain that was covered with snow, but from that vantage point she could see the Deadly Desert. She ran toward it as fast as she could and in a wink-and-a-half she was in the market stall with the astonished cobbler.

"I'm back!" she cried as she dug the leather parcel of dragon scales from her bag. She presented them to Mr. Bucklebelt, who accepted them with reverence, his eyes alight.

"They're perfect!" he declared as he examined them. "Let me have the shoes so that I may sew them on."

Nyla hesitated—of course she did—and it hurt her heart to have to take off the shoes and hand them over, knowing that she might not get them back. But they really did belong to the cobbler. He had only lent them to her, after all.

Even so, the cobbler gave her a strange look as she handed them over.

"You'd give them back to me?" he asked. "Freely?"

"I guess so," she said, and then sniffed away her tears.

The cobbler held the shoes for a long moment and Nyla was totally unable to understand what emotions flitted back and forth in his eyes.

"There aren't many people who would give away anything magical."

"But the shoes don't belong to me."

"Some might say that they belong to whoever has them," said the cobbler. "But…that is another matter. You've given them to me freely and I accept them freely. And yet I don't know that I can recall a single time in all my years when something of a magical nature was given away with such innocence and trust." He shook his head. "Perhaps I don't know as much about the Winged Monkey people as I thought."

Nyla did not blush because Monkeys cannot blush, but she lowered her eyes.

In truth the cobbler's words were as much a mystery to her as the dragon's words had been. They seemed to refer to behavior that was so different from the way her people acted.

"I'm only a little girl," she said, because she didn't know what else to say.

The cobbler nodded, but it was more to himself than to her. He set to work on the shoes and Nyla watched him, sitting once more on the ball of yarn. It took more than two hours for him to sew the new scales in place, and as he did so, Nyla saw that the old scales around them suddenly flashed with a new luster. Even the worn sole and heel no longer looked as battered and weathered as before. The cobbler only stopped working once. His eye strayed to the silvery leather in which the scales had been wrapped. He frowned, picked it up, rubbed it between his fingers, sniffed it, stretched it between his hands, then grunted as his bushy eyebrows rose high on his head.

"Did the dragon give you this as well?"

"He used it to wrap the scales," said Nyla. "I suppose he gave it to me. He didn't say he wanted it back."

"Did he not," mused the cobbler distantly, "did he not..." Then the cobbler straightened, fished in his pocket for a coin, and handed it to Nyla. "This will take a while longer. Go and get us some fresh strawberries for a snack."

She was off in a wink—realizing that she was very hungry, not having eaten in hours—but she discovered that the strawberry stand was on the far side of the market and there was a long, long line. She fretted as she waited, and danced in agitation because a very fat lady in front of her wanted to examine every single strawberry before making her selection. Two Winged Monkey boys her own age flew past the stand and then soared high onto a jeweled parapet, where they sat making jokes about her wings and calling them down to her.

Nyla bought the strawberries and trudged back to the cobbler's stall, feeling very low and dejected. And when she returned, she saw that the dragon-scale shoes were completely done.

But they had changed in more than appearance.

"Oh no!" she cried, dropping the strawberries and covering her face. When she could bear to look she saw that apart from the silvery shine that gleamed from every single polished scale, the shoes themselves had grown. They were now slender and graceful and perfectly suited for the foot of a grown woman. A human woman.

Mr. Bucklebelt smiled sadly at her. "Oh, poor little one, I was afraid this would happen. With the magic restored, the shoes have grown to suit the foot for which they were made."

"The dragon warned me that this might happen," said Nyla, "but…oooh! I hoped it wouldn't. Now I'll never go traveling faster than the wind. I'll never run from one end of Oz to the other, and I'll never see all the wonderful things there are to see. I'll always be a little Monkey girl without wings and all I'll see is what's down here on the ground."

Yet, even in the depths of her despair, Nyla did not whine and did not shout about the unfairness of it all. She despaired, but she accepted these things. After all, the dragon-scale traveling shoes were not made for her feet.

"I'm sorry, little one," said the cobbler, and she could see from his face that he truly was sorry. "Magic is a funny thing and we can't always predict what will happen."

"But what will happen to the shoes?"

"They will wait for the right feet," he said. "They've waited this long, they can wait longer. That's the way of shoes…they are used to waiting for the right feet."

Nyla nodded. She started to turn away, but stopped. "Thank you for letting me wear them for a little bit. I'll never forget your kindness and trust. And…I got to meet a real dragon!"

"Ah," said the cobbler, "indeed you did, and that dragon must have liked you very, very much."

"Why? Oh…because he gave me the scales so you could repair the shoes."

"Not just that." Mr. Bucklebelt reached under the counter for something. "That dragon gave you more than his trust. He gave you a very great gift."

"A…gift?"The cobbler removed the item from under the counter. It was the silvery leather in which the scales had been wrapped.

"Do you know what this is?"

"Just a piece of leather. You can keep it if you want. I have no need for it."

The cobbler laughed. A soft, warm laugh.

"Are you so sure?"

He held the material up and Nyla gasped to see that the cobbler had worked on it. The leather had been snipped and sewn and stitched into a pattern that looked like…

"Wings?" she asked in wonder.

"Wings indeed," said the cobbler. "And magical wings at that, for the gift that the dragon gave you were pieces of his own wings. I don't know how this leather came to be detached from his wings, or why he would give it up, but as you see there is more than enough here to make a very pretty set of wings."

The wings were sewn onto a harness that was small enough to fit her. He had her take off her vest, and the cobbler snipped a slit in the back of it. After he'd helped her buckle on the wings, he pulled the silvery leather through the slit so that the wings lay draped over her own tiny, useless wings. Then he gently tucked each of her wings into pouches he'd sewn into the leather.

Then Bucklebelt stood back and pursed his lips for a moment before he nodded approval.

"They're very pretty. Thank you very much," said Nyla, though her voice was still a little sad. "Now at least people will be able to admire my wings, even if they are only leather and thread."

The cobbler arched one furry eyebrow. "Do you think so little of dragon magic, my girl?"

"W—what do you mean?" stammered Nyla.

"At the very least try flapping your wings."

"No! The leather is too heavy and it will break my little wings."

"Will it indeed? And am I a villain who would make something that would injure a little Monkey girl for my own sport? Is that what you think?" His words were sharp, but there was a twinkle in his eye.

"But…but…"

"*Try*!" urged the cobbler.

Nyla took a breath and braced herself against the pain she knew she would feel. She'd made cardboard wings before and tied them to her own wings but she could barely lift them. And once she had made wings of cloth and sticks, but when she tried to fly, the extra weight hurt her back. She cried all that afternoon.

But she did not want to be rude or appear weak.

So Nyla gritted her teeth and flexed her wings.

And something incredible happened—the silver dragon wings expanded out as high and wide as the greatest wings on the biggest eagle in the forest.

The cobbler clapped his hands in delight.

"It doesn't hurt at all!" cried Nyla.

"Flap then," said the cobbler. "See if they'll flap."

She tried, still bracing against the moment when her little wings would collapse from the strain.

There was a huge *crack,* but it was not of the bones in her wings. It was the powerful flap of her dragon-leather wings.

She flexed again and there was an even louder crack.

And another and another.

When Nyla looked at the cobbler for an explanation, she was shocked to see that he was not there.

He was many feet below her, looking up, pointing and dancing with joy.

The wings cracked and cracked and cracked, and up and up and up Nyla went, soaring above the cobbler's stall, up above the market square, up beyond the tallest spires in the Emerald City. Her laugh was high and clear and it bounced off of the lofty towers of the Wizard's castle.

The gift of the dragon and the skill of the cobbler brought forth the magic that lay sleeping in the leather. Wings that had broken off of the old dragon now lived again, and to Nyla it felt like they were a part of her.

She swooped and soared and fluttered and dove and rose up to meet the golden sun. She flew past the two Monkey boys by the strawberry stand and laughed at the goggle-eyed expressions they gave her. Then she swooped back and dared them to follow her.

They goggled a moment longer, then they laughed and threw themselves into the wind. The three of them swirled and chased each other and flew away toward the forest. But as fast as the two Monkey boys flew, the little Monkey girl flew so very much faster.

-7-

The cobbler dabbed at a happy tear in his eye.

Then a shadow fell across his counter and he turned to see a tall figure standing there. It was a woman wearing a green cloak trimmed in black, and the cowl of the cloak hid her face. A battered umbrella was hooked over one thin arm.

"That was a kindly thing," said the woman. "You changed that child's life."

The cobbler's smile melted away and he hastily adjusted his apron and stood very straight.

"She…she certainly changed mine, my lady," he said.

The woman leaned forward slightly and placed her hands on the counter. The motion caused her cowl to slip so that her face was partly revealed. She was old and wrinkled, and she wore an eye-patch that shimmered as if covered with oil. Three gray-black pigtails hung within the shadows of the cowl.

"And has that child changed *my* life?"

The cobbler licked his lips nervously, but he bobbed his head.

"Yes, my lady."

He turned and opened the chest and removed the dragon-scale shoes. The sight of them, restored and whole, shining with living silver, made the old woman gasp.

"At last…after all these years…"

The cobbler looked right and left to make sure no one was watching, then he raised the shoes and offered them to her, head bowed in fear and respect.

The woman hesitated for just a moment, her fingers seeming to claw the air above the delicate shoes. Then she snatched them from him. She kicked off her own shoes and put the silver shoes on. Her robes seemed to ripple as if the shoes gave off waves of energy. The strawberries Nyla had bought suddenly withered and turned rotten.

From far above the sound of innocent laughter floated down. The old woman raised her head to listen. "All this time I thought the Winged Monkeys were nothing more than curious freaks." Her eyes took on a calculating look. "Apparently they're useful after all."

Before the cobbler could ask the woman what she meant, the crone tapped the shoes together once, twice, and a third time and took a single step away.

And was gone.

The cobbler wiped sweat from his face.

Gone, he knew, but not from Oz.

He stood there for a long time, trembling and frightened, considering what it was he had done. And for whom. She had been his princess long ago and might one day be his queen. His allegiance was owed to her.

But he looked up into the sky and saw the little Monkey girl with her beautiful silver wings swooping and dancing on the wind. In the end, he wondered, what would be the most powerful magic here in Oz? The dark arts of the witch who once more had her silver shoes, or the goodness of a child?

"Fly, little one," he murmured. "Fly and fly and fly."

He sat on his stool and spent all of the rest of the day watching the sky.

ACKNOWLEDGMENTS

Many thanks to the following:

Inspiration: L. Frank Baum. (Of course.)

Publisher: David Pomerico, for acquiring and editing the book; Karen Upson and Jill Taplin, the production managers; Katy Ball, Justin Golenbock, and Patrick Magee in marketing, publicity, and author relations, and to the rest of the team at 47North.

Art/Design: Galen Dara for providing not only amazing cover art but also individual illustrations for each of the stories, and to the team at Inkd for adding in all the most excellent design elements that took the artwork from being mere images and transformed them into *books.* (And for making the interior look so good too!)

Copyediting and Proofreading: Lisa Kaitz, Carissa Bluestone, and Miranda Ottewell, for Catching all the errors *we* didn't Catch, and for helping us sort through L. Frank Baum's Maddening use of Random capitalization.

Agent: Joe Monti, for being awesome and supportive, and for finding a home for this project. To any writers reading this: you'd be lucky to have Joe in your corner.

People Who Helped Us Wrangle Authors and Contracts: Deborah Beale, Kathleen Bellamy, Kristine Card, Elizabeth Harding, Emily Prabhaker, and William Reiss.

Mentors: John thanks Gordon Van Gelder, for teaching him the ways of editing, and Ellen Datlow for revealing the mysteries of anthologizing. Doug thanks Jeanne Cavelos, who gave him the editorial foundation that made everything that followed possible, Shawna McCarthy, who gave him his first chance to practice the editorial craft with professional writers and for adding to his knowledge over the years, and Warren Lapine, for helping advance his career with his unwavering faith through thick and thin. We couldn't have done this without your tutelage.

Family: John thanks his amazing wife, Christie, his mom, Marianne, and his sister, Becky, for all their love and support, and their endless enthusiasm for all his new projects. Doug thanks his parents, Joyce and Gary, and his brother, Brian, for exactly the same.

Friends: Robert Bland, Desirina Boskovich, Christopher M. Cevasco, Jordan Hamessley, Andrea Kail, David Barr Kirtley, Matt London, Nicole Mikoleski, Jesse Sneddon, and Michael Spensieri, for being there for us when we're not anthologizing, and for, you know, putting up with us while we nattered on about the project incessantly.

Readers: John and Doug both thank all the readers and reviewers of this anthology; we hope we've done the Land of Oz proud. (John would also like to thank all the readers and reviewers who loved his *other* anthologies, making it possible for him to do more.)

Writers: And last, but certainly not least: a big thanks to all of the authors who appear in this anthology.

ABOUT THE CONTRIBUTORS

Dale Bailey

Dale Bailey lives in North Carolina with his family, and has published three novels, *The Fallen, House of Bones,* and *Sleeping Policemen* (with Jack Slay Jr.). His short fiction, collected in *The Resurrection Man's Legacy and Other Stories,* has won the International Horror Guild Award and has been twice nominated for the Nebula Award.

Orson Scott Card

Orson Scott Card is the best-selling author of more than forty novels, including *Ender's Game,* which was a winner of both the Hugo and Nebula Awards. The sequel, *Speaker for the Dead,* also won both awards, making Card the only author to have captured science fiction's two most coveted prizes in consecutive years. Recent books include *The Lost Gates, Ruins, Earth Aware,* and *Shadows in Flight.*

Rae Carson & C. C. Finlay

Rae Carson is the author of the *Fire and Thorns* trilogy. Her debut novel was a finalist for the Morris, Norton, and Cybils awards and won the Ohioana Book Award for young adult fiction. C.C. Finlay is the author of the *Traitor to the Crown* trilogy. His short stories have been finalists for the Hugo,

Nebula, Sidewise, and Sturgeon awards. Carson and Finlay are married. They live in Ohio, where they are working on their next collaboration.

David Farland

David Farland is an award-winning, *New York Times* best-selling author with nearly fifty science fiction and fantasy novels to his credit. He has won the Writers of the Future International Gold Award for best short story of the year, the Philip K. Dick Memorial Special Award for Best Novel in the English Language, the Whitney Award for Best Novel of the Year, and others. He has worked with some of the largest franchises in the world—writing novels for *Star Wars* and *The Mummy.* Dave worked for many years as the judge for one of the world's largest writing contests, as an educator teaching creative writing at Brigham Young University, and thus has trained dozens of other *New York Times* best sellers, including Brandon Sanderson, Brandon Mull, and Stephenie Meyer. Dave currently lives in Saint George, Utah, with his wife, children, two cats and a cocker spaniel.

Jeffrey Ford

Jeffrey Ford is the author of the novels *The Physiognomy, Memoranda, The Beyond, The Portrait of Mrs. Charbuque, The Girl in the Glass, The Cosmology of the Wider World,* and *The Shadow Year.* His story collections are *The Fantasy Writer's Assistant, The Empire of Ice Cream,* and *The Drowned Life. Crackpot Palace,* a new collection of twenty stories, was recently published by Morrow/HarperCollins. Ford writes somewhere in Ohio.

Theodora Goss

Theodora Goss's publications include the short story collection *In the Forest of Forgetting*; *Interfictions*, a short story anthology coedited with Delia Sherman; *Voices from Fairyland*, a poetry anthology with critical essays and a selection of her own poems; and *The Thorn and the Blossom*, a novella in a two-sided accordion format. She has been a finalist for the Nebula Award, the Crawford Award, the Locus Award, and the Mythopoeic Award, and on the Tiptree Award Honor List. She has won the World Fantasy and Rhysling Awards. Her website can be found at www.theodoragoss.com.

Simon R. Green

Simon R. Green has written over forty books, all of them different. He has written eight Deathstalker books, twelve Nightside books, and thinks trilogies are for wimps. His current series are the Secret Histories, featuring Shaman Bond, the very secret agent, and The Ghost Finders, featuring traditional hauntings in modern settings. He acts in open air productions of Shakespeare, rides motorbikes, and loves old-time silent films. His short stories have appeared in the anthologies *Mean Streets, Unusual Suspects, Powers of Detection, Wolfsbane and Mistletoe, The Way of the Wizard, The Living Dead 2, Those Who Fight Monsters, Dark Delicacies III,* and *Home Improvements: Undead Edition.*

Kat Howard

Kat Howard's short fiction has been performed on NPR as part of Selected Shorts, and was included in *The Year's Best Science Fiction & Fantasy, 2012*, edited by Rich Horton. You can find her work in *Lightspeed, Subterranean, Apex,* and various other magazines and anthologies. She lives in the Twin Cities, and you can find her on Twitter as @KatWithSword.

Ken Liu

Ken Liu (http://kenliu.name) is an author and translator of speculative fiction, as well as a lawyer and programmer. His fiction has appeared in *The Magazine of Fantasy & Science Fiction, Asimov's, Analog, Clarkesworld, Lightspeed,* and *Strange Horizons,* among other places. He has won a Nebula, a Hugo, a World Fantasy Award, and a Science Fiction & Fantasy Translation Award, and been nominated for the Sturgeon and the Locus awards. He lives with his family near Boston, Massachusetts.

Jonathan Maberry

Jonathan Maberry is a *New York Times* best-selling author, multiple Bram Stoker Award winner, and Marvel Comics writer. He's the author of many novels, including *Assassin's Code, Flesh & Bone Dead of Night, Patient Zero,* and *Rot & Ruin*; and the editor of *V-Wars: A Chronicle of the Vampire Wars.* His nonfiction books range on topics from martial arts to zombie pop culture. Since 1978 he has sold more than 1,200 magazine feature articles, 3,000 columns, two plays, greeting cards, song lyrics, poetry, and textbooks. Jonathan continues to teach the celebrated Experimental Writing for Teens class, which he created. He founded the Writers Coffeehouse and co founded The Liars Club, and is a frequent speaker at schools and libraries, as well as a keynote speaker and guest of honor at major writers and genre conferences.

Gregory Maguire

Gregory Maguire is the author of *The Wicked Years,* a four-book cycle including *Wicked, Son of a Witch, A Lion Among Men,* and *Out of Oz*—all *New York Times* bestsellers. *Wicked: The*

Musical is soon to celebrate its tenth anniversary on Broadway, and is one of the top dozen longest-running shows in Broadway history. Maguire has written five other novels for adults and two dozen books for children, and has written and performed pieces for National Public Radio's *All Things Considered* and *Selected Shorts.* His novel, *Confessions of an Ugly Stepsister,* was an ABC film starring Stockard Channing.

Seanan McGuire

Seanan McGuire is the best-selling author of two ongoing urban fantasy series, both published by DAW Books (the October Daye adventures and InCryptid). She was the winner of the 2010 John W. Campbell Award for Best New Writer. She also writes medical science fiction under the name Mira Grant. Between her two identities, she is a five-time finalist for the Hugo Award, and has been nominated for the Shirley Jackson and Philip K. Dick Awards. Seanan is the only woman ever to appear on the Hugo ballot four times in a single year. She is a founding member of the Hugo award-winning SFSqueecast, an ongoing adventure in mild positivity. Seanan likes horror movies, abnormally large blue cats, and cookies. You can find her on Twitter at @seananmcguire, and on the web at www.seananmcguire.com. Seanan thinks sleep is for other people, and is still waiting for her twister.

Rachel Swirsky

Rachel Swirsky holds an MFA in fiction from the Iowa Writers' Workshop. Her short fiction has appeared in venues including *Tor.com, Subterranean Magazine,* and *Clarkesworld Magazine.* In 2010, she won the Nebula for best novella for "The Lady Who Plucked Red Flowers beneath the Queen's Window."

Robin Wasserman

Robin Wasserman is the author of several books for children and young adults, including *The Book of Blood and Shadow*, the Cold Awakening Trilogy, the Chasing Yesterday Trilogy, and *Hacking Harvard.* Her books have appeared on the ALA Quick Picks and Popular Paperbacks lists as well as the Indie Next list, and her Seven Deadly Sins series was adapted into a television miniseries. She is a former children's book editor who lives and writes in Brooklyn. Find her at www.robinwasserman.com or on Twitter @robinwasserman.

Tad Williams

Former singer, shoe seller, radio show host, and inventor of interactive sci-fi television, Tad Williams established himself as an international best-selling author with his Dragonbone Chair epic fantasy series. The books that followed, the Otherland series, are now a multi million-dollar MMO launching in 2013 from dtp/realU/Gamigo. Tad is also the author of the Shadowmarch books; the stand-alone Faerie epic, *The War of the Flowers*; two collections of short stories (*Rite* and *A Stark and Wormy Knight*), the Shakespearian fantasy *Caliban's Hour*, and, with his partner and collaborator Deborah Beale, the childrens'/all-ages fantasy series the Ordinary Farm novels. Recently, with *The Dirty Streets of Heaven*, Tad has begun publishing the Bobby Dollar novels, noir fantasy thrillers set again the backdrop of the monstrously ancient cold war between heaven and hell and following the adventures of a certain maverick angel. Tad is also the author of *Tailchaser's Song*: his first novel spawned the subgenre of cats and fantasy that we see widely today. *Tailchaser's Song* is in production in 2013 as an animated film from Animetropolis/IDA.

Jane Yolen

Jane Yolen, often called the "Hans Christian Andersen of America," has published over 325 books. Two of her short stories won Nebula Awards. Her books and stories have won the Golden Kite Award, the Caldecott Medal, two Christopher Medals, the Jewish Book Award, and the California Young Reader Medal, and been nominated for the Hugo, the National Book Award, and dozens of others. She has been voted Grand Master of the Science Fiction Poetry Association, and Grand Master of the World Fantasy Association. Six colleges and universities have given her honorary doctorates.

ABOUT THE ILLUSTRATOR

Galen Dara has done art for Edge Publishing, Dagan Books, *Apex, Scapezine, Tales to Terrify, Peculiar Pages, Sunstone, Lovecraft Zine,* and *Lightspeed Magagzine.* She is on the staff of BookLifeNow, blogs for the Inkpunks, and writes the Art Nerd column at the Functional Nerds. When Galen is not online, you can find her on the edge of the Sonoran Desert, climbing mountains or hanging out with a loving assortment of human and animal companions. Follow her on Twitter @galendara.

ABOUT THE EDITORS

John Joseph Adams is the best-selling editor of many anthologies, such as *The Mad Scientist's Guide to World Domination, Epic: Legends of Fantasy, Other Worlds Than These, Armored, Under the Moons of Mars, Brave New Worlds, Wastelands, The Living Dead, The Living Dead 2, By Blood We Live, Federations, The Improbable Adventures of Sherlock Holmes,* and *The Way of the Wizard.* Forthcoming work includes *Wastelands 2, Dead Man's Hand,* and *Robot Uprisings.* John is a four-time finalist for the Hugo Award and the World Fantasy Award. He has been called "the reigning king of the anthology world" by Barnes & Noble, and his books have been lauded as some of the best anthologies of all time. In addition to his anthology work, John is also the editor of *Lightspeed Magazine* and *Nightmare Magazine,* and he is the co-host of Wired.com's *The Geek's Guide to the Galaxy* podcast. For more information, visit his website at johnjosephadams.com, and you can find him on Twitter @johnjosephadams.

Douglas Cohen is the former editor of *Realms of Fantasy Magazine,* where he worked for six and a half years. In the magazine's final year, they published their 100th issue, won a Nebula Award, and were nominated for a second one. Multiple illustrations he solicited for the magazine have appeared in the prestigious *Spectrum Art* series. Douglas is also a writer, and his stories have appeared in or are forthcoming in *Fantastic Stories of the Imagination*, *Interzone*, and *Weird Tales*. He recently finished writing his first novel. *Oz Reimagined* marks his first anthology. Find him on Twitter @Douglas_Cohen.